I0818113

LEVEE

VAST COLLECTIVE X

Nicole Hayes

Iona Print

Library of Congress Control Number: 2022916759

ISBN (Hardcover Edition) 978-1-7378379-8-5
ISBN (Softcover Edition) 979-8-9908310-3-2
ISBN (Ebook Edition) 979-8-9868220-0-6

Printed in the USA

Iona Print
nicolehayesauthor@gmail.com
https://nicolehayeswriter.com/

THE VAST COLLECTIVE SERIES

Last of Daylight
By the Pale Moonlight
Asylum in Firelight
Nox's Verse
Glass Chains
Pyrite Prison
Restraining Silver
Korac's Verse
Thirst
Levee
Flood
Xelan's Verse
Cascading Light

In loss, we find our greatest strength.
Never let go.

TRIGGER WARNINGS

Please consider my entire series 'Rated R.' These books are meant for readers sixteen years and older. Read with the following triggers in mind:

- Graphic Violence
- Graphic Language
- Graphic Sex Scenes
- Deep Dive into Mental Illness
- Abortion
- Gaslighting
- Domestic Violence
- Threat of Cannibalism
- Battle Scenes
- Colonization
- Genocide

CONTENTS

Acknowledgments........ix

01 Blade, Fire, And Nacre—
My Vengeance Is Absolute........01

02 Dark Fire That Blazes
Through The Vein Of This Life........27

03 Take Out The Source;
Stop The Cascade........43

04 Shine A Light On Lost Shadows........51

05 Cultivate Victory Beyond
The Next Ordeal........79

06 Hope Lies Beyond That Darkness;
It Awaits Your Rescue........119

07 Best Laid Plans, And All That........141

08 Light The Way To That Lost Shadow........159

09 Brilliant Facets Of
This Cursed Plot........169

10 Try As You Might,
Effort Is Measured In Action........187

11 Your Faith, My Courage,
And Their Weapons........207

12 Revelations From A Weeping Statue....................225

13 Miracles Among Predators
Are Readily Devoured....................245

14 On And On,
The Nightmare Stretched
Into The Horizon....................257

15 Walk The Fine Line Between
Justice And Vengeance....................267

Epilogue....................283

Time Line....................287

Author's Note....................289

Flood....................291

ACKNOWLEDGMENTS

Here, at my tenth book, I want to take a moment and thank my mother. She taught me to read when I was three. Dr. Seuss' *Are You My Mother* was the first book I could read on my own. I remember the way her face lit up the first time my brain connected all the dots and read the entire thing without her help. It was the same look on her face every time she offered to type my books for me, long before Scrivener and Google Docs.

From the publication of *Last of Daylight* to the completion of *Cascading Light*, I regret never letting her read my stories out of selfish teenage mortification.

Batman and Firefly tell me often how mom would've loved my characters and the world I built, but I'm still sad I'll never know.

So thank you for being here when she couldn't be.

Enjoy this wild ride while it lasts because the end is coming.

Soon.

ONE

BLADE, FIRE, AND NACRE—
MY VENGEANCE IS ABSOLUTE

{EARTH}

"ANDREW, WHAT'S WRONG?!"

Andrew knew it was Lynn without seeing her, but the rest of his brain couldn't make sense of what was happening in front of his eyes. Neon halos surrounded the woman kneeling over him in varying shades of her vibrant lives. Her skin shifted in every saturation of brown. Her eyes were almond-shaped, perfectly round, hooded, deep-set, and almost feline all at once—every human color imaginable. Full lips on the verge of kissing, thin and bordering on angry, down-turned and surrounded by tears—every expression was on her shade-altering countenance at once.

Beyond Lynn, the scenery kaleidoscoped from a pagoda to a stone temple and into a Tudor palace. All of it grand, but none of it felt true. More faces surrounded him and churned in a cascade of vacillating features.

Andrew closed his eyes. Elden, what the fuck happened to the Probability Matrix?! What if Andrew reached out to Lynn and...

Get him some water.

Kiss him and tell him it'll be all right.

Check his temperature.

Did Imminent do something to him here on Earth?

When a hand touched his arm, Andrew jumped three feet into the air and scrambled back. All her voices—all the very different emotions behind them—felt too strong with physical contact. Lynn was all of those thoughts, but only one belonged to the friend Andrew knew.

With his heart pounding in his chest, Andrew opened his eyes. All the Lynns and all the Lamassau's held their hands up, trying for harmless. Colors lined their faces like Andrew forgot his 3D glasses at the movies. He shut his eyes again and shuddered against the solid surface behind him.

This was too much.

And to think, only yesterday Andrew died to see more Probabilities. Now…

"I take it back."

A silence filled the room, which could only mean Lynn and Lam exchanged a "what should we do" glance. Andrew was fresh out of ideas to offer them. Because this was it. What Zero described to Sagan. Razor to Xelan. What Imminent was all about.

Chaos.

At once, Andrew was terrified and alive—more alive than ever in his existence. He felt the birth of a new star in the fiery waters of Cascading Light, and the essence of their promise seeped into him. It married with his soul and exacted only the price of a hunger he'd ignored until now. A desire—a need—to create more. To feed on it as the light fed on him when he joined the ranks of Imminent.

And this line would never end.

Andrew licked his lips, took a deep breath, and let it out on more of a shiver this time. An electric tremor. He pressed his head back against his only solid anchor—whatever it was—grateful for its sentry as his mind drifted along the waves of black flame.

Who was this new initiate? Could Andrew see them? See their place in this fragmented world—

Blue eyes found Andrew adrift in the future-seeking sea. Bright blue and filled with tears. Not tears of joy or sadness. These were tears of pure fear and loneliness.

Rayne.

Those eyes glared with a white light—true, magnesium white. Brighter still. And brightest, until the light consumed her. One last breath and the light released what remained of his best friend—his sister, really—in tiny fireflies of pure phosphorous sparks. All of Enki was taken in her shine.

"No!"

A billion times, Andrew watched her die. The same way each time. It was the last sight on the edge of a lightning-struck horizon. Rayne died alone and afraid, and she destroyed Enki in the process.

It never changed.

"Andrew, how can we help you?" Lynn inched closer.

Andrew knew without opening his eyes that she'd stretched out a hand. By all that was Shadow, he took it this time. He opened his eyes to find hers wide and unsure. He pulled her in for a much-needed hug.

Lynn gripped tightly and muttered against him, "It's okay. We won't let anything happen to you. Can you tell me what's wrong?"

Lamassau waved his arms across the room. "Yeah, is it safe for me to move yet?"

"Please," Andrew started against Lynn's locs. "Please, don't let go yet." The two friends weren't really *this* close, but at the moment, her earthy moisturizer smelled like home. Like Shadow.

Someone entered the room behind Andrew. "Uh, does Doc Pablo know about this?" It was Cypher.

Lamassau dismissed the soldier with a wave. "I think her husband will make an exception just this once."

Lynn sounded like she was rolling her eyes as she said, "There won't be any exception to make if Conscience, here, can tell me what the fuck is wrong."

Right. Andrew sniffled and let her go with an apologetic smile. "Sorry. I… I don't know how to describe it. Someone new touched Cascading Light, and I don't think this is the only Probability in which this particular person joins Imminent. It felt so familiar. Anyway, I guess I'm affected when someone dives into the Probability Matrix."

Cypher walked into Andrew's line of sight and looked him over. "Are you okay?"

Andrew couldn't imagine how he looked. Was he pale from the shock or radiant from the feeding? Overall, the only way to describe how he felt was alien. "I'm… alive, but I don't feel quite right."

Lamassau leaned back against the far counter of the Brethren's lab facility and crossed his arms. "Well, can you tell us who it was? Or what you saw?"

Ashamed of his shortcoming, Andrew shook his head and grit his teeth. "No. Nothing, but the end."

They all shared a glance. Everyone knew "the end" meant Rayne dying. Everyone looked equally sick about it, too.

Andrew met Cypher's eyes and said, "Since we can't reach our people on other planets, we need to get back to the villa on Reipon. I think something's gone horribly wrong with our plan." He checked with Lynn and Lamassau. "Any protests to returning?"

They exchanged a glance before Lynn answered, "You won't see me complaining about checking on Pablo right now."

Lam shrugged with a look of pure understanding. "Nor me on Tumi."

They knew not to fuck with the Probabilities ever since Razor attacked the Shadow with copies of themselves from alternative universes where they defected to Imminent. Repeatedly stabbing someone wearing their own face had scarred them, with a particular trauma impossible to replicate outside of their special brand of bullshit.

Cypher headed for the door, where he paused and turned to say, "I'll let Tempest, Dolor, and Colton know.

We'll pack you some goodies for the trip home. I hope everything's all right." With that, he left.

Lynn stood and shuffled around the lab. "I'll pack these samples. Lam, grab the rifles."

Lamassau did so without sass. Things really were taking a turn for the worst.

Each of them moved with a nervous energy and vibrated with apprehension. They felt it, too.

Something momentous waited for them at home.

Something that would change their lives.

Andrew only wished he could see it before it took them by storm.

{REIPON}

A bad thing happened here. Bethany knew it in the faces of the people left behind to guard the house. Bones, Caedes, Pehton, and the other Lyriks waited in solemn silence, surrounding the tree in the foyer. They waited for Sagan to Seamswalk the others home. Bethany watched from above, dangling her legs from the second floor banister. The same spot she sat with Pax earlier when they saw the Shadow off on their dangerous mission.

Who knew the danger would find them here?

Xelan and Tameka's toddler had often sat with Bethany. He played with her hair or drove his toy train, Iron Hope, over her thighs, making steam engine noises. Sometimes he asked her to blow the whistle, but Bethany made no noise. Nods and shakes of the head were all she could muster through the din of Razor-sharp static in her head.

Much like this quiet which infected the house.

Bones sat with his knees wide, his hands clasped tight, and his head lowered. Pehton and Caedes stared forward beside him. Both of them blinking in time with each other without the other realizing. Long, shocky blinks. Pehton left occasionally to check on Triss, comatose in her pregnancy.

The rest of the Lyriks circled the tree on the floor with their legs crossed. Their faces full of meditative mourning.

Pax's kidnapping was an event to grieve and to rally against. This time, Bethany would join her brother and sister—They would all go to retrieve Pax. The Shadow didn't understand "surrender" or "meeting demands." This was not a ransom to answer.

But first, Bones put himself in the very unfortunate position of breaking the news to the adoring parents. The shame which slumped his shoulders implied self-blame. In the last few months that Bethany had spent under this roof with Tameka and Xelan, she didn't believe for one second they'd let him carry the shame for long. They were people of action. Not wallowing in turmoil without exacting restitution.

So they waited.

With a hoarse voice, Bones broke the silence without lifting his head. "Do you think they'll forgive me?"

Pehton clicked her tongue and kindly admonished, "Do you seriously think those two will blame you for Imminent's actions? Even for one second? Please. We'll get him back, Bones."

"Immediately," Caedes added in his gravelly voice.

Bones sat straighter. The Lyriks lifted their chins higher. So it didn't surprise Bethany when Pehton hopped to her boots and ordered, "Instead of sitting here waiting for them to come home, let's prepare for the move. And hurry. We've got to make this a smooth operation for Tameka and Xelan to carry out."

Caedes stood with sparkling eyes and clapped his hands once, twice. "Come on, ladies. You heard your Warden. Let's move out."

Bethany climbed out of the banister and rushed down the stairs, putting herself in line with the others to receive orders.

Pehton pointed and assigned duties. "You three, mobilize the Infirmary. Careful to collect anything Pablo said would help with Triss. You two, the nursery—grab everything essential to a newborn. We'll have to come back for the rest. Bones, gather weapons and armor—Anything we can't miss. Caedes—"

"Ma'am." He came to attention.

Pehton grinned at the bald Icarus in a way Bethany could only describe as goofy before she shook it off. Her voice was firmest for him. "Pack up Pax's things for our leaders. Let's not ask them to endure that."

Caedes' eyes darkened, and his jaw set. He saluted Pehton with his fist to his chest, and it hurt Bethany to see him do it. She'd heard around the house Caedes had raised Pax like his own during the two years Xelan was gone.

Everyone here carried this loss, and Bethany wanted to help. For Iron Hope and tree adventures. So when Pehton finished doling out orders while kindly ignoring Bethany, the mute girl refused to let her go on.

Bethany whistled, and the house fell silent. All of them whirled midway through their tasks. Concern plain on their faces. Their attention on her increased the sharpness of the static in Bethany's anxiety-addled mind, but it could never grow louder than her quiet grief. She whistled again and jabbed a finger to her chest.

Lyriki eyes were hard stones of varying colors. Pehton's were red, like carbuncles. A glare reflected from them and brightened when Gait's Executive Warden smiled. "You want to help, Bethany?"

Bethany nodded.

Bones called down from the third floor, arms full of blades and rifles, "Thank Elden, girl. You had us all worried to death."

She almost winced at his candor, but understood he came from a warm place.

Pehton's voice rang through the mansion with authority. "Keep working. We don't have time for sentimental huggy shit." All the while she beamed at Bethany, to whom she said, "Help me prep Triss for transfer. We don't know what the next safe house will be like, but we can't assume it'll have the same luxury we've entertained here."

Bethany nodded and followed Pehton to the infirmary. There, they entered the pregnant woman's room. Tortured for years in Razor's Emporium of Exotic Experiences, Bethany had plenty of motive to kill his unconscious woman. As she stared down at the emaciated near-corpse of the Aegis incubator, she only felt pity. Triss would never live to see the daughter she wanted so badly to give Razor. The daughter Korac and Sagan wanted to raise as their own. If Triss died now, that would constitute another tragedy.

Bethany wouldn't allow that.

Pehton pulled back the sheets to reveal the bed sat on locked wheels. Reaching for something, she said, "It separates from the other half of the bed."

With a nod, Bethany went to the other side and found the connecting locks. With the bed separated, they both wheeled it from the wall. Pehton grabbed all the nearby supplies, explaining, "This oral medicine is how Pablo keeps her in this coma. She can't sustain an IV with her blood vessels bisecting and her bones turning into glass and..."

They both looked at the cube shape in Triss' protruding belly. Hard angles stretched her skin to almost bursting.

Bethany swallowed.

"Don't worry, Bethany. She deserves every second of torment." Pehton's voice was full of pure conviction, pouring over the words like acid.

While it was true, Bethany understood Triss' dependency on Razor. His world only made sense because all other worlds melted in his presence. Consuming. He burned in Bethany still—

Bones ran into the infirmary, breathing hard and pointing down the hall. "A conduit opened."

It was time.

{PIL}

Ross regained consciousness, looking into Miy's beautiful hard eyes which matched her black and orange feathers. Beyond her, the red sky told Ross they were still on Pil, helping with the rescue effort. But something went wrong. What was that again—

Para.

Controlled by Remorse, Para confronted them here, and Jack convinced the crowd to subdue her. To rescue her from Imminent's clutches. Then Ross overloaded her memory abilities and—

"You're missing one amazing fight," Miy admonished.

Ross turned her head, following the Lyrik's line of sight. There, Jack faced off with an ancient Tritan wielding a Valkyrie's body like a weapon. And when did he get wings?

In midair, Jack evaded a left hook and a right jab, speared headfirst into her middle, and knocked them both back to the ground. A cloud of dust and debris surrounded them, but Ross heard their grunts from here. While the Valkyrie was smaller and more agile, Jack was beyond strong—bordering on his sister's capabilities. He used it to his advantage, but somehow restrained himself to prevent harming Para.

When Jack punched her face into the dirt, her neck didn't break, for instance. Para reached up and tried shoving her thumbs in his eyes. He easily brushed aside her arms and waylaid her again without crushing her face.

"I can't affect Remorse's memories from within her." Devis' voice came from Ross' left as he explained, "It's one of the more savage elements of volition and how Celindria stayed in control of T.A.O. despite my efforts."

That explained a lot.

Amid the scuffle, Para escaped and burst into the sky, throwing Jack back.

"Allow me." That was Twenty-One's voice.

Ross looked up in time to see him aim a rifle at Para and fire. Direct hit.

Hell. Yes.

The Valkyrie plummeted from the sky, caught mere feet from death by Jack and his really pretty black wings. Ross wanted to touch them—

"For the Shadow!" Miy cheered.

The crowd of Pil Dwarves—merchants and restaurant owners—repeated the chant, giving Jack room to pass with Para.

Devis held out a dark-complected hand in Ross' face. "Can you stand?"

She took it. "I'm willing to try." The sound of her own voice grated. "Water. Can I have some—"

Miy handed her a canteen, and Ross drank from it without taking her eyes off Jack as he drew closer, looking for all the worlds like an avenging angel. When he was close enough to see—really see—him, Ross noticed for the first time that his hazel eyes were lighter than her own. That his hair looked soft and touchable as opposed to simply practically cut and fitting to his face. A handsome face, one he grew into more every day.

Ross set the canteen down and met Jack, seeing for the first time the admiration he held for her in his eyes.

"Are you all right?" he asked Ross, while carrying an unconscious woman. Looking quite heroic, in fact.

"Everything's making more sense now," Ross answered without thinking. She shook herself. "I mean, do you need help with her?"

He laughed. "Nah, she weighs nothing, but I think we should check her for injuries while we wait for Sagan."

Miy patted the pallet Ross was just using. "Right here. We'll get to work." Jack laid her down as Miy further instructed, "Devis, do you think you could scrounge up where she's been and what we need to expect when she wakes up?"

"On it."

Twenty-One set the rifle down beside Devis and helped with the triage. The massive Icarus said, "I'm not a bad shot for a man who never fought a war with guns."

"You were amazing," Ross said with a smile for him. A smile she turned on Jack and felt her face grow warmer before saying, "So were you."

Jack beamed at her and a faint blush crept on his cheeks. Lowering his eyes, he shook off her compliment. "Nah. I'm only doing my job."

Ross took a chance and dared to touch his hand. His eyes met hers again as she muttered only loud enough for him to hear, "I know all about your concern with restraint. You were amazing."

"Ahh!" Devis returned from the memory-walk with a shudder, a grimace, and a groan. "Elden, what... What's wrong with her? Why is she acting out?"

Miy exchanged a glance with Twenty-One before peering questioningly between Ross and Jack. Everyone stared and waited for Devis to clarify.

Devis swallowed and licked his lips before elaborating, "Celindria. She's... she's out of control. The things she and Remorse subjected Para and the others to—I've never known her to act so hateful."

Ross ignored the sympathy on Celindria's behalf and asked, "Anything health related? Anything to explain why Para's still unconscious?"

Devis shook the ghost out of his head. "No. I'm unsure. Much wasn't said in the presence of the captives."

That made sense, but unfortunately set them back.

Jack placed the back of his hand to Para's cheeks and forehead, gently check her vitals, and sat back with a sigh. "We'll simply have to wait. On her and on Sagan."

Twenty-One arranged Para's wings around her like a cocoon without saying a word. A battlefield gesture for the fallen, perhaps? He took his eyes off Para to meet Ross' gaze and offered a nod, as if she asked her assumption aloud.

Miy stared out at the waiting crowd. "They need direction. Have we established a temporary hospital yet?"

"Yes," Jack said, sitting in the dirt across from Ross. "We also connected them with The Brethren supply line. Tempest and Dolor can afford to help more now that Cinder is fully evacuated."

As they discussed diplomacy, Ross admired the way Jack leaned into his experience from his regency of Earth. Admired how proud his sister would be if she could see him right now. And also admired the certainty in the authority of his voice.

There was much to admire about Jack Callahan.

Why had it taken Ross so long to see it? And the next question was, when would there be a right time to tell him?

{MONARCH 3}

Ishkur.

Celindria said Silence—the Mother of all that was Imminent—was looking for Ishkur.

"Tameka." Xelan knelt across from the woman he loved and squeezed her tawny hands. Again, he tried to reach her through the shock, maintaining a soft tone to prevent her further retreat. "Please. We must leave so we can find Pax."

Pablo muttered, "Her nacre should prevent shock, yes?"

Xelan shook his head, staring into Tameka's Atramentous eyes. He refused to look away from her as he responded, "No one can exchange nacre energy the way she just did."

Somewhere behind them, Iuo whispered, "Fury killed everyone upstairs. Everyone but us."

Kyle, louder, declared, "She saved our asses."

While the conversation carried on around them, Tumu and Korac formed a perimeter to guard their unlucky position, an intersection of corridor. In the middle, Sagan stood ready to Seamswalk them to Reipon, so they could evacuate their home.

Celindria.

Xelan's truest failure. His ultimate sin. There was never time to address her properly. Never time to work through her traps and walls—to make her see. That Xelan was wrong, and he was sorry—

"We have to save our son no matter the cost." Tameka squeezed Xelan's hands, finally. Her words left her in a firm oath. "She doesn't get one full day with him, do you hear me? We're saving him, today."

Xelan searched Tameka's eyes as the Atramentous seeped away, leaving shards of green glass in its wake. They still had work to do, and he hated reminding her of it. "Not one day. Let's finish this mission first. There's still people who need us"

Sagan knelt beside Xelan and smiled sadly at Tameka. "We'll get him back. Xelan, where's your contact—"

"Right here."

Korac's voice traveled down the hall, skeptical. "Wingmaster, this Monarch Queen... is she the one from our first misadventure there?"

Xelan heard the smile in Tumu's voice without seeing his lipless mouth. "That's right. F8, how's the hive?"

Kyle sounded as suspicious as Korac when Kyle asked, "F8?"

Iuo and Pablo, standing beyond Tameka, shared a curious look.

Sagan turned and gasped.

Tameka's eyes were still too wide and unfocused. Xelan was afraid to look away from her, but the commotion behind him demanded his attention.

Feet, hundreds of pairs of boots, stomped behind them. A woman's rich voice cut through the din, familiar and welcomed. "Gather the drones and their queens. Remember, these people know nothing outside of this gas farm. Be easy with them. Prince of Cinder, I demand an audience."

Xelan grinned. F8 was a handful, and he'd looked forward to introducing her to Tameka, but certainly under better circumstances. "The calvary's here, Tameka." Concerned by her silence, he pulled her to him and kissed her forehead. Only quiet enough for her to hear, he vowed,

"Today, Tameka. Help us move this along, and you, me, and Pax will sleep in the same bed tonight."

Tameka shifted then and pressed on his shoulders to stand. Xelan followed her up, catching her line of sight. F8 stood amid her drones, busy corralling confused members of their species born and raised in Imminent captivity. A butterfly in every sense of the word. F8's black and red wings draped off her back like a cape for her matching battle armor. Antennae twitched and sensed above her multi-faceted eyes. Where her drones had needle-nosed mouths, her lips were like all the other females of the species across the Vast Collective. Currently, the regal pout formed a line of determination and even a little disgust. This wasn't what F8 wanted for her people.

"I thought surely you'd exaggerated." The twenty facets of F8's eyes reflected the light in a diamond shimmer as she shook her head in disdain. "I knew Enki performed experiments at my old hive, but I never imagined…" Her gaze shifted from Xelan to Korac and scanned him with an assessing glance. "Been some time, General."

Korac looked at Xelan, then back to F8, disbelief on his face. "You truly survived."

F8 smiled sweetly with a predator's threat hidden beneath those lips. "I never forgot you or Prince Nox. Before I heard your Verse, I was sure the next time we'd meet I'd kill you—"

Sagan stepped up beside her… man, who gripped his axes.

"—But I've reconsidered my position on the matter. You tell a good tale, child."

Pablo went to Tameka and changed the subject. "I need to check you over, okay?" He started with her pulse and flashed a light in her eyes. After blood pressure, he smiled at both her and Xelan. "I'd like to run some additional tests, but considering the circumstances, you're battle ready. And I'm needed inside." He gathered his bag and headed deeper into the underground facility, where drones were scattered, to collect lost souls.

Iuo approached F8 with his hands empty, and his bipedal form relaxed in one loose muscle. Friendly and unassuming. "Queen F8."

"Prince Iuo, the Porn Baron. Word of your fairness precedes you."

With a bow of his head, Iuo said, "It's lovely to meet you. I've employed many of your people over the millennia. With your permission, I'd like to record the events here—"

"Can you fly?" F8 asked with a glance over his sincere face.

Iuo shrugged apologetically, "No."

F8 placed hands on her hips and shook her head. "We're relocating them to foster hives immediately. I need air travel. But please, do record the history with some regard for accuracy. Don't hide the abhorring truth of your Tritan masters—"

Kyle stepped up, interrupting her diatribe that Iuo was no doubt accustomed to hearing by now. "I can't fly either, but the faster we help these people the sooner we can save Pax."

F8 pointed into the gaseous field beyond the shattered nacre barrier. "Big drone. Goes by 'Seps.' He'll put you both to work." Once they wandered inside, following the other rescuers, F8 turned back to Xelan and Tameka. "Am I receiving the message clearly? Has Imminent stolen your son?"

Xelan started to answer when Tameka took control of the situation by saying, "They did, and we're getting him back. Do you want in?"

F8's insect eyes scanned Tameka. Fierce gaze, clenched fists, set shoulders, and the chain dart holstered on her hip. After another moment of this regard, the Monarch Queen quirked a brow and asked, "You're taking on Enki?"

Xelan felt the air shift and a momentous occasion would be marked by Tameka's answer.

"Yes. In thirty-six hours, meet our forces at Cinder's shrine."

Over his shoulder where he and Korac still stood guard, Tumu said, "The anti-nacre weapons might pose a problem."

"I'll drain them all." Iron will rang in Tameka's voice. "I am done. F8. Korac. Pass onto our allies that we attack Enki from Earth, Cinder, and Reipon."

Sagan returned from helping migrate some of the rescued drones in time to overhear. Resolute, she assured, "I'll see them there personally."

Thirty-six hours wasn't much time to plan. Xelan was worried Tameka wasn't giving herself space to process the loss of control in the situation and compensated with an utter taking of it. But then, he caught Korac's gaze over the others. The General gave one firm nod with grave eyes and erased any of Xelan's doubts. They could do this. To Mon3's ruler, he said, "Thirty-six hours, F8. We'll stop Imminent."

The Monarch Queen's eyes illuminated as she gave a radiant smile. With a small bow, F8 said, "I believe you will."

Xelan and Tameka exchanged a confused glance.

Why did F8 bow? There was something significant to it.

"Not that this isn't an empowering moment..." Korac's elegant cadence interrupted their huddle. "But how many troops and what kind can you supply? I need to know before we finish here."

F8 met each of their eyes one-by-one, bewildered. Eventually, she placed a delicate hand on her chest. Disbelief lightened her voice. "You mean, you don't know?"

Tameka tensed beside Xelan in frustration. He felt it and understood completely, but they needed patience with their allies. He pulled Tameka against him to shoulder some of her burden. In turn, she nuzzled her face against Xelan's bicep where he felt her hide a tear.

Anything...Xelan would give anything to take this pain away from her—

At their exhausted silence, F8 kindly elaborated, "Word of the Traitor Prince's return has united Caprents, Dwarves, Luks, Yun, and drone alike. Even the Lamias, like your Porn

Baron, are rallying to support the Shadow. Especially now that the King Regent confirmed Primary Rem was responsible for the disaster at Pil. When your allies learn Pax was taken, they'll say the crusade belongs to Fury. They—we—will follow you into the storm." She put a fist to her chest in salute.

"To end it once and for all."

The pure vehemence in Tameka's voice convinced Xelan that this was truly the end.

{MONARCH 3}

"You're the key to Ishkur."

Tameka hadn't forgotten Celindria's parting words from T.A.O.'s mouth, but now wasn't the time to get into it. Nor was it the time to ask Xelan why a flicker of recognition lit his eyes at the mention of the word. Or why Tumu tensed and froze at it.

Instead, they stayed and helped with the rescue efforts. The Shadow and F8's people transferred thousands of drones and dozens of queens with no nacres and no concept of "outside" to her hive so far away that Sagan Seamswalked entire herds of people to save travel time. Kyle, Iuo, and Pablo covered medical and practical assistance. The entire mission stole precious hours from their hunt for Pax, and for that, F8 was more than enthusiastic about arranging troops with Korac. Tumu, Xelan, and Tameka joined the conversation to discuss strategy.

F8's wings folded and fluttered on their own, brushing against Tameka's arm as the butterfly Queen pointed out, "Enki's such a vast mystery. We don't even know the grounds well enough to designate a battlefield."

Korac silently looked from her to Tumu and quirked a brow.

The Tritan stared back, uncharacteristically laconic. In fact, Tameka noticed a lot of quiet from Tumu lately. So she answered instead, "Between Caedes' rendering of Enki and the map Razor provided us, we can put schematics together and send word in two hours' time. Does that work for you, F8?"

Xelan grinned at Tameka, and it kind of bothered her. She knew he was affected by Pax's abduction, but more despair and less terror. Almost as if he trusted Celindria not to damage Pax or leave traumatic scarring on their son by the abduction alone.

Tameka didn't share those assurances.

F8 tilted her head at Tameka and asked in confusion, "Your majesty, did you just say you have a map provided by Razor? The *dead* Pain Curator?"

"Uhm." Damn, it was weird that a Queen kept referring to her that way. Tameka said, "Yes. It's a long story."

Xelan explained, "It should lead us to the bridge."

Before Tameka muttered that she suspected it was a trap, Korac said, "Razor spoke the truth. The map should lead us there."

Finally, Tumu spoke up. The depth of his voice and the abruptness of his speech rang in the corridor. "The Primaries never found the bridge, but trust an Aegis to know its location. It was the last frontier they withheld in Enki, to the point we believed the Dyson's Sphere ran on some automated system."

Sagan Seamswalked into the middle of the conversation, looking a little strained around the eyes and the line of her mouth. Without preamble, she slumped her face against Korac's shoulder. Muffled, she said, "Okay. All done. Can we go home now? I still have to pick up the rest of us so we can… move."

Sagan's knees almost gave, and Tameka noted it. They couldn't afford an exhausted Seamswalker right now. "Thank you, Sagan."

F8 seconded. "Yes, thank you." She saluted with a fist to her chest before turning back to Tameka and Xelan. "Your majesties, we are honored to join you in this fight. Thirty-six hours from now, we will arrive in Enki by Cinder's shrine once we rendezvous with Sagan for the location of the battlefield."

With his hot hand pressed in the middle of Tameka's back, Xelan bowed his head to F8, and Tameka mirrored him. After, he said, "Korac will join Sagan and further discuss the attack. Tonight we break bone and shed blood together in the name of peace. We could not ask for better allies. Thank you, F8. Pass our thanks onto Seps and the other Generals. Until we can thank them in person once the battle's won."

A chorus—an ear-drum busting unison of Mon3 voices—grunted their approval behind their queen.

Tameka placed a fist to her chest and wanted to scream. She held it together for everyone, for her son. But every part of her shook with the need to strangle Celindria and Remorse. To drink their nacres dry and feed their essence to the nearest star. Or perhaps feed it to everyone of their nearby minions until they burst.

Swallowing the emotion, Tameka turned away and felt a smaller hand lace with hers. Sagan stood at her side and asked softly, "Ready?"

"Elden, yes."

The conduit opened to their villa on Reipon. This beautiful mansion—one of Xelan's safe houses—was no longer safe. Bones was the first to greet them, running down the infirmary hall. Pehton and Bethany followed, holding medical supplies. Bones looked paler than usual, and his shoulders held a great weight.

Bones licked his dry lips before opening his mouth. Closed it. Tried again. Eventually, he shook his head and croaked, "Elden damn me, I'm so sorry."

Xelan and Tameka stood across from one of their son's guardians. The others appeared from around corners and along the multi-story foyer's balustrade, arms filled to the brim with everyone's belongings. Everyone was aware this place was contaminated now. All of them were stricken in their puffy eyes and flushed noses.

But it was Caedes—loyal, noble Caedes—and his arms full of Pax's clothes and toys which unmade Tameka. She fell to her knees in the house that smelled of Pax's spiced honey scent. She shrieked until her throat went raw and her lungs begged to collapse.

This was their *home*. God damn it. They were meant to bring Rayne back here and live together as one giant family. Sagan and Korac with baby Echo, and Pax's natural curiosity of the infant. Pablo and Lynn perfecting the shield and the sword, saving nacre-bearers from malicious tampering. Xelan writing his Verse and reading it to her, while snuggled near a fireplace. Kyle, Andrew, Tumu, Bones, Lamassau, Twenty-One, and luo playing games and competing over media trivia. Jack and Ross growing into adulthood and learning their powers. Bethany speaking again and returning to normalcy. Fuck, Caedes and Pehton figuring it out—

All of it gone in an instant—

Warm arms enveloped Tameka, and she fought every instinct to bat them away, to kill the person touching her because every part of her knew it was Xelan. Then thinner arms with smaller hands—Sagan. A tentative squeeze on her shoulder with the typical stink of marijuana smoke. A stronger hand squeezed the other shoulder, smelling of must and desert. luo. Another person touched her hand. Male and a lighter brown than her own could only mean it was Pablo. Comforting smells and warmth. Her family.

Bones fell to his knees across the way and hung his head.

No. Tameka wouldn't have that.

She surged forward and let the people she loved fall behind her to form a wall of pure goodness at her back. When Tameka reached Bones, she crouched and squeezed both his shoulders until he looked up at her. Then she hugged this funny and kind Icarus. He sobbed against her, the guilt racking him.

"Shh. Sh... You'll have to tell me what happened, but you don't have to tell me it wasn't your fault. I already know."

Pehton answered from behind Bones, "We fell unconscious—all of us. Caedes and I... We were in the middle of a conversation. The Lyriks were meditating. And

Bones was making a fort with Pax. Even Bethany went under."

The teenage girl beside her nodded earnestly.

Caedes finished telling the story, with concern adding gravity to his hoarse voice. "When we came to, Pax was gone, and Imminent was carved into all the windows."

Korac cursed from behind Tameka and Xelan.

With urgency in her voice, Sagan said, "I'm pulling the others from the field. Korac, back me up."

"Right."

With Tameka's back to them, they left. Bones finally cried himself out and let go. She wiped away his tears with the sleeve of her jacket and tried to give him some firm, reassuring eye contact. "We're getting him back today."

Bones wiped a hand over his face and swallowed his tears. He said, "Yes, we are." Already, his voice sounded firm with confidence.

Tameka ordered, "When Korac returns, I want to meet with him, Tumu, Caedes, and Xelan. We'll designate a battlefield. You hear me, people. We're going to war."

"Hell, yes. I've got some news from Earth." Lynn exited the conduit with Sagan, Andrew, and Lamassau. She wasted no time crossing the foyer to hug Pablo.

He whispered the bad news to her, and it got around fast. After some whispering between them, Pablo said, "I'll pack my infirmary." The Doctor rushed away with Pehton and Bethany to prep Triss.

Lamassau went to Tumu's side and muttered, "Have you told them what it's like to invade Enki?"

Xelan answered for Tumu, "No. But you're joining us in the war room to tell us."

The green Tritan nicknamed, "The Chef," for his fire breath, nodded curtly.

After lugging some sample nacres to the infirmary and returning, Andrew pulled Tameka in for a hug. "You're damn straight we're getting him today."

She squeezed. There was something special about hugging those with her from the beginning. It felt more at home than even this beautiful house. Than even Xelan's arms. When Tameka let go, the connection lingered, and they shared a sad smile to celebrate it. "Today—"

"We've got Para!" Jack announced on the way through the conduit with the unconscious Valkyrie in his arms.

Ross, who followed behind him with Twenty-One, Devis, and Miy, said, "We can't wake her."

Xelan checked her vitals while Korac and Sagan backed against the stairs to let them have room.

With a glance at Para and one for his sister, Kyle asked, "Have you tried accessing Para's memory?"

Shivering, Ross said, "First thing, but…" She glanced between Kyle, Tameka, and Xelan. "There's nothing there."

Iuo looked up from his stenography equipment. "Imminent erased her memories? Like their other expendable soldiers? Doesn't that mean…"

"No. At least, I don't think," Ross said with an uncertain shake of her head.

Tameka felt Tumu's great height step up beside her to contribute his two cents. In that deep Primary voice, he said, "Then volition must affect their memories. Kyle, is that your experience?"

"Somewhat." He finished inhaling the joint which manifested magically in his hands. "I think I'm different because of…" He tapped his temple, indicating his memory gifts. "But it makes sense, seeing as the controller assumes first position in all functions except pain. They might keep the memories after expulsion."

This irked Tameka. "I want more certainty than a hypothesis. Xelan, can you wake her?"

"I was worried about this. It's why I wouldn't let you shoot T.A.O. with the nacre disabler. I think Celindria installed fail safes. Ones which wipe memory banks and leave the host useless."

Of course, she would, and now Tameka felt better about Xelan jumping between them. No one wanted anything else to befall the volition victims.

Bones offered, "We can put her with Triss. Keep them comfortable."

A little hesitant, Andrew asked, "I'd hate to bring this up, Wingmaster, but does the new safe house have everything we'll need? Or..."

"Or" was likely, Tameka judged from the crestfallen expression on Xelan's face. They were lucky for these last few months of luxury, even if they were never home long enough to enjoy it.

Iuo emerged from the lounge with his arms full of board games. As he threw them in the "move" pile, he said, "The next plan was to use my palace, but I think we can agree I was ousted. Tumu, do you have any hideaways?"

"In Enki." They all whirled to him, including Lamassau, who glared upside the giant Tritan's head. Tumu ignored him and said, "It's risky, but since we'll all be there, it also makes the most sense."

Without hesitating, Xelan asked, "Where?"

Three hours later, Tameka sat on Tumu's bed built for a sixty-five foot Tritan surrounded by pools of Cascading Light and the same white stone and glass which typically covered Enki. A little strained from the last twelve hours, she croaked, "And you're sure they won't find us in your original sanctum?"

Lamassau plopped onto the bed and folded his hands behind his head. "Nope. We spend most of our days here. And nights." He didn't have any eyebrows, but Tameka swore he bounced them at her.

She got off the bed, resisting the urge to cringe.

"I removed all the external conduits and locked it from the inside before I left. They can't access it, but I left everything as it was." Tumu decompressed to thirteen feet and pointed at an invisible barrier in the northernmost point of the room. "My private lab has medical supplies for Triss and Para. Pablo, you'll find it through the conduit there. Food, through there. And space to spread out over there." He pointed all around the temple designed in his honor.

Pehton, Bethany, Ross, and Jack went with Pablo, aiding Triss and Para.

Miy offered, "We'll make food for everyone." She and the rest of the Lyriks headed through the eastern conduit.

Farthest from Cascading Light, Devis' shrunk in on himself, but still said, "We may need bedding for the wounded. War and all that. I can help with it. Does anyone else volunteer?"

Pleasant as ever, Twenty-One raised his hand immediately. "Aye. Let's unpack and set up."

Bones, or a shade of his usual self, also raised his hand and shuffled over to the baggage behind Lynn. She and Andrew exchanged an uncomfortable glance before he prompted, "Go ahead. They need to know."

Tameka looked between them, feeling a sudden spike in her already maxed anxiety. "What is it?"

Lynn explained as she crossed the space, "Smith, he uh... He let Imminent inside to collect the Tantamount. The colossal Tantamount."

Xelan frowned. "The one from your memory, Tameka? From Volcano Day?"

"That's the one," Lynn confirmed, with her dark eyes grim.

Korac and Sagan stepped over to the quiet conversation. Lam nudged the blond with his toeless foot where he lay on the bed, and she stuck her tongue out at him.

Because these were adult conversations.

"There's a failsafe." Korac, for once, brought reassurances instead of more bad news. "You know it, Lynn. You and Pablo tried to deactivate it, but Nox never fully assembled it."

Lynn rubbed the back of her neck and nodded her agreement, stressed. "Yes. But it requires a significant amount of blood. More than he and I assumed. According to my analysis, it would take the volume of at least four nacre-bearing beings. If you want them to live and regenerate. Three if not."

The conversation carried on, but Tameka couldn't hear it anymore.

The room spun until the pools of Cascading Light surrounded her in a claustrophobia-inducing hurricane of black flames. So much horrifying news and all at once. Now, they were expected to make camp in the heart of enemy territory, smelling of sterility and loneliness.

Drain it all.

End everything.

Save Pax.

But first... try not to pass out—

The white stone floor switched places with the starless abyss above. So tired...

"I got you."

Xelan, please don't let go.

Even as she thought it, Tameka knew he never would again.

TWO

DARK FIRE THAT BLAZES THROUGH THE VEIN OF THIS LIFE

{ENKI | NEAR 130,000,000 YEARS AGO}

REMORSE BROUGHT HIS STROLL WITH THREE TWO FOUR TO A HALT, STARING OUT ACROSS THE LAKE IN QUET'S SANCTUM. Cascading Light gathered and pooled in ripples timed to their steps. Black fire with no heat. What had it felt like for Surra to swim in it? To feel its forbidden burn?

Three Two Four with his white hair, white skin, and white eyes split by two crescent pupils, held his hand above the flames. He sounded more curious than concerned. "So Project Surra escaped through here? Touching the fire we forbade you to touch?"

Twenty million years ago, she somehow freed herself and invaded a delicate ecosystem on the Tritans' most promising planet for their salvation. Fret, that's what Remorse felt. "Son, I cannot expound upon the incompetence of that Primary." True, Remorse never learned Three Two Four's age, but referring to him in this familiar way came naturally after all these walks.

"And the one who went in search of her was never to be seen again? Quet, yes?" Three Two Four straightened and fixed a wrinkle in the strange pants he wore, seamed in a fashion unfamiliar to Remorse. The Aegis prodigy often dressed strangely. Smartly, but strangely. Brilliant, Three Two Four logically devised the missing details with ease. "He went in search of her at your insistence and with the compression suit you loaned him. The one you asked if I could mend to your sixty-five feet of height."

Remorse said nothing now. Only stared out at that black lake, not of water but of flame, and wondered…

Quietly, Three Two Four shoved his hands into his pockets and correctly observed, "You are curious about it. You think Surra gained something from it."

Did she see or feel something that aided in her freedom? How had she used whatever she gained to sway the Icari? To evolve them? But this light was off limits. Remorse said as much. "Well, there must be a reason the Aegis warned the Tritans to dismiss it."

"We cannot be certain of the reaction." Three Two Four scrutinized Remorse closely now, although the Primary kept his gaze on the lake, but the old Tritan watched in his periphery as the other man continued, "Most of the test subjects died, but the few who survived went mad. We never knew one to remain whole. She must be very special."

Special.

Yes, Surra was the womb from which the Tritans birthed a galaxy. Ever since her escape, Primary Rem cursed Quet for granting her sentience. What being—higher being, at that—would tolerate the slavery she'd endured? Still, she'd lived comfortably in the luxury of a Dyson's Sphere, far from the poverty and sickness which evolved her children even now.

Ungrateful.

Now Surra possessed a gift, something that bested a Gargantuan Tritan and led to her maker's undoing. How…

Remorse reached out to find the answer, hesitated and retracted his arm—

"Reach out to the light, Primary Rem. Surra survived it. I have every faith a higher being such as yourself will, too. I will see that you do."

{MONARCH 3 | NOW}

What would Vi think of Remorse now? Would his wife even recognize him?

Not inside Karter's skin—

Why was Remorse having all these thoughts of ghosts long dead? They'd recently plagued him even on assignments. He watched from a great distance as the Shadow evacuated the gas farm. Meanwhile, Celindria did nothing to prevent it. Was she intentionally antagonizing the Shadow? Did she want the plant destroyed?

And what of Silence? Her suggestion to sacrifice Para to divert them from preventing Pax's recovery seemed very much like relinquishing a hostage.

This stank of the same rebellion that emboldened the Tritan women to commune and develop a secret government. With Abresson as his only company, Remorse found himself more and more lamenting the loss of Three Two Four. The young man possessed so much genius and innovation, a lost commodity in today's nacre economy—

Xelan.

Remorse's son flew off with F8 and Tameka, ferrying rescues back to the hive. Damn, F8 was meant to be dead. Two million years, and it was still a forgivable offense. What wouldn't Remorse forgive in Xelan? Born to a woman so like Remorse's Vi, Xelan represented all the hope the Primary placed in all his schemes.

Celindria mourned Nox's intended return. When Xelan resurrected in his place, Remorse felt the closest thing to happiness since before Vi's obliteration.

Still, it was bittersweet. Xelan was Shadow, after all, and he worked every waking hour to dismantle Remorse's Imminence. All the while, Remorse wove his son's lover into a thread of restoration and birth. Without her consent—

You will fail, you will die, and Fury will take your head.

Primary Rem rolled Karter's neck and shoulders, exorcising loud cracks from the tension. Within her mind, he let Karter see how little she impressed him with her thoughts.

That damned Valkyrie stood tall and proud. Everything about her straight and perfect. Black and green eyes clear, avian. Karter smiled, and it was predatory. No one withstood volition like this warrior. Most mewed on the floor in a puddle. Never had Remorse seen one so steadfast.

"You know, I find myself quite captivated by you in this moment. I think when we return to Enki, I'll express my attraction."

Karter folded her powerful arms and jutted out a full hip. Naked, confident, and sassy. "The same way you expressed it to Savis? No, thanks. I prefer my sex lively."

Remorse ignored his host and returned to using her body to spy on his son and Imminent's enemies. He'd rather return to Celindria's lab and watch over his grandson's sleep.

Everything became so complicated. So muddy. And this was a Probability of firsts. Nox exhaustingly rebelling against his orders, including assaulting Rayne. Her asking to spend fifty years in the Martyr Complex. Korac surviving Volcano Day. Andrew initiating into Cascading Light. Silence returning from slumber. Xelan resurrecting instead of Nox. Sagan killing Razor and bisecting Gait. Pax meeting Xelan.

Some of it was entertaining. Some of it was beautiful. But most of it pounded a furious geyser of octane into Remorse's heart. So much so that even now he was verifying if Rayne still slept in the Martyr Complex, using his true body to check. When he'd asked after her, Silence had remarked that the sleeping King no longer required a guard.

No.

Rayne roaming around Enki on her own was the last thing Imminent needed.

{ENKI | NOW}

"Primary, do you think she's already escaped?" Abresson asked, as they rushed through the conduits, shrines, and landings that separated New Cinder from the Pantheon. He sounded enticed, not threatened.

Remorse, furious to leave his grandson's side, couldn't bother with a reply. Celindria refused to lend T.A.O. to transport the two Tritans faster across Enki's immensity. She cited that Seamswalking Karter's body away from the Shadow and back to Enki took precedence.

Dread occupied all of his thoughts.

Silence was unpredictable as ever. Dangerous, even. They needed to rein her in, but with all her particular and exceptional abilities, she could melt Remorse for merely suggesting her judgment diverged from their aims.

Eternity help Remorse if Silence confronted him for meddling with her descendants.

"Sir, are you cold?"

Abresson looked Remorse over head-to-foot, incurring the older Tritan's irritation. In a flat voice, he ordered, "If she's missing, you will scour the entirety of Enki to find her. Use whatever resources necessary. Begin with the areas we least want her near and circle out. Start with the depositories."

Living up to the villain stereotype, Abresson excitedly rubbed his indigo hands together, scattered with scars. Scars from T.A.O.'s defense of her decimated virtue. Ever reliable—unfortunately so—Abresson answered, "Yes, Primary."

As long as he stayed useful, Remorse would use him, but Abresson was one minion he couldn't wait to execute. Maybe he'd feed him to Squilly? Or lose him in Torrentus, to wander forever in a perpetual storm?

Abresson hated storms.

"Here we are."

They rounded the last aisle that led to the old Aegis throne, granted to Silence upon her return. Mostly at Celindria's insistence. Another female in their ranks with an excess of power and not enough consistency. On several historical occasions, Celindria almost took Remorse's life, but it was never over his failure to complete a mission or to attain an asset. It was always the reminder of her missing soul. Remorse had learned a valuable lesson to never—ever—call that woman soulless. The ten million years she stole off his life accounted for it.

While Remorse was lost in these thoughts, they'd crossed the room to the Martyr Complex's dais. He knew without looking it was vacant. He also knew Silence had left Rayne unguarded, intending her freedom.

Abresson caressed the box, no longer lit from within. Softly, he said, "Is the Mother toying with Rayne?"

That was one theory. Not a bad one.

No matter how much the child railed against it, Rayne's fate ended here, destroying Remorse's well-earned home.

"The Mother works in mysterious ways." Or whatever nonsense it took to shut Abresson up—

Disheveled books close to the throne captured Remorse's attention, and he tilted his head as if it would help him to better discern their identity. An Overseer barreled above in its worn vigilance as Remorse crossed the space and opened the first book.

Vi.

Quet mentioned the love of Remorse's life in these entries. The dead Primary wrote these before... just before...

But someone tore out the page accounting for the race-altering event. Reduced to eighteen elders and a few dozen young bulls in one glorious and staggering second. The disaster which transformed Remorse into a being of pure pragmatism. Reason governed his every action, and sense formed the bars of his isolated prison.

"Shall I begin searching the depositories, Primary?"

Never alone, but always lonesome, Remorse nodded without turning back to acknowledge his lackey. The other man's footsteps echoed from the towering shelves as he marched to perform his duties.

Reading the entries brought back old memories. In all his time living here, the one wish Primary Rem repeated—for Vi to see this place, all its technology, life, and history—resurfaced and echoed in his old heart filled with black...

Remorse.

{ENKI}

Chris knew T.A.O. wasn't on her way to retrieve Karter. In fact, T.A.O. hadn't returned from her last mission at all. He knew this because Celindria muttered a single utterance about four hours ago.

She'd said, "Damn."

Afterward, Celindria parked Chris in a room and vacated his conscience. Stood with his back against a wall, Chris couldn't move his hands or feet, but could use his own eyes again.

It was a dark room with a big bulky thing he eventually recognized as a bed. He only figured that out because tiny snores filled the room from it. Toddler snores.

Pax.

Alive and well, praise Elden, but what in the hell did Imminent plan to do with Xelan and Tameka's son?

Chris overheard them mention initiation and a lot of confusing conversation about things being different "this time." Whatever that meant.

If this stint at guard duty granted him a few more hours without Celindria's molestation, Chris gratefully accepted the scenario. It afforded him time to consider their chances of escape and/or survival. Thanks to Silence, the Shadow recovered Para, but some of the ancient intelligence living behind Celindria's eyes implied a potentially sinister pitfall to the rescue.

Despite any of Celindria's schemes, Chris prayed the Shadow saved Karter next. Primary Rem spent more and more time with her, and when both bodies were present, the old Tritan regarded Karter with curiosity of the sexual variety. He even asked Celindria to check the Valkyrie's fertility cycle—

Look at that. Chris controlled enough of his bodily functions to cringe.

But what was all the drama before Celindria left Chris here? Something about Silence no longer guarding Rayne. Remorse took Abresson and hoofed it out of Celindria's lab.

What beautiful mercy that'd be if the Sleeping King awakened and destroyed these fuckers—

Light entered from a crack in the door.

"Celindria, please let Pax go back to his father!" Andrius' cries carried into the bedroom from deep within the adjacent lab.

Celindria's voice was closer to the door. "His father shouldn't exist. He should be grateful for this much time with his son. Pax is home now." She closed the door on any further protest.

With her regal carriage and sweeping skirts, the First Progeny glided majestically into the room, accompanied by a soft glow which emanated from an orb in her hand. Chris tried to open his mouth and tell her to stay away from Pax, but no volition, no words. Unhindered, Celindria sat on the edge of the bed and tenderly brushed Pax's red curls from his closed eyes. Those long red lashes softly curled on his tawny freckled cheeks, extra squishable with baby fat.

With everything in him, Chris strained to intervene. Still, nothing.

With eyes as bright a blue as her descendant's, Celindria gazed at the sleeping child, contemplative. As Chris looked on in his helpless state, a terrifying darkness shifted in her eyes. Something tried to press its way out. It raised goosebumps on his neck and tensed every responsive muscle in his body.

Attack!

Stop Celindria from—

From what?

When Celindria leaned forward to kiss Pax's cheek, an echo or a shadow of herself—multiples of her—followed.

It was as if every one of her existences folded the blanket back over Pax and covered him once more in a prismatic effect.

Her eyes flashed to Chris, and he resisted the urge to squirm under their haunting scrutiny. As if indulging in his discomfort, Celindria formed inside his conscience.

"Mother wants me to relegate you to guard duty, but I find you a hard temptation to resist."

Chris let himself shudder this time before quipping, "Do you always do as 'Mother' says?"

To call the smirk that formed on her generous lips wicked was a tremendous understatement. Evil learned everything it knew from this vile monster. Shadow clung to her malignancy, spurred by the dark room.

The phantom of Celindria vanished from this plane and exited the room as gracefully as she'd entered without another look or taunt for Chris. Which suited him just fine as every second with her exhausted any ounce of sanity left in him.

Xelan.

Tameka.

Rayne.

Please. Hurry.

{CINDER | 150,000,000 YEARS AGO}

Project Surra's Icarean companion grasped the universe, but only the singular one. Nacre-imbued Elden couldn't see multitudes of instances—blind to the Probabilities, the threats, and the lives outside their own. She could tell by the wonderment on his face. His gaze was absent of Cascading Light's exhilarating stimulus.

Elden stared into Surra's eyes, tilting his head left and then right. Cautiously, he reached a trembling hand, charcoal in shade, for her cheekbone. Exploring his heightened vision, he traced along the sharpest point of her soft skin, gazing all the while. Hot, his touch nearly seared Surra. It widened her eyes, and Elden mistook it for rejection. He let his hand fall.

"No!" Surra brought it back and leaned into it.

Contact. Real congress for the first time in her life. It brought tears to her eyes, which Elden brushed away with his thumb.

"I am honored for your grace, Surra."

For being born illiterate and mute, Elden spoke eloquently and in a beautiful baritone from the moment he swallowed Quet's nacre. His words held a significance which Surra wanted to explore. "You have reveled in my presence, and the moment you can speak, you speak only of me. What does Elden desire?"

Unabashed, confident, and a little cocky, Elden's lips turned in a smirk. "You." Still cupping Surra's cheek, he leaned in and pressed his lips to hers.

A sun blazed in this Icarus. A completely new experience to Surra, and it seared, burned for hours.

The night the Icari swallowed her maker's nacre, Surra spent it in Elden's arms. During their union, he asked her so many questions, filled with the precious curiosity had drawn him to her.

"Do the foreigners pursue you for your gifts?" "Will more arrive?" "How can I shelter you," and "How might I give my people wings?"

Surra answered all, but the last. There was a desperation in him, an indomitable need, to elevate the Icari to his intelligence. Elden reached for them with his attempts to educate their small minds and curb their impulsive behavior. They reached back, and Surra's martyr lover took their hands with fevered tears which begged for their evolution.

It broke her heart.

Surra knew how Elden could give his people wings, but she selfishly withheld the answer for over a hundred million years to keep him with her a little while longer. For once she taught him to splinter his nacre and share, the resulting cascade would drown them both in an endless wave of choices.

{Enki | Now}

Silence looked into the expansion of fate and encountered the same end. Pax's initiation sponsored a starburst of Probability activity. Fresh outcomes in the Matrix. Unfortunately, they still ceased with Rayne's demise. Unpredictable results yielded several threads where Silence faced the unthinkable.

Her end.

In thirteen thousand Probabilities, Silence died at the hands of a Shadow member. Once they learned she was beyond saving, Sagan destroyed Silence via conduit splitting, Tameka in her intolerance for condemned souls drained Silence's nacre dry, and Kyle...

Poor Kyle.

"I've never seen you shudder before," Lucas muttered for her ears only, standing at her side. Silence's initiate.

Also at her side, Lucas' initiate, Smith, smiled in his quiet regard for the screen projected in the room's center.

After Pax's initiation ceremony, they strategically withdrew to Silence's favorite space in Enki. A secret her father once divulged. An egg-shaped chamber of ambient-shifting colors—purple, blue, green—filled with droplets of water that traversed a helix of antigravity in a perpetual dance that encompassed the entire room. She stood on a transparent surface at the heart of it.

At Lucas' observation, Silence wanted to hold her chin higher, but she knew it would simply acknowledge his accuracy. She wasn't ready to engage him in that conversation—the one about betraying people they came to love—just yet. Instead, she said, "You haven't seen me for almost six million years. How was it for you?"

Smith chuckled, as if he already suspected the answer wasn't a positive one.

Lucas stamped a foot on the glass twice. A clear lounger rose from the surface, and he draped himself in it with a sigh. He looked uncomfortable in the battle gear, surely missing his finer attire. Pinching the bridge of his nose, he said, "Where do you want to begin?"

As if the other man's informality gave him permission, Smith relaxed his stance and adjusted the view on the screen.

Silence followed suit and also summoned a chair only to climb onto it, sitting with her butt on the back of it and her bare feet on the cushion. The color of the room transitioned into a rose red, and she knew how to answer. "Tell me how we've deviated so far."

"Oh, Silence. That's a journey too long and too sad to share."

She quirked a brow at him.

He sighed and shook his head. Beside her, Smith chuckled again. Surrendering, Lucas leaned his head on his resting hand and said, "I have never discerned the timing of events. Mind you, I pieced this together—Smith and I. What you suspected of Remorse was always true. He never fully aligned with you. Sabotaging your stasis chamber was only one event in a long history of deceit. All the while Remorse came to you for leadership, he conspired with the Exalted's son—Razor—"

"I wished I'd seen Sagan cut that fucker in half." Smith's first words in hours.

Silence brought her legs up and crossed them under her. Perched on the back of the chair, her hands idly played with Pax's chain around her neck. "What of Elden and my daughter?"

Lucas huffed and slouched inelegantly across the chaise. "You're really insisting I tell you—"

Silence's eyes flashed Atramentous, and he held up his hands. "Fine. Fine. Eternity take me. You told me Umbra would take power somehow and in the process wed your daughter, but I don't think you expected Elden to ever… See, it's upsetting you."

Damn him for reading her so well even when she controlled every muscle on her face, but Elden always said the steel in Silence's eyes betrayed her. She waved for Lucas to go on and returned to fidgeting with the necklace.

Smith shook his head and tsked.

"With his Primary status, Remorse convinced Bol and Tumu—barely Tumu—that the Icari posed a threat. When Tumu and Wiw went off-world for an unknown mission, the other Tritans expanded Li via its nacre. You know this much from Nox's Verse."

Smith spoke again without taking his eyes off the monitor. "Rated five stars. Best damn book I'd read in three millennia."

Silence shot him a look, but he never glanced her way. Nox's Verse said nothing of the fighting force that Primary Rem wanted decimated. "My fighters?"

Lucas shook his head, golden eyes flat with gravity. "Between Umbra and Remorse's influence and simulations in the Probability Matrix, they positioned the desired survivors and the intended victims with immaculate precision. Savis was never in any danger, but they wiped your armies from history."

It hurt to swallow the humility. Silence lost an invaluable gambit to a Tritan. "You? How did you survive?"

"I heeded your warning and went into the galaxy undercover in one of Umbra's secret smuggling operations." When Lucas continued speaking, mischief sparkled in his eyes. "Reipon was fond of sleigh oil."

Silence frowned. "Why is that?"

"Lubrication."

Both of them glared at Smith this time.

Lucas cleared his throat before continuing. "Moving on. What else would you like to know?"

Not much remained. Tumu's subsequent demotions obviously resulted from his investigation into Remorse's motives. A dangerous game. Wiw operated by inconspicuous means, retaining his Eminent status while performing some good in the galaxy. Lance preferred ignorance for his conscience's sake.

One thing occurred to Silence. "Why were Celindria and Xelan on Thailea the day of the cataclysm?"

"Ah," Smith muttered.

Lucas sat up for this one and rested his elbows on his knees. With his fingers steepled over his mouth, he said, "We don't know, but we would all like to."

Nacre ore? Or something more sinister? Silence knew one thing for certain. "It wasn't for the Atheneum. I believe Xelan already knew it was Korac by then."

Biting his lip, Lucas considered for a moment. Eventually, he nodded. "Yes. Although it was uncertain in the Probability Matrix, the Prince was far too close to Razor and Korac not to know."

Korac.

Silence loved Sagan, and Sagan loved Korac. It seemed so cruel Silence would see them apart, but her mission beckoned. Speaking of... "How is she, Smith?"

"Rayne is fifty klicks into the first leg of the map. She's fast. They'll never catch her."

Lucas beamed before he could hide it from Silence. She wished he didn't feel the need. These two men spent time under Rayne's leadership, and they vouched for her prowess and virtue.

As if on cue, Lucas said, "She'll give them hell if they're so unfortunate as to try."

Smith grinned back at him.

With Rayne free and Pax captured, Celindria's and Remorse's hands were full. And therefore, out of Silence's way. The Shadow were certainly inevitable. Tameka would rescue her son and bring every ally in the Vast Collective to help save him. Unfortunately, Remorse and Celindria had considered this in their calculations. When Rayne destroys the Dyson's Sphere, she'll destroy the only defenses against pure Imminent control throughout the galaxy.

Silence hopped off the chair and walked over to the projection. Smith stepped aside for her. They both watched from the vantage of a hijacked Overseer as Rayne ran across the continent-sized Pantheon. Tireless, raw, and beautiful. Her biorhythms were synced perfectly with the layers of living existence which surrounded her. In true holographic harmony, billions of Probabilities interlaced over one girl.

As well as the billions of fates hanging on Rayne's last breath.

THREE
TAKE OUT THE SOURCE; STOP THE CASCADE

{ENKI}

"DOES IT FEEL LIKE I'M BEING WATCHED?"

Rayne's skin itched ever since leaving Silence's throne room. Her bones tingled with prickling nerves. She stopped dead center in an intersection connecting miles of identical white shelves, reaching for the silver sky above.

Beside her in mind only, Nox said, "Something feels wrong."

Yes. It did.

Rayne ran thousands of miles over the last two hours under this irritating sense of scrutiny. Someone followed her without impeding her mission. They—and she could only guess it was Imminent—either wanted her to succeed or wanted to learn from her performance.

"Rayne."

In all ways possible, she closed her eyes to the weight of her name from Nox's voice. Every time he said it, the leagues of history between them crashed into her like a tidal wave, and she struggled to keep her head above the confusion. Instead of acknowledging it, Rayne licked her lips and said, "What do you think? Continue following the map or take another route—"

Calibrated.

Optimized.

Stabilizing...

Unable to stabilize.

Warning: Sixty-eight hours and thirty-two minutes until maximum destabilization.

Frustration nearly clawed a growl from Rayne's throat—a scream, even. A war cry to deflect would-be contenders that watched from the shadows. There wasn't time to get lost in this chalky library. She needed Xelan. Would give anything to hear him say—

"Open your eyes."

Without question, Rayne did and took in her surroundings. Nox searched through the screen that acted as her vision within the mindscape. His keener eyes, more avian than her own, often glimpsed things before her. The mercury waterfall across the way, for instance. He pointed at it before she realized why. Reflected in the sheer falls was one of those clunky metal security boxes that hovered over the Pantheon, lingering miles behind her.

That's how.

Nox narrowed his gaze, and Rayne saw the calculation in his black eyes. "You can take it down with the nacre rifle, but I advise against it."

"Because it's Silence, and we may still need her? And keeping it around would eventually reveal her motivations for helping me?"

Respect flashed on his handsome face and pulled the corners of his mouth. Nox didn't bother asking her how she'd guessed. No. While Rayne surprised him with her intuition, he trusted it in a way she came to appreciate. After another second, Nox said, "She's not your only pursuer, but she's your only perceived ally. Lean into that as we have no other direction to speak of and face a labyrinth of epic proportions."

With a countdown, no less.

But neither of them mentioned it. The fuse updated Rayne frequently of her diminishing lifespan. "Right." She stepped up to the waterfall and took in her reflection. Running at this speed was hell on her ponytail. After adjusting it and her armor, she turned inside her mind to smile at Nox.

He shook his head at her incredulous behavior with a slight... was that a smirk? Nox wasn't simply different in the last twelve hours. He was transformed—

"Is there something on my face, your majesty?"

They both knew that wasn't possible in her mindscape, but Rayne took the hint and looked straight ahead. "Sorry. It's just... I can't tell if you're liberated by Korac's Verse or relieved that Enki's end is nigh."

This time Nox *did* smile, and Rayne admitted a small thrill went through her at the sight of this six-foot, five-inch behemoth grinning with an abandon he'd never known in his lifetime. It even silkened the baritone of his already rich voice as he said, "Why not both?"

Rayne saved a small smile for herself, a happiness she embraced instead of buried, despite the hopelessness inspired by the fuse. Even that couldn't take away from the win which was this man's unfettered humor. So she ran, pressing onward, following a map of conduits to lead her from this place and to... wherever. Here and there, glimpsing the reflection of the Overseer across the Pantheon's many shiny things perched precariously on shelves.

"I hope no one ever lets a cat in here." Inside her head, Rayne snickered at her own joke.

With his heavy arms folded in a tough-guy pose, Nox quirked a brow at her.

Rayne snickered even more.

{Enki}

To Nox, Rayne's laughter chimed like a cheerful bell. A sound only given in freedom, and she rang it in Hell.

He loved her for it.

Which hurt him to think that his current elation stemmed from impending altercations. How could Nox tell Rayne he was excited at the mere thought of feeling her strangle an opponent with those dainty but powerful hands? Confess he wanted to feel the splash of warm blood on her face from a well-executed nacre-ectomy? Express how he lamented he couldn't see her doused in her opponent's carnage and relish in their defeat? Hair mussed, chest heaving, bright blue eyes sharp for more.

For all the good this rehabilitation did Nox's soul, nothing could sate the fighter in him like pure, skillful violence. Rayne was the best at it. Nox should know.

Thousands of miles passed down this path of repeating shelves and mercury pools. Rayne never tired, and the exertion hardly affected her breathing. The Tritans built quite the nacre they installed in this killing machine with a precious smile. Gargantuan—Primary class—and weaponized. Her heritage contributed to it, mostly unbeknown to the many of those Tritans involved in her making. Primary Rem's DNA from Xelan no doubt bestowed some gifts combined with her nacre. Who knew what Rayne gained descending from Celindria, seeing as no one knew the extents of the First Progeny's abilities.

A god. The reincarnation of Elden. And Rayne's eyes sparkled whenever Nox smiled.

He closed his eyes.

Time and place. If they survived, Nox would continue living in her consciousness. Her ease with it surprised him and implied a bizarre but mutually comfortable future ahead. Focus on it. Not on his feelings or his attraction for her.

Which was damned hard to do with Rayne smiling like that.

Nox shook himself and said, "You're approaching the first conduit."

"Right." Rayne straightened her shoulders, shoring herself. The slight clench of her jaw said as much. "What do you suppose is on the other side?"

Enki was vast. Sized to house several million suns, but in his lifetime, Nox counted less than two dozen Tritans. He'd wondered about the Aegis population, and why they considered building this Dyson's Sphere. But at least he knew the likely answer to her question. "Tameka reported to you that the Shadow estimated several billion identical ocean 'landings' comprises most of Enki's maze. I imagine you'll encounter one early in this excursion."

Outside her mindscape, Rayne slowed to a halt. The aisle which served as a major artery to the ancient archives ended at a columned arch of white stone, framing a shimmering wall of energy. She said, "We're about to find out. This is the first of hundreds of conduits on this map."

Rayne took a breath, held it, and stepped through.

For the first time in Nox's life, the glimpse of the Seam between conduits wasn't monochromatic. The cathedrals ceilings of the once bone-white hall were every shade of purple, vibrant and beautiful. He wondered at the majesty of it.

Rayne beamed at it. "Sagan did that."

The Progeny were truly gifted.

Once through, they both took in Rayne's surroundings. Ocean stretched in three-hundred and sixty degrees around the marble square platform she stood upon. Blue cloudless skies hovered above the flat blue water. Softly, she said, "You were right. A landing." After a thoughtful moment passed, Rayne added, "I don't know why Enki fears me. They should fear Tameka."

No doubt. They stole her son. Curious, Nox asked, "What kind of fighter is she? I'm afraid I've only had the pleasure once, and I was... distracted." By Rayne. On Volcano Day, he'd only wanted to fight with Rayne and completely alone. And, because of Nox's Verse, Rayne understood why.

A touch of pink kissed Rayne's cheeks as she took his meaning. Sticking to the subject, she crossed the landing to the next conduit and explained, "The name 'Fury' suits Tameka. She never held back, even in those early days. When she swung, she intended to knock your teeth down your throat. She's good with her legs. Kicking. Grappling. But I've seen no one work a chain dart like her. Just amazing."

Yes. The back of Nox's head vividly recalled Tameka's weapon. The blow had nearly killed him, but he'd avoided its gilded blades by mere centimeters.

"But it's not why she's a fury to fight..."

Nox let Rayne see the curiosity in his glance.

She took the intended encouragement and continued as Rayne stepped through the next conduit onto another generic landing. "Never come for the people she loves and leave Tameka alive. She has no patience for redemption, no grasp of mercy. I think I read something once like, 'To know your enemy is to love them.' Or vice versa. I can't remember. But either way, Tameka leaves the knowing to someone else. She's not here for that shit."

Another conduit yielded another landing, and as Rayne strode across it, Nox considered her words. "The five of you make such a balance. The three women, especially. Sagan of grace, Tameka of pragmatism, and you of sacrifice."

Rayne winced, and Nox immediately wished to take it back—

"No, it's okay. I know what my strengths and weaknesses are. It's only that..." She sighed and ran through the next conduit. "I don't think I would trade mine for something else. Everything I've gone through has taught me so much— You know I still hear Xelan's voice telling me lessons in my head? All this shaped us, and I like who we are. And do you know what else?"

Nox raised a brow for her to continue.

"I think you, Korac, and Xelan are settling into who you want to be, too."

Another revelation here with Rayne. The Verses... They were an admission that now was the time to write of their lives because only now do they feel balanced, right, and... good.

A warmth encompassed Nox, familiar only in ancient memories, but he felt it more and more in Rayne's presence. He opened his mouth to tell her as much when something caught his eye.

A movement in the otherwise flat water. A shade swam the length of the landing as Rayne ran across it to the next conduit marked on the map.

As if she'd sensed his tension, Rayne whispered, "What is it?"

Nox wet his lips and said his next words carefully. "Don't show alarm, but glance to the edge of the landing on your left."

When Rayne glimpsed it, only the slightest hitch of her breath gave her away. "How long?"

"Two conduits back was the first I noticed it." While half of Nox hated the tightness around her eyes, the other half of him hoped this was an exotic beast soon to meet its bloody end at her capable hands.

Inside her head, Rayne nodded over her shoulder. "The Overseer is still behind us, too." Her voice was airier than before.

Accelerated heart rate, constricted pupils, shallow breathing—

"Rayne, are you afraid?"

Her pulse fluttered as Nox noticed it did when he used her name. He tried to refer to her as 'your majesty,' but her name came too easily from his lips.

Still, Rayne answered with a firmer tone than Nox had expected. "No."

Interesting. If she wasn't afraid then... Almost in a whisper, he said, "You can tell me."

Soft, so very soft, Rayne confessed, "I'm excited."

Now, more so than ever, so was Nox.

FOUR

SHINE A LIGHT ON LOST SHADOWS

{ENKI}

BEING IN ENKI BROUGHT BACK PAINFUL MEMORIES FOR PEHTON. The last time the Lyriks were all gathered here was when the Primaries decommissioned them. These arrogant blue bastards created a species of near-mechanical women to use and discard at will. Ugliest pink slip ever. Two million years ago, and it was the only time Pehton had ever admired Triss.

"Why are you punishing us all for Gale's mistake?" Triss' yellow eyes glinted like citrines as Primary Bol stared down at her from his sixty-five feet of bulk, sat on his alabaster throne. She was unimpressed. "Condemning us to death for one Lyrik's delusions of grandeur is grotesque."

Pehton gasped behind her hand. The former Executive Warden had actually spoken out against their makers. Miy broke rank to show solidarity. Oleen followed. Then the others. They stepped forward for their lives under Triss' desperate defense.

Pehton was so impressed at the time, but now she knew the truth. It was Razor, wasn't it?

Bol, solely concerned for repopulating the Tritan race, spared his precious time to berate the battalion of tiny, constructed females. Disdain hardened his voice as he said, "You are all complicit in her activities."

Activities? Pehton narrowed her eyes at the word. Plural. Gale was the first and the most loyal of all Lyriks. She was the strongest—forewoman of the Siren's Gale.

Triss seemed less surprised as she said, "You have no proof of this. How should we know Gale would ask us to act outside your interests? You sent her on secret missions frequently. That one instance—"

"Forty-eight." Mouth shut, Triss fumed as Bol continued. "Forty-eight counts of conspiracy against your makers. Gale freed our test subjects and smuggled our weapons' technology to rebel forces on numerous occasions."

Fists clenched, teeth grit, Triss said, "You sent her to her death on Cinder. You knew Nox would destroy her."

"We had hoped it would be Korac who would execute her." Primary Rem—Remorse—entered the conduit into Bol's sanctum where the women faced persecution.

Elden, in hindsight, Pehton noticed so much more. Triss relaxed the moment the compressed Tritan entered the white bone and translucent glass space because she already knew the news he brought to their sentencing.

Surprised to see the other Tritan, Bol managed a polite gesture of greeting to the highest ranking Primary. "Remorse, are you joining the proceedings?"

Remorse shook his head. "Nothing to proceed here, old friend. Their fates are decided."

The Gargantuan recoiled and took a moment to recover before asking, "What is it to be?"

Facing the women, Primary Rem spared Pehton, the mother of his two beautiful children, an indiscernible glance. Regret? Grief? She'd never know because he said nothing to her. Instead, he announced, "Their punishment is to live solely in the employment of Gait as Wardens. No other commissions, ranks, or privileges."

Pehton knew this condemned them to Razor's service because she signed their volition to him. All but Triss, unbeknown to Pehton, who beamed at the news.

In the present, sitting in Primary Tumu's kitchen, something about the story only now struck Pehton.

"You were helping Gale."

Xelan, Caedes, Lamassau, and Korac stiffened and turned. Not Tumu. He carried on as if Pehton had never said a word, compiling Razor's hand-drawn map with Caedes' three-dimensional rendering to find the battleground Tameka promised their allies.

Korac's eyes widened from their narrowed consideration as he searched Pehton's face. It was as if he knew her well enough now to recognize a chord was struck. "What is it, Executive Warden?"

Pehton tried to drill a hole in the back of Tumu's head with her gaze. Korac noticed and tapped Xelan's chest with the back of his hand, directing the Prince of Cinder to the old Primary.

Lamassau took the weight of their stares and, with a roll of his eyes, flicked his Tritan lover. "Yo, she's talking to you, and you know it. Spit it out, Tumi."

"Yes. I was helping Gale. Can we please return to the impending galactic apocalypse?"

Caedes made an approving humph.

Korac and Xelan exchanged a look before the former asked, "How do you mean?"

Lam whispered something in Tumu's ear hole, while Pehton answered for him, "Gale was a double agent. All that time as the Primaries' personal guard, she took advantage of the resources in Enki to free research subjects and smuggle technology out of Enki."

Xelan's mouth dropped open.

Korac frowned hard enough to nearly wrinkle his perfect face. Given his history with Gale, this news was tragic.

Caedes met Pehton's eyes. "So your leader wasn't a villain?"

She opened her mouth to answer when another interrupted.

"She was my friend."

Every one of them glared at Tumu's back.

The oldest Tritan kept it to them as he elaborated, "Gale was much like you, Pehton. She couldn't stand suffering. Fed up with the mistreatment of Bol and Quet's experiments, Gale came to me for help. The first Seamswalker wasn't born yet, so a Primary would do. Using Aegis blood, I created conduits to Reipon, L. Capra, and Yu. Iuo, Kombuchi, and Legir helped the victims. I told no one because Gale feared retaliation. She thought to make an ally of the Icarean Princes, but her liaison with Korac unearthed some anxieties she never once considered."

Pehton held her breath when Tumu turned around with a sad look on his featureless face.

Korac met the Tritan's stare with his usual icy mask. This was a sensitive subject they all learned in Korac's Verse recently. That Gale was the Icarean General's first lover, and she mistreated him after.

"Apparently, your encounter changed Gale's perception of her life. She confided in me about it. About how she never had a lover thrill her as much. How it made her contemplate her own happiness, for once, over the thousands Gale had saved. It rattled her trust in herself. Gale couldn't ally with you because her distraction with you would endanger her mission. And it did. She slipped one scale in Cinder's favor, and Primary Rem noticed. He rightly feared she'd considered activating the Chorus to destroy Enki. So he sent her with scant forces and sabotaged gear to face the galaxy's deadliest weapon, and Nox executed her proficiently."

Xelan looked at Korac, who turned his face away. Everyone else followed suit. This was a regret which couldn't be mended, and the hurt it caused chilled the room.

Tumu stepped into Pehton's field of vision and forced eye contact. "When another promising Lyrik came asking for my help to free the enslaved children across the Vast Collective, I knew I couldn't resist."

"No matter how much I asked." Lamassau was staring at his hands as he said, "You took so much of Gale's death on yourself, Tumi. I worried about you." He reached out and squeezed the bigger Tritan's bicep.

With a shadow in his eyes which belied his extreme age, Tumu stared into his lover's face and pat the hand on his arm. Stiffly, he turned back to the map. "We're all here now. It all culminates in this. Let's talk strategy and let the long-dead rest for one day."

Korac and Xelan returned to business, but Caedes stared across the three-dimensional image at Pehton. Did he feel it too? The weight of all these bricks stacked and mortared over them, waiting to fall?

"Are. You. All. Right?" He mouthed.

Pehton almost snorted. A man of few words. Literally. A light warmth reignited in her heart despite all this heavy shit. That's how the Shadow survived all these trials. It wasn't magic or special endurance. It was surrounding themselves with people who eased the strain.

"Yeah. I'm. Fine."

Inappropriately, Caedes raked his eyes over her tiny stature. Pehton felt them on her shoulders, breasts, and hips as if he'd used his hands instead. It burned her cheeks. He nodded. Not smirked. Not grinned. It was a single dip of his chin, affirming they were on the same wavelength. Caedes was thinking of Pehton in the thick of this mess, and he wanted her to know it.

Someone cleared their throat, and Pehton's eyes flicked to the source.

Fuck her. It was Korac. No smirk on his lips, but it sparkled in his eyes. He gestured to the cosmos-affecting strategy as if asking, *"Is this boring you?"*

Asshole. Pehton would never pick on him if he were flirting with Sagan—

Pablo rushed into the kitchen, and Xelan spun to face him. They spoke at the same time. "Is she awake?" "Tameka's conscious and asking for you."

A burden lifted off the Icarus, and the Traitor Prince glowed like a sun before he checked the others.

Tumu waved him off. "Return with Peaches. She should be here for the empire she's building."

Pehton caught the ghost of a smile on Caedes' lips. He'd lived with Tameka for two years, resulting in a close friendship which Pehton respected, but it wasn't that kind of smile, and it wasn't only on his face. Lam and Korac also shared this secret expression. Even Pehton felt a twitch at her lips.

Tameka, Fury, promoted from Sovereign Ambassador to your majesty, raised as a human and trained to kill Icari, blazed a reputation across the galaxy. The Vast Collective needed a leader like her. Like Xelan.

Pehton couldn't wait to see what Tameka would do to Remorse. She only hoped to get a swing in before he met his overdue end.

{ENKI}

Xelan entered the space to find Tameka talking with Miy, as she and the Lyrik exchanged armor. The mother of his child, accustomed to communal showers, slipped out of her tactical suit. Goosebumps formed on every inch of her naked skin. Bones, Pablo, and Jack looked anywhere else in the room. Miy, as comfortable with nudity as any other Lyrik, didn't rush to hand over the change of clothes. There was no hurry to lace the elements together.

Here Xelan was, concerned over her welfare, while Tameka was gearing up for the battle ahead, and doing a fantastic job of it. Miy laced black bracers which hugged Tameka's corded arms up to the shoulder caps. There, a bright blue fabric cascaded from it. More of the black leather covered her breasts, tied like a corset. They threaded black shorts over her hips, with the same blue material gathered at her waist and draping down her legs like pants to meet black boots. With every leggy step, the gossamer cloth parted, revealing her tawny skin. It would add an amazing effect to her use of the chain dart holstered on her hip.

"We'll do hair and makeup when you're ready," Sagan offered from where she sat, staring at Triss' comatose body. She'd already changed into a bright blue halter and black leather pants. The attractive and impractical battle gear matched Tameka's outfit, but not the expression on Sagan's face.

Grim. That's how the Seamswalker looked.

Xelan crossed the room, gripped Sagan's shoulder gently and kissed the top of her head.

Tameka glided toward the door and called out to Sagan, "After the strategy meeting, we can do hair." To Xelan, she said, "Let's do this." The very picture of health—

Oh. Of course. Tameka was familiar with sipping from Enki's abundant sources of energy.

As if she knew Xelan had figured it out, Tameka winked at him on her way out of the medical zone. Xelan waved to Pablo and Lynn before following the enticing and capable redhead to the war room. He caught up to her and pulled her behind a column before they entered. He searched her green eyes and resisted kissing her black freckles, all fifteen of them. He'd counted. "I want to hear you say it before I assume—"

Fire blazed in him, energizing Xelan's blood with electricity until his eyes water and he gasped from the power surge. When he could see again, no longer blinded with power, Tameka's eyes had transitioned into her Atramentous. Solid green with a black slit for a pupil. She pulled him close during the power feed, and bergamot blossomed between them.

Breathy, Tameka's voice came out in three pitches. "I'm managing. It's the best I can do. Now that I'm back in my territory of power sources, I'm a live wire. I want to fuck you while draining Enki's star and experience that curiosity. But I can't get Pax off of my mind. I'm not sure how you're compartmentalizing so well. I won't lie, it's almost disturbing."

Xelan winced, but valued her honesty.

"I know it's your millions of years of learning to react from a calmer place, and I'm afraid I just lack that. So I might pass out again. I might cry and scream, but I know we'll get through this together and save him." Tameka cupped both sides of Xelan's face. "Until then, that's how I'm doing. Please don't ask me again because it disrupts however I've managed to cope in the moment."

Xelan kissed both her palms. "I understand completely."

Tameka's eyes transitioned to normal, and her cheeks flushed as she stepped away. "Sorry for the mixed signals."

Goofy grins felt a certain way when they formed. Too much stretching and a slight bashfulness which burned. That's how Xelan felt. "I accept all of your signals."

"Are you two returning to save the Vast Collective, or does Peaches need a minute?"

Tameka rolled her eyes at Tumu's intrusion and blew the air from her cheeks. "Are you ready?"

Xelan held out the bend of his arm. "As I'll ever be."

They entered the kitchen/war room. Andrew and Kyle arrived at some point, preparing snacks for everyone.

Pehton and Caedes nodded to Tameka. Korac moved over to make room for her. Lamassau circled a finger at her ensemble and gave her a thumbs up.

Tameka's smile was half-crooked, as if she spent all the energy she'd gathered to appear "okay" for them. She took the center of the room and searched the map. As was her way. "That's Primary Rem's sanctum, entry to the Pantheon. Razor's map takes us to the heart of it for this specific conduit." She tapped on it. "This is it. Enki's most sacred ground is our battlefield."

Korac looked over the area and asked, "What about the stacks?"

Lamassau circled a vacuous space around the conduit. "No stacks there for miles. It could work. We won't meet any resistance there. It's not guarded."

Across the three-dimensional rendering, Caedes adjusted the map with an occasional glance over Tameka's shoulder at Pehton, who muscled her tiny way in between all the giant males to say, "But there's a reason this conduit isn't guarded, right, Tumu?"

The past was still chasing Xelan. This conduit was the basis of so many nightmares.

Andrew and Kyle stopped messing with the replicator to listen to the Tritan's explanation.

An explanation which started with a heavy sigh. "Torrentus."

"Now you're just making up words," Korac accused, folding his arms with an unconvinced frown.

Despite himself, Xelan held back a chuckle and shook his head to hide his instinctive grin. That Icarus could always make him smile.

Lamassau clicked his tongue. "He's got you there, Tumi. It's a terrible name."

A frown almost replaced Xelan's smile. He actually quite liked the name.

Tameka pointed to the next location the extra special conduit led to. "Torrentus is there, and it's a deterrent?"

"Peaches, do you remember when you first came to Enki, and Sagan pointed at a storm over a continent?"

Xelan certainly remembered when he brought the five Progeny to Enki.

"See that storm over there?"

Tameka, already overwhelmed without the aid of a nacre, groaned as if turning to look made her head spin. A big swirling mass of dark gray clouds spread across another oil painting of a continent. "That's several thousand times larger than our whole planet."

"Torrentus *is* the storm." Tameka pieced it together.

Lamassau said, "And the conduit leads to it. It's the only stable space there.

Pehton went into more detail. "Say Sagan Seamswalks us all into Primary Rem's sanctum, and then we make our way to the center of the Pantheon. Anyone who goes into this conduit will never come back. None of the prisoners have, anyway."

Andrew asked, "Prisoners? I thought they went to Gait."

Xelan hid a wince and tried to think about anything else.

Tumu explained, "Not the bodies of research. Remorse wouldn't let them out of the Dyson's Sphere. Again, this is all conjecture based on—"

"Why do you feel the need to cover for them?" Tameka searched the Tritan's voids when he looked down at her.

Xelan almost felt the need to intervene when Tumu answered, "There are so few of us left. They are my people. And I hate thinking one way about a person only to learn later they weren't as bad as I thought."

Like Gale. Like Korac. And maybe like Nox.

Kyle pointed a joint at the image and returned the conversation to the topic at hand. "So this map says the bridge is on the continent under Torrentus, and this storm, I assume, is always going?"

"It's not simply a storm. It's terraforming," Lamassau said. "But it went wrong when..."

"When we sealed the Aegis inside Gait." Tumu's many sharp teeth gnashed together, and Xelan understood it.

Regret.

The Prince of Cinder stared at the screen and bit his thumbnail. Terraforming. Dangerous atmospheric instability, but operated somehow. "It's a device?" He was already certain of the answer.

Tumu nodded.

Tameka got there before her lover did. She asked, "Does Torrentus have a power source?"

"That's my girl." Xelan grinned.

{ENKI}

Korac, along with the rest of the room, turned and looked at the powerhouse who was Tameka Phillips. He couldn't help but notice the pride in Xelan's eyes as he gazed at his girl with pure respect. It amused Korac that Caedes shared a similar expression. Long-term exposure to Fury had a catching effect.

Hell, even Tumu's voids glimmered regarding her fantastic suggestion of draining the storm. "Yes. Torrentus should respond, but I warn you. The experience under that catastrophe might be so intense you can't reach your ability in time before it overwhelms you. It was a byproduct of Ishkur."

That word again. It rang in Korac's bones.

Recognition ignited Tameka's eyes in green fire. "What is Ishkur? Why did Celindria say I was the key to it?"

A flicker of something passed over Xelan's face before he answered, "Ishkur is a project the Aegis abandoned."

Tumu elaborated, "I never saw evidence of its completion."

When Razor cycled into Korac, he told Sagan of projects the Aegis abandoned because of Inanis and eventually Tritan intervention. Was Ishkur one of them? Korac said, "The Aegis left several endeavors unfinished because of Razor's experiments with his Probability army."

Something pressed against Korac's mind, nearly interrupting his thoughts. Something he'd experienced before. He spared a glance at Andrew. It was happening more frequently lately and only when this Progeny was in the room. When Andrew met his eyes for a brief glimpse, Korac knew it was him. So much guilt inside. Was Andrew tearing himself apart over Lucas? Testing their intentions because he forgot how to trust?

Tumu carried on with details about Tritan security. Andrew left the room with a wave. Kyle stayed behind and offered his joint to Lam, who whispered a flame onto it, reducing it to ashes. Pehton followed the conversation from her height deficit, looking for all the world like a sexy penguin. Tameka's eyes fluttered, and she shook her head. When she took two deep breaths, Xelan touched his hand to her back.

The Shadow was burnt out. Phase III came too soon after Phase II, and planning wasn't exactly regrouping. The Prince's comforting gesture to his mate reminded Korac of an important promise he made to himself. He said, "I need to check on Sagan. I like what we have here so far. Tritan hallowed ground as a battlefield—What a concept. I'll formulate units once we get this information to Lady F8."

"Wait," Xelan grabbed his arm and... well, things were complicated. As if he sensed it, too, the Traitor Prince dropped his hand and said, "I may or may not have smuggled some Tritan weaponry—"

"Excuse me?" Tumu took some offense.

"—Into my stronghold on Earth. Colton and Cypher told Lynn and Andrew that it's structurally sound. Can you and Sagan grab them for me? There's not many. Nothing you can't carry." As if to make his point, Xelan's eyes flicked to Korac's substantial biceps.

An awkward silence settled in the room. Everyone watched Xelan and Korac's interaction. A side-effect of airing all of their dirty laundry. As the unnecessary tension mounted, Korac muttered a curse and walked out on the past which haunted Xelan's eyes and went in search of his future.

Sagan sat across from Triss, staring with dark circles under her eyes. Elden, Gait's royal couple stole so much from his girl. He wanted a way to return her peace of mind.

"Sagan?"

She startled in a room full of her favorite people and blinked a few times at Korac as if trying to recognize him. Or check whose eyes were in his head. After a second of this, a gorgeous smile—goofy, too—spread over those soft lips.

When watermelon diffused the air, Korac knew she liked his battle gear almost as much as he liked hers. A purple Icarean robe which matched her eyes, cinched at the waist by a silver wide-link chain. Black leather pants which matched her own tucked into embellished motorcycle boots completed the ensemble.

Sagan stood and drove the point home, running her small hand over his pale exposed skin where the robe intentionally gaped. Warm fingers traced the designs he'd painted beneath. With her free hand, Sagan tugged gently on one of Korac's ornate braids that fell from his sliver ponytail. She smiled and said, "Hey there, handsome. I was just imagining the rest of our lives together."

Shit. It was never a good time to ask her. Phase III came upon them fast, but "rest of their lives together" sounded nice. Korac took Sagan's hand from his chest and brought it to his lips. Soon. "We have some errands. They shouldn't take long." He let his eyes wander to the sweetheart neckline of her deliciously revealing halter top.

Yes. Pink, glowing cheeks. That's what Korac wanted. Sagan stopped playing with his hair and swatted him. He kept the wince to himself. Progeny women were fucking strong.

"Where do they need me to go?"

After thirty minutes of checking with everyone to see if they needed anything on this run, Korac and Sagan arrived on Monarch 3, where they met with F8.

"The Pantheon."

"Yes."

"As a battlefield?"

"Yes."

Inside the viscous fluid-lined hive, the elusive Queen of Monarch 3 sat on a black blossom which formed her throne. Seps stood at her right side, while a legion of other drones lined the walls, standing at attention like excellent soldiers. With her head tilted in contemplation, F8 asked, "Was this Tameka's idea?"

Sagan's mouth gaped in surprise. "How did you—"

"She's bold and this is an idea only thought up by someone possessing such bravado. Can you get us there, Seamswalker?"

Sagan stepped forward like the confident General who Korac loved. "I'll retrieve you and the rest of the forces from Cinder's shrine. There *are* other forces, yes? With our current situation, we're out of touch, so we've no idea how far the declaration of war has carried."

F8 smirked and glanced at Seps, who also smirked. She leaned into him and muttered, "Shall we tell them or let it be a surprise?"

Sagan tensed beside Korac, so he pressed his hand against the exposed skin of her back. He could see what she couldn't. F8's pulse pounded, her heavy breathing expanded her ample chest, and the woman's multi-faceted eyes glimmered with warm light.

Pure exhilaration.

Korac recognized it from many of his partners. After all, with gags, blindfolds, and masks, they'd learned to communicate without words.

Sagan looked a question at Korac, and he whispered in her ear, "It's good news. I'm still uncertain how good, but we'll see the support we need."

"You have no idea." F8 sounded satisfied and elated. "This will be the battle to end all strife across the Vast Collective, and we move under the Shadow's banner. Please... pass on my respects." The Queen bowed at the neck, but her people fell to one knee and pounded a fist to their chest.

Thousands of drones paid their respect to the Shadow.

On a final note, F8 said, "The Tritan makers, all their dominating schemes to subjugate the women they'd created, will see their worlds undone at our hands." She held her tiny feminine hand to her face and clenched it into a fist.

All the leaders of the planets were such drama queens.

Korac was still contemplating this when Sagan Seamswalked them into the study of Xelan's desert stronghold. A hexagonal room lined with rosewood shelves and furnished with plush leather sofas plus one massive desk custom-made to mount along one half of the room. A small flame of Cascading Light burned in the fireplace.

It was called "taste."

Sagan went over to the desk and rummaged through some books. "Can you believe—"

One latched and the wall with the desk revolved into another room.

"—That Xelan's this cheesy."

Korac gaped incredulously and swore to never accuse the Traitor Prince of having taste again. As Sagan disappeared, Korac followed the desk into the next room. "Before Imminent had attacked Iona Medical and the Arsenal, I would have called it redundant to house a secret vault in a stronghold miles under an empty desert."

Taking in the room, Korac could see why. A variety of goodies hovered over a dozen podiums set throughout the otherwise bare room. One of which he recognized. Pointing at the gun, he said, "Remorse held one like this at me when I confronted him after you went... missing."

Sagan shot him a sweet smile. This way and that, she tried to show she was recovering. Korac only wished she'd never endured it in the first place. She bent her knees to read the podium's label under the handheld cannon. "Aegis Deterrent. Yeah, no shit. How big is this thing? Oh . . ." Sagan blinked and read, "Forty-five kilograms. Aw, thanks, Wingmaster. These labels are nifty."

Korac smiled to himself all the while to Sagan's chatter. He scanned a few labels of some interesting blades and something which looked like a riding crop. Interesting. Reading the label, he said, "This one is electric." Maybe it vibrates? Glows?

Oh.

Nope.

Touching it, the throng sparked and buzzed. Korac caught Sagan's wide eyes staring as he held it. He smirked and said, "After we've won, we'll put it to good use." He almost added "if you're up for it," but realized reminding Sagan of her progress wasn't helpful. She needed the distraction and fun. Korac could deliver that in spades.

"What do you think they're doing to Pax?"

Sagan's question put a cap right on Korac's intentions. He answered honestly, "I wish I knew."

Sagan plucked another weapon from the podium and added it to the trunk. "Tameka will kill them all, including Silence. I hate feeling this conflicted about the enemy."

"You shared hope with her. That's a precious thing to the Shadow. It hurts to have such a pure, intimate experience spat on, and I can tell you that you'll get through it and there's more after this, but it's not good enough. It shouldn't be this way."

Across the way, Sagan looked at him like...

Well, it was a hard expression to describe. Gratitude. Understanding. Ah. Korac smiled openly for her as he interpreted it. "I love you, too, amos." Now was the time—

Fuck!

Fuck, Korac left it with all their shit back in Enki.

He must have groaned because Sagan stopped smiling and asked, "What's wrong?"

Korac was an idiot. That's what was wrong. "Nothing. Just exhausted. Forgetting things and the resulting frustration."

"Tell me about it. I forgot to bring a bra." A playful glint shone in Sagan's eyes.

Elden, love her, Korac nearly melted on the spot. "Well, we can't take advantage of that now, can we?" He crossed the short distance between them and bent down to meet her soft lips. Warm. This was home—

"Cut her out of me. I am my own. Korac!"

He broke the kiss and whirled to find T.A.O. entreating him with her arms outstretched, soaked in red blood.

"T.A.O.!" Sagan cried, before rushing over to her. "Oh, Elden. Are you all right?" She frantically searched the smaller Seamswalker.

The tears spilling from her broke Korac's heart. "Can you hear us, T.A.O.? Are you, yourself?"

It was her. There was no way Celindria could imitate the warmth in those Atramentous eyes, but otherwise, T.A.O. barely looked like herself.

Fuck, Korac hated all the strappy bondage shit Celindria dressed her little sister in. At least Celindria left T.A.O.'s hair long and wavy. He cupped the volume of it to her face and touched something wet and warm. Korac's hand came away from her skull, covered in blood.

Even injured, T.A.O. kept herself from marring his clothes. Frantic, she spoke in that strange talk of hers. "I cut her out of me. I am my own. My blood. My power. My brothers, oh, Elden... Korac!" She looked away from him and into Sagan's eyes. "You let him have you. I couldn't stop it. Never let her have you. I couldn't... The boy..."

Sagan caught the dark elfin woman when she collapsed. Distraught, his lover looked to Korac for guidance. "Do we take her to our people and risk that she's a sleeper?"

Any way out of this was a bad idea.

What would Wingmaster do?

{ENKI}

Ross finished helping Pablo make Para comfortable on one of several dozen pallets which Lynn, Twenty-One, and Bones assembled. Those beds were like tombstones in a graveyard. She sat down on the glass floor and pressed her back against a glass wall—all of it surrounded by Dyson's Sphere tech.

"Do you think we'll need them all?" Jack's voice was sad, but not hopeless.

He sank down beside Ross, folded his arms on his knees, and then rested his chin on his arms. Jack's side profile looked handsome against a pool of Cascading Light. Earnest and sincere.

Ross realized he'd asked her a question. "I hope not. Para is stable, though. Xelan isn't sure how to wake her." Now wasn't the best time to tell Jack Ross woke up and saw the potential in him, but she was doing it, anyway. "Jack, I like—"

"We got an emergency here, Doc!" Korac and Sagan Seamswalked into the makeshift medic corner. The latter was holding a bundle—Holy shit, the bundle was bleeding.

After laying the woman out, Sagan opened another conduit. "I'm getting Xelan."

Usually perfectly collected, a slight edge strained Korac's otherwise smooth voice. "Thank you." Sagan nodded to him as she left, and Pablo approached. Korac explained, "She's bleeding from this side of her head. She said a few things to us before she passed out."

The Doctor gaped at the woman. "That's T.A.O. Is she free? Oh, wow." He switched into professional mode and checked the bleeding injury.

Andrew called, "She's free. I can feel her intentions are her own and aren't hindered by Celindria."

Ross stayed put as Lynn and the others came to verify for themselves it was the first Seamswalker. Jack remained sitting with Ross, and this was good. They were better off out of the way.

Sagan Seamswalked out of thin air again. This time she brought Wingmaster. He took one look at the woman on the table and slipped his medical hat on. Xelan asked, "What are her vitals?"

Pablo packed gauze around the wound on her head and answered, "Thready pulse. Her nacre is healing the damage too slowly. Xelan, I—I think she tried to cut something out of her brain. See here, and here..." He indicated points along her skull which Ross couldn't see from over here.

"Of course..." Xelan started with his thinking and pacing. Talking to himself, he said, "And a drill... Yes, she would know where in my lab to find those things..." He went on for another minute. As he often did in these trances, Xelan nearly bit his thumbnail until he saw it was covered in her blood.

Sagan watched with bated breath.

Korac glared at him and said, "Do you mind sharing your findings with the rest of the class?"

Pablo licked his lips. Lynn's eyes flicked to them as the doctor said, "It's a theory we've been discussing about Para or anyone else inflicted with the Tenements of Volition, but I cannot imagine the horrors which drove T.A.O. to attempt brain surgery on herself."

"Brain surgery?!" Sagan cupped a hand over her mouth. Ross always thought she looked pretty when she did it, even in distress.

Korac pulled Sagan against him and chafed her arm in a comforting gesture as he continued to look Xelan upside the head. "Elaborate."

Xelan answered while turning T.A.O.'s head for a better look. "She cut into her motor cortex and..." He swallowed. "Carved out the voluntary motor function. Her nacre isn't healing because Celindria would think of this. Fail safes." He tossed a nod over his shoulder at Para to indicate a second example of such precautions.

Jack called from where he and Ross sat on the floor, "What about Gargantuan Tritan blood? Tumu cured my disabled nacre with it."

"I'm happy to volunteer." The spoken of devil walked into the room. "We can try."

Ross asked, "If it works, will we try it on Para?"

Xelan turned and gave Ross a proud smile. "Very quick. Yes. If it works. Tumu?"

Korac stepped out of the way to let the Tritan next to the bed.

Lynn removed a wet rag from where she was tending T.A.O., soaked in her blood. She and Pablo shared a hopeful look.

Even with his back to her, Ross still knew what Tumu was doing. Cutting a black vein and feeding his ultra special blood to T.A.O. Ross looked over to see Jack had closed his eyes as if praying. Shoring up all of her nerve, she reached over and took his hand. He opened his eyes and stared at her with a grateful and astonished look. Within one squeeze of Jack's hand, Tumu stepped back from the table, finished.

Xelan kept his hand on T.A.O.'s pulse. Pablo and Lynn returned to cleaning her. Better to see if she was healing without all the mess in the way. Sagan took Korac's hand and squeezed it. They all knew after listening to his Verse that Korac shared a special friendship with the endangered ancient Progeny in question. And everyone couldn't wait to see if they could save Para and the others this way—

"There." Xelan sounded elated. "T.A.O.'s pulse. It's stronger."

Lynn cried, "Her wounds are knitting."

Tumu stepped back, and Korac touched his arm. "Thank you."

With his lipless mouth, the Tritan smiled warmly. "No tiny women are dying on my watch. Not if I can help it."

Tameka stood in the doorway, leaned against it out of the way. She glanced over at Jack and Ross, who couldn't miss the warming of her eyes as she took in their hand holding. A smile touched her lips. Lam appeared behind her, watching over her head. Twenty-One and Bones even stopped mid-construction to watch.

Everyone held their breaths.

One heartbeat.

Two.

Those surrounding the table relaxed and let out their breaths on relieved sighs. Xelan muttered, "Thank Elden."

"Korac?" T.A.O. croaked.

He positioned himself in her line of sight once more. "I'm here. I never left."

"I cut her out of me—Father?!"

Xelan leaned over and did something Ross couldn't see. Probably kissed her forehead or something very Wingmaster-y.

"I got you."

Yup. Wingmaster-y.

Jack smiled at the catch phrase—No. The entire room lit up at it. So did Ross.

It was a sign of hope. Of making the impossible possible. And it wasn't going anywhere.

T.A.O. sounded beyond traumatized as she told her story. "When she called, I couldn't say no. Unless in the Seam. The bones of the old ones protected me. But only there. Still, I knew. I watched over all of you. Forgive the stolen. They are burdened with her ways. But it was the boy. I could bear it no longer—"

"My son?!" Tameka rushed to the table.

Xelan placed his hands on her shoulders, gently restraining the woman known as Fury.

T.A.O. possessed enough strength to sit upright and face Tameka. "Trains and bears. Bear the burden of this born soul. He waited so long... Longer than the rest of them."

Tumu moved up behind Tameka. Korac flanked her other side. They looked ready to grab her. Ross couldn't see, but the woman's shoulders trembled, either with tears or rage. Or both.

"What have they done to Pax?"

T.A.O. searched the other woman's eyes. "So long without the others. Won't let Remorse touch him. Shines with love at Karter, Chris, and Para."

That seemed to soothe the room.

"And sister."

The comforting moment ended.

Xelan whispered something in Tameka's ear which made her shake harder, and when she spoke, sobs strangled her voice. He said, "Please, T.A.O. Have they hurt him?"

"Never. No one would ever hurt your cub." Without reservation, T.A.O. reached out and cupped Tameka's cheek. "You will find him... when it's time."

Ross felt the heartache from over here as Tameka slowly lowered her head into her hands and cried. What did it say about their lifestyle that Ross thought it was a good thing Sagan hadn't done her makeup yet?

Activity overtook the room once more. Xelan and Pablo rushed over to Para's bed. On the way, Wingmaster said, "We'll get more clarity from Para. Let's start immediately."

Sagan pulled Tameka into her arms, and Korac stayed with T.A.O., who looked at him in an interesting way. Like Korac was a beacon in a dark abyss. Twenty-One and Bones went back to work. Tumu and Lamassau hung out, waiting to treat Para post-operation.

And Ross was still holding Jack's hand.

Crushes, war, and brain surgery.

The Shadow excelled at everything.

{ENKI}

Tameka refused to give Imminent one more drop of her tears. To solidify the pact with herself, she asked Sagan to apply her makeup and style her hair. It was more for the comfort than the aesthetics, and that's truly why the others were doing the same. Everyone was preparing.

Meanwhile, Xelan and Pablo waited at Para's bedside. Bones joined their post-surgery vigil. He looked grave.

As Sagan positioned a few red coils to frame Tameka's face, she asked softly, "Do you think they had a thing going?"

Para and Bones? "Looks like." In the same vein, Tameka spared a glance over at Ross, who still held hands with Jack. "They aren't the only surprise couple today."

Sagan gave a half smile. "I know. I'm happy they got around to it. You wanna matchmake? I think Iuo and Twenty-One would make a cute couple."

Tameka rolled her eyes. "I don't think a Lamian Prince referred to as the 'Porn Baron' needs our help getting a partner."

"I've got two thousand credits that say Iuo's not into his own work." Kyle emerged from somewhere behind them, rolling a joint.

Andrew came with him, saying, "I don't know. Iuo walks such a fine, polite line. I can't tell what's on either side." He sat on the floor beside Tameka and patted her leg.

Sagan ruffled the brown mop growing out of Kyle's head. "I'll take you up on it. I wonder if any of the Lyriks will test him for us."

Tameka shook her head, smiling at their incredulous behavior.

That's right. The four of them together always made her smile. Tameka asked, "You guys remember the gorge in Yosemite?"

With a sigh, Sagan sat her chin in her hand, elbow propped on her knee. "Do I ever. Cleanest water I ever swam in."

Andrew got a faraway look in his teal eyes. "Yeah. And the food. Elden, I'd give anything to have that picnic again."

"We can."

They all turned and looked at Kyle. Tameka raised her brow at the Progeny male as he flipped his hair out of his eyes in a long forgotten gesture. With a joint between his lips, he explained, "I've been working on reconstructing memories for multiples, not only individuals. We could return together. All of us but…"

Rayne.

Tameka wished she could hug her best friend. Her sister in all but blood. Until then, she pressed Kyle, "How?"

"I have to touch you and then you touch Andrew and so on. Ready?" He held out his hand to her temple.

With a final glance at the makeshift infirmary, Tameka nodded her assent. Once his fingers touched her skin, she did the same to Andrew and he to Sagan.

Kyle instructed, "Close your eyes."

Tameka did and took a deep breath. A breeze touched her cheeks, an impossible one.

Sounding a little pleased with himself, Kyle said, "Okay. Open them."

They were standing on the cliffs high above their secret valley. Red sediment rocks stratified the canyon walls, acting as a basin to the gorge. Their waterfall thundered below in the most pristine lake Tameka had ever seen. Deep green trees stretched out beyond the beach into a vast forest.

The sight of the perfect summer afternoon took Tameka's breath away. She could even smell their picnic food, replay their fun, and hear Rayne's laughter.

"We will always remain."

Kyle slipped his hand into hers. "Damn straight. No matter how much Imminent keeps kicking us and stealing all our hot G.I.L.F.'s."

Andrew gave him a bewildered look. "What's a 'G.I.L.F.'?"

Sagan snickered.

Tameka didn't need any help to figure this one out. "'Grandma I'd like to fuck.' Silence."

Kyle winced at her name, but managed a goofy smile when Andrew gagged.

"That's right." Kyle hit his joint pretty hard before adding, "I slept with Wingmaster's matriarch. Nox's, too. Now there's a bonus. I swear that's the only upside to this bullshit."

By now, Sagan almost fell out on the ground, gripping her sides in laughter. Her voice was full of giggles as she squeezed out, "Elden, you're killing me."

Tameka rolled her eyes and shook her head. The wind picked up in the high altitude, carrying the scent of pine. It reminded her of their errand. She squeezed Kyle's hand. "Ready?"

His grin was sad, but he still squeezed back. "Ready."

Andrew nodded and smiled. "Set."

Giddy, Sagan cried, "Go!"

The four Progeny—their training, their growth, their lovers, and their grief—jumped off the cliff and chased the waterfall down. Sure, three out of four of them could fly, but that's not what this jump was about. This plunge invigorated their mortal thrill still attached to their humanity from before this life of nacres, committing to each other despite whatever came next.

They splashed in the water hard enough to lose their grip on each other. After several heartbeats, they surfaced one by one, laughing from the exhilaration. In their combined memories, the water was just as warm in the August sunlight, filtered through Rayne's Sphere. The smell of spicy fried chicken and sweet potato mash called to them from shore.

Andrew swam over first, clothes drenched and dripping. "Oh, my Elden. It's been too long." He bit a chunk out of a chicken leg he'd prepared for this picnic and moaned in satisfaction. "Oh yeah. Replicated food can't compete with this."

The remaining three surged from the water and joined him. Tameka ate a forkful of potatoes and groaned. "Does it taste better because we're eating it here?"

"Yeah, everything tastes better in your memory. It's a kink I haven't figured out yet," Kyle said as he dipped a piece of chicken in ranch dressing. "Too spicy, you fucker. You know I can't handle spicy food."

Sagan smiled at him. "I guess we all thought you'd work up a tolerance."

Tameka added, "Like Rayne."

It got quiet. Each of them turned to the empty spot around the fire they'd made. Rayne was with them in spirit.

Kyle's voice carried a heavy weight as he asked, "Do you think she's left the Martyr Complex yet?"

Andrew pointed a piece of chicken at him. "You know she's already out in Enki somewhere taking it over, but she'll need our help."

"Especially yours, Tameka," Sagan added.

Tameka frowned. "Why mine especially?"

Kyle finished drinking a glass of milk to say, "Who else would someone team up with to bring down Enki besides the person who already dims its power?"

They all stared at Tameka with an unexpected amount of respect on their faces. She wasn't sure how to take it. "Does everyone know something I don't?"

Then they all looked away at once. Sagan muttered at the sand between her toes, "It's X and Legir."

"Tempest and Dolor," Andrew added, drawing circles in the sand with a stick.

Kyle chafed his arm, looking guilty of something. "Tumu and luo share a part in it, too."

Tameka sat up on her knees. "What is it? Why is F8 calling me 'your majesty?'"

Sagan took Tameka's hand and squeezed it. Her voice soft with the gravity of her words. "Unfettered, you are the most powerful being in the galaxy."

Unable to help herself, Tameka scoffed. "Yeah right. Andrew can make us all line dance. You split an entire planet in half. And the memory Progeny can reduce hundreds of soldiers in an instant—"

"You reduced millions on Volcano Day in front of all our allies," Sagan pressed. "Tumu knows you put Enki through rolling blackouts. Fury, you're it—"

Tameka made to protest, but Sagan shook her hand, insistent.

"—And you're an amazing leader. Everyone looks up to your grace and fortitude. Your practical nature. You and Xelan make an unbeatable match. The Vast Collective knows you'll win against Imminent, and they're coming to stand beside you for it and for what comes after."

Swallowing hard to digest this information, Tameka searched Kyle and Andrew for confirmation.

Andrew said, "It's true. They want you to use all that resilience to lead them."

"And not just through the battle," Kyle added. A sudden spike of anxiety hit her, and he must have seen it on her face. "You won't be alone. We'll be right there with you. Wingmaster's 'got you.'"

Okay. That made Tameka laugh away some of the nervous energy. All of it, in fact.

This was a lot. She said, "It's too much right now. I need to save Pax, do you understand? We need to rendezvous with Rayne somehow. And everybody's in line to kill Abresson's sick ass."

All three of them lifted their drinks to her. "Cheers to that." "Here, here." "Fuck yes."

Something stronger to drink sounded good right about now. Instead, Tameka looked out at the untouched space which was all theirs. "We need to come back here with Rayne, Xelan, and Pax."

"Oh my Elden, can I jump down with Pax?" Sagan's eyes sparkled with violet excitement.

Andrew chuckled. "If he doesn't leap off on his own."

Kyle scoffed. "You kidding me? That kid's going down on *my* back."

This warmth. There was nothing like it. Tameka's family. "I love you all."

A quiet fell on their group after. Their eyes softened. This battle... It was different this time. They all knew it.

Tameka opened her arms, and Sagan flew in for a hug. Andrew and Kyle followed. They sniffled and squeezed.

Softly, Kyle said, "They need us back there."

"Can't wage a war without the Progeny," Andrew agreed.

Sagan sighed. "It does have a way of finding us."

"Let's go back and win this for all the people counting on us. We'll save Pax and keep Rayne from dying. We swear it?" Tameka shook them a bit.

Kyle, Andrew, and Sagan grunted their assent.

The gorge melted away, and they returned to Enki—

Surrounded by a ton of people. Their friends sat in a circle, protecting their Progeny in their huddle.

Pehton asked Caedes, "So the palm devices will all have the maps installed?"

He nodded.

Devis told Lynn, "I can help you build a weapon which steals memories."

Her dark brown eyes sparkled. "That would be fantastic."

Jack, Ross, Iuo, and Twenty-One played a game of cards while Bethany watched. Probably Go Fish.

Outside the protective circle, Korac sat at T.A.O.'s bedside as the First Wave Progeny rested. Tameka wasn't surprised to see his intense stare on Sagan, who smiled and waved at him.

Tumu and Lamassau smiled from the end of Para's bed. Pablo waved before stepping aside to reveal Xelan and Bones talking to a conscious Para.

Two wins in one day. Their odds were looking up.

Now, time to plan the mission to recover the others.

Tameka stood and said, "I need volunteers to rescue Chris and Karter."

FIVE

CULTIVATE VICTORY BEYOND THE NEXT ORDEAL

{ENKI | GAIT}

"WAS SEAN CONNERY IN IT?"

"Matt, I swear the anti-inertia meds are making you high. No. Sean Connery was in *Meteor.* Getting colder, man." While Puk spoke, his voice dipped here and there as he knelt and either scavenged something or placed an explosive charge.

Across the district, Matt did the same all the while pondering which movie all this planet-wide demolition reminded him of. He was 'O' for three on guesses and distracted by Lucy's absence. He missed her sweet voice on the morning calls. Lux and Yito tried, but there was nothing melodic about their tenors. And then there was the question of what was Lucy doing in Enki all this time? Hopefully having some fun, but not too much without Matt—

"Yo, you see this?" Awe permeated Puk's voice. "I know you got human vision, but surely..."

Matt imagined his friend gaping and when he exited the abandoned space scraper—holy shit—Matt could see why. Almost too distant to make out, but close enough to understand what it was, he stared at the end of the line.

One half of the planet formerly known as Gait hurled toward the star at Enki's center. The half Matt and the demolition team were scouring hurdled toward one of the Dyson's Sphere's outer walls. And there it was. He blinked, trying to make sense of it. On the horizon, Matt made out swirling clouds and peeks of an ocean through that. Days from impact.

Over his earpiece, he injected plenty of alarm in his otherwise flat voice as he confirmed, "I see it." Someone was always listening. Best to be careful.

"Ginger, Puk. Come in. Over."

It was the engineering team, monitoring the situation, safe and sound from a nearby shrine. A combined effort of Pil Dwarves, Tritans, and Monarch 3 drones.

Among the rubble of a fallen building, Matt set another charge on the pavement. "This is Ginger. Go ahead. Over."

Whoever was on the line—Matt didn't care to learn all their names—assured, "We know it looks bad, but we're way ahead of schedule thanks to the excellent team Puk's cousin sent for the job. We're just passing on kudos from the higher-ups. Keep up the good work and don't let morale suffer because of the view. You're making it happen. Over and Out."

Encouragement. Razor and Justice Lee were good with that, too. It appeared the villains were well aware of how to manipulate subordinates in the right way to boost their self-esteem and enroll them in the franchise for evil.

Not Matt.

He rolled his shoulders, releasing several cricks in his back. Leaned his neck to the left and then to right for a satisfying pop. Lastly, as Lucy had told him lately, he rubbed the mandible joint of his jaw to relieve the tension from grinding his teeth.

Deep breaths. In and out.

When Matt closed his eyes, Gait's remnants spilled away, replaced by a rancher's estate in Iowa. The horses kicked up a wild dust storm to escape the flames engulfing the squat barracks.

Matt was worried about Lucy. Not about the filthy lout on his hands and knees at Matt's feet. The degenerate begged, "What do you want? I can get you anything. The Icari will grant you anything. Just let me live."

Blood dripped from Matt's knuckles, busted and used. He'd left the bone protruding from Justice Bell's cheek, and he was nowhere near finished.

"If it's that little bitch you want—I swear I didn't lay a hand on her. She's lying if she says I did. She—"

"She's back."

Matt wouldn't take his eyes off the groveling scumbag to see the smile he heard in Lucy's voice. A horse chuffed behind Matt close enough to muss his hair. Lucy's small giggle made him smile.

This widened the eyes on the Justice's face to a painful degree, bulging out from his head with corneas red from smoke inhalation. Funny, that normally didn't happen until Matt started crushing their skulls, but no matter.

From atop the comical beast, Lucy tapped Matt on the shoulder with a length of good rope.

When Bell saw it, tears spilled down his face. "What're you planning to do with that?" Desperation kicked the pitch of his voice up a few notches.

Matt took it and knelt before the good Justice. Feeling nothing but the buzz of anticipation, he said, "The Cult of Night hasn't served the Icari since Volcano Day. You lie to your congregation. You also claim to recruit for an assassination attempt on King Rayne. Sinner, we're your punishment, and it's long overdue."

The man squirmed then and screamed for help, long reduced to ash.

With all the strength imbued in Matt from his nacre, he pinned the man to the ground and tied the rope around his waist and wrists. A handcuff knot. He and Lucy learned so many interesting knots over their time taking down CoN, taught to them by Collectors who now salted the

Earth. The men and women who stole people for CoN recruitment.

Dismounting, Lucy handed the reins to Matt with a sweet smile. "I only want a quick word with him."

"Be my guest." Matt understood. He climbed the horse after an iffy first attempt and smiled awkwardly down at her raised brow. "I got it."

Lucy wore those stupid Promoter robes. Justices always cited her youthful allure and her eloquent speech for placing her in the role of spreading the CoN rhetoric for recruitment. Black fabric draped over every inch of her, but left her breasts almost completely exposed. For the coup, she ripped the skirt to expose the length of her tan, toned legs, splashed in the blood of their enemies. So slick Matt wanted to wash her clean, while reclaiming the heaven denied to him after months of this undercover work.

Dressed like this, Lucy stood before the Justice. Nearly hogtied, Bell still rolled his eyes in his sockets to look up at the blood-soaked blond who incinerated his compound. Her dark blue eyes glinted, reflecting the firelight of his kingdom in flames. Even so, Justice Bell looked straight at her breasts.

Matt smiled.

Lucy laughed at her prey, turned, and Matt asked, "Ready?"

"Wait, wait, wait—Please, don't do this." Bell tried to reach for Lucy with his bound hands, missed by an inch, and sobbed on his failure.

Matt leaned forward, expecting Lucy to climb up behind him, but she surprised him by swinging her leg over in the front, straddling him. She met his eyes with an openness to her secret smile meant only for the finale.

So this was how Lucy wanted it.

Matt experienced only certain kinds of excitement. Crushing a skull, bringing down an evil franchise, and the first time with Lucy after weeks of deprivation from her soft... everything. Lips, hands—everything. Holding

Lucy again was the only thing which made Matt shiver in anticipation.

Lucy felt it, and her eyes darkened. Shyly, she dipped her chin and peered at him through thick blond lashes. When she bit her lip, Matt couldn't take it anymore. Months apart, this kiss melted him to her, and she gasped into his mouth, feeling the same.

It was fucking magical. Made all the better when Matt squeezed his thighs, and the horse took off at a trot.

Lucy broke their kiss for a gentle, "Yip!" But only for a second. She quickly reconnected and touched him everywhere with those soft hands he'd missed so much. It was the only time he was grateful CoN wouldn't let him wear a shirt.

Behind them, Justice Bell started off with a groan which grew into a lot of swearing across the open field, and into a shriek when they cantered onto the gravel drive. Keening, loud, and overlaid with an arrhythmic thudding which turned his every sound into a ragged, staccato performance.

"P-p-p-l-l-e-e-e-a-s-s-e-e! S-s-s-t-t-o-o-p-p!" Over and over again.

Meanwhile, Lucy whispered how she thought of Matt every night and wished there were no cameras in her cabin so she could touch herself while thinking of him. Her hands slipped down his shirtless front and went for his fly.

No lie, this was physically difficult to manage. The extra endowments from their nacres helped make it less hard. Well, something remained hard for her, but the position, the rocky ride—

Lucy gripped him after some maneuvering, and Matt's eyes rolled back with a teeth grinding groan. Months. Without her. They were only cantering along the circular drive. Surely, they could figure this position out—

Oh.

God.

Every word Lucy said was gospel. She was ready for this and, with a determination set in her eyes, she moved for him, nearly sending Matt over in a puddle of perfect stimulation.

They were fucking on horseback while keelhauling a half-dead bad guy on a gravel road behind them.

A good hunt.

Matt opened his eyes to an ocean on the zenith, soon to disappear as this half of Gait made another rotation. He'd spent a few months on this project now without Lucy. Without a hunt. She taught Matt these meditative exercises to help him cope. About every four days or so, Matt took a minute to stem the hunger in him. With as many CoN compounds they'd taken down over the years, Matt possessed an arsenal of satisfying kills to relive. He'd yet to touch his time at Razor's Emporium of Exotic Experiences. But nothing quite substituted the real hands-on experience.

Still, Matt tried and managed. Miles of space-scrapers and derelict warehouses were spread out around him. There was no one to kill this time.

Mount another explosive charge, pop another anti-inertia med, and check in with Puk to maintain sanity.

How funny it was Matt's life had changed so much in a single day, years ago now. He would argue for the better, and thanked whoever was up there every day that he tracked Rayne down at her bookstore three years ago on Invasion Day.

The last of the impending ocean vanished around the curve of Gait. Massive and impossible—beautiful, really. The scale of it should astonish and arrest Matt, but it failed to move him. Little did. Yet, even with his emotional hindrance, he still understood. This was enormous.

It was the crux of this entire mission, wasn't it? This wasn't a compound of zealots or a den of endorsed vice. It was different this time. Bigger than Matt and Lucy. Bigger than Earth. The waning view confirmed it.

Everything was about to change again.

Fortunately, there was nothing Matt and Lucy couldn't survive together.

{Enki | Tumu's Sanctum}

It was different this time.

Pax was stolen.

The Vast was getting all Collective against its common enemy.

The Shadow gang was all together. Well, minus a few key players. Kyle wasn't sure whose absence hurt more. Rayne's or...

Fuck Kyle for always thinking of Silence. Some voice in his head berated him, "She betrayed you, dude! Get over it." But another voice muttered, "What if..." What if there was something to the last gaze they shared? Or Lucas' quiet message to Andrew?

"Keep your faith in me a little while longer."

That one kept Kyle up at night. It wasn't the first time the Shadow had heard the peculiar reassurance. The lack of sleep made it hard for Kyle to focus on his role during the day. Pablo warned him to take care of himself, but honestly, who the fuck had time for that in the middle of a galactic war?

And on that note...

"Okay. Okay. We can get started." Kyle sat beside T.A.O. She smiled at him with concern in her Atramentous eyes. It hurt him to see her so distraught. "Are you sure you don't want Devis to do this?"

Devis sat on the other side of her bed, holding her hand. "I don't mind, sister."

T.A.O. held up their hands, her arms muscled but so thin every striation stood out in stark relief. To Devis, she said, "You keep me here." Korac was originally meant to anchor her, but he was needed on the mission with Sagan, Tumu, and Tameka. Now there was a party of awkward relations Kyle would pay to see in a memory replay.

Xelan sat down and clamped a hand on Kyle's shoulder. "I'm tagging along." He gave T.A.O. a reassuring smile.

Her eyes glittered whenever Xelan came around, like she saw something other than a man when she looked at him. "Yes."

Kyle took a deep breath and blew out some massive burnout which he resisted at every turn. Yet at every turn, something or, more recently, someone waited to gut punch him. "Ready?"

Devis nodded, Xelan squeezed Kyle's shoulder, and the small woman in the makeshift hospital bed tugged on Kyle's hand. He jumped inside her memoryscape.

In theory anyway.

For Korac and Pehton, the plane of their memories resembled an art gallery where they could jump in and out of memories on display. Andrew's scape was a kaleidoscope of transitioning, potential memories within refracted Probabilities in his mind like a prism of existence.

T.A.O.'s memory was a labyrinth of mirrors. Literally. Purple floors and mirror walls stretched to the silver sky. It was like nothing Kyle ever saw before. And of course, they didn't enter together.

"Hello! T.A.O.? Xelan?"

No answer.

Well, fuck.

Kyle wandered down the—

"Ouch." He smacked his face into a mirror. Off to a great start. With both hands stretched out, his finger grazed reflective surfaces on either side. Every now and again, he called out to the others, and although his voice carried and echoed, he heard nothing from them.

Still, something unnerved him.

This was a mind. He wasn't in danger here, yet Kyle felt watched. Judged.

"I swear if there's a minotaur—"

A glint caught his eye. Sans joint and trapped in someone's mind, Kyle turned slowly to capture—

There it was again.

Was T.A.O. always trapped in this place, catching glimpses of things which might chase her? How terrifying.

And there it was again. It was not with him, but in the mirror. Kyle stared and tried to see it again. Like watching someone turn a corner right before catching sight of them.

"T.A.O., I want to show you something."

Oh, that could only be Razor's voice.

"Hello?" Kyle wasn't sure where this was headed, but if this guy was involved—Shit.

A man with white skin, white hair, and white eyes, fancy business suit, and more gel in his hair than a ballistics lab—Razor—was behind Kyle. He spun, suddenly full of adrenaline and the desire to punch a cut jawline—

Oh.

Razor was inside the opposite mirror and walked up to the surface. He was like a much more impressive and put-together reflection of Kyle. He held out a hand without fingernails.

"So, would you like me to take you?"

Uh. This was probably against the rules, but Kyle tried and succeeded in putting his hand through the mirror. Razor took it, and the scenery took on shape and color. Black glass and rock—the room was carved of obsidian and onyx. Kyle knew this place from Korac's Verse. The Obsidian Palace. T.A.O. lived here as Razor's friend and employee. The room was warm and comfortable—Couches, glass bookshelves dividing the room, a black desk. Honestly, Kyle had heard no complaints about the Pain Curator's sense of fashion or decor. Just his sense of right and wrong.

Still holding Kyle's hand, which in the memory was warm and familiar, not at all frightening, Razor led him into a secondary room with only one thing: a fireplace filled with black flames.

"Yes, it's pretty, isn't it?" Razor said as if responding to T.A.O. "Sit with me for a while. You can look into it, if you want. It won't hurt your eyes."

No wonder Sagan fell prey to this bastard. He was perfectly warm and genuine-seeming. Kind. Everything about his voice and posture said, "It's okay to feel comfortable around me." Kyle was happy when Razor let T.A.O.'s hand go.

This was an odd memory walk for him. In his mind, Kyle knew Razor was capable of terrible things, and kept expecting him to do something unsavory. But in T.A.O.'s heart, he felt perfect trust. The man known for pain would never hurt her—

Something changed in Razor. A shift, an anticipation—something. His body was poised, and his white eyes gleamed. The Last Aegis licked his lips before saying, "It won't burn if you want to touch the light."

No. Red flag. Not good. Touching Cascading Light exposed the victim to the Probability Matrix. Like what happened to Andrew a few months back. He'd not been the same since.

Coaxing, kind, and warm. "Of course. It's safe. It won't burn you."

No. T.A.O.—

But before Kyle could pull himself from the memory, he reached out and touched the black fire. And thank Elden, nothing fucking happened. Shit, this was involuntary as hell. Instead, Kyle experienced everything from T.A.O.'s perspective. Which wasn't much of anything before she blacked out.

Not for long though, as if the memory skipped this time. Her vision returned, and Kyle found himself in a massive swimming pool-sized bed. His instinct was to crawl out immediately and scrub his skin off, but T.A.O. was safe here.

Razor's stupid, handsome face appeared between her and the black rock ceiling. "I'm sorry. I should've known better than to—Are you all right? How do you feel? Can you see, T.A.O.?"

She could, although Kyle couldn't see what she saw. Surely, the world looked to her the way it did for Andrew. All blurred lines and different colors and textures. But for some reason, T.A.O.'s memoryscape was absent of elements involving herself. Kyle got her emotions, but not her words. The view from her eyes, but not exactly what she saw.

It was time to leave this memory. While Kyle was sure no one knew T.A.O. had touched Cascading Light, he came here to review the time she'd spent in Celindria's captivity.

As Kyle walked back to the mirror's surface, Razor called out to him, "Steer clear of Abresson for me. He's taking a liking to you, and I don't trust him. I know how much you like having friends, but please do this for me. I'd hate for anything to happen to you."

Kyle shivered as he stepped out of the glass.

Therapy. They all needed therapy.

With the comforting knowledge that the mirrors represented T.A.O.'s memories, Kyle tried to glimpse them only long enough to see if they were during her captivity. If not, he'd respect her privacy and move on. It hurt. Most of T.A.O.'s life was spent in Razor's diabolical care, or Celindria's merciless captivity. Then there was Abresson. Kyle barely glanced at that memory before hurrying along.

Hundreds of memories denoted T.A.O.'s good nature. Penguins, Hellkittens, some weird fuzzy spherical creatures on Pil—Over and over, T.A.O. buried herself in animal cuddles. But Kyle's favorite memories involved elaborate and hilarious setups for pranks. The Seamswalker regularly walked into houses of great planetary leaders—Legir and X, among them—and rearranged a chair before they sat down so they fell on their asses. Or opened all the doors in their homes, only to close them moments later.

Silly things.

It made coming to T.A.O.'s recent memories more painful.

Celindria was a fucking monster—

"I love her."

Kyle turned to find T.A.O. and Xelan walk up behind him. She held Xelan's hand like *he* kept her on this plane. Not Devis. The mirror failed to reflect them because it wasn't a mirror at all. What had she said again?

Oh.

Kyle asked, "Do you think of her as your sister?"

T.A.O. tilted her head to the side. "She wants to feel our hearts, but they don't beat for her."

Surely what T.A.O. said wasn't nonsense, but was senseless to Kyle. The memory behind him played of her crawling all over Chris' captured body, threatening to perform oral sex on him against their wills. Elden, Kyle couldn't imagine being in Chris's head at that moment.

He shuddered.

Xelan looked right at the memory with a frown on his face. It wasn't the look of disappointment. It was... fear? Was Xelan afraid of Celindria—

"I'm so sorry, T.A.O." Sincerity emanated from Xelan's words. Almost as if he were apologizing for her entire life.

The small woman shook her head and gestured with a wave of her hand at the mirror. The memory changed, mercifully. Now it was a memory of Celindria and a Tritan which could only be Remorse. The last time Kyle saw the Primary, Silence had put him in his place, and it felt like a hundred years ago.

Celindria sounded fed up with Remorse's shit. "Your son wasn't meant to be there. Where is Nox?!"

"You'll have to manage without him this time. He—"

Celindria—Were Kyle's eyes playing tricks on him?

For a second, the light surrounding Celindria dimmed. Not like a power surge. More like she absorbed the spectrum. What was more unnerving than that?

Primary Rem took a step back.

Celindria's voice was chilled but not in Atramentous. Pure ice dripped from her full lips. "Nothing can separate us. We are the Eternal Bind, and I want Nox returned to me."

Swallowing, Remorse visibly shored himself to say, "He is not the way to obtain your soul, nor has he ever been. Try this once without him because there's no means to recover this. We'll take Pax soon. He'll need you as mother *and* father, now."

Shadows converged around Celindria, and the ice in her voice threatened murder. "Someone will pay for this mistake."

Kyle's brows shot up, and he couldn't help but glance at Xelan.

Said mistake scrutinized Celindria's paused face as if he meant to decipher a means of defeating her from it.

T.A.O. waved her hand and scenes fast forwarded in the mirror. Celindria taking advantage of Chris, arguing with Andrius, and bossing around Remorse.

Primary Rem walked into Celindria's lab. "Have you made any progress with increasing Seamswalking distance?"

Without looking up, she admonished him, "You don't ask about my progress with any of my endeavors, Remorse."

Sly, he sidled up to the counter she leaned over. "But I come bearing good news. We can trade." The Tritan tried to imbue his voice with silk, but it sounded more like spider's thread. Sticky.

Celindria sighed almost in disgust before relenting. "Very well. I've almost made a breakthrough which will increase distance from a city to a continent, but still no interplanetary travel."

"That's excellent." Pleased, Remorse rapped his knuckles beside Celindria. "We've confirmed Tameka was the source of the power drains a few months back."

Celindria looked up then, something shining in her bright blue eyes. "We can deliver Ishkur to Mother—You know I can see the twitch in your voids whenever I speak of Silence. Tell me, do you fear her wrath or do you fear she is righteous in it?"

That was the most disgusted Kyle had ever seen a Tritan look. In Remorse's deep primary voice, he said, "She won't let us integrate Para and Karter into the breeding program."

Needling him, Celindria argued, "And you can't tolerate that her logic is sound. Those warriors are creatures of violence, not incubation. I agree with her."

"Female solidarity."

With far too much satisfaction, Celindria said, "You of all people should fear it, Tritan."

Shock and anger passed over Remorse's face. He opened his mouth as if to tell her as much, but thought better of it. Instead, he said, "Once, you were pleasant company."

"No. I merely fooled you then as I do now."

Remorse sighed. It was heavy and mournful, as if lamenting something he lost. "As you choose."

More memories like this one passed along. Sometimes, the heads of Imminent left the room to discuss affairs away from their captives. Cautious. It was smart.

After some time, Xelan pulled T.A.O. into a hug. She was so small the top of her head met his ribs. In their embrace, he said once more, "I'm so sorry."

This was enough. "Let's go back." Kyle needed a joint and possibly a stiff drink before the war started. Andrew was nice enough to volunteer and roll him a stash like in their last battle.

Xelan nodded. "Take us out."

Voices and commotion replaced the hollow of T.A.O.'s labyrinth. People were shifting around and organizing for the upcoming strife inside Tumu's sanctum.

Devis beamed at his sister. "How do you feel?"

T.A.O. let her smile answer for her. For the first time in a long time, she was free, and everyone here intended to keep it that way.

Speaking of…

"Let me give you this shot, T.A.O." Pablo appeared with a syringe. "It won't hurt much."

Lynn, too. "All of you need a booster."

Kyle bared his arm for more of the doctor's goodwill and looked around at the activity.

After her shot, T.A.O. smiled at all the men surrounding her bed and asked, "Fury returns?"

With a touch of a frown, Xelan said, "On a brief mission. Why?"

"Pax is waiting for her. I can take her there."

That's exactly the morale boost they needed. Para and another Seamswalker.

Things were looking up.

{ENKI | TRITAN RESIDENCES}

Tameka stood with her hands on her hips and tapped her boot, replaying her life for any other mentions of Ishkur. Why was she the key to it? Would Celindria hurt her son for it? How much of this was a trap?

Their plan was risky, and it started with Eminent Lance.

Hence all four of them standing in his apartments, waiting for him to return from his shift on the Tribunal. That's right. Enki continued to function despite chaos reigning throughout the galaxy. Fucking Imminent—

"How long do you plan on doing that?"

Tameka's back was to the rest of them as she ruminated, but there was no mistaking the irritatingly smooth cadence. Should she stop tapping her boot or should she turn around and pick a fight? What was more productive, and what would make her feel better in the interim?

Childish.

The boot tapping stopped. Taking a deep breath, Tameka inhaled more than oxygen. She sipped of Enki's star and fed it to herself. Too late, she considered more energy might not help with the fidgeting. Some part of Tameka wanted to confess to the room how she was feeling, but everything she'd felt was expected of her circumstance. Airing it and compounding their anxieties with her weakness wouldn't make them feel better about her as their leader. Neither would nervously tapping her boot.

Another deep breath. Another sip. Tameka glanced over her shoulder where Korac perched on an empty pedestal in the room like some bird of prey. It suited his battle gear. Captivating and unnerving—and he was staring right at her.

"What?" Without a trace of irritation or frustration, Tameka managed to keep her voice steady and kept her nerves to herself.

Tumu looked up then and glanced between the two while Sagan went through all the strange things in Lance's room. Lots of empty furniture. Bureaus with no clothes. Cases with no shelves or mementos. Outlines of frames on the walls, but nothing there.

Korac gave a cavalier shrug to Tameka's question, but kept staring at her.

Confused, she frowned. "Are you trying to provoke me?"

Sagan quit taking in the room and inched toward them. Tumu shook his head at her.

After another moment hanging between them, Korac abruptly stood on the pedestal, clocking the ceiling at sixteen feet or higher. Balanced with one motorcycle boot on the slender column, he made for a majestic and intimidating sight. Yet he showed no strain. Even his voice was fluid as he said, "Only months ago, I was in a similar position as you—part of Imminent's designs, unbeknown to myself. A wealth of unlucky significance which rained down on me all at once. Atheneum. Savior of the Aegis. Half Ancient. It was... devastating. It took a Verse and Sagan's kindness to breach the surface. Now look at you, your majesty."

Sagan looked ready to intervene, but Tumu leaned all the way down to whisper in her ear. Whatever he said was reassurance enough because she stopped approaching.

Which left Tameka staring at Korac, trying to see his point. "What about me?"

"I can see it." Korac hopped off the column and strode over to her with a certainty in his eyes. "Even with Pax missing and all this extra weight, you're keeping your composure and building strategies to approach the problem from a place of calm and intelligence." He stopped only a step outside of her personal space.

Tameka frowned in confusion and searched his strange eyes. "What can you see?"

As if *this* were an appropriate time for it, Korac smirked. The next he said so quiet only Tameka could hear. "I can see why he likes you."

Korac. Icarean General, the Aegis Atheneum, and the love of her best friend's life was giving Tameka shit to distract her. There was no other explanation for this mess, and the longer she stared at him, the wider his smirk spread as if he knew she'd figured it out—

"Ow!"

"You'll get another swat if you ever come at me like that again. We are in the middle of some real shit, and you are fucking with me."

Sagan snickered and said, "You deserved it, babe!"

Tumu sighed. Heavily.

Korac went into a block stance and mused, "It stopped you from tapping your boot for another hour—"

The nacre barrier released on a sigh and the door opened.

Before Lance could step into his apartments and get on with this mission, Tameka glared once more at Korac and mouthed, "I'm. Telling. Xelan."

Did he—Did he just stick his tongue out at her?!

Lance, the shortest Tritan Tameka had ever seen, swept into the room with a surprise in his wake.

"Lucy!" Sagan cried before Seamswalking across the expansive space and throwing her arms around the blond guest.

The unknown Tritan beside Lucy blinked the film over his voids in utter confusion at the crowd waiting for Lance in his home. A famous crowd at that.

Warily, Tameka gestured at the three new arrivals. "What's going on here?"

Lance shook off his heavy ceremonial Tribunal robes to reveal a carbon fiber jumpsuit fit for battle. He said, "We're organizing. What are you doing here? Officer Tumu—"

"I think you can refer to me as Primary from hereon." Tumu didn't sound angry, more matter of fact. "We both know I never left my responsibilities behind."

To Tameka's surprise, Lance let out a massive sigh of relief, easing his tense shoulders and took the frown off his face. "Thank, Elden."

Now the entire room went quiet. Tritans thanked Eternity; never the Icarean martyr made famous across the Vast Collective. "What the hell is happening here?" Korac took the words out of Tameka's mouth.

Lucy and Sagan beamed at each other before the blond with the empty blue eyes stepped forward. "I've enlisted these fine gentlemen to help with our assignment."

Lance's face filled with black blood as he flushed, and the new Tritan beamed down at Lucy.

Ahh. So they were in on it now. Tameka smiled. "How resourceful of you."

Tumu took the floor. "So you've chosen a side?"

Sagan returned to Korac, and Tameka took up leaning against the wall. The unknown Tritan watched his two elders interact like it was a tennis match.

Lance ignored their concentrated gazes and returned his robe to a rack with a casual air. "You know I've no tolerance for injustice, *Primary* Tumu. Now I prepare for an existence without my home. The one we destroyed a species to obtain—I will pay for my crimes."

The next, Tumu said without an ounce of surprise. "You're the one who suggested they give Rayne a Weaponized nacre, aren't you?"

Okay, this escalated quickly. "You what?" Tameka tried to keep her voice calm, but the energy of a star welled in her. She stepped away from the wall and in Lance's direction.

Sagan touched her shoulder to stave her. Korac watched with his piercing gaze, and Lucy's empty eyes scanned the room.

Lance turned around and faced them, a man defeated. He ran a hand over his bald head and blew the air from his lipless mouth. "We meant for the shortened fuse to end her life before she destroyed Enki. We were trying to reduce the number of Probabilities, to uncomplicate the Matrix. To save the Dyson's Sphere for our people. All of our research..."

Tameka was grateful for the fed up tone of Tumu's voice when addressing one of the few supposedly good Tritans. "You arrogant hypocrite. How many times did the Exalted tell you? Only the Eternal Bind can—"

"That is a fairytale." Lance dismissed Tumu's reprimand with a wave of his hand. Tameka imagined he was frowning with all the demoralization in his voice, but his back was to her, facing only his accuser.

Tameka tapped on his shoulder. "Hey Lance." He turned and faced her with the exact expression she pictured. But this interrogation wasn't over for Tameka. "Let's get back to you intentionally harming Rayne to save your precious Matrix." She kept her eyes on him while gaining some confirmation. "Did you know anything about the Weapon, Tumu?"

Lance stood eye-to-eye with Tameka.

Tumu answered, "No, Peaches. I knew only of the Gargantuan source."

Tired and haggard, Lance said, "I confess. It was me. Primary Rem suggested I scour Prince Xelan's lab for powerful upgrades to infuse into the Gargantuan nacre. I infused her with the Weapon created by her mentor."

Tameka winced.

While the Eminent Tritan gazed at her, he missed the person walking up behind him. Korac placed both hands on Lance's shoulders, startling him. Either he didn't put up a fight or Korac used an impressive amount of force—either way, Lance went to his knees at Tameka's feet. Korac nodded at Tameka.

"Eminent Lance, you've committed atrocious crimes against the Vast Collective, unleashing a weapon of mass destruction with no hope of recovering it—her—Rayne." Tameka swallowed back the sudden overwhelming emotion. She knew her eyes shifted into Atramentous in her pause when Lance gasped, staring into them. "How do you plead to your crimes and what punishment do you suggest?"

As Lance lowered his head as if heavy with a burden, Tumu, Sagan, and Lucy crossed the room to stand at Tameka's side. The unknown Tritan stared in quiet fascination, but not in defense of his Eminent.

In his brilliant blue shade of Tritan complexion, Lance returned his gaze to Tameka with black tears. She'd never seen a Tritan cry, nor imagined their voice filled with so much regret. "I am guilty, and I accept death as punishment for my cowardice and abuse of my Eminence."

Something flashed in Korac's eyes across from Tameka. She barely glimpsed it, but… it left an impression. She understood. That's when Tumu leaned forward and whispered in her ear with his impossibly deep voice. "Remember the Verses, Peaches."

Yes.

Those lessons helped Tameka forgive Kyle. Allowed her to keep her heart open to Silence. Let her save all this concern about Xelan's involvement with the nacre Weapon until he was ready to talk about it.

Tameka inhaled a deep breath and let it out. "Eminent Lance, I won't kill you. Not when you can be of use to the Vast Collective." He looked up at her, shocked, and Tameka continued. "I can't promise you a path to redemption. That's really up to you and Rayne, but I'll give you an avenue to seek it. The Shadow need your help. Imminent permeates Enki. Did you know that?"

Lance frowned and glanced at Tumu.

The Primary said, "Yes, the organization is real and very close to home."

The Eminent on his knees turned back to Tameka with his eyes so wide they spilled tears. They smelled of coconut and pineapple. Lance guessed, "Eminent Abresson?"

Korac chuffed from behind him, startling the rattled man.

Sagan answered, "Yes. And Eminent Celindria and Primary Rem."

"They had Eminent Wiw killed, and they physically control Eminent Karter." Tumu knelt in front of his frightened brethren. "Haven't you noticed lately that they've outvoted you three to one?"

The puzzle worked itself out in Lance's voids. "On every issue."

Lucy finally said something, "They voted to construct a colossal Tantamount, but Celindria and Remorse already stole ours."

The quiet Tritan raised a hand. "Hi. I'm Yito. I work on the Gait demolition project. That's how I met Lucy. We came here to discuss the latest ruling with Lance and how it affects Lucy's assignment."

Tameka held her hands up to stop them. "Before we go much further, Lance, do you choose to serve the Vast Collective properly? To fight alongside those dedicated to freeing it from Imminent?"

Lance met the eyes of everyone in the room and settled on Tameka's. He nodded. "I swear I'll do whatever I can to rid the Vast Collective of Imminent until such time Rayne has her revenge."

Korac patted his shoulder. "Attaboy Lancey."

The Tritan jumped out of his skin. His voice was shaky. "Lance, please."

Korac's voice was icy, but his irritating smirk at Tameka belied the humor. "Nope. Your name is Lancey now."

Tumu looked a question at Tameka, ready to reach out to his kinsman.

"Stand, former Eminent." Tameka backed up a step. "Welcome to the resistance."

"To the Empire!" Sagan called with conviction.

"The empire!" Tumu and Korac joined.

Lance stood looking as bewildered as Tameka felt.

She blinked. What Empire? No. Her sanity told her to ignore that rabbit hole. Instead, she said, "Uhm... Yito... you mentioned the latest ruling."

Tameka wasn't sure why, but something about Yito's complexion or the sharpness of his eyes gave away his youth compared to the other, more seasoned Tritans. Even his voice carried a healthy ring. "First, I just want to say how cool it is to meet all of you. The guys would be so stoked to hear about this—"

"All right, number one fan." Why was Korac such a... Well, Tameka didn't have a word for his brand of charisma which oozed from him as he continued saying, "We get it. If you want to join the super cool Shadow club, get to the point."

Tameka rolled her eyes, but mostly because he said what was on her mind. And she really hated that. "He's right—"

"Bet that hurt to admit," Korac mused.

Sagan kindly suppressed a giggle.

"—We don't have a lot of time. What do you have for us?"

Lucy touched one of the azure striations in Yito's forearm. "Like we talked about."

"Yeah, but who knew you were Shadow?" Yito stared down at her, nervous. When Lucy shone a radiant smile at him, her eyes still didn't light up, but it had the intended effect. He faced Tameka once more. "Sorry. You're right. The other three Eminents voted against Lance to pay the demolition team on Gait. Instead, I heard Abresson boast they planned to eliminate them."

Lance gaped. "I knew nothing of this. Sometimes we have repairs done around the Dyson's Sphere. Remorse says the experience and the addition to their vitae is more than payment enough. I don't agree with that. But… No…" Both his hands covered his mouth as horror lined his face.

Tumu's voice sounded lost when he said, "You've never heard from the employees after they completed a project. Yes. The nightmare I've lived with since I was ruling Primary: our people are not great. They are deeply flawed. Ever since we murdered our females."

Tameka couldn't stop herself from gasping and staring with the same horrified expression as on Lance's face. Korac and Sagan echoed her.

Yito took a step forward. "What… what did you say, Primary Tumu?"

Tumu sighed and touched his ear. "Xelan, are you listening?"

"I'm here, old friend. Are you finally prepared to tell me?"

Weary, the old Tritan looked as if he carried bones of lead under soaked muscle. "Make sure everyone is on their earpieces. I want to tell this story only once."

{ENKI | TRITAN RESIDENCES}

Wow. This would make one hell of a story time.

Sagan went to Korac's side and took his hand. She found it chilled compared to his usual comforting warmth. Even with his careful composure, his brows were up and his mouth was open—shocked. Tameka hugged herself. Lucy watched the room with a careful consideration in her gaze. Her friend, Yito, looked positively devastated and visibly braced himself for the story to come.

Lance was the only person in the room without shock on his face. Shame emanated from him in waves of depressing failure.

Same as Tumu.

Sagan took the memory capsule Tumu offered her, and the rest did the same. Korac was the last, hesitant.

She mouthed, "I. Trust. Him."

He nodded and downed it.

As it took effect, Tumu began narrating their journey. "We came here so long ago, we Tritans. Traveling across the stars in search of a home after plague decimated our own. The rumors are true. An enemy chased us."

{MILKY WAY GALAXY | TWO GALACTIC YEARS AGO}

"Primary Rem, we should surrender. Their terms are fair!"

Sparks exploded above Tumu's head from the station's secondary navigation panel. At this speed, the bulkheads would compress and fail. None of this equipment was meant to withstand the pressure of a chase. But try telling that to any of these headstrong fools.

"Primary Quet, reconsider."

Piloting the station, all the Primaries were slid down into their interfacing pods. The station's hybrid organic mechanics encased them in a membrane cocoon to absorb impact. They operated the bridge through a connection in their biorhythms and telepathic suggestion.

The station was alive and very blue.

But it wasn't impervious.

Especially after half of it was shed away in an escape vehicle equipped for emergency colonization in case the Tritans crashed onto a planet without means of escape. Now, their own colony vessel with a three-billion Tritan capacity attacked them with weapons designed only for defense.

The station was helpless. No defenses and their adversaries masterfully disabled their weapons before the mutiny.

Mutiny.

Was this really happening?

Tumu tried again. "Primary Bol, tell me you hear me—"

Rem's voice cut him off. "We all hear you, Primary Tumu. We are considerably busy piloting the ship to secure our escape. Your near-treasonous pleas are a distraction against our survival."

Disgusted, Tumu snarled. "Treasonous?! Only you would consider mending ties with our females a treasonous act!"

"They refuse to relent," Primary Bol reminded. "We gave them viable options—"

"Slavery is not an option, Bol!" Again, Tumu heard the revulsion in his own voice. "We should consider their counteroffer."

The sliver of a pod slipping open had Tumu rolling his voids upward. Rem exited his cocoon to stand over Tumu. Not a flattering angle, especially with that venomous look on his face. "We will not cater to their whims. They know this is for the good of the race, and they mutinied. Nearly marooned us in this infant galaxy. And you expect us to capitulate—Fuck!" The most recent impact sent him staggering across the bridge.

A voice came over the comms then. Female, stern, and in a tone not much different from her mate. "This is Vi. Rem, surrender. We want our men safe to save our race—"

"Mate, mine." Primary Rem sounded more composed than during this entire journey. "See reason. Only *we* can manufacture the perfect breeding program to reinstate female offspring—"

"You and Quet reduced us to this. Why in Eternity would the females trust you to recover it while we live as pregnant stock?!"

This was going nowhere.

While they bickered, the firing ceased. Tumu exited his pod, crossed to the east side of the bridge, and shoved his hands into a viscous gel to access their trajectory for any objects—

"What..."

Scans returned an unbelievable mass over four hundred and eighteen million kilometers wide. Spherical in shape. It was too heavy to be a star.

Bol asked over Tumu's shoulder. "Have you found something?"

Quet cried from his pod, "Give us a heading, Tumu!"

"Rem, you're only alive because we wish it." Vi's voice denoted perfect calm and calculation. "The females engineered every centimeter of the station, its stasis lab, and the colony vessel. Our crew knows where to shoot to finish you. And what will you do without us? I find it unlikely any of you will learn complex organic engineering to repair the station. You need us."

Rem walked over to Tumu and shoved his hands into the viscous gel, too. Plugged in, he called out the galactic coordinates of the sphere. The others slid back into their pods. Rem glared at Tumu before doing the same.

This was it.

Tumu walked to the center of the bridge. "Hello, Vi."

"Hello, Tumu." Her voice warmed in her response to him.

Exhausted, he hung his head and sighed.

She heard and asked, "Rem returned to his pod, am I correct?"

Why was this happening? "You know your mate."

Anyone else might sound sad at that reminder, but not Vi. She sounded set and determined. "We will pursue you. All of you. Tumu, I know you see our terms as fair, but we will make an example of all the Primaries."

"Yes. Do as you must."

"Goodbye, Tumu."

"Goodbye, Vi."

The comms died, and the firing continued.

Primary Rem ordered, "Return to your pod, Primary Tumu. We are within orbit of the sphere."

No glass. No visual. Sensory awareness came from a kind of sonar which only gave the impression of the massive non-planetary object.

Defeated, Tumu slid into his pod and prayed to Eternity they all survived somehow. As he prayed, the blows to the station came harder and more frequently. Sparks rained down from everywhere now. They wouldn't make it—

Quet called to the bridge, "Something is moving down there. Opening! A bay!"

"Quick, maneuver us inside." Bol squirmed with excitement from within his pod.

Tumu barely piloted his effort—

Rem ordered through gritted teeth. "Pick up your share, Tumu."

So very done, he relented, "Maybe you should wake up the other Primaries to pilot—"

"Greetings!" A voice called over the comms. Friendly and energetic. "Welcome to Enki, new friends—Oh, my. Is that ship pursing you?"

Bol answered, "Yes, they are armed! They keep firing at us!"

The friendly voice kindly directed, "No worries. Dock in bay twelve if you have skids. Land on pad four if you have hydraulics."

Uhm. "Does anyone know what kind we have?" Quet asked.

They were so fucked without their women.

Tumu sighed and took control, sliding on their skates into bay twelve. Only then did it occur to him, he could read the number twelve and understand the strangers at all. "Do they have translators?"

"We can ask when we meet them." Quet seemed equally curious.

Primary Rem wasn't just curious. Almost enthralled, he exited his pod and opened the hatch, calling out, "It's so vast. So advanced." The hangar was enormous and encased in an unfamiliar metal with a seamless surface. The rest climbed out of the station together.

Uninterested, Bol said, "Let's hope they can solve our reproductive dilemma. Come now. This way." He headed down the only corridor.

"But for a moment." The friendly stranger held some massive weapon on them. "We need to disarm you first." White hair, white eyes, and white skin. The pupils of his eyes... were they—

They were bouncing. Up and down in time together.

Two more men with the same characteristic but varied pupils frisked the Primaries. "Do you have more on board?"

With technology this advanced, they must know and expected an honest answer. Tumu lowered his hands and said, "Yes. We have a few dozen asleep in stasis."

The friendly stranger lowered his gun once the search produced no weapons. "Very well. Come this way. We are dealing with your pursuers. They are only minutes away."

As the Tritans fell in step behind their new acquaintances, Quet asked, "Why can we understand you?"

"The sphere. It translates all of our communications. Even writing."

Tumu stopped listening because he lost sight of Rem. That was never a good thing. When he looked back, he found the other Primary gazing at everything with an unexpected wonder. And as they transitioned from the bay into an open bridge, they all gaped.

There was a star inside of Enki. Behind them was a rounded wall with an ocean from top to bottom of the shell. It was hard to make out, but walls lined the ocean and land masses bordered it on either side.

"Oh, yes." The friendly stranger nodded solemnly. "Plenty of this to see—Here we are." He pointed to the gaping entry of the Sphere's shell.

Tumu's voids widened as the colony vessel bearing their women entered the Sphere. So tiny compared to the surrounding mechanisms and the space between.

Primary Rem warned, "They will shoot us. We have to reason—"

From all around the Sphere, light triangulated into one central column and unleashed on the colony vessel. For one horrifying moment, the ship was engulfed in white light. The next breath Tumu took was in a world without their females.

Eradicated.

"Wow, few people have seen the Chorus," the friendly stranger announced. "Satellites harness the energy and then combine it within the Sphere's center—What... what is the matter? You look... Well, you look quite devastated."

Quet gripped the rail of the walkway with his mouth wide open and his voids bulging from his head. Bol looked away. Rem's reaction shocked Tumu.

The Tritan fell to his knees and black tears gushed from his eyes. In a broken voice, Rem cried, "V—Vi!"

Tumu wasn't mated, but the strangers obliterated many of his friends in an attempt to rescue the men from their pursuers.

What an ugly mess this was.

Tumu knelt beside Rem. Stilted, frightful, the younger Primary, the one who'd just lost his spouse of many generations, faced Tumu with abject horror in his voids. Rem said, "My... my mate. Tumu. Our females. Our race."

"They were superior to us, and I hope you feel the remorse you deserve."

{Enki | Now}

"Primary Rem showed no signs of blame or regret afterward. Instead, he fell headlong into the lab the Aegis offered us to compensate for killing half of our species in a misunderstanding. The other Primaries, Eminents, and Officers settled into life on Enki while we kept our young bulls in stasis to preserve their pre-nacre lifespans.

Gargantuans lived longer than any Tritan, and we were few. Not long after, the other Primaries established a small dynasty in Enki and created ecosystems on our test planets. Strife between the two major races followed. A war to claim Enki for themselves.

"And that's it. Our women died in a ridiculous feud, a civil war."

The room was quiet as everyone emerged from the memory capsules. Sagan sniffled, feeling Tumu's regrets. Tameka kept her head down, probably overwhelmed with bad feelings in the last twenty-four hours. Korac regained some of his composure and pulled Sagan against his side, which she cherished.

Lucy rubbed Yito's back. The poor guy fell to his knees at some point. Choked with emotion, he asked, "Why do they keep this from us?"

Lance answered, "Would you want to admit your complicity in such an event? I struggled so much to understand why I awoke a widower. My beautiful Maz. We had three daughters. Every one of them . . . gone." He wiped away his tears and swallowed hard.

Pity washed over Sagan. Some part of her wondered how she had any capacity left to feel for those who'd wronged them. Was it never ending, this well in her? Lance condemned Rayne, but he was a man in a desperate position—

Sagan buried her face in Korac's side and let out a shuddering breath. This was too much. She totally got why Rayne would rather fight through everything. Violence was easy.

While Sagan hid, Tameka took a powerful step forward and put a hand on Tumu's arm. When he looked at her, she said, "Thank you for sharing your story. I'm sorry."

Xelan said over the earpiece, "I'm sorry, too. We have more than a few teary eyes here."

Tumu touched Tameka's hand. "Thank you, Peaches."

Gently, she pressed on, "Now I need to ask, where are the rest of your race? Like Yito."

Yito answered, "They keep us asleep still."

Lucy helped him stand and gave him a reassuring smile. Again, it didn't reach her eyes.

"I want them evacuated, and I want the demolition teams evacuated. War is coming to Enki again, and I don't plan to leave it whole when I'm done. You get me?" Tameka sounded like a ruler.

Sagan smiled in admiration.

Tumu nodded solemnly. "I think Enki has had its time. We can't derive its functions with the Aegis gone, at any rate." He cast a cautious glance in Korac's direction.

Ignoring him, Korac said, "We came here to ask about the bridge."

Lance recoiled. "That's a myth." At their stern stares, he asked, "Is it not?"

Korac chafed Sagan's arm as he said, "As it were, it happens to be real."

"And under Torrentus," Tumu finished.

Tameka declared, "We plan to enter it from the Pantheon—"

"Oh, you can't," Lance said. "That conduit is bio-locked—like the Pretiosum Cruor locked Cinder—to Celindria." After a thoughtful pause, he added, "But I have an idea."

Xelan said over the earpiece, "I vote we trust him."

Tumu nodded.

Korac shrugged.

This was momentous. It was different this time. Bigger. More important. Tameka glanced at Sagan for her to weigh in on this decision. Place their faith in another person with a history of betrayal. Take a chance and trust again.

Sagan moved out of her retreat at Korac's side. He peered down at her without pressure, but also without his opinion. As if he wanted her to make this decision on her own. She looked at Lance, Yito, and Tumu. Three potential Tritan allies with murky histories.

It was different this time. Insiders. That's what the Shadow needed.

Decided, Sagan faced Tameka and smiled with her nod.

Tameka returned the expression before addressing Lance, "What did you have in mind?"

{Enki | Tumu's Sanctum}

Everyone around Xelan looked tired of revelations, but he held back more questions. What sort of plague wiped out the Tritan homeworld? How many other species were capable of space travel, given the Aegis prepared a variety of docking facilities? Was Imminent aware of how to operate the Chorus?

The last posed a terrible risk to their current plans.

Xelan, Pablo, and Lynn finished vaccinating members of the Shadow hiding in Tumu's sanctum. Each of them had closed their eyes and spared a silent prayer to Elden that they worked. Meanwhile, Lance finished describing the most dangerous plan Xelan had ever heard.

It was exactly what they needed.

"Can you handle it, Fury?" Xelan hoped his grin infused his voice. There was no mistaking how Tameka would answer.

"Hell. Yes."

"That's right," Lynn murmured across the way with her own grin lighting up the room.

Pablo shot her a thumbs up from the other side.

Kyle took his joint from his mouth to say, "As if Tameka would answer any other way," on a cloud of smoke.

Andrew rounded the corner from the kitchen to say, "In all the Probabilities which lead to this moment, Tameka answers the same. There's a reason she's one of my pillars."

"We're heading back," Sagan announced over the earpiece before a conduit split the space.

As people filed through, Lucy waved through the Seam at Xelan with her entire body thrown into the gesture.

He waved back, calling "Hey Morning Star! I'm so proud of your team!"

"I know, that's why I'm grinning so big! We'll see y'all soon!"

Xelan liked when Lucy smiled like that. It was the only time her eyes held any shine. That and when she stood anywhere near Matt. With Korac as the last one out, the conduit closed on Lucy's hopeful face.

Without a second wasted, Xelan approached Tumu and opened his arms. "It's been a while, Primary."

"I never thought I'd hear you call me that again." The Tritan compressed further from his thirteen-foot height to seven feet, and they embraced, with Xelan speaking into the other man's chest.

"Why didn't you ever tell me?"

Sagan nudged them both, unsteadying them. "Because Tumu wants to write a Verse."

Tameka laughed. "That would be one massive tome."

Tumu ruined Sagan's structured curls by ruffling her short hair. "Only if you—"

"Hey!"

"—took my dictation, Star." He let go of Xelan, and they both smiled down at her nose, scrunched in anger.

Korac answered for her. "No way I'd let you keep her for so long."

That's right. If everything goes like they'd hoped, Korac and Sagan would raise a little girl soon. Xelan wanted to see it happen. He wanted to see their daughter playing with his son and the dozens of children Pablo and Lynn would no doubt have once everything calmed down. Swing sets and forts—

Xelan frowned while Tumu and Korac fought over Sagan's free time beside him. Pax was building a fort with Bones when Imminent took him. Para said she remembered falling asleep before Celindria captured her, Karter, and Chris. Imminent mercifully left Pax then, but why...

"What's wrong?" Tameka's warm hand slipped into his. Smaller with softer skin in the most beautiful complexion.

Quietly, so the others wouldn't hear, Xelan confessed, "I worry about the mechanism Celindria's employing to abduct our people." He bit his thumbnail as he thought more on it.

Tameka nodded and confirmed, "Falling asleep and feeling drained when they wake. It's almost like my ability."

Xelan smashed his fist into his other palm. "Exactly. Is it artificial? And if so, why does Celindria insist you're 'the key to Ishkur' when she may already possess a semblance of your ability?"

"Are you sure Merit was a null?" Tameka used the word Xelan gave for the inert Progeny descendants.

It was a good question, given what Tameka knew, but Xelan was sure. "Completely. If Celindria weaponized your ability, she must have manufactured it without a source. I think that's why it's only good in small doses—Can I just say how impressed I am with how you handled Lance?"

Xelan liked the pretty way Tameka blinked at the sudden change in subject. With them one step closer to finding Pax, some of the anxiety had lifted from her face. After a second, she beamed at him. "Yeah?"

"You make one hell of a galactic leader, Fury."

There she went again. Tameka frowned anytime someone mentioned leadership or an upgrade in her status. Was she really unaware—

"I volunteer for the rescue." Para had changed into a combat jumpsuit and armed herself with psi daggers. "I want to get Karter and Chris back. And Andrius, too. He doesn't deserve to spend his life in a cage."

Tameka asked the right question. "Are you sure you want to put yourself in Imminent's sights again?"

Xelan's chest warmed with pride for his girl.

Para, ever the lethal warrior, spun the psi daggers and holstered them. "You're damn right I do. I want a shot at the Primary. And Abresson."

"Get in line." Caedes stepped up to the group, looking ever the gruff killing machine. Xelan wondered how much of it was Korac's camp and how much of it was simply Caedes' nature. The gruff Icarus said, "Pablo and Lynn asked Twenty-One, Miy, and I to cover them here at the sanctum. Bethany is helping them prepare supplies for the wounded."

Tameka took Caedes' hand and ignored the blue flush all the way to the top of his bald head. "We'll get Pax back to his Uncle."

The blushing Icarus cleared his throat as an acknowledgment and politely withdrew his hand. He and Para left with a nod to prepare for their respective missions.

There were so many good people here and on the way. Xelan's heart swelled with it. They would win this day.

"So that makes me, Bones, Devis, Para, T.A.O., Ross, and Jack." Tameka counted the souls off on her fingers before frowning at him. "You know, Rayne would kill us for letting her brother risk himself."

Xelan was ready for this counterpoint. "Jack Callahan will make all the difference. Mark my words."

That shade of sorrow appeared behind Tameka's eyes again, the lost look in them. Xelan cursed Celindria for bringing it on. Cursed her for so *many* reasons. Tameka asked, "What about your team?"

Xelan pulled Tameka over to a ledge, sat on it, and positioned her between his knees. All the while, she followed on autopilot, focusing only on the mission ahead. Xelan kissed her wrist, and she looked at him, this time actually seeing him. He answered, "Our Generals will escort us—Kyle, Andrew, Lamassau, and Tumu—to Cinder's shrine. From there, we'll ferry F8 and our troops to the Pantheon. We'll wait for your signal."

"If we do our jobs right, my signal will be a lot of non-responsive static and clear skies, but I know I'll deliver."

Xelan appreciated that even with the last twenty-four hours, Tameka still soldiered on. He cupped her cheek and smiled when she leaned into it. "I know you will." Her makeup dramatically accentuated her green eyes and glossed her full lips. He wanted to kiss her, but buried the impulse. Not with Pax missing. Making Tameka more uncomfortable was the last—

She leaned forward and sealed his lips with hers, seeking comfort. Comfort Xelan easily gave. It was nearly chaste and purely warm. When Tameka broke it, she buried her face in his neck, and Xelan enveloped her in his arms. He wanted to offer words that helped with the anxiety. Reassurance.

"Tameka."

"Yes?" She kept hold of him.

Xelan swallowed before confessing, "You've been patient with me about the Weapon project. I only wanted to assure you I didn't know what it was or how they would use it." Or who they would test it on, but mentioning this would simply raise more anxieties.

Tameka pulled back to search his eyes. Hers shone with understanding and love. "I believe you, and thank you for telling me. You want to explain some things in mass. I get it, but it means a lot to me that you confided in just me."

"I love you, Fury."

"I love you, Wingmaster."

After they rescued Pax and saved the Vast Collective, when she was ready, Xelan would explain to Tameka about the galaxy's plan for them.

A tall agenda, but Xelan knew they could accomplish anything together.

Even unification.

{ENKI | TUMU'S SANCTUM}

It was different this time than all the millions of times before and all the simultaneous ones and split from here—

Heads.

Andrew shifted between the seams of the blazing realities and practiced focusing on the one with his corporeal body. The one in which Tameka and Sagan had dressed Andrew in a blue jumpsuit with black elbow, shoulder, and knee pads. They braided strands of blue ribbon through his hair. After much protest, even Kyle couldn't escape the girls, forcing him into an inverse of Andrew's ensemble. It was a grooming ritual similar to painting the black band across their eyes for the Volcano Day battle, distinguishing Progeny from the average soldier. They all prepared in their own ways.

Tameka snuggled against Xelan. Caedes and Para separated to their respective groups, with him meeting Pablo and Lynn at Triss' bedside. There, Miy wiped away the perspiration from the comatose woman's brow. Twenty-One, Bethany, and all the Lyriks finished carpeting the floor with beds for the wounded. Devis meditated on the floor, while Para joined Bones in explaining what supplies they needed to T.A.O., Jack, and Ross. Tumu walked in with Lamassau, probably after some more *alone time,* and met Kyle, Iuo, and Pehton on their way to Sagan and Korac at the weapons cache. All of them under one roof.

It was the perfect time to make Andrew into a fucking prophet. Predictions and the Probability Matrix. He couldn't afford to wait, so Andrew stepped up and said, "Every—"

His voice failed him with a serious case of performance anxiety. Lucas was the diplomat. Andrew just tended the crops—

Xelan caught his eye from across the room. Tameka, too, with a warm smile. Cheesily, the Icarus who'd codenamed himself "Wingmaster" gave Andrew the most dramatic thumbs up since the T-800 self-terminated in *T2*. It was almost enough to make Andrew groan and roll his eyes. It was perfect.

"Everybody, listen up." With renewed confidence, Andrew took to the center of the room and met everyone's curious glances. It damned near crossed his eyes as the Probabilities blurred into one layer plus or minus a member of the Shadow. Clearing his throat, he continued. "The Probability Matrix gave me some insight into our next missions. If we don't act immediately, we fail in all but two hundred Probabilities. That's out of hundreds of thousands."

Sagan, frowning, raised her hand. She even bounced so Andrew would see her over all the six-foot energy in the room. Korac smiled openly at her cute behavior, and Andrew felt an unfair pang of loss in his chest.

"Go ahead, Sagan."

She asked the same question in one hundred and fifty Probabilities. "I get you're saying Tameka and the others need to leave now, but what about our mission?"

Kyle lit another joint and blew out some smoke. "Yeah, what about F8 and all that?"

Across the way, Xelan opened his mouth, paused, and closed it. He pulled Tameka against his side and waved for Andrew to go on with a reassuring smile.

Andrew appreciated all the support, but he'd never felt more alone. He wet his lips before saying, "They've already gather at their shrines, waiting for Tameka to disable the weapons in Cinder's station."

Tameka frowned. "Aren't they monitored—"

Lamassau cut her off with a laugh.

Tumu cut him off with a glare and said, "There's not enough of us. Cinder was the first planet to outright abuse our passive surveillance. Eventually, we assigned someone to monitor that single conduit at all times—Yes, General, we knew of every pirate and smuggler you entertained."

Korac shot a knowing smirk over his shoulder at Xelan, who gave Tumu a shameless shrug.

Sighing, the Primary folded his arms and continued. "But the Icari required more force. Once Peaches drains the nacre-turrets, there won't be any defenses left. And you're saying it's time, Andrew?"

Their eyes returned to Andrew again in all their varying shades and shapes. Each held a wealth of respect and curiosity. Andrew ran a hand through his hair before blowing the air from his cheeks. "Yeah. Yeah, I am. We go now, or there's a real chance we don't win."

"Then we go."

The Shadow mercifully turned their collective eyes to Tameka, who truly glowed under their trusting gazes. Xelan beamed behind her as she said, "This is it. Gear up.

I'll go with Sagan now to prepare the shrine, then we split up and get it done."

With all their backs to him, Andrew flipped his coin.

Heads.

Relief washed over Andrew in such a sweeping force it knocked a sigh out of him. "Thank, Elden," he muttered. A glance upwards caught Tumu watching him with something unidentifiable in the depths of his voids.

Arms still folded, the Gargantuan Tritan dipped his chin in a nod of… deference? Why—

"…Is everyone's role clear?" Tameka met all their eyes as she finished.

Assent rang through the Sanctum as the Shadow moved off into their assigned groups. Tameka took a step toward her team, but Xelan pulled her back to him for a kiss which left Andrew aching with concentrated envy. A shade stepped over him, and he turned to find Tumu towering behind him. Andrew asked, "Sup?"

"They'll need you to tell them the most likely outcomes."

Tumu's suggestion had occurred to Andrew who asked, "But won't that effect the Probabilities in someway?"

Lamassau, who was aggressively packing a bag with snacks, said, "Not if you tell them several outcomes and keep it vague. That's how the Tritans use the Probability Matrix. Likely Imminent, as well—Whoa!" The bag slipped out of his hands in an uncoordinated explosion of chips and ramen. "Aww, man. Tumi, help me." A whining Tritan.

Ignoring his lover, the Primary gripped Andrew's shoulder. "You're doing good."

The words cut like a hot knife. There was too much warmth in them not to hurt. Andrew blinked back tears and swallowed to say, "Thanks," in a strangled voice.

"Don't worry, Lam. 'I got you.'" Tumu went to help the Chef, who groaned at the use of Xelan's catch phrase.

Iuo laughed abruptly at it.

The green Tritan rolled his eyes. "Come. On."

Taking a deep breath, Andrew crossed the room to Tameka's group. "Hey, I think I should tell you some things which could help. Jack, too."

Hearing his name, the teenager stopped helping Ross pack and came to attention. "I'm listening." His hazel eyes were so serious and so young, even compared to the Progeny when Xelan first started training them.

Empathy, not pity, warmed the cold emeralds in Tameka's eyes as she squeezed Andrew's bicep. "You have our attention."

Bones and Para inched their way over to catch the briefing. As for The Afflicted One... Well, T.A.O. was watching her skirt as she twirled in the blue dress she borrowed from Sagan.

Andrew closed his eyes and sifted through the outcomes, their threads glowing in a white light which followed a black flame across his vision. Prophet. Freak. "Someone else may be there. Don't engage the target until Celindria's alone. Otherwise, in thirty-eight Probabilities, everyone dies. Watch each other's backs. Give nothing away. Answering any questions with the truth ends badly in thirteen Probabilities. Just avoid answering, if you can. Jack, when it's your time, you'll know it. You're almost always successful." Opening his eyes, the group surprised Andrew with their expressions. Not horrified or freaked out. Just impressed.

As if she sensed his reticence, Tameka pulled him into a hug. "Thank you."

Ross said from behind Jack, "Yeah, that's pretty cool, Conscience."

"What about..." Bones paused mid-sentence and glanced at Para, who shared the concern. "Will we successfully rescue Karter, Chris, and Andrius? Are they okay?"

Without hesitation, Andrew said, "They're alive, but I can't answer more than that. Trust yourselves."

Sagan Seamswalked over and smiled at him before turning to Tameka. "Ready?"

The redhead asked, "Oh, Andrew. Will Sagan and I manage the turrets okay?"

Both girls beamed at him with love and confidence. Warriors. Leaders. Family.

"Trust in each other, and nothing will stop you."

Andrew didn't need the Probability Matrix to see that. Sagan's and Tameka's eyes burned with it.

They couldn't lose.

SIX

HOPE LIES BEYOND THAT DARKNESS; IT AWAITS YOUR RESCUE

{ENKI | CINDER'S SHRINE}

IT TOOK THE WORK OF A MEMORY TO LOCATE CINDER'S SHRINE. SAGAN OPENED A CONDUIT TO THE BLACK CORRUGATED METAL STATION, CONTRASTED AGAINST THE USUALLY SERENE, SEAMLESS GLASS FOYERS TO OTHER PLANETS. That's right. The Tritans built the post which guarded the planet they ruined to match Gait's prison. Plus one extra detail.

Horizontal, rectangular boxes with a split down the middle. The nacre detecting sentries added real menace to the harsh red glow of the perimeter lights against all this bleak darkness.

As Sagan and Tameka stepped through the conduit, the blond Progeny placed her exposed back against a chilly wall to peer around its corner. "Shit."

The redhead crouched, prepared for a roll to the next zone. "This place is the size of a football field. There must be dozens of those things."

Sagan raised her brows and made a face which reflected her words. "Well, you're not wrong. Try hundreds. I don't remember seeing this many when Tumu led us here for the Pretiosum Cruor."

"Let's not bring that day up ever again. And..." Tameka took a deep breath which steadied herself before darting her head around and back as quickly. No pew pew energy sounds. "Yup. Hundreds." She sat back, peering up at Sagan. "I have an idea, but you won't like it."

Nerves fluttered in Sagan's stomach. She trusted her girl, but... "What happened to draining them?"

Tameka ducked her head, conceding to the turrets. "There's too many. I think I might overload, so I'll do the opposite."

Wow. "Like at the Queen's Fare?" Sagan felt her eyes widened, impressed with her bestie. "I got your back." She reached out a hand.

Tameka clasped it and closed her eyes. One deep breath in, and one long breath out. When she opened them again, the green irises swallowed her corneas, and Sagan wondered why Imminent was ever dumb enough to challenge someone as powerful as Fury—

A tiny explosion followed. And another and another. They thundered from the expansive corridor around the corner. Sagan grinned at all the smoke. "I think it worked." Still holding Tameka's hand, she risked a glance around the corner.

Sure enough. Two dozen turrets, lining the winding passage, were reduced to scorch marks. Sagan let out a cry of triumph. "You did it!"

"Take me down the corridor, and I'll smoke the rest." Tameka stood and squeezed Sagan's hand, strong and confident. "Like I said. We'll get it done."

Damn, her smile was infectious. "Yes, ma'am." Sagan opened a conduit, and they passed through into another corridor—

A dash of light speared by them. And another—

"Ow, Fuck! I'm hit!" Tameka let go to apply pressure to her wrist.

Sagan tackled her through a set of conduits to safety outside the passage. "Sorry! Are you okay?" Little pelts sounded against the corner as the sentries battled their impotence out of range. At least eighty of them lined the corridor. Sagan ground out, "I *know* there weren't this many last time."

Tameka peeled her hand away from her arm and wiped the first blood of the battle on her shorts. "It was a glancing shot. The damned thing nearly ruined my bracer, but it's already stopped bleeding. I'm fine." After Tameka took another deep breath, Sagan recognized the increasingly familiar thunder from the turret's exploding. Glowing with energy, Sagan's best friend said, "We'll need to be more careful this time. There's not much of my gear to destroy." Tameka smirked.

"It is a fantastic outfit." Sagan had to agree. "Come on. Next one, we'll tuck and roll out of the conduit, like spies in an action movie."

Both girls dove through it and rolled out into another alcove with zips of energy firing on all sides. They pressed their backs against their safety wall, and Sagan wanted to test Tameka's multi-tasking concentration. It was one thing to focus her ability in these more controlled circumstances, but soon, they'd face an army. Could Tameka drain and overload things while distracted?

Sagan hugged herself and said, "I'm really glad you've found a place for Kyle in your forgiveness." She meant every word. The two of them being at odds since high school was a real detriment to their group. And okay, yeah, Kyle messed up pretty bad, but he tried to make up for it. That mattered.

Tameka took a deep breath and focused. She answered with the thunderous roar in the background, "Well, after Silence, I guess I decided he'd had enough punishment. When Rayne gets back, I'll be the first to petition he gets his wings. Although, I understand her position and reasons."

Right. Silence. Sagan frowned because that was one piece in this sliding puzzle she'd swear wasn't turned right. "Even after everything I've been through, I couldn't imagine falling for someone who sided with people capable of... all this..." She opened the next conduit and bent her knees.

"I know." Tameka did the same. On three, they both jumped, rolled, and repeated the process of finding cover. "Have you noticed Andrew lately?"

Poor Andrew. Sagan sighed. "How could I miss him? He wears his heartache in his eyes."

Explosions thundered. Tameka nudged her as she teased, "After helping with his Verse, are you picking up Korac's way with words? Or is this one of those things where couples become more alike? Please don't start smirking, too. Xelan's getting enough shit from one General."

It was warm and familial, but Sagan still halted the casualness with a serious touch on her friend's arm. "I loved Lucas, too."

With a hard swallow, Tameka looked away. Smoke from the destroyed sentries clouded Sagan's view of her best friend as Tameka confessed, "I can't. I can't look at everything more seriously than I'm already addressing it. You know what I mean? I'm taking the steps to do the things I have to do, but if I spend too much time dwelling on it, then Pax is really . . ." Sagan felt like an asshole when Tameka gave her the full weight of her Atramentous gaze. Tameka's next words came out in three pitches. "I have to move forward to get to him."

"I'm really sorry, Tameka, I—"

Her best friend dragged Sagan into a hug with that grip of hers. Softly, Tameka assured, "I'll get to Pax. You'll get our army to the battlefield. Hell, maybe Rayne will be waiting for us."

Sagan squeezed back. What a beautiful notion. All of them together and finishing it. "Do you think so?"

"There isn't a doubt in my mind. This is when we bring the family together. Now, come on, Seamswalker." Tameka pulled them apart to smile for Sagan. "We've got less than a hundred sentries to go."

It was different this time.

The Vast Collective would unite to back the Shadow as they finished Imminent for good.

Rayne.

Pax.

"Let's get it done, Fury."

"That's my girl!"

{ENKI | TUMU'S SANCTUM}

Flushed with victory, Tameka walked hand-in-hand with Sagan back into their makeshift infirmary. She announced to all their people amid preparations, "All clear."

Mid-conversation with Pablo beside Triss' bed, Xelan stopped talking and beamed at them. "Good work! I never doubted you."

Sagan squeezed Tameka's hand before meeting her lover halfway and melting into Korac's arms. A smile spread across Tameka's lips, despite the heaviness of everything. As the Icarus handed over Sagan's axe, they looked good together sharing the mated weapons.

Inspired and in need of her chain dart, Tameka crossed the room until she stood so close to Xelan she needed to crane her neck to meet his eyes. "Admit it. You worried a little."

"Only this much." He held up his pinched fingers before placing a kiss on her forehead, reseating Tameka's weapon on her belt.

Warm and sweet, she soaked it up. There was no telling how long until the next time she saw him, but staring into those eyes, Tameka knew without a doubt, this wasn't goodbye. "Look for my signal."

Andrew lingered at the corner of Tameka's eye, distracting enough to make her look over. He gave a solemn nod. It was time.

Xelan's warm finger crooked under Tameka's chin and brought her back to him. "Take from me what you need."

The sincerity in Xelan's eyes, the utter confidence—It was so much Tameka had to swallow her emotions before saying, "Give to me what you want." Hot tears squeezed from the corners of her eyes.

Xelan pulled Tameka into a tight embrace and whispered in her ear, "Until Eternity takes me."

"I'm yours."

Drawing all the strength from him without actually affecting his nacre, Tameka pulled them apart and touched her fist to her chest. She let it fall to her side before stepping away and calling, "My team, with me." Her people—Jack, Ross, Bones, Devis, T.A.O., and Para—crushed in around her, checking their earpieces.

Xelan circled a finger in the air, and the second team rounded up. Their group—Iuo, Pehton, Tumu, Lamassau, Andrew, Kyle, Korac, Sagan, and eleven more Lyriks—performed the same checks.

The two leaders met gazes and nodded.

Tameka called, "Seamswalkers."

On her command, two conduits opened. Sagan's went to the Monarch 3 shrine, and T.A.O.'s led to the continent of New Cinder. The two women peered at one another over the manifestations. Physical contact wasn't required to enter the younger Seamswalker's conduit as she'd far surpassed her ancestor, but T.A.O. had lived a longer life practicing the ability. Both were assets which Tameka was happy to see on the Shadow's side.

The small waif of a woman reached out her hand.

This was it—

"For Pax."

Tameka whirled to see half the room staring at Caedes.

The normally silent Icarus led the rally and nodded at Tameka.

"For Cinder." The second voice was unmistakable. Korac met Tameka's gaze with the intensity of a few million years steeped in vendetta.

Para called next, "For the people we love."

"For the ones we lost." Tameka couldn't even see Pehton, but recognized her voice.

John.

Oleen.

Nikki.

All they'd endured thickened the moment until it hurt to breathe. Tameka's heart ached with the sharp clarity of it. This wasn't a moment for the Shadow alone. She touched her chain dart and proclaimed, "For the Vast Collective!"

The group grunted and followed their Seamswalkers to their destinations.

Elden, keep them safe.

After a glimpse of the Seam, Tameka stepped into a black cave, one hand clasped in T.A.O.'s and the other in Ross'. Kyle's younger sister pulled Jack through. Then Bones, Para, and Devis followed.

As they filed out, Tameka took a better look at their surroundings. Black, basalt rock like Nox's castle. Not completely dark, a faint glow emanated from the... Wow, was that red water? It was beautiful. Tameka knelt at a nearby pool to admire the phosphorous light emitting in the clean smelling springs. Flowers were nearby, their wild scent filled the cavern.

Tameka turned to find her team smiling, equally taken in by the scenery, but there wasn't time to sightsee Cinder before Li's expansion. Quietly, so her voice didn't carry on the rock, she asked, "T.A.O., is it this way?" Tameka pointed, following the water.

Those amethyst Atramentous eyes met Tameka's and blinked. "Been here before?"

Devis gently touched his sister's bicep. "It's a logical assumption." To Tameka, he said, "And yes. There will be a land bridge over a waterfall, and beyond that is her laboratory. Are you confident in this?"

Across the way, Bones raised a brow as if acknowledging what they were all thinking. He kept his hands near his sword at the ready.

Jack answered, "I am."

Para's hands hovered over her psi daggers. "That's good enough for me."

"We're with you, Fury." Ross, too young to be out here risking her life, adjusted the strap on her nacre disabling rifle.

Was this what it was like for Xelan to lead Tameka's Progeny into Enki the first time? How could she forget how eagerly they'd followed him into such a chaotic end? But… things had a way of working out…

Tameka gave the hand signal, and they followed her in careful formation through the tunnel. As Devis had described earlier, she inched her way to a fork which opened into an enormous chamber. The viscous red water fell from a crevice in the ceiling so gently that it made little noise splashing into the pool below. Orange flowers ivied the walls in a fresh fragrance so unexpected in what was otherwise a dank cave. No, that wasn't accurate. The cave pulsed with life, and Tameka couldn't wait to bring Xelan here.

The bridge led to only one exit. Narrow. They would need to single-file through it. On Tameka's signal, they followed her across the expanse without hiccups. Once through the tunnel, they encountered another fork.

When she glanced back, Devis mouthed, "Right."

After a few turns, the scent changed. Not alive here, but cold and sterile. Tameka stopped and signaled for the others to line the walls behind her. She glanced at T.A.O., who'd paled from her usual deep, almost blue complexion. Tameka wished they could've left her behind, but a second Seamswalker was too valuable—

No.

That wasn't fair thinking, and that line of thought stole credit away from the smallest Progeny. T.A.O. volunteered to save her brother and free the others. Brave and confident in their chances.

Tameka gave her a reassuring smile. Devis took T.A.O.'s hand and nodded at Tameka with gratitude in his eyes. Para and Bones signaled they were ready on her mark. Jack watched as Ross concentrated. When the girl opened her eyes, the hazel Atramentous shifted her corneas to a golden brown with a green slit for a pupil. She held up three fingers.

Right.

The chain dart's pommel fit Tameka's hand in a familiar, comforting grip. Cautiously, she peered around the corner. It was as she suspected. Stainless steel and glass surfaces furnished the lab, covered with instruments Tameka didn't recognize. Along the south wall, bars formed a cage with a figure trapped inside. The human-sized lump lay across a cot, sleeping. Or seeming to. That must be Andrius. Aside from him, the lab appeared empty, with only one door on the far side.

Tameka took a deep breath and sought the other nacres.

There.

On the other side of a door. Tameka considered draining them, but doing so without visual confirmation risked Karter, Pax, and Chris. No, she had to do this the hard way.

Letting her breath out on a nervous shudder, Tameka ran into the lions' den and prayed their jaws claimed her alone for their next meal.

{ENKI | MONARCH 3'S SHRINE}

As her team made their way through the conduit, led by Xelan, Pehton's last conversation with Caedes replayed in her head. The one he initiated right before Xelan called roundup.

"If you get a chance, take Abresson out for me." The gravel in Caedes' voice thickened so much he cleared his throat before adding, "I'm afraid I won't get much in his way while I'm guarding the ICU." Beneath his request was a carefully veiled concern.

Pehton laughed in his face, surprising him, judging by the widening of his eyes. Once she collected a few breaths, she said, "I'm sorry. I'm so sorry. It's just... haha... They did it. They sapped you."

Caedes' eyes darkened as realization dawned on his face. He clenched his jaw and gave a big exhale. "Shit."

Refreshed from the break in all seriousness, Pehton touched his arm. "Now. For your orders—"

He seriously straightened to attention and his dark green eyes sparkled down at her.

"—I command you to guard these people—yes, even Triss—from the hordes of bullshit heading this way. To the death or to your shame. Do you understand me?"

Quiet passed between them. It was an important moment with Caedes staring in her eyes. His expression was intense. The tension stretched so tight that when he reached out to brush his fingers in her feathers, Pehton startled. Cue the truly annoying but very male smile on his face as he said, "What do you like for breakfast, Pehton?"

She frowned. Breakfast? "What... Why?"

"So I know what to make you tomorrow morning after we win, and once I've spent tonight doing everything I've thought about doing to you. At your *command*, of course."

Welp, that's all Pehton could think about. Yup. They were heading into battle, and her head was full of a gravelly voice in her ear during all the times Caedes had pinned her in their training games. It occurred to her Caedes would be Pehton's first lover with no hair. What would she grip her fingers in?

They'd figure it out.

"Psst." Someone nudged her from behind.

Pehton turned to crane her neck up to glare at Korac, who'd found his signature countenance once again. Cold and confident, but his pale eyes glittered with mischief as he said, "Head in the game, hussy." Her cheeks warmed as he said, "That's right, I heard you two. Focus on the battle. We'll need your mind on your Siren's Gale to defeat Enki, not on how you like your eggs. Scrambled or over bald heads."

This would be worth it. Pehton swung one good jab at Korac's ribs because it was the highest she could reach on him. When she did it, Pehton knew the moment Korac could block because he was simply that fast. Instead, the cavalier General let it land and even faked a wince on her behalf.

"Ouch! No wonder your new boyfriend has a thing for redheads. So feisty."

Another punch. This one landed in Korac's gut. He pretended to stagger back from it. "Oh no! Not my abs. Sagan will never forgive you."

Pehton growled. "This is so patronizing—"

"I find it quite amusing."

They both looked at Sagan, who grinned and waited at the front of the group with Xelan. Beyond them was the Monarch 3 army, led by the black-and-blue-clad Queen, F8.

The ruling butterfly smiled with entirely too many teeth in her pretty, petite mouth. F8 ducked her head. "General Korac, I find I like you much more in recent years. And Executive Warden Pehton, I've only heard of you from Tumu, but I appreciate your attitude. However, if the two of you don't mind, we need to assemble the other armies at their respective shrines. Prince Xelan?"

Grateful to see the attention had moved from their embarrassing misbehavior, Pehton offered an apologetic smile to Sagan. She hid a snicker with her hand for both the Executive Warden and her errant lover.

There was that feeling again. Belonging. Love. Whatever drove the Shadow to be so huggy and sappy—Pehton got it. She'd die for them. Hell, she might.

Korac plowed by Pehton, almost knocking her over on his way to the front.

Fucking juvenile.

Once Korac reached Xelan, he asked with a severe brow quirked, "Armies?"

Xelan turned and reassured, "I suspected your Verse might encourage some of the others."

F8 chuckled. "'Some,' he says. You knew exactly what you were doing. It's why I like you so much."

Sagan raised a hand, and three heads turned to her. Korac's smirk for his lover was so warm. Pehton almost let out a cheesy sigh at how much she admired the couple.

"How many people am I transporting?" Sagan asked a reasonable question.

The widening of F8's eyes fluttered Pehton's pulse even before she answered. "My armies are the most immense in the galaxy. I cannot give you a number. The Caprents numbers are more exact. Then Pil might provide accurate estimates but with the mech suits—"

"Pil? L. Capra?" Incredulity warmed Korac's voice.

Pehton's eyebrows raised as F8 continued without acknowledging the astonished faces around her.

"—The healers of Yun are on Cinder with the Icarean troops and human forces. Iuo, do you know how many are in your private army?" The last F8 called over the crowd to the Lamian Prince.

"Five million. You know? Standard." He smiled in his friendly, unassuming way, while the rest gawked at him.

"Oh," F8 added, "I almost forgot X is meeting us with Lukemore's forces at the Pil shrine. Then, of course," she turned and smiled at Pehton before continuing, "Your army is short in number, but mighty in spirit. I look forward to seeing your Lyriks fight, General Pehton."

General Pehton. What…

Why was Korac smirking at Pehton? Even Xelan beamed at her with pride. Dear Elden, fighting alongside Icari was dizzying, especially ones with a tendency for dramatic theatrics. Only Sagan's touch on Pehton's elbow grounded her enough to say, "We're ready." Of their own volition, her Lyriks whistled behind her in a demonstration which swelled Pehton's chest.

Lamassau explained, "Tempest and Dolor assembled the Two World armies with Colton, Six, and Cypher leading the humans. It was a precaution we arranged on Earth."

Kyle looked at Andrew. "Good thinking."

Andrew said, "Actually, it was Tumu's idea."

They all turned and looked at the old Primary. He ignored their curious faces and asked, "Star, can you manage all this?"

Sagan smirked, and Korac's lips broadened into a grin, once again melting Pehton. The Seamswalker said, "No problem."

A conduit opened, and F8 ordered, "March!" Her queens stepped through first.

As the Monarch 3 army funneled into Cinder's shrine, Pehton overheard Xelan whispering to Andrew. "...their intentions?"

"They're telling the truth," the Progeny confirmed.

Pehton tried not to eavesdrop, but she couldn't help overhear Xelan say, "You sound surprised."

In a distraught voice which nearly broke the Lyrik's heart, Andrew confessed, "Let's just say I'm struggling to keep my faith in people, lately."

"Hey, that's something I wanted to talk to you about." Kyle sounded intrigued. "How many times have we heard that phrase? You know... 'Keep your faith in me a little while longer'?"

Korac's slightly exposed chest entered Pehton's field of vision. She looked up at his smirking face. Good and caught. In an attempt to defend herself, Pehton opened her mouth to say, "I swear, I wasn't trying—"

"Eavesdropping. Tsk tsk. Although, I suppose I'll let it slide this once. It's a skill you no doubt found useful on Gait—"

Gait.

Pehton knocked into his knees as she pushed past him to reach Sagan. "Hey."

Sagan searched her eyes. "You need me?"

"The drive. The one Razor gave you..." Pehton crossed her fingers, hoping.

Sagan patted a pocket in her leather pants, the existence of which Pehton found surprising given how tight they fit her. The Seamswalker assured, "I brought it. One of the times, Razor—" Sagan swallowed, and Pehton almost kicked herself for bringing him up. "Ahem. He said it might decode for an Aegis Terminal in Enki."

Xelan stepped up beside them. "What's on it?"

Korac answered from behind Pehton, "A dossier of all the members of Imminent. You're so brilliant for thinking to bring it amid all this chaos." He leaned to the side and kissed Sagan's cheek. She blushed.

Pehton gagged. Yup. She'd met her limit. Rather than beg the two to stop being the perfect couple, she looked up at Xelan. Hmm. Interesting. As the coupliness of them increased, a little vein strained on his forehead—

"Xelan, I brought something for you." Tumu turned and took something from Lamassau. It was folded and made of a black material. "I believe you left this the last time I arrested you in Enki."

The Prince of Cinder's eyes widened as he snatched it and let the folds fall open—

It was a frock. An actual pirate frock with folded cuffs and blue-stitched details on the buttons and lapels. It looked like a cheesy movie prop.

And Xelan luxuriated in it, sweeping it on with a flourish. His voice held an excited wonder. "I thought I'd lost it."

To Pehton's fine-tuned ears, Lamassau sounded a little displeased when he said, "You left it in Tumu's Sanctum millennia ago. You remember? When you stripped naked to enter the Pantheon."

Korac's brows shot up with a glare at his ex, Tumu held up his hands to stave his lover, and Xelan stammered on his explanation—

"General Pehton."

Called, she turned away from the unfolding drama to find F8 standing behind her. Tiny, like the Lyriks, the butterfly queen held out her impossibly small hand. "Escort me through the conduit? I'd like a chat."

Pehton glanced between the smiling leaders surrounding her before accepting the woman's hand. "Of course. What's on your mind?"

They walked together to the conduit as millions of the queen's people filed inside. The drone soldiers fell back for the monarch, allowing them a pocket to pass through. As they walked, F8 said, "Soon, we'll convene with the other generals to discuss strategy. Do you have formations for your soldiers? What about the Siren's Gale? Are you the only one blessed with—"

"Okay. Slow down, your highness." Pehton staved F8 with her free hand. The aggressive butterfly quirked an amused brow in response. Then the woman's eyes scanned Pehton's body. The black net weave of her Lyriki armor was the same brilliant blue as her soldiers, but maybe this queen saw something else. Regardless, Pehton set F8 straight. "I'm working with the Icari. With Xelan and Korac. Although I have some maneuvers in mind if we're facing Imminent soldiers from across the galaxy, I'll put my girls where it best serves the entirety of our forces. I suggest you do the same."

"We all are."

Wait. What. "Pardon?"

F8 squeezed Pehton's hand gently, but tense enough to hint at her disproportionate strength. In a reassuring voice, F8 said, "We will follow them into battle and long after. They are what we need."

So it was true.

"Okay, then why ask me—"

"I'm only curious as to your fighting style." F8 patted Pehton's hand and released it, stepping back into a black metal alcove. Her army's boots reverberated with each step on the corrugated metal. The station at Cinder's shrine was truly oppressive, made more so by the faint smell of the burnt planet's ashen breeze. F8's clothes blended into the walls as she continued to explain, "As someone tragically confined to an entirely male army, I'm curious how women get along. The Valkyrie interest me as well."

Oh.

The drones lined the vast space in perfect formations with perfect posture, led by Monarch 3's tiny queens. Pehton frowned. She almost asked why not form their own army out of the women, but the answer was obvious. If they died, their race died with them. In that spirit, Pehton said, "I look forward to giving you a demonstration."

F8 nodded her approval, staring out at her soldiers. "I look forward to seeing it. In a few brief hours."

Yes. It would be over soon.

Pehton looked forward to French toast with Caedes and learning exactly where to grip him when the time came.

{ENKI | TUMU'S SANCTUM}

"Thanks, Caedes," Pablo said as the two lifted another crate of Earth nacres. Before the others considered fighting with a human army, Pablo figured it was best to test these puppies. "This makes three."

The bald Icarus humphed, as Pablo had expected him to reply, and helped open the crate.

Twenty-One wandered over after tearing sheets into rags. "So you test them for Tritan tampering?"

"Like how they tampered with the sleeping King?" Miy asked as she set another IV bag of Aegis blood for Triss.

Gathering a handful of nacres to test, Lynn answered with a smile at Pablo, "That's right. It was Tumu's idea, too. If he can't trust his people, then..."

Right. How was there any hope for the rest of them? Pablo collected a few samples as well. "We're checking their nacre banks for the operating system and memory, searching the code for any initiatives outside normal perimeters."

"I'll pretend to care about the technical stuff while I fend for my comatose friend who you're all praying delivers a healthy baby you can steal once she dies." Miy always sounded so... bitter to Pablo.

Bethany looked up from sorting Aegis blood and nutrient bags. Twenty-One, Pablo, Caedes, and Lynn exchanged a look. The massive Icarus shrugged and approached the sour Lyrik. His presence was a gentle one, despite how he came by knowing them. So Miy hardly paid him any attention as he took a fresh rag and wiped away the perspiration from Triss' forehead.

The pregnant woman was a nightmare to behold. Dark bruises marred her already black complexion under her eyes, the hollows of her cheeks, and randomly across her body. The swollen belly took on an abnormal shape. Cubed rather than rounded. Occasionally, the cube pulsed and pressed along the corners and sides like the baby wanted to escape its prison. Her lips stayed dry despite hydration drips. Her vitals were erratic and implied a substantial amount of pain.

Miy was right, though. Korac, Pehton, and Sagan were less than sympathetic toward Triss' condition. As her physician, Pablo retained some objectivity, but frankly, it hurt to see a patient go through this. No matter who they were or how they lived their life.

Almost as if she followed his exact train of thought, Miy murmured without looking at him, "I'm sorry, Dr. Suarez. I know you try. I wasn't being fair. The rest of you can go straight to the Wrong Side of Eternity for all I care."

"All of us?" Twenty-One asked with a curious lilt.

She sighed, heavy with frustration. "Well, no. Not you. You were one of their prisoners, and now they've brainwashed you into one of them."

"What about those of us who weren't prisoners?" That was the most words Pablo had heard from Caedes at once.

Across the way, it even made Lynn raise her brow at him.

Miy let her hand, IV bag and all, fall to her lap with a defeated sigh. "What can I say? I haven't had what I consider decent sex in six million years. I lost one sister, and now I'm looking at losing another. Not long from now, I'd say. Honestly, I just feel like being a bitch."

Twenty-One stared at her long enough to raise Pablo's curiosity. After another heartbeat, the big man stepped over to Miy and whispered in her ear.

Pablo blushed from what he could hear of it and found the crate on his table very interesting.

Lynn looked away sharply, focusing all of her attention on the samples and the terminal used to access them.

Bethany appeared oblivious.

Caedes chuffed and went about his work, but Pablo noticed the small smile on his face.

None of them met each other's eyes as Miy set the bag to drip and left the room with Twenty-One, who politely nodded as they let themselves out.

Lynn sat down beside Pablo and muttered incredulously, "Time and place, people."

He almost laughed in her face. Of all the people… "I love you."

"I love you, too." It showed in her smile. "Now, let's save the worlds. Again."

No Tantamounts this time, thanks very much.

{Cinder | Li Mountain}

Xelan wished he was at Tameka's side, rescuing their son. Instead, he gazed out over the barren wasteland of his homeworld and the race he abandoned looking to him for command. On his mountain. Only a few steps from his memorial—A two-meter tall monument of stacked rocks.

"Korac put it up for you," Sagan had told Xelan. After which, she left him alone with his thoughts.

Everyone organized and worked to funnel the Two Worlds' armies into the conduits Sagan had opened throughout the station which acted as Cinder's shrine. Everyone afforded Xelan this second to see how every moment in his life led to this. If Rayne hadn't claimed the title, this would mark the moment the Traitor Prince became the King of Cinder. But it was bigger than that.

Tempest and Dolor kindly conceded their supervision to Korac, no longer "former" General. Likewise, Cypher, Colton, and Six happily relinquished command to Sagan. The Progeny and the Icarus led their worlds as true equals in authority. They were a model for things to come.

Pax.

The best thing to happen to Xelan since Tameka and, before that, Rayne.

"Elden, please let them be all right." His words went to the wind.

"Come to take in the view, your highness?"

Xelan closed his eyes. That voice on this rock brought a rush of emotion he thought long dammed until he read his General's Verse. He opened them to look out at Umbra's Spire. Its thin shade cast along those entering the conduit at its base. Xelan swallowed the dry lump in his throat to say, "Tell me, Korac, did you ever think while we were dreaming over there that we'd find ourselves here, leading our people against Enki?"

Korac took the last few steps to the edge, between Xelan and the memorial, and peered out. Confident and solid, he said, "I always knew you and Nox would lead us to salvation. I'd only hoped we'd all be together."

To the heart of the matter. How like the man Xelan knew so well. Truth be told, Xelan had thought of Nox many times since reading his brother's Verse and now Korac's. Since he learned Rayne truly defeated the King of Cinder despite whatever feelings she harbored. He thought of all the sacrifice and trauma the three Icari had suffered over the last three millions years. Six for Nox. What did it amount to?

Then Xelan looked out at the people below, the mingling of human and Icarus. The promise of the loyalty from those worlds which gathered in concert. All to release the Vast Collective from Imminent and ultimately Tritan rule.

But it all started with Primary Rem's intervention on Xelan's species, which led to the direct ruin of his family. Of three brothers who could never communicate enough how much they valued each other. To address Korac's observation, Xelan asked, "Do you remember the time Nox's hair caught fire?" He put on the expected grin and turned to the General.

Korac narrowed his gaze, scrutinizing the Traitor Prince. Incredulity weighed the smooth cadence of his voice. "Oh, you mean the time he tried to put out the fire you started to prove sleh oil was, in fact, flammable?"

Xelan dismissed him with a wave. "It wasn't that bad—"

"You blew up the Spire's stores."

He frowned. That wasn't right, was it? "The entire store? It was only one barrel."

Korac balked near to gripping his hair. The next he said as if explaining to a child. "No, you lit one barrel out of fifty. It spread faster than Many Feet's gas through one of mother's parties."

Xelan held his ribs and laughed like he couldn't remember the last time he'd laughed so hard. Maybe not since he was a teenager. No, that's not true. Since the first night he taught Rayne to drive. Or maybe it was the first time Tameka broke his arm.

Korac let out a chuckle. Then a little laughter. Finally, he leaned on the memorial and let it hold him as he went into a fit of laughter. Between breaths, Korac said, "And then... and then... Nox had to explain to her why you had an Icarean firestick in the first place. Do you remember?"

Oh, did he ever. Xelan fell to his knees, laughing to tears. "I was supposed to... supposed to light it in case Umbra caught us switching his off-world liquor with Hellkite piss."

"And who had to collect all of that?" Korac's tone suggested they both knew full well the answer.

Xelan tried to open his mouth and answer. Once. Twice. But he couldn't gather enough breath, he was laughing so hard. He managed to point at his personal guard.

"That's right. Me."

Although his decorum wasn't very befitting of a Prince or a King, Xelan cherished the lack of oxygen, near to giddiness in this moment.

Until Korac took two steps and put his face in Xelan's, where he sat on his knees. Too close in this mindset of reminiscing about another lifetime they once shared. So close he made out the flecks of gray in Korac's otherwise white eyes. For one second, it took Xelan's breath away.

"My Prince." Korac fixed a few errant strands of Xelan's hair while the Prince searched his General's eyes for the meaning of this. Then the blasted Icarus smirked. "If you ever give me your fake smile again, I'll leave you crippled in your laughter."

How…? This entire time… Korac drew this recollection out on purpose only to make Xelan smile. He opened his mouth to say something, but Korac held up a finger.

"And I don't think it's fair you use that smile on Tameka. She's too young to know the difference." Korac let go and moved back to let Xelan stand. The General said, "The Progeny can see your mask, and I share their sentiment—We don't like it."

Xelan looked out at the army, saying, "It's rather hypocritical for you of all people to tell me when I can't shield what I think and feel from others."

"That's ridiculous." When the Traitor Prince whirled back, Korac continued. "Everyone is entitled to concealing their grief from time to time, but only in a moment which is earned. Coming back from the dead. Fine. Earned. But let Tameka see how much Pax's abduction affects you. She needs it. Now, your majesty, let's return to saving him and winning this war."

So much about Korac had changed after meeting Sagan. Xelan grinned. "Let's." He went to Korac's side and pointed at the memorial. "Nice marker, by the way."

"Stuff it, your highness."

After the laughing fit Korac had subjected Xelan to, the Prince wanted a little payback. "No, really. You made it yourself, right? I'm honored."

Korac rolled his eyes and opened his wings. "You always were a fucking tease."

They jumped off the cliff toward the conduit, where Tumu stood below with Kyle and Andrew. Legir was walking away from Kyle and into the conduit. Sagan went Seamswalking to unite luo with his army. Pehton stayed behind with the Lyriks in Cinder's station. Lamassau stayed with F8 to help orientate all the troops of the difference between Tritan and Imminent.

Good luck.

In a much better mood, Xelan alighted with Korac. Into an interrogation.

"Does Peaches know?" Tumu's almost expressionless face drew lines of concern at the corners of his eyes and mouth.

Kyle stopped screening the army's memories and faced the other men. "What does Tameka need to know?" He gave a suspicious, sweeping glance over Korac and Xelan.

While screening human intentions, Andrew said, "In two hundred and twenty Probabilities, she doesn't know. The ones where we succeed, anyway."

Korac remained quiet. Only his cold gaze contributed to the conversation.

Xelan understood their concerns. He worried, too. "No. I don't think she realizes, and I plan to tell her once she finishes this mission. I didn't want her distracted with the pending responsibility."

"What responsibility?" Now Kyle sounded a little offended on Tameka's behalf.

Tumu stared at Xelan for a second, as if considering his answer. Eventually, he nodded to Xelan's relief.

This time, Kyle's voice took on a harder tone. "No, really though? Is it dangerous?"

Andrew assured him, "No more dangerous than her current mission. More like a lifetime of paying back all these people for helping her recover Pax."

Again, Kyle asked, "There's a price?!"

Xelan feared this exact conversation with Tameka, but there was no other way to describe it. A price. With a heavy heart, he answered, "The absence of Imminent and what takes their place. That's the price Tameka and I must pay."

SEVEN

BEST LAID PLANS, AND ALL THAT

{ENKI | TUMU'S SANCTUM}

"I FOUND IT. PABLO, I FOUND WHAT'S WRONG WITH THE NACRES." Lynn gaped at her own discovery on the terminal's projected screen.

Pablo hopped from his station over to hers, and Caedes crossed the room after checking their weapons. He kept a nacre knife on his hip. Bethany sat with Triss while Miy and Twenty-One continued their "break."

Lynn's husband read with his chin resting in his hand before snapping his fingers. "There. Wow."

Caedes peered over their shoulders. "What is it?"

Still halfway astonished, Lynn pointed at the line of code on the screen. "Right here. See that?"

"Well, I'll be damned." The Icarus looked between the two of them. "I'll let them know." He pressed into his earpiece. "Wingmaster. This is Caedes. Over."

Lynn was fine with not being the bearer of this bad news.

Pablo took her hand and squeezed it. Softly, he assured, "It'll be all right."

"Go ahead, Master Graveller."

Caedes cursed.

Lynn stifled a snicker.

Pablo, laughing, said into his earpiece, "We found the fault in the Earth nacres. There's a tiny trigger that makes them more susceptible to volition control. Something so small the Tritans wouldn't know to look for it. Imminent was careful."

Tumu came on the line. "Was it in the code?"

"That's right. In the Operating system."

Xelan said, "Good work. Any other concerns?"

Lynn wanted to answer this time. "We should be all set. We'll keep searching in case there's more. Good luck out there. Over and Out."

Caedes gave her a nod with his eyes full of respect.

Pablo kissed her forehead. "You. Are. Amazing."

"I know." Lynn nudged him teasingly.

They all looked when Miy and Twenty-One returned through the threshold. Lynn had to keep from shaking her head. They didn't even bother checking a mirror before this walk of shame into a life or death situation they were all in. At least the Lyrik was glowing, and the big Icarus walked with some swagger. Jeez. They both stopped by the weapons cache and loaded up on knives and nacre disabling pistols.

Pablo went to check Triss and her supply of Aegis blood. Lynn watched him move in that combat suit and wondered if she preferred him in scrubs or this. She was so distracted with his ass that she missed some of what he said.

"...And I hope Matt and Lucy are making out okay. Their mission was more rigorous than ours."

Lynn rubbed the back of her neck, stiff from staring at nacre data. Would she rather be out there fighting or here doing this with her husband? Pablo smiled at her from across the room as if he'd shared the same thought. While those full lips beamed at her, Lynn knew the answer. Definitely here with him. With a sigh, she said, "Now there's nothing to do but wait—"

Bethany looked up, her honey brown eyes wide with... Terror.

Lynn cried, "Code Red!"

Someone was coming.

{ENKI | TRITAN RESIDENCES}

Lucy adjusted her technician gear: white leggings and a blue smock. Not much to work with, but she put the push-up bra she borrowed from Para to good use. Her black non-slip shoes squeaked on the floor as she and Yito hurried away from Lance's unfurnished residence. All the blond hair she'd curled was swept back from her face at the speed of their departure. The way Yito pulled her by the arm hurt, and he refused to slow down.

As if responding to Lucy's thoughts, he muttered, "Any minute now." Every inch of his blue body was tense, the muscle constricting to reveal a deeper blue striation where his skin showed beneath his armor.

In these moments, Lucy missed Matt the most. The craziness of a crisis. A plan gone wrong. Their version of improvising would frighten a Navy Seal. Especially when Matt applied some elbow grease. The boy was good with his hands—

"There! She's with the Shadow!"

Yito whirled with Lucy to find Lance surrounded by Tritan guards, pointing at the pair from down the hall. She widened her eyes and quickened her breath. Terrified, looking from Yito to Lance to the scary assault guns in the guards' hands.

Busted.

The lack of a brow furrowed on Yito's face, and hurt poured into his black voids when he looked down at Lucy. "You… Morning Star, you're with the Shadow? But how…"

Lance took an arrogant and dangerous step closer to Lucy, saying, "She's one of their agents."

Visibly upset, the Tritan at Lucy's arm asked a good question. "What about her husband?"

The Eminent shook his head, clearly finding all this regrettable. "That human is pretending to be her husband. I'll deal with him, myself. Arrest her."

Yito clutched Lucy's arm harder while she entreated him with her eyes. "Please. Do you know what they'll do to me?"

He squeezed the clear lenses over his almond-shaped voids to shut her out. When he opened them again, he swallowed his resolve. "Lucy, with the authority granted to me by the Vast Collective, I detain you to provide testimony before the Tribunal for war crimes committed against the Collective. Until you testify to your crimes, you have no ownership of self. Do you understand?"

Head lowered in defeat, Lucy held out her hands. "I understand. I'm sorry."

Yito's breath hitched as he locked her wrists in nacre cuffs. He led her by the arm to Eminent Lance. She wished a few times the old Tritan had fit her target type, but his eyes never wandered and his thoughts remained on business. It was kinda refreshing.

Stern, more disappointed than angry, Lance said, "I want the entire guard to escort you. Any member of the Shadow makes for a dangerous prisoner."

"Your Eminence, if not you, then which Eminent will take her into custody?" Yito was careful in questioning his superior. Lucy heard it in the deference of his voice.

She stared at Lance's toe-less feet as he answered, "I should think Eminent Abresson, since he's responsible for all Shadow-related interrogation. He and Primary Rem should get some information out of her." He clasped a hand on the younger Tritan's shoulder in a friendly gesture. "You're doing the right thing, Yito."

"Sir!"

That was it.

Lucy, Yito, and her fancy escort made their way to some dungeon. There, Abresson would interrogate her using Elden knew what means. The Tritan's reputation was well known throughout the Shadow. T.A.O.'s story came to Lucy's mind. Or John's death.

When she shivered, it wasn't out of fear.

The walk was a long one, made longer by the chilled silence and icy expressions. Lucy kept her head down mostly, letting them capture her. Meanwhile, her thoughts once again drifted to Matt. How could she spin this in her favor? She asked, "What will happen to the one who betrayed me—"

Black blossomed in Lucy's eyes as the butt of a gun made a play for the teeth in her jaw.

Yito pushed the responsible Tritan back. "Get. Off. Do you think Eminent Abresson wants someone as fresh as her damaged by an underling like you or me?! You know how he is about 'purity.'"

"Oh, shit. My bad." The offending soldier gripped her chin roughly. It hurt where she was tender, and Lucy knew if she spat in his face it'd spray red. Still, he continued to agitate her. "You're okay, aren't ya? There. No need to tell the Tribunal of my misconduct."

Lucy let the moisture in her eyes from the sting build until all her dark blue irises were swimming in tears. Blood trickled warm out of the corners of her mouth. She shied away from his attempts to placate her.

"You fucking suck, Dolton," one said.

Another guard wrenched Dolton's hand off her. "Let her go before you bruise her more. I don't want to hear about abuse from the Eminents." This one put his face in hers.

Lucy gave him wide, terrified eyes. Like a doe in headlights.

"Are you sure she's a Shadow agent? She's kinda . . ."

"Weak," Dolton said. "It should take more than one strike from a gun to soften up an agent of the Shadow this much. Tell us, sweetheart. Did you piss off the guy on Gait, so he sold you up river with a phony story?"

Lucy kept her eyes down, remembering Rayne's old habits which saved their skin now and then. Twenty-six Tritan feet. Counting Yito, that made ten additional guards. Not bad numbers with some King blood, but alas, Lucy was fresh out.

"Please . . ." She gasped on a sob.

They drew closer to listen.

Lucy met their gazes with tears streaming down her cheeks. "I don't know how everything got so messed up. I liked him. He told me he could get me a job. And now..." Two sobs, and she cried into her chest.

"That's cold," one of the nice ones said.

Dolton cursed. "Yito, you know her best. Does she seem like a super villain to you?"

Yito knelt and used his thumbs to clean away Lucy's smeared mascara. Softly, he said to her more than to them, "She's my friend."

Lucy swallowed blood before smiling into her friend's face.

With a sigh, Dolton gently gripped her by the arm and eased her onto her feet. "Look. I'm sorry I hit you. The Shadow have caused us a lot of frustration here. They want to end our race, for Eternity's sake, but I believe your story. The hard part now is convincing Eminent Abresson because believe you me, sister. He'll eat you alive."

"Can you help me?" Lucy added some extra breathiness to her distraught voice.

The Tritans peered around at one another before the nice one—Praw, she heard one call him—said, "We'll coach you on the way. Eternity knows it's a long enough walk."

Yito returned his grip on Lucy's arm, and the walk began again. On the way, Dolton, Praw, and the others were too busy teaching her how to handle Abresson to notice Yito's thumb gently graze Lucy's arm in a show of solidarity and consolation.

Ten men in one hour. Matt would be impressed.

{ENKI | NEW CINDER}

Bones held his breath as Tameka led the sweep into the proverbial lions' den. A.K.A. Celindria's lab. He clocked the lump lying on a cot in the cell and the door on the far wall. Ross said she knew three nacres were nearby. The others must be through there.

At Tameka's signal, they broke rank and stealthily entered the room in pairs. Para on Bones, Ross on Jack, and Devis on T.A.O. The latter went to the cell while the rest kept their nacre disabling rifles on the entrances.

"Andrius," Devis whispered, and it sliced through the room.

Elden, no one wanted to alarm Celindria as to their presence.

Well, sorta.

T.A.O. called next, "Andrius?"

The lump on the cot shifted in Bones' peripheral vision. Andrius startled and rolled over to find his brother and sister waiting for him. His skin was shiny, putting Bones in mind of Karter after her super hero prosthetic replacement surgery on Enki. Bones recalled Devis telling him stories of Celindria carving the imprisoned Progeny like roasted meat—

Great, now Bones would never eat again.

The relief in Andrius' voice already jerked some tears from Bones. "T.A.O., Devis, are you really here?"

The small Seamswalker gripped his hands through the bars. "Here."

Devis searched for the mechanism to release him. "Do you know—"

"You shouldn't be here." The sudden terror in Andrius' voice brought all their heads around. "She'll take all of you. This is a trap. Can't you see? We're the bait."

Tameka inched toward the door, giving the "on me" signal to Jack and Ross.

Softly, Devis tried to assure his captured brother, "What is the purpose of freedom if not to free those in captivity?"

Bones liked Devis.

What he didn't like was the increased tension in the room hauling up the hackles on the back of his neck the closer Tameka got to that door. Rankled. That's the word.

Para was a statue aimed at the tunnel they entered, ready and alert. While Bones appreciated her intensity as a Valkyrie and an Icarus, he hated the fear behind it which Celindria put into her. The fear Celindria might soon put into all of them if she found them there.

Tameka reached for the door, paused, and asked, "Andrius, who's in here?"

"Chris, Pax, and Celindria. It's her bedroom. Get away. Get far away!" All of this, he rasped in a hoarse whisper.

T.A.O. Seamswalked into the cell with him and put his hand on her face. "No more fear. Everything ends today. Father, Fury, and Li will see to it."

While Bones kept one eye on that touching moment, the other eye watched Tameka open the door. Her gasp told him she found something. He prayed to Elden it was only Pax and Chris.

"Tameka, maybe we shouldn't try to wake him," Jack sounded unsure.

Ross sounded even less certain. "And Chris… do you think she can see us through him?"

Para's confident answer twisted the knife in Bone's heart. "Definitely. Be careful, Fury."

No one remained calm when Devis swallowed audibly and said, "Oh, it's far too late."

Disembodied blue eyes glowed from the darkest corner of the lab, at about the height of an average human woman. They stared out at the Shadow infiltrating the space. The collective breath they held filled the room with an ear popping tension.

The eyes blinked.

They gasped, shouted, and jumped away.

Tameka was the first to train her weapon on Celindria. The crazed angel stepped out of the shadows with one pistol trained on Tameka and deftly shot T.A.O. with the other.

Andrius caught T.A.O. and checked her pulse. "She's alive. Only unconscious."

Celindria aimed a gun at Jack and kept the other on Tameka. "I'd never kill my most valuable doll."

Bones shuddered.

Para cursed.

Ross concentrated, as her hazel eyes shifted into a brown and green Atramentous outside of Celindria's line of sight. If she could knock her out with a memory spill, then maybe—

"Cease, girl, or I'll shoot the young Callahan with a lethal round which simultaneously disables his nacre."

Tears spilled from Ross' eyes before she hung her head, defeated.

Tameka took a step toward the statue which was the First Progeny. Unafraid, Fury demanded, "I want my son, Celindria."

Bones spared a glance at Para, and his chest swelled with pride. Fearless despite their current dilemma. Jack faced an enemy weapon with a fierceness his sister would respect. Devis and Andrius' faces, however, unnerved Bones. Pure. Fear. They were terrified of the monster in the room. All the while, Bones wondered what those on the other side of the earpieces gained from the encounter.

Celindria tilted her head to the side, listening to ancient things elsewhere. Her eyes remained sharp as ever on her quarry. No opportunity there. Instead, she straightened and said, "You still don't know. Good. Back up to the cage."

Jack used a tone Bones had never imagined from the young man. "I will bend those bars and—"

"Before you bend them far enough to escape, I will paralyze you and force you to watch as I take Ross' volition and use Chris to pleasure her. Or Devis. Bones. Maybe all of them at once. Now drop your weapons and back into the cage."

Ross winced, and Bones felt it.

They all dropped their weapons and took a step back.

Tameka was the only one who lingered. It wasn't anger that rolled off of her. It was intolerance. Eventually, she, too, backed to the cage along the south wall.

Andrius laid T.A.O. on the cot and shifted to make room. It wasn't a cell big enough to accommodate eight people.

Para cried out, and they all turned to find Chris holding another weapon on them from the room's doorway. Apparently aimed at them all the while. No wonder Celindria was so confident.

Using a mechanism along a counter, Celindria slammed the cell shut before walking to the cage. She didn't look smug or satisfied. She looked like she knew this would happen. "To save one another, as only the Shadow does, you'll sign your volition to me one by one. But first, relinquish a sample of your blood."

Bones chafed Para's arm as each member of their team let Celindria prick their fingers. The Valkyrie wasn't necessarily in shock, but her icy skin told him she wasn't far.

"Comfort doesn't exist here," Celindria assured.

Andrius scoffed. "You are as wrong as ever. Knowing Devis and T.A.O. were safe from you was comfort enough. Knowing one day you might come to your senses—"

"Sense I have in plenty." Celindria turned her back on them, taking their samples to her workstation. She held up a test vial and looked into it as she said, "What I lack, you can't grasp."

Devis countered, "I can."

Celindria peered over her shoulder at him with cold eyes. "Then why do you continue to challenge me? Betray me?"

Devis' silence raised some suspicions for Bones. Why all this back and forth?

Tameka made it worse by asking, "How did Xelan wrong you?"

The other two First Wave Progeny in the cell groaned and shook their heads at Tameka's naivety.

Celindria broke the vial in her fist and stared at the wound—

Whoa.

What the fuck…

Despite all the glass in her skin, there wasn't any blood. The wound healed before Bones could blink.

Bloodless, deranged, and beautiful.

"I am the monster he made of me."

{CINDER | ENKI'S CONDUIT}

Kyle hated the stupid matching armored suits. He spent the last apocalyptic battle in a Hawaiian shirt, as Elden intended. The girls always liked coordination, but don't the good guys wearing black and blue let the bad guys know who to kill? Besides, there were so many pockets in the damned thing he kept losing the stash Andrew made him.

The gear fit his form too well, all bulging biceps and thick quads—

What would Silence think?

Kyle literally slapped himself. Slowly, he glanced over to check and see if Andrew—

Yup, he caught that. And now, he was raising a brow at Kyle.

Perfect.

Another Shadow pep talk.

All this chatter in Kyle's head should've distracted him from the threat to his sister. He had intentionally tuned out of Ross' frequency, electing to watch Xelan for developments on their team.

"She'll be all right. Tameka knows what she's doing." Andrew wandered over, after all.

Kyle raked a hand violently through his curly mop and tangled his fingers at the ends. Frustrated, he wrenched through the strands with a growl. "How can anyone claim to predict Celindria's actions? I spent a week with her in my head and still couldn't tell you a damned thing about her motivations or plans. This is reckless."

Andrew patted Kyle's shoulders, biceps, forearms. The frisk went to his sides before Kyle shoved him. "What—Oh."

Conscience held out a joint to Story Taker. "Please. Before I have to watch you slap yourself again."

"Thanks." Kyle lit it and took a hit, ashamed of his weakness. "I should be with her. And Bethany..."

Taking the joint from him, Andrew hit it next. "Look, you need to trust Xelan knows what he's doing, and your sisters can handle themselves. Even little Bethany. Did you see her helping out? She's coming out of her shell."

Yeah, she was. Kyle was reluctant to admit it, but Korac did good with her. Ross could level a garrison with a passive flex of her memory muscle. Jack and Tameka wouldn't let anything happen to her, which Kyle was also reluctant to admit about Rayne's little brother. It's just...

"I want them to live in a world where people aren't trying to kill us all the time. There was that break after Volcano Day, but two years isn't long enough. Not to mention where Bethany's been since the invasion happened. I want... They deserve some—"

"Peace." Andrew sounded sad, tired, and finished. He sounded as if he understood.

Kyle glanced at him and nearly flinched at the sorrow in his eyes, staring out across the army entering Sagan's conduits without seeing a soul. Well, maybe one with golden eyes.

Yeah. Andrew got it.

Kyle went back to work flitting through memory banks of hundreds of thousands of nacres. So many lives. And no sign of Imminent. "Anything on your end?"

"Naw. Their intentions are pure. Looking for peace as much as the next person."

They carried on that way for another hour before Xelan stepped up. The look on his face...

"No. Is she okay?!" Kyle couldn't keep the edge of hysteria from scratching his words.

Andrew placed a gentle hand on Kyle's shoulder as Xelan said, "She's unharmed, but Celindria has captured them."

Kyle shut his eyes. Every second in that woman's presence was a reminder of his fragile mortality. Stone. That's what she was. Old and impervious to all but time. "Andrew, what are their chances?"

"If Celindria's alone—"

Xelan nodded.

"—That only happens in one hundred and sixty-two Probabilities. Out of those, Ross returns unharmed in one hundred and twenty-one."

What was that? Under seventy-five percent. That was a "C" average. His sister's odds of survival should look better than Kyle's GPA.

When Xelan spoke, Kyle opened his eyes. "Tameka has her talking. Chris, Pax, and Andrius are alive. No sign of Karter yet, but we know from Para that Remorse has control over her. Not Celindria."

Andrew let go of Kyle's shoulder and raked that hand over his face. "The good news is Celindria talking increases their odds. Don't ask me how. It just does."

Good news. Celindria talking is good news—

But it made some sense, didn't it? When she'd possessed Kyle, something shifted in her anytime she engaged him in his attempts at banter or probing. Almost as if she sought an audience for… what?

Xelan walked up to Kyle and let his shadow fall on him. A familiar place. When the Icarus knelt, he looked up into Kyle's eyes and the warmth there nearly choked him. They'd never really gotten along, but despite that, the younger man knew the ancient alien cared. As if to show it, he held out an earpiece. "Do you want to listen?"

Well, for one, Kyle sported his own earpiece. For another, "I don't need your freaky alien wax in my ears, dude. It might infect me with stick-straight hair and the inability to tan."

Andrew, stifling a snicker behind them, made Kyle smile at Xelan's grinning face. The Prince of Cinder said, "We can't have that, now can we?"

Tumu came over in the same coordinating colors: black and blue robes. He clasped Xelan's wrist to help the Icarus stand up. "Peaches has a way of getting under Celindria's skin. No doubt she'll leave this encounter with more questions for you than answers."

Xelan sighed and a flash of something passed through his eyes.

It wasn't doubt or worry. More like…

"You're as exhausted as we are." Andrew beat Kyle to it.

Tumu barked out a sarcastic laugh. In his impossibly deep voice, he said, "Well, he's been at it a lot longer than you. And I longer than him. We all deserve a break."

"You can say that again, Tumi." Lamassau strode up behind his lover. The green Tritan wore the inverse of Tumu's robes. His voids scanned the endless parade of soldiers into the conduits. "One way or another, it's coming soon."

Xelan pressed his fingers to his earpiece before saying, "Korac wants us to join him for a summit with the other generals. I want you both there to screen them for us. If you're up for it, of course."

Kyle looked at Andrew, who blew the air from his cheeks and said, "My life is seeing into people and the worlds that press into this one. I don't much care now what else I do."

Everyone's faces fell.

Except Kyle. He threw an arm over Andrew's shoulders and pulled him in for an uncomfortable squeeze. "You and me. That's all we need. Maybe we could fanfic this and look at our current predicament as more of an opportunity. What do you say, Conscience? Can you see me that way?"

Andrew, famously bisexual, peered at Kyle between big, wide blinks.

Kyle shook him out of his shock. "Well, I'm not saying I can compete with your history, but I'm willing to try—"

"Get the fuck off me, asshole!" Andrew pushed him away and straightened his jumpsuit. "Besides, I prefer my partners pretty."

"Are you saying I'm not pretty?"

"No. I'm saying you're not pretty enough."

The group headed for the nearest conduit. Lamassau chuckled into Tumu's sleeve, and Xelan shook his head incredulously.

"Well, excuse me for not having a fashion sense."

"Oh, and like I'm a chick that could definitely kick your ass. Yeah, we've noticed you have a type."

Tumu sighed. "The Vast Collective is in such good hands."

{Enki | Tumu's Sanctum}

Twelve nacres.

Outside of Tumu's door.

They entered, yelling. Bethany didn't hear what they said or see what they looked like. She was safe under the hood over her head. A metaphorical garment, it came to her whenever she closed her eyes, bidden by her fear. Everything under this hood was meant to happen.

Struck, burnt, frozen, sliced, and bled.

So when a hand grabbed her arm, Bethany was safe. She let him corral her with the others. Familiar, warm hands which checked her over.

Fine. Bethany was fine.

She ate a person once, and she was fine.

Tonight, she'd do it again.

The shouts from both sides couldn't penetrate the fuzzy static in Bethany's ears, but before long, those familiar hands pushed her forward and led her somewhere. She let them. It took a long time.

The twelve new nacres hovered on either side of their grid formation, locking the familiar people in place with her. It'd be easy. Quick.

But Bethany wasn't allowed, so she followed and ignored the fuzzy conversation around her.

It wasn't her time yet.

Not even as they arrived in a space less vast than Tumu's sanctum, but broader than the corridor. Remaining good, Bethany lifted the hood and cracked her eyes.

Beds everywhere. A bank of terminals lined the far wall. Machines big enough to hold a person took up the center of the room.

With the hood lifted, Bethany could hear.

One of the new nacres, a Tritan, said, "Place her there. Now!" The skin on him looked like Tumu's, but shorter and darker.

He was talking to Lynn and Pablo, two people Bethany liked very much. They lifted the mother of Razor's baby up from a cot and placed her in one of those person-sized machines.

The nacre from earlier shooed them off and settled the pregnant woman in the device. "Get back. Over there by the rest. That's right."

One nacre with a gun trained on them said, "Don't even think about it, Shadow scum. We know you're here to kill our Primaries, and we take great offense to that. So give me an excuse to blow your head off or await your interrogation and execution obediently. We'll find the others soon."

Another one joined the scorn. "How could you ever think Eminent Lance would work with the likes of you—"

"That's enough talking to the prisoners." The first one said as he stared at a projection screen. "Good. The baby's heart is beating. The mother's a mess though." He looked at Miy for the last "Who's the father?"

Bethany didn't care anymore and put the hood back on. This place, with all its medical equipment, was exactly what the Shadow needed.

Twelve nacres without names. Bethany opened their memories and let them flood into her. Eleven fell to the floor.

Birth. Academy. Job designation. Courting. Pairing. Pairing went wrong. Forced to sleep in the suspension pods. Awakened. Informed of the loss of the entire female population. The new Tritan Prerogative. Resentment. Consigned to guarding Enki. Called by Lance to locate and detain the Shadow, hiding in the Dyson's Sphere. The pride of finding the intruders. Honey brown eyes. Danger—

Nothing.

Bethany lifted the hood and stared at the last Tritan standing. He gaped with his mouth open like a goldfish. Prepared for this, Lynn, Twenty-One, Pablo, Miy, and Caedes aimed the fallen guards' weapons at him.

Lynn took a step toward the lone Tritan. "Now. You told us these guns can turn you inside-out with or without a nacre. If I shoot, you die. But I don't want to shoot a fellow soldier for only doing his job."

Yes. But they weren't soldiers. Bethany saw. This one was a second level physician. He fell in love with a Tritan girl named Kip. He liked the way she always served him extra food at the supper line. The way she cheated at their games. Kip promised to take him to the stars, but that was the night the Primaries locked the younger Tritans in the pods.

Qas never saw the stars.

Bethany crossed the room, paying no mind to the others exchanging glances. Qas stared down at her with a frown on his mostly featureless face. This was not his best day.

Slowly, carefully, Bethany held out her hand.

The frown never left his face as he peered down at her. A moment passed between them, long and curious. Strained and confusing. When no one fired a gun, and Bethany didn't attack, Qas cautiously lowered his hand into her smaller one. Bethany took it and pulled him along to the others, hoping to convey with her eyes what she wanted them to understand.

None of these men were evil.

They were sad.

Well intentioned, Lynn and Pablo stared at her. Twenty-One and Miy looked at one another, shrugging. It was Caedes who took a step forward. In that rough voice of his which Bethany quite liked, he explained to Qas, "We kept you awake because we need medical help. That woman is not well. Bethany, here, thinks you can help Triss. Will you?"

Bethany felt Qas' confusion as he met everyone in the eye. With that frown entering his voice, he said, "But you're Shadow."

Pablo tried. "As one physician to another, I know helping people takes priority."

They all glanced as Twenty-One spoke up. "These people were once my enemy. I fought against them in battle, but they aren't what I was led to believe. Likewise, you think they're evil because you were told so. They're not here to kill your kind. They're here to stop Imminent."

Confused, Qas tilted his head. "Imminent is a myth."

Lynn took a less gentle approach. "And they're mythically kicking the Vast Collective's ass. They're hiding behind Enki to do it. Bethany screened your memories, and in them, she saw someone worth knowing."

Qas peered down at her again.

Please. See it.

Lynn's hand slipped into Bethany's, and the girl understood.

A walk in an enemy's shoes was rough, but there was no better way to understand them.

Korac taught Bethany that.

EIGHT

LIGHT THE WAY TO THAT LOST SHADOW

{ENKI | OCEAN LANDING}

NOX NEVER FELT THE CONFINES OF HIS SECOND LIFE AS CONSTRICTING AS IN THIS MOMENT. The shade swimming alongside Rayne as she ran could only be one of Enki's famed leviathan, and there wasn't a damned thing he could do to help her.

Not that Rayne needed it. The capable warrior whose mind housed him ran thousands of miles an hour with immense strength in those powerful legs and arms. Her unshaken core laid the foundation for a perfect battle against an epic creature.

Nox wanted a piece of the action.

"Do you think it's under Remorse's command?"

Rayne asked intelligent questions.

Nox didn't need to consider it. There was only one correct answer. "Absolutely."

A little sigh escaped from her. Between the Overseer which chased them all the way from the Pantheon and the sea monster along her stride, Nox understood Rayne's growing frustration.

They could both do with some violence.

"Nox."

What could make her voice sound so—Oh, this looked promising.

Rayne stopped and faced a small army. At least a hundred men and women from all over the Vast Collective were dressed in black and brandishing weapons. Guns, swords, axes, electric prods—An entire arsenal.

In front of them stood Abresson.

The sniveling waste of skin boomed, "Where do you think you're going?"

Rayne straightened her ponytail and loosened her neck muscles while quipping, "Oh, you know? Taking in the sights." She finished limbering up with a balanced stance and without reaching for the rifle.

Abresson jeered in a smug smirk. "I must confess. I've looked forward to your waking." He turned toward the ocean.

Rayne looked in the same direction and muttered aloud, "Those are some big bubbles."

Foam roiled and splashed until a massive thing surged to the surface. Ocean water sluiced away to reveal a giant serpentine monster rising and rising. A white dragon with six sets of long whiskers lined back toward its ears. Sharpened quills marked its mouth in rows like a shark. Nacres glistened where they nestled in its pale scales.

Not that Nox needed more reason to love Rayne, but the strongest warrior in the galaxy took a step toward the creature with a few breathless words. "It's beautiful."

"It is a 'he,' and he has a name. This is Squilly." The leviathan spoke the words himself with the familiar tone of one always in power. "Squilly's monitoring your flight across Enki while I tend to other affairs."

Six million years of pure venomous hatred slammed into Nox. He spat, "Primary," through his teeth.

Aloud, Rayne ground out, "Primary Rem."

Abresson ordered, "Return to the Martyr Complex, King Rayne. Don't force us to put you in it."

Inside her head, she looked up at Nox. He scanned the line of soldiers. "Assuming the Primary keeps his pet out of the fight, subdue the projectiles first. You can take them easily. Shoot Abresson with the rifle, then engage the others in hand-to-hand."

Target engaged.

Combat initiated.

Calculated duration: Thirteen minutes.

Rayne's voice changed inside her head to the extreme three pitches. Her eyes danced with anticipation. "This should fill me up for a while."

Nox folded his arms, eager to watch Rayne repay Imminent for locking her in that box and hurting her people. His people. To stand at the edge of retribution beside its emissary was glorious.

Rayne took a step forward.

The army took a step back, frightened of the sleeping King.

Nox peered down at Rayne, wondering at her composure. Her eyes glittered with excitement, staring out at her enemies, and her lips moved as she quietly computed who to attack first and what move to make. Fast, so fast that Nox barely made out Rayne's strategy. Imminent made her into a machine of death, and she was here to repay them.

Within the work of a second, Rayne crossed the platform, kicked one sniper hard enough to shatter his arm, and ripped the throat out of the next one. Shots were fired from the others, but she moved faster than their nacre-disabling rounds. Rayne jumped over one sniper, rolled him across her back, and threw him into another. Their bones made audible cracks when they collided. An axe swung from the side, and she fell into a backflip, kicking the assailant's jaw into pieces along the way.

More came. Rayne took them all out with ease. Her agility impressed Nox. It was something he had worked toward, but which came naturally to her slighter frame. She sidestepped to avoid a round while simultaneously launching a retrieved sword at the sniper. Someone grabbed her from behind, and she opened her wings with a battle cry. Their gossamer silk threw the fighter off her back. Rayne buffeted her wings, pushing back her enemies in a circle around her. Taking advantage of the break, she closed her eyes and opened them in Atramentous. The light from them spread in a white, searing wall which swallowed the platform.

When Rayne next closed and opened her eyes, they'd returned to Li's surface—A red giant blazing in her eyes. The surrounding soldiers cried out in agony and rubbed their empty sockets. They were blind, and their nacres wouldn't heal it. Most weren't upgraded high enough to survive at all, but a few remained.

They circled Rayne. She ignored them, storming across the battlefield to the spineless Tritan only meters away.

Desperate, Abresson ordered, "Stop her! Kill her!"

Maybe three dozen soldiers remained upright. Nox gained so much satisfaction when Rayne punched through the chest of the closest one and threw their useless nacre at the one behind her, hard enough to go through their skull. She flipped back from the next one, who swung a sword. Mid one-handed cartwheel, she shot the nacre-disabling rifle and hit Abresson, using the remaining rounds to take out her nearest opponents.

Restabilizing.

Warning: Seventy-two hours until maximum destabilization.

There was some good news.

While Rayne decimated an entire army, Nox kept a lookout on her peripheral vision for the Primary's pet. A weakened Abresson shouted at the beast, "We must retreat!"

The nacre-studded leviathan spoke his master's words. "Go, and empty the depositories. I'll deal with her myself."

Squilly lifted its great heft out of the water and onto the platform. Eight sets of clawed feet carried the leviathan on land impossibly fast and right for Rayne.

"Rayne!" Nox shouted in her head, only to find her elbow deep in a dozen assailants.

No. This was *not* happening.

When the shade of the sea demon fell on Rayne as it opened its jaws, Nox could take no more.

{ENKI | OCEAN LANDING}

A shadow towered over Rayne. No, not the first one. A second enormous shadow. This one burned and stretched from her. She broke the person's neck in her hands and turned.

It was Rayne's shadow. She stared open-mouthed at it. It grew taller and broader, very broad. Muscle cut the shape of the silhouette. And long hair. Almost as long as hers. Taller and bigger. A man—An Icarus.

"Nox."

Wings spread from his back, made entirely of shadow, and carried him higher like a plume of smoke. He met Squilly head on. Literally head butt the leviathan, grabbed its tongue, and pulled, extracting a terrible roar from the injured monster. It backed up.

No, too far!

"Nox!"

Rayne screamed and chased after them, but not fast enough to catch the creature from dragging Nox into the water with it. "No!" Surely, the sea monster fought better in the water. "Nox!" She shouted again at the surface.

Someone was dumb enough to run up behind her with a triumphant cry. Rayne let them swing whatever weapon they had, ducked, and tripped them over the platform's edge. At the last second, she caught them from falling into the water, only to break both their arms before dropping them in—

Squilly broke the surface. And... floundered. He writhed and spewed gray fluid—presumably blood—in a spiraling arc. Rayne crouched to avoid the spray and to make out the source of pain on his back. The screeching and crying almost brought tears to her eyes. The poor creature was a victim as much as any Imminent pawn.

With one last roar, Squilly's long neck sagged and fell into the water. From this angle, Rayne made out the wound. Ripped open, and the spinal cord was bisected.

Bare hands.

"Nox!" Rayne called out to the ocean. He wasn't in her head, and the water grew darker in its depths. Would the absence of light erase his shadow construct? Could he… would he… die?

"Nox!" Rayne's cry was more desperate, reverberating off the dead bodies littering the battlefield at her back. "Nox!"

"Behind you."

Rayne whirled to find him standing there. In her shadow. Her voice was breathy, surprised. "You're all right."

Nox gazed at his hand as he lifted it to his face and flexed a fist. "Much better than all right." When he looked at Rayne, he smiled.

Black smoke, veiled specter—A shadow smiled at her. It suited Nox and took Rayne's breath away. "How… how?"

"The constructs you taught me. I—"

Calibrated.

Optimized.

Stabilizing…

Unable to stabilize.

Warning: Sixty hours and thirty-two minutes until maximum destabilization.

No. That couldn't be right. It was full only seconds ago.

Oh.

Rayne gazed at Nox with a horrible truth dawning behind their eyes. She shut them from facing it.

This wasn't fair. Of course Rayne's Weapon burned more fuel powering two bodies, but… This was working out so well. She and Nox could take Enki together. There was a poetry to it that Rayne wanted to hear more of—

"Rayne."

How did a shade make such a beautiful baritone? Swallowing her distress, Rayne opened her eyes.

Nox stood over her with a patience in his gaze she'd attribute more to his younger brother. "The price is too high. This is how it must be."

So many thoughts. The first and most obvious one was, "This is *not* fair." The second was, "Wow, he's handling this a lot better than the Nox of even a year ago." And the final thought was, "How can I keep him with me?"

The last one stirred something in Rayne, confusing and deepening the moment all at once. The look in the smoke of his eyes further confounded her.

Happy. Nox looked happy.

A tear spilled from her lashes and burned her cheek. She rubbed it away harshly and confessed, "I was worried Squilly had dragged you down too far and... I don't know. Extinguished you or something without the light to fuel you."

"I *was* dragged down too far, and the construct returned me to you. To the shade you cast."

With time slipping away from them, Rayne stared up at Nox. "You're my shadow."

"You're my light" hung in the air.

Calibrated.

Optimized.

Stabilizing...

Unable to stabilize.

Warning: Fifty-eight hours and fifty-four minutes until maximum destabilization.

Rayne cried out in frustration and a little bit of fear. "What?! What do we do?"

"Face the sun and close your eyes, your highness." An edge of sadness tinged Nox's voice and broke her heart.

The scalding tears made it hard, but Rayne turned and closed her eyes, trusting in him.

A warmth pressed against her back, firm and adamantine. Her heart raced with it. More so when the warmth went through her skin and into her bones. It seeped into her blood.

His name left Rayne's lips on a breath. "Nox?"

"Open your eyes."

Inside her mind, Nox towered over Rayne once more. Gratitude washed over her and sent her to her knees in tears. "I was so worried. Worried how to fix it." Truthfully, the transformation in him overwhelmed her. Nox could've let Rayne self-destruct. Fought her, kept her from her mission, and wasted her time until there was none. Instead, Nox traded his first taste of freedom for her peace of mind without hesitation or ceremony.

Never mind, Rayne feared her own loneliness. When she thought he'd vanished, she almost couldn't process the loss. No more company, and an unfit end for all the time they'd invested in his reeducation.

Nox held his hand out for her. "Every battle deserves a good breakdown, but save it for after you win. You need to catch up with Abresson. Remorse sent him after—"

"The depositories." Rayne clasped Nox's wrist, ignored the warmth of it and the way his hand swallowed hers, and let him haul her off the ground. "I caught it, too, and I think the depositories what's at the end of this map. I'll get there."

Something passed over Nox's eyes. Curiosity or consideration—either way, he asked, "You knew the dragon was there. What would you have done if I couldn't manifest myself as a construct?"

The grin that spread across Rayne's lips was pure fun. "I guess you'll have to wait and find out. I'm not a damsel that needs saving." His face fell a little, and it made her duck to meet his lowering eyes. "But I'd much rather fight by your side."

Staring at her, Nox said, "You cry so much. You fight so hard. In less than fifteen minutes, you wiped out an army. Now it's time for you to lead us to victory, King Rayne."

She wiped away the tears and any trace of her desperate fear at the thought of a future without him. That was too scary to unpack, and there was no sense wasting time interviewing Nox as to his motivations for helping her. It was in his eyes. Even without his Atramentous, they reflected Rayne.

He loved her and placed all his faith in her.

Rayne set on Abresson's trail to prove it wasn't misplaced.

All the while, the Overseer watched. She hoped they liked the show.

NINE

BRILLIANT FACETS OF THIS CURSED PLOT

{CINDER | 6,000,000 YEARS AGO}

"WE CAN COMBINE FORCES. YOU, THE FIRST OF US. AND I, THE ELDEST PRIMARY IN ENKI."

As Remorse came closer to begging for his life, he kept looking away from Surra's glowing blue eyes to the stars winking out behind her. They pulsed in time to the azure surge under her deep gray skin. All those worlds—Each of them cultivated by him and populated by her. On his knees, he spared this proposed arrangement a considerable amount of thought.

Surra's army of nacre-imbued Icari could make the difference against the Aegis, who clung selfishly to their Dyson's Sphere, but she insisted her soldiers were meant only for locating Ishkur and defending Cinder from Enki's interference. Remorse counted on that. "You cannot find Ishkur without the Exalted. He has responsibility in your design. Together, we can bring him to his knees."

Surra unlocked the sickles from Remorse's neck, letting him breathe. Black blood trickled onto his clothes as he stumbled off the audience house's red floor and onto his hands and knees before her, cowed before Surra. Dressed in armor and kitted out in weapons, even pregnant, she made for a fearsome sight. The blue streak of her hair was left out from her braid, swinging to the back of her knees. It swayed with her as she stepped back.

Sharp silence filled the space between them, honed for more explanation.

Remorse considered this a boon and tried for more. "It was I who sabotaged Quet's suit and sent him to Cinder alone. I sent him to you because we may not have always fought on the same side, but now we can both see the optimum future and should work toward it together. With you leading us."

Looking unconvinced, Surra glared at him. Her six-octave Atramentous resonated a tremor deep in his chest. "You wish Enki to end?"

"I wish for power, Surra. You gave us that with Cascading Light." All truth. Most of it.

Surra cocked her head to the side in an avian gesture and repeated, "Us?"

Remorse winced and gently approached the explanation of the organization he'd created. "We honor your discovery of the window into the Probability Matrix. We—"

"Silence, Elden seeks you—Oh, Primary, forgive me." Umbra went to one knee and bowed.

To a man he shouldn't know.

That was one way to introduce Surra to Imminent.

{Enki | Quet's Sanctum | Now}

Remorse spun and screamed, circling to see the wound gushing in his back. To see the mortality leaking out of him like a geyser. "NO—"

He collapsed on the floor of Quet's Sanctum in a painful spasm as powerful and impossible hands wrenched into his spine and stole what kept him whole.

"I relent!"

Disconnected, Remorse slammed back into his physical body and soaked in the moment, lying on the glass, feeling his own skin and intact spinal cord. On a growl, he cursed, "Nox!"

This development was unexpected. How was Nox in Rayne's shadow, and what were the implications—

Celindria could never know.

This. Was. New.

Impossible.

And entirely Silence's fault. She was to blame for the extreme disparities between this and the other Probabilities. No doubt to Celindria's immense delight.

No.

Remorse would keep this from them all and resume his search for Project Surra. That's how he found himself here, in her father's sanctum. The lab which created her. He needed to confront Silence about freeing Rayne before her time. And wouldn't that be ugly business? There was no questioning the Mother to her face. Entirely too dangerous. Although she'd never risk her mission to find Ishkur, she'd easily cause trouble to inconvenience Primary Rem for his treachery.

Vi would call that "good business."

Remorse stood in the lab meant to discover Tritan salvation. Zero's words echoed off the walls, haunting him. *"There is no recompense we can offer to replace the females of your species, but perhaps we can help you begin anew. In this lab, we will assist you in rebuilding your race. An embryo is all you need. One such as this one. Surra."*

Zero was right, of course. Project Surra seeded every planet under their surveillance. Life which the Tritans cultivated into the Vast Collective. Remorse and Razor carefully omitted the Mother from Enki-approved histories. No need for the galaxy to learn of its creation from the womb of one experiment.

One ridiculously overpowered rogue experiment.

Then came Celindria, the next most powerful being Remorse had ever met. Why was it always in the hands of a woman? No matter how much he touched Cascading

Light, it never endowed Remorse the way it gifted those two females.

Which begged the question, what would happen if Rayne touched the black fire?

Remorse shuddered at the thought.

No.

This was all a distraction from his tasks before Rayne ended Enki.

Deploy the Tantamount.

Check in with Celindria.

Throttle Abresson.

Locate and confront Silence.

And if Rayne interfered in any way, Remorse would demonstrate to her how the Tritans defeated the most technologically advanced race in the cluster.

{ENKI | GAIT SHRINE}

It took Remorse an additional hour to reach the Tantamount lab while remaining conservative with his supply of Aegis blood for creating conduits. Two Caprents, one Pil Dwarf, and a Luk were gathered in a Shrine fixed in the path of Gait's trajectory.

Strange.

Remorse had intended to collect Lucy for the reproductive program after Celindria approved her, but… "Where are Yito and the human girl?"

The Pil Dwarf, a male tall for his race, answered, "Eminent Lance checked in on our progress a few hours ago and took her with him. Yito escorted them. They should return any minute."

What would Lance want with Lucy? And without Yito, this station went unguarded.

No.

Remorse didn't like this. "I'll see to their return. In the meantime, what will you use to affix the Tantamount to Gait? I understand it's gained in speed as it nears the ocean."

One Caprent, with his backward-bent joints, beamed. "Dukki," the Dwarf, "engineered appendages like those in his mech suit to a drone designed by Primus." He nodded to the Icarus when he finished.

As he explained, a three-dimensional model projected in their terminal. It was a wing-ed mech suit, fully remote operated from this station.

"Impressive." Remorse meant it.

They grinned ecstatically, as one does before a pleased god. The Icarus bowed. "Thank you, Primary."

The Luk interrupted the congratulations to say, "I contributed my electric jelly to power the suit. We're at ninety-five percent capacity. Another hour, and we can deploy it. Do we have your go ahead, sir?"

This was the first good news Remorse had heard since he learned Xelan was resurrected, which was immediately ruined by the decimation of Gait and Razor's death.

For the first time in weeks, Primary Rem smiled. Not out of cruelty or jest, but out of elation. "Job well done, team Tantamount. You should all be proud of yourselves. Yes. Proceed with the launch sequence once ready."

The last thing Imminent wanted was for another catastrophe to befall Enki before Rayne could destroy it, and if Remorse had his way, Rayne would only end herself while the Dyson's Sphere he fought so hard for would remain.

The Dwarf clapped his hands together. "Thank you, Primary! We'll notify the demolition team to withdraw their members from the rock and—"

"No. I'll notify them myself." Lies. "Everyone performed commendably on this task, and your counterparts deserve to hear that in person, as well."

Again, this team shared pats on the back before seeing him off. As he stepped up to the conduit, the Luk said, "It was Lucy's idea to combine our talents. We don't want her to miss out on any credit."

Over his shoulder, Remorse assured, "I will see she gets her due."

{Enki | New Cinder}

Remorse wore Karter's body to Celindria's lab. Like always, the stalwart Valkyrie stood naked and proud in her mind, impregnable. Her bizarre eyes recorded every task he attended with rapt ferocity. To confuse her recollection, Remorse took a more complicated route and intentionally circled a portion of the maze twice.

Through the tunnels of exotic flowers, over the land bridge, and into Celindria's lab, Remorse from within Karter announced, "We have an unpleasant complication—"

Karter's mouth hung open as Remorse gaped.

Shadow, including some very important Progeny were locked in Celindria's cell. What a fascinating development.

The nightmare in white called to him from her workstation, "Look, Rem. I found some flies in my web."

Delicious. Truly.

Karter's body walked over to them as Remorse met Tameka's fuming glare.

"Don't get any ideas, Remmy."

He smirked with Karter's lips. What fire in her. Tameka was unshaken, and oh, how he looked forward to rocking that foundation of hers. "If it isn't Fury. Near to the top of our most wanted list." He took a bold step closer to the cage, certain they wouldn't harm Karter's body. "I regret I never found time to spend with you while you resided here in our home, but now I can compensate for that."

Tameka rolled her eyes and glanced over at Celindria. To Remorse's extreme irritation, Celindria also rolled her eyes in commiseration. Over their irritation with him.

Females.

Instead of dignifying their treachery with a response, the Primary walked Karter over to Celindria. "Are there more of them?"

The annoyingly intellectual First Progeny kept her eyes on the weapon she examined as she answered, "Undoubtedly. I disarmed them of these. Very good design. I desire to have a chat with Lynn Renee."

Frustrated with Celindria's nonchalance, Remorse folded Karter's arms over her ample breasts, which he quite liked with the jumpsuit partially unzipped.

"Thanks for ruining them for me."

Remorse closed his eyes in Karter's head to shut out her quips. She was entirely too much her own, and his imagination remained too limited to invent a suitable treatment without Para to punish.

But perhaps...

Inside her head, Primary Rem asked, "Do you think Jack would accept a male partner if it was one to which he held a prior relationship? Such as guard to the King Regent. What would that be like to have a man you loved like an older brother assert himself on you? Shall we find out? I'm sure Celindria is game. In fact, I hesitate to mention the threat aloud as I worry I wouldn't be able to stop her once the idea got in her head."

Karter's thoughts assailed Remorse.

You're so weak without someone to hurt. Soon, the Shadow will send you to Eternity. Coward.

Remorse wagged his finger at her. "No, child. I am millions of times older than the combined age of your Shadow. Eternity no longer seeks me. I will grant you that I am prone to hurting people weaker than myself, but it's not due to cowardice. I simply enjoy when you cry, but I commend you for not giving voice to your thoughts. So I will leave Jack's sexual inexperience intact. For now."

Outside Karter's mind, Celindria asked, "What are these complications you speak of?"

Remorse glanced at the cage filled with Shadow and back to Celindria. He hesitated to communicate Rayne's freedom in front of her people. It might inspire them, and Eternity knew what the Shadow were capable of with a little inspiration.

Instead, Remorse said, "I've already arranged for the disposal of the demolition team, but we need a clean erasure of the Tantamount engineers. One of them is missing. Lucy. The human girl you interviewed for the breeding program."

Celindria blinked. "Missing?"

Remorse dismissed her ire with a wave. "She's with Lance for some reason. We'll need to collect her and clean the engineers. Silence, on the other hand, has vanished. I can't locate her."

Still tinkering with the gun, Celindria shrugged. "If the Mother wishes to be found, she will be. I'll see to the engineers and your Lucy."

Remorse wouldn't go so far as to call that predator "his." Something ravenous starved behind her eyes.

"What will you do with us?"

He turned Karter's body to face the cage once more. The young woman with curly brown hair and extraordinary eyes between brown and green asked the question. Remorse said, "You must be Ross. Razor spoke highly of you and your abilities."

Para put a protective arm around the girl.

Quite rudely, Remorse laughed at the gesture from inside her lover's body. "You know better, Para."

The small Valkyrie shuddered visibly, but kept her arm around Ross.

How Shadow of her.

Remorse gestured at the cage and announced, "With the Mother away, we can induct the females into the breeding program immediately."

Celindria slammed the weapon on the counter and stood in such a fashion that Remorse stepped Karter's body back. Sweeping aside the excess of her white skirts, the First Progeny turned and faced him. He wished she hadn't.

Those cobalt eyes were empty. Hollow. And like a portal, something stretched and yawned behind them.

A breeze picked up from... where?! They were underground. It flowed through her skirts and the fabric draped from the bangles on her biceps.

The pressure rose and rose until Remorse needed to pop Karter's ears—

Too late.

Blood trickled from the blown eardrums and from the capillaries in her nose.

No!

Karter shouted inside her mind, "What's happening?!"

The pressure squeezed and condensed the very marrow of the Valkyrie's bones. Tendon and ligament contracted muscle until the tissue shrank off the bone. Blood vessels constricted to thin cords and twisted.

Remorse felt all of it.

Vi's voice came to him then. *"From every painful lesson, you must accept the cost with the wisdom to make yourself a better Tritan."*

"I relent!"

Why were all of Remorse's lessons so costly?

{ENKI | NEW CINDER}

"All the Tritans ever speak of is their foolhardy breeding program. I grow so tired of their limited minds. When he can go a week without mentioning it, I'll grant him one of you as a reward. Like training a pet."

Celindria—scary, terrifying, and impossible Celindria—was no longer focused on her work. And Chris couldn't share with the Shadow exactly how fucked they all were now because of it.

Back in the driver's seat, Celindria piloted Chris' body to carry the unconscious Karter into the cage. The actual Celindria trained two guns on the Shadow, and they backed away to make room for Karter. He used this time to gaze at her dark gray skin, the thick fans of lashes on her cheeks, the mouth he spent hours appreciating in bliss—

"Karter? Karter!" Para's broken cries bruised Chris' heart.

Tameka wrapped her arms around the Valkyrie in a hug from behind, but also to placate the crazy woman with the guns. Tameka said, "Shh. We'll get her to Xelan and Pablo. They'll take care of her like they did you and T.A.O."

Never had Chris ever been so simultaneously happy and scared shitless to see a group of people in his entire life. As Celindria used him to lay Karter on the cot beside the small Seamswalker, he checked out the family which graciously came to his rescue.

Jack looked good. Healthy. Pissed mostly. But he held hands with Ross, so things were looking up in that area. Devis looked whole and mostly concerned for his brother and sister. Bones pulled Para into his arms and brushed his fingers through her short hair. Maybe they'd get more serious after this.

Then there was Tameka. Her name was Fury for a reason. As their leader, Chris trusted her to turn this around somehow and get them the hell out.

With that in mind, Celindria chuffed in his head, unconvinced and eavesdropping on his thoughts, though she offered no additional commentary. Instead, she removed Chris from the cage—

Para's fingers brushed down Chris' arm in a wordless gesture, sending pure love straight to his heart. After being deprived of touch from someone he loved and trusted for months, Para's gesture sprung tears to his eyes.

Celindria stilled inside and outside of his head. Carved from beautiful black rock, this statue—this genius enemy of theirs—reflected nothing but pain. Yet, for one spellbinding moment, she held her breath, waiting…

Unaware of the significance of Celindria's silence, Ross interrupted the moment to ask, "How did you do that with the Primary and Karter? I thought the one with volition couldn't feel the host's pain."

With the quiet spell broken, the First Progeny exhaled the held breath and triggered the switch to close the gate. Celindria set the guns on the counter and stepped up to the cage. Her full attention on them was not what they wanted, despite whatever they had planned for her. This was bad.

Para muttered to Ross, "Remorse felt everything I did."

Tameka stared at Celindria as she elaborated, "Kyle said Celindria didn't feel a damned thing."

The First Progeny's eyes flashed.

Were they trying to get Celindria to talk?! No. Stay small. Don't let her pay any attention—

Devis gripped Tameka's arm hard enough to indent his fingers into her skin. His eyes were wide when she turned to his emphatically shaking head.

Andrius cautioned, "That subject is forbidden."

Chris sighed with relief. At least two people here possessed some sense. Meanwhile, Celindria scanned them with her eyes and some tech device. She left Tameka for last and paused the device over the other woman's green eyes.

Tameka put her face to the bars. "What're you doing, Celindria?"

"Shopping."

Chris shuddered. He loved Tameka's ability and fire, but so much had happened since Pax arrived. Although she and Remorse—and even Silence—kept everything on the down low, he overheard mentions of preventatives against Fury's draining ability. Something to do with Pax testing it for them. It implied the worst-case scenario Chris did *not* want to give too much thought. It would devastate them.

He was about to do something stupid. Something to distract Celindria and pull her away from the Shadow long enough—

Ah. Maybe this. "How are you and Nox the Eternal Bind when you betrayed him like he described in his Verse?"

Inside Chris' mind, Celindria closed her eyes and exhaled. She eased her neck to the left. Then to the right. Deep inhale. When Celindria opened her eyes again, she set her sights on him. "I believe it's time for a reminder on decorum."

Chris' body walked over to a wall lined with mirrors. The caged Shadow watched him go. He saw their concerned faces in the reflection, unable to look away. Celindria, herself, grabbed a tool from her workstation behind him. Without seeing it, he knew what it was and how she intended him to use it. They'd played this game the first week of his enslavement, but to do it in front of them...

"Did I strike a nerve, Celindria?" Antagonizing her would only make it worse, but dammit, Chris would grit his teeth and survive this.

Her actual hand, soft and caressing, delivered the tool. Celindria kissed his neck with soft, full lips and a warm wet tongue Chris couldn't wait to rip out. The tool was metallic and thin. A scalpel. She wouldn't let him focus on it, keeping eyes focused instead on his family, trapped in that cell.

Inside his head, Celindria stepped over to his naked, prone body—The manifestation of his indentured exhaustion. Her eyes to his, she said, "I need not explain my relationship to you. You understand how a woman must be cruel to be kind, to shape him into the man this galaxy needed. I made Nox into a god."

Chris spat on the floor at her feet. "That's some toxic bullshit, and he didn't seem grateful for your charitable education."

Pissing Celindria off here was better than paying attention to his hand raising the scalpel with a deliberate pace to draw out the fear of her audience. Inside, she remained silent. Majestically, she turned and swept away from him.

But Chris wasn't done yet. "What makes you think he and Rayne aren't the Eternal Bind?"

Celindria stopped. Stopped everything. Walking *and* breathing.

Chris kept pressing, despite what it would surely cost him. "Nox *loved* Rayne. I've never read the unredacted copy of his Verse, but it's obvious by it simply existing." Chris whistled, as if impressed. "And boy, I wouldn't want her for competition. She's beautiful, smart, loyal, and kind. Sure, you have two out of four of those traits, but why would he ever have settled for *you* when he could have *her*?"

The scalpel stopped, poised to puncture Chris' eye. Close enough that his lashes blinked on the blade. Involuntary tears leaked from his strained eyelids. Inside his head, he swallowed hard. The tension mounted the longer it took Celindria to act—

Wait.

Her shoulders were shaking. Was she... was she laughing?

Celindria's soft laughter reached him then. It held an edge as sharp as the scalpel. It tinkered on the inside of his skull, louder and louder.

The pierce of the scalpel drew a wail from inside his head immediately as his eyeball exploded. Behind him, the Shadow screamed and begged her to stop, but there wasn't any outward reaction from him. Not even as he pulled it out and shoved it back into the socket.

Chris swallowed the sharp metallic pain, only to gather enough air to scream again.

Celindria laughed and laughed. Not even cackled. No, her laughter was beautiful and cold. Just like her.

If Chris could vomit, he would. The blade slicing along the pulped nerve sent a message to his brain to run, cower, and cry. Instead, the white and red ruin gushed down his face and dripped from his jaw without a single twitch of a muscle on his face.

Tameka screamed, "Celindria! Stop! I swear to Elden I will send you to the Wrong Side of Eternity!"

Again, Chris stabbed himself in the eye.

Ross hid against Jack's chest. The King Regent had busted the bars to the cage, leaving Celindria pointing a gun at his head. Andrius and Devis stared with the same expression. They'd seen this before. Para and Bones glared at Celindria, ready to do something about it.

Fury watched Chris shove the scalpel back in and dig it around, with tears spilling down her face.

That's as much notice he could pay them, but Chris was ready to pass out. Surely Celindria would let him shut down long enough to heal. How could he be any good to her, exhausted, with a missing eye?

Celindria stopped laughing. The hand holding the scalpel fell to Chris' side. She folded his body down on his knees in front of the mirror. The hard rock floor cooled into his skin through his gear. It wasn't soothing. It was just hard. Like her.

Ross made a good point earlier. How could Celindria not feel any of this when Chris was near to blacking out?

"You will never ascend to a high enough elevation of existence to understand my motivations or capabilities. You've seen what happens to those who try. Until your nacre heals you, you'll see now for certain. As best you can see with one eye, and that's the best anyone can ever hope to see me. From an inferior plane. Good night, toy."

Celindria's sudden absence was a rare mercy. Chris' body grew stiff with shock in a kneeling position. His eye throbbed with each beat of his racing heart—

The Shadow caught his attention in their reflection. T.A.O., Para, and Karter had all recovered their free will. Although they said Karter needed to see Xelan to complete the process, Chris still considered this a win. With their combined abilities, surely they were more than capable of bringing Celindria down—

"You will never ascend to a high enough elevation of existence to understand my motivations or capabilities."

Celindria's words put a halt to Chris' positivity. Her abilities seemed limitless. What if she wanted them here?

Tameka flagged him in the mirror, subtly. He focused on the look in her eyes and the strength within them. With only a nod, Fury restored Chris' faith in the mission. There was no way in hell she'd lead them to defeat.

Now if only they could wait until Chris' eye stopped throbbing and regenerated. After all, he deserved a little revenge.

{CINDER | 7,000,000 YEARS AGO}

Surra told Elden of Enki and the Tritans. Of their schemes and her part in it. Of her desire, not for revenge, but for freedom which neither she nor the people of the Twelve Worlds could obtain as long as those men still held power in Enki. Ishkur was their only hope.

But Elden heard other words from her lips. He wanted to negotiate with them and broker peace through words. No matter how many times she explained the Probability Matrix and how no thread ended in peace that way, he believed in a fate outside of Cascading Light's reach.

They worked together to split the nacre and upgrade the species. They worked together to build an empire. But Surra worked alone to build an army. In such time, Elden came to call her Silence.

A name apart from her identity as Project Surra. One that threatened an end to all things. A name she loved in secret.

While Elden played leader with his Coalition, Silence trained and organized the Icari—specifically the females. It seemed poetic to bring peace through their underestimated and nurturing nature on a battlefield.

Then Remorse came.

Silence stood over a humbled Primary and glared at the Icarus who'd interrupted them. "Umbra, I demand to know how you recognize this foreigner?"

Also on his knees, Umbra bowed deeply to the floor. "Mother, we—"

"Mother?!" How could he know of Silence's old life? Her purpose?

With his face kissing the red floor, Primary Rem answered, "I have done much in your name, seeking your praise. You who created a galaxy and who led the way to Cascading Light. Initiates such as Umbra come from far and wide to be in the service of the Probabilities. Of creating more."

Imminent.

Silence kept them on their knees as she considered his words.

As if sensing the direction of her contemplation, Primary Rem pleaded, "Who else would send your father with a sabotaged suit to 'reason' with you?"

His words reverberated through the very hall where Silence conceived for the first time of her own design. Not the Tritans'. They took so much from her, she never thought she'd desire another child enough to carry and deliver again.

Silence stood now before him, pregnant and still unafraid. "What do you gain, Primary Rem?"

He braved raising his head to meet her eyes. "In my sorrow for the wrongs I've committed against you and so many others—I can see it now in the Matrix—I claim a new identity much like you, Silence. Please call me Remorse."

Could a Tritan even grasp the concept of guilt and self-doubt?

The Primary, on his knees, searched her eyes. "Tell me about the black fire. What did it say to you?"

Silence understood now. "You've embraced it and drew others to its beckoning?"

Umbra dared speak to the floor. "Only a select few are shown its mysterious. We all desire to know the influence and outcomes of our lives."

The pulse in Remorse's neck fluttered at Umbra's audacity before the Primary said, "You were the first being to know. You are the start of it all, and it saved you from Primary Quet's oppression. What did it tell you? And does it oppose my proposal for an alliance? For Ishkur?"

Cascading Light unveiled mysteries, but could two men such as these ever understand the simple message Silence sought from it? The pitiful need that gnawed at her and the base of every being? In truth, Remorse's alliance—this Imminent—presented new and advantageous Probabilities to Silence's pursuits.

So, she answered their question. "It told me I could be happy."

{Enki | Opal Mezzanine | Now}

On the projected screen, Remorse's pet rose onto the platform, making its way to Rayne with alarming agility. Silence expanded the screen to watch its approach. Smith and Lucas stared with equally rapt attention—

"What is that?" Lucas asked, frowning and staring harder.

Smith pointed and exclaimed, "Do you see Rayne's shadow? It's moving—Is that Nox?! Silence, that's your grandson."

The girl's freed shadow took the shape of a man Silence had never met, but empathized with, sprung on Squilly and rode him back into the ocean. Meanwhile, Rayne screamed after Nox, disposing of the remaining soldiers in an army she decimated on her own. Truly, the girl's shrieks grew more desperate, bordering on terrified.

With a thunderous roar, the beast broke the surface and released a beautiful spiral of gray arterial spray. The wound was impressive and fatal, sending it crashing back onto the water's surface without a pulse.

And still Rayne screamed for Nox—

"There." Lucas gestured at Rayne's back.

Nox's outline, painted on the platform, took on a three-dimensional form, and stood at her back. Meanwhile, she called to him three more times before he announced himself. "Behind you."

Style.

Something Nox clearly inherited from Silence. She appreciated it, but their interactions bewildered her. Lucas and Smith both focused on Silence's face, while Nox and Rayne played beyond them. Affection. Warmth. Sacrifice. They shared these things between them. It suited the smile they exchanged.

Noticing her observers, Silence raised a brow. "Yes?"

Lucas answered while Smith smiled in his quiet way. "We understand your reticence to support Rayne when she executed your kin, but it seems as if she gained your ability to hold multiple nacres. She *chose* to hold his."

This was similar to Silence's making. One she didn't understand until Remorse explained to her about Primary Xhi and Lon. Absently, Silence touched a hand to her chest and absorbed the rest of the scene. Rayne closed her eyes and looked out to the sun while Nox pressed his back to hers and took a step back until he melted into her.

Smiling.

Savis' eldest son had a beautiful smile.

Has.

Silence fidgeted with the pendant of Rayne's blood over her nacres. Regarding their observations, it was true. Her main concern for distrusting Rayne dissolved with that smile.

But what more could Silence do? Rayne was free, Para was released, and the others were on their way to rescue Pax—Including the Atheneum. Everything fell into place with minimal damage to the Shadow.

So far.

Soon, Silence would emerge to complete her mission. Smith and Lucas would take care of the rest. In the meantime, let Remorse, Abresson, and Celindria entertain themselves as the last members of the befouled Imminent. In their last hours.

Cascading Light's truth waited for Silence.

TEN

TRY AS YOU MIGHT, EFFORT IS MEASURED IN ACTION

{Enki | New Cinder}

TAMEKA GRIPPED THE BARS OF THEIR CAGE, SAGGING NOT IN DEFEAT, BUT IN IMPOTENT RAGE AT THE INJUSTICE SHE COULDN'T STOP. Chris deserved better than this torture. No matter how she tried, Tameka's ability had no effect on Celindria. Ross', too.

When organizing this mission, Devis warned them this might be the case, but Tameka didn't want to believe it. "Celindria's capabilities are unpredictable. Neither Andrius nor myself have ever successfully subdued her. That's why I have this." He held up a memory drive like the ones they retrieved from Razor's Emporium of Exotic Experiences. "With this, I might reach her."

Ross peered at it. "What's in it?"

Jack kept his eyes locked on Devis'. "It's a memory that's important to you, right, Devis?"

The First Wave Progeny nodded. "It will sway her."

Well, Celindria needed a little swaying right now. "*Unpredictable capabilities*" explained why Ross couldn't detect Celindria's nacre. Elden, Tameka nearly fainted at the sight of the woman's eyes in the darkness, but she swore she'd checked that corner. Another mystery to go unsolved.

Since assaulting Chris, Celindria returned to her workstation, tinkering with their guns and running some simulations on her terminals. If Tameka looked close enough, the three-dimensional renderings of Tameka and the others on that screen chilled her blood because she wasn't behind the wheel in those simulations. Celindria was. Or Remorse. Honestly, sitting in this cage, one found themselves contemplating which parasite was worse. The homicidal angel? Or the tyrannical hypocrite hellbent on reproduction?

Poor Chris.

And what about Lucy? Both Remorse and Celindria were on her trail. The couple with the highest body count swore to Tameka and Xelan they could handle themselves before embarking on their dangerous mission. She would have to trust them on that.

All the while, Xelan had listened through the earpiece, careful not to distract Tameka with any response. It must kill him to listen to all this—All his people in danger at the hands of his first creation. She wanted so badly to reassure him, but she wanted to rescue her son even more.

Pax laid peacefully asleep in Celindria's Spartan bedroom. The bed was big enough to swallow his small body. Tameka tried her best not to speculate on what went on in those sheets and focused on her son's breathing instead. He was fine. Alive. It begged the question.

Why?

A shuffling movement beside Tameka distracted her thoughts. Bones handed Andrius an earpiece. They brought more spares for Karter, Chris, and Pax—Really for anyone else on their side, including one for Rayne when they found her. Each group grabbed an extra earpiece meant for her, looking after each other.

An idea occurred to Tameka. She was well-acquainted with Enki's star. Drawing a bit of energy, she glanced over to see if Celindria noticed somehow.

No reaction.

A little more energy, and Tameka filled her well. Easy, carefully, she fed the energy into T.A.O., hoping to wake her. Maybe she could get Ross, Karter, and Para out of here before Celindria noticed. They didn't need to be subjected to this.

The small woman's lashes fluttered until T.A.O. opened her eyes. The others stood back, but Tameka tried to keep her down. She shook her head at the Seamswalker. Let Celindria think she's asleep.

T.A.O. nodded and closed her eyes.

They'd get their chance.

No matter how much energy she fed Karter, the Valkyrie remained asleep thanks to Celindria's fail safes.

Now. For Chris. Tameka took a sip from the star and fed it to him, hoping to speed his soft tissue repair system. This was risky. With Celindria inside him, Fury risked exposing her attempts to revitalize her team. With that in mind, she fed everyone else.

Andrius, the longest in captivity, gained some vibrancy to his deep skin and mouthed, "Thank. You."

Devis nodded his thanks at her.

Ross took Tameka's hand and squeezed it.

Bones tapped his fist to his chest.

Then Para pointed at the mirror. In the reflection, Chris' eye re-inflated in a terrifying but encouraging spectacle. Jack kissed Tameka's cheek and hugged her from behind, clearly withholding a cheer of gratitude and relief for his friend.

A small, yet much needed celebration—

The sound of Celindria slamming something down startled all of them. Afterward, she reached for a vial, popped the lid off, and poured the blue liquid into her mouth. When it hit the air, it turned red. Human or Progeny blood.

Tameka *knew* it. "So that's why I can't affect you with the power drain, but if you're using Rayne's blood, you full-well know her nacre is locked."

Celindria set the empty one aside next to a rack, holding dozens of identical vials filled with non-oxygenated blood. Magnanimously, the queen of evil divulged, "Unless I acquired it before our Mother administered the virus." She turned and met Para and Bones' eyes. "You two were instrumental in making Rayne available to me during several shifts."

They both looked away, faces flushing blue with shame.

Oh.

Guard duty got boring, or so Tameka was told. Was she angry they left Rayne unguarded to make out? Not really. Especially when Rayne intentionally requested a light surveillance in hopes Imminent would take her to their hideaway. Guess their King didn't consider Celindria might steal doses of her blood. Or maybe Rayne did. Maybe her blood was having some adverse effects on the First Progeny, but judging from that superior attitude, Celindria was doing just fine.

A pretty, yet horrifying smirk spread across Celindria's lips as she switched her attention to Tameka. "You always perform so well with my tests. My toy is good as new. Now, we'll see how many wounds you can heal at once—"

"'So evil, he isn't permitted light.'" Tameka blurted the line from Xelan's time in the resurrection casket that bothered her the most, hoping like hell to distract Celindria. "Why 'evil'?"

The First Progeny cocked her head curiously to the side.

Encouraged, Tameka continued. "The Tritans, Tumu... they described Xelan as 'So evil, he isn't permitted light' when he was in the resurrection casket. Why 'evil'?"

Celindria sat on a stool with her back straighter than an exclamation point, legs crossed under her skirt, and hands patiently laced in her lap. Regal. She brushed the skirts aside until a gap in them exposed the length of her dark thigh against the white fabric. All the while, her expression remained contemplative. Eventually, she said, "I wouldn't call father evil. I'd call him reckless."

Tameka wondered what Xelan thought of that on the other end of the earpiece—Anyone listening, for that matter. She licked her lips before pressing, "May I ask how is he 'reckless'? From one woman to another; he fathered my child. I would like to know these things."

"He created us, after all. Like an excellent scientist, he researched and experimented until he learned how. Then he did it, but he didn't consider all the consequences of our making. Fortunately, he created me first, and I could make the later iterations without the same... kinks."

With Xelan listening, Tameka asked, "But the answer is in there, isn't it? Why you hate him—"

Devis clutched her arm, and Tameka recognized the signal by now. She didn't finish her question.

Celindria swiveled on the stool and returned to her work. At first, Tameka thought that was the end of it, but with her back to them, Celindria said, "Hate is not within me."

This time, Andrius also grabbed Tameka's arm. A fierce warning to back the fuck off.

Only then, it occurred to Tameka. Both brothers knew more about their sister than they had let on. Especially Devis, who spent the most time with the Shadow without divulging much of Celindria's secrets. There was still loyalty there for her.

It didn't matter. Tameka woke T.A.O. and helped Chris without further punishment from Celindria. The last twenty minutes were a win, lessened only by the unpredictability of the next twenty minutes.

Breathe and survive this.

Tameka prayed to Elden the vaccines would work.

{ENKI | GAIT}

"Hey, Matt, you hungry?"

The ginger nearly laughed. They broke for lunch only an hour ago. It seemed the faster they hurdled toward Enki's hull, the hungrier Puk grew. "Sure. I'll take a snack. Hey, do you have your anti-inertia pack—"

"Yeah, yeah. Can't eat without taking one. I swear we've sped up more than they told us," Matt's partner observed.

Astutely.

Indeed, Matt swore the horizon would bend to the sight of that less-distant ocean any minute now. He sat on a concrete pillar which once stood upright and supported a space scraper. In his supplies case, Matt counted three more squeeze tubes of nutrients. They stopped receiving solid food when the speed exceeded seventy thousand klicks per hour. At the rate Puk and Matt were eating, he'd run out of food in a few hours.

"Engineering team. This is Ginger. Come in. Over."

Puk came over his earpiece then. "Hey, get me some, too. I need about a hundred more charges if they got 'em. I might be done after that."

"Hey, Ginger. This is Engineering." Lots of laughter and chatting carried on in the background. "Good to hear from you. How can we help? Over."

Matt finished squeezing some food into his mouth. At the speed they went, some of it flung away in a weird anti-gravity experience. Wasteful. "We're running out of food out here. And charges. Can you send some supplies? What's going on up there? Have you heard from Lucy's team? Over."

A span of silence followed. Long enough for Puk to eventually ask, "What do you think is happening?"

"I don't know. It sounded like they were celebrating—"

"Ginger, Lucy's team is organizing some nifty drill thing. A Tantamount? Yeah, that's what they called it. Pretty cool stuff. You should be proud. And of course we can send supplies, but we think it's almost over. The Primary sent some food and music to our shrine—We're having a party to celebrate. We'll save some stuff for when the surface peeps finish. Won't be long now. Over and Out."

"Matt. The food."

Puk's voice held the appropriate weight. Matt felt it, too. It begged the question. How were he and Puk supposed to get off this rock? Matt said, "Lucy will get us. But you know what this means?"

The Monarch 3 drone practically nodded on the mic. "Phase III."

With a Tantamount in the mix, there was no telling how wild this ride might get. The last time Matt was on ground this shaky, Lucy came to his rescue.

Albuquerque, New Mexico CoN compound. The cold of winter. Once the alarm rang and Enforcer turned against Enforcer, things went sideways. Someone shot the water tower with Matt beneath it. The entire thing exploded, and he barely managed to dive out of the way of the worst. Instead, he was shirtless and barefoot in shorts—the Propagation Cycle uniform—on the hunt for anyone that came at him.

A middle-aged Promoter charged at him. Matt easily swung the scythe he stole from the barn and cut the dude in half. Next comer was a Collector with short-man syndrome. *He* could fight. Rather than blindly tackling Matt, he rolled and took out Matt's feet. Fucking short people. The scythe was useless in hand-to-hand, and Matt found himself on his back in the freezing mud.

His opponent got in one good punch.

Two.

But a nacre made all the difference. Barely phased by the blows, Matt gripped the enemy's throat and squeezed until his eyes bulged out. He fell dead on top of Matt, who lay there a second under him. "Good fight, buddy."

Then a roar ripped through the night, and flames covered the barracks.

No fucking way.

Matt hurried to his feet and ducked behind some cover, searching. When he found what he'd suspected, he gaped for a good minute.

Napalm.

The Justice went and got herself a fire cannon. Now *that* was impressive.

Matt picked up his scythe and strafed his way from building to building—quickly burning around him—until he was beside her. Without a sound, he rushed into the open courtyard and swung at her. At the last second, she turned and—

Matt never came so close to meeting Eternity.

Thinking quickly, he slid down into the mud at her feet beneath the flames burning above him and hungry for flesh.

Justice Abigail, "But *you* can call me Abby," stepped back and aimed the nuzzle at him. "How dare you violate the sanctity of our gods?! You and that whore!" Her finger squeezed the trigger—

Nothing happened.

She tried again, frustrated and panicked—

"Hey, Abby?"

The Justice froze at the sound of a voice Matt would never tire of hearing.

"This whore just killed you."

Without knowing what she'd intended, Matt burst onto his feet and ran. Hard. He wasn't sure how he knew Lucy had cut the line to the Napalm tank or even how he knew she planned to ignite it, but once lit, that fucker blew.

It knocked him into a pile of pallets meant for the participants in the Propagation orgy. There were worse and better places, but Matt didn't care. Especially as Lucy picked her way across the ruined ground to him. He stretched his arms out to her. Not to help him up, but to help her down onto him.

Lucy straddled and kissed him all in one movement. And Matt loved it.

Because he knew she'd always come for him.

The scenery of that derelict compound traded places with the approaching ocean on Matt's horizon. This mission might be their greatest—

"Was it *Volcano*?"

Puk gave a disparaged sigh over the mic. "Now, you're not even trying."

Matt stood from his break and went back to work while saying, "What? Isn't that the space movie with Tommy Lee Jones?"

"Elden, this is getting embarrassing. *Space Cowboys. Space Cowboys* had T.L.J. in it. Fucking amateur."

{ENKI | CINDER'S SHRINE}

Korac's neck was stiff with tension as Tameka engaged Celindria over their comms. The Progeny female impressed him with her tact and restraint. It was unfortunate about their abilities. He'd been looking forward to hearing the First Progeny fall to her knees at Tameka's feet. Instead, he had to endure the sound of Celindria injuring Karter's body enough for Remorse to abandon it.

Korac's mother's body.

Something unendurable had also happened to Chris. It was hard to say without a visual, but judging by the Shadow's reaction, some fresh nightmares were born today.

Everyone suffered in Celindria's wake—

Another conduit opened, and Iuo led his army into the blackened shrine. They lined up in one of the few available spaces left, but with the combined armies, their staging area filled fast. Multiple conduits remained open to accommodate the armies too vast to fit into their designated stalls. All the soldiers wore black, and all the Generals dressed to match with accents of blue.

Sagan had come so far in the last few months. Korac left his vantage point, gazing out at Torrentus, to find her. He shoved a hand in his pocket to ensure he packed some food. It was there, right beside the box he kept for the perfect moment. Locating her took the work of a moment as she was with the General from L. Capra, Kombuchi.

The Caprent, with his backward joints dressed in a toga, beamed down at her. "We've all waited a long time for this—Ah, General Korac. I haven't seen you since we defeated your army on Earth."

Korac smirked and crooked it further at Sagan's gentle nudge. "Yes, what a battle that was. I've never been so relieved to voluntarily concede in my life." He kissed her on the head and held out the reason for his errand. "Here. You need to keep your strength up."

Sagan beamed at him as she took an unladylike bite from the nutrient bar. "Thanks, babe."

Kombuchi's smile was friendly and filled with affection for the Seamswalker. "This is quite impressive, General Sterling. *You* are a goddess."

That had a certain ring to it. They all took a moment to appreciate the number of conduits open, and the people funneling into them. To their right, Pil Dwarves and their engineered mechanizations formed legions in blocks of ten thousand. The rest of the armies filed into similar ranks. Monarch 3 in hive formation took up the middle, Reipon soldiers swayed and slithered to the left of them, then the Lyriks, Icari, and humans gathered at the far end. Yun healers were dispersed throughout each army for support.

Korac muttered in awe, "How many remain?"

Sagan finished gnawing on the chewy, flavorless Vittle supplement and pointed to an empty lot. "Lukemore is the last one. I'm just on my way to get them." She climbed on her tiptoes to kiss Korac's cheek, warming his icy facade in public. "Thanks again. I'll be done soon." She flitted off to mobilize the next army.

"Did you ever imagine the likes of this?" Kombuchi mused at the sight. "You. Here. Working with the entire Vast Collective to bring down Enki?"

No. But… "The Shadow have this irritating way of drawing people together and seeing shit through." With his guiding star, Korac found his people, his home. As if on cue, another enormous conduit opened, and X, a Luk Korac knew by reputation, walked in with an army of the jellyfish-capped, whispering aliens with Sagan leading the way.

Her hair stylish, her eyes sparkling, and her smile dazzling, Sagan walked up to Korac and said, "I love the way you look at me."

Wishing they were alone, Korac leaned down and whispered in her ear, "That's my line."

"Are you two sure you don't want a film?"

With a groan, Korac separated from Sagan's sweet watermelon scent to glare at Iuo.

Ignoring him, the Porn Baron continued with his pitch. "You'd look gorgeous together. Pablo and Lynn can vouch for the quality."

Pehton's voice came from behind. "I can't say I wouldn't watch it."

Her good humor pulled a radiant burst of laughter from Sagan which Korac nearly thanked Pehton for. He smirked, instead, noticing Pehton still blushed despite whatever bald Icarus courted her. What a compliment. A compliment Korac would treat with dignity, not with a flip of his ponytail and a brilliant smile.

Look. Pehton's mouth gaped open—

"Ow!" Korac cried out when Sagan swatted him a second time. Seamswalkers were strong. "I did nothing wrong—"

Sagan put a finger in his face. "You know exactly what you were doing, and as much as I enjoy it, there should be a law against glamour warfare."

Iuo chuckled, and Pehton snickered in her hand, saying, "Thanks for having my back, Sagan."

"Anytime. So have you and Caedes made it official yet?"

Comically, Sagan waited until the Lyriki Warden took a drink of her water flask to ask the question. Pehton choked.

It was Korac's turn to chuckle.

Iuo said, "It's sweet, really."

"Yeah, we're all rooting for you two," Lamassau said on the way over from briefing Lukemore's army.

X came with him, dressed in a blue jellyfish kilt. He whispered, "Quite the turnout."

It truly was.

Sagan pulled on Korac's hand. "C'mon. I want to watch for Tameka's signal."

Korac let her lead him to the view, followed by all the Generals in their coordinating outfits. He approved.

Pehton peered around with a frown. "Where's Xelan?"

Lamassau answered, "He and Tumu are discussing exit strategies for the trapped Shadow since their abilities are useless."

It was quiet over the comms. The silence unnerved Korac the longer it stretched on.

Iuo blew the air from his reptilian cheeks, his black and blue eyes shifting to each of their faces. "I'd put my money on Fury any day."

"Here, here." Sagan toasted with another nutrient bar she slipped from Korac's pocket.

The group shared approving nods and gazed out at the view. The pale storm clouds spiraled in an impossible hurricane, so immense it covered an entire continent. According to Razor, the Aegis stationed the bridge there before the storm failed to terraform the plane's atmosphere. It wouldn't surprise Korac if his villainous brother had caused the failure in the first place.

Korac glanced down at Sagan. This would require the Atheneum, and every time he called Razor, the Pain Curator lingered too much on her for Korac's liking. Fortunately, she was more than capable of killing him.

Again.

Korac only hoped it wouldn't come to that.

{ENKI | MEDICAL BAY}

"The terminal recognized her DNA, but I can't believe it. You said the father was an Aegis?"

Qas understandably balked at Triss' results.

Pablo was doing some balking himself at the machine that stabilized her with ease after his significant efforts to do so until this far in her term. He nodded at the Tritan doctor's question. "The last one. We've figured the baby's physiology is dominating her. That it's converting her mother's blood to yellow Aegis plasma and her bones to nacre ore. It started with the womb and spread out from there."

Across the multi-tiered room, Lynn, Twenty-One, Caedes, and Miy made the unconscious Tritans more comfortable, hoping they'd wake in a mood willing to listen.

Bethany's quick thinking had surprised them all. The Progeny with memory gifts were truly exceptional.

As if sensing the trajectory of his thoughts, the quiet young girl caught his eye and nodded.

Qas adhered a patch to the back of Triss' hand. Pablo watched as tiny, nearly microscopic wires from the machine connected to the patch. The Tritan explained, "These will feed her nutrients and anesthetize her. See this reading here." He pointed to a line chart on the three-dimensional projection.

"Yup." Pablo guessed at their purpose. "Is that..." He frowned and narrowed his eyes at it. "Pain? You can measure pain?"

Qas nodded solemnly. "It's spiked. She's been suffering for a while."

This brought all kinds of conflict for Pablo. On the one hand, he listened to the entirety of Korac's Verse. Triss didn't come out looking so good. Truly, with every atrocity she had committed alongside Razor, she was a villain. But Pablo hated to see any patient in pain. Especially one as dedicated as Triss to bringing a rare and special life to this world.

A half-Aegis, half-Lyriki baby. One with a wonderful childhood ahead of her, with Sagan and Korac as her parents.

Pablo asked, "So, we're reducing her pain with the patch? And feeding her? She needs Aegis blood. We brought intravenous bags of it."

As if already ahead of him, Qas pointed to the projection. "That reading is here. Yes, she's low on blood cells."

Pablo turned around to ask for them and nearly ran into Lynn, who held an entire arm full of bags. The smile she gave him made him want to marry her all over again. Lynn didn't like Triss, but she liked the way Pablo took care of people and would never stand in the way of that. She understood him.

As he took a bag, Pablo planted a kiss on her soft lips and turned back to Qas, who was watching intently before looking away. But not before Pablo caught the grief in his eyes. Pablo was moved by Tumu's story about the females dying while some of these "lesser" Tritans slept. It moved them all. It certainly brought the Tritans' attempts to recover their species into perspective.

Qas was no different from that.

The Tritan cleared his throat and pointed to a cylinder connected to a chute attached to Triss' machine. "Open one and pour it into there. It will sanitize it first before sending it through the patch."

Cool. Sanitizing blood before exposing the recipient to anything carried by the donor. Why didn't Pablo think of that? He emptied the bag into the cylinder, saying, "This is some amazing technology. To think, I ran a lab kitted-out with a few gadgets and gizmos from Enki, but nothing like this."

"They gave you Tritan devices. These are Aegis works. They're far more advanced. The Primaries and the Eminents try to copy it, but they don't allow any fresh minds into the engineering labs." Qas peered about the facility as he spoke with such admiration.

Pablo was grateful they found someone with such a passion for medicine to help with Triss.

"What should we do in the meantime?" Miy called from below the multi-tiered room.

Twenty-One and Caedes stared at Pablo as if he were in charge. Even Chief Lynn gave him a similar look with a shrug. "You're the boss, Doc."

Pablo liked her saying that entirely too much.

Twenty-One must have noticed because he chuckled in that sizable chest of his.

Right.

"How many more machines like this are there in this bay?" Pablo asked while checking some of Triss' readouts.

Without a word, the Tritan stepped up to the dark glass beyond the readout projections and flipped a switch. Bright perimeter lights illuminated one identical bay after another and another in a growing circle of medical facilities. Qas said, "There are one hundred beds in each bay, and several more facilities like this one around Enki. Are you expecting company?"

Pablo stopped gawking to answer. "More like an army. How do you feel about joining the Shadow, Qas? We won't restrict you from our research. In fact, I'd welcome another doctor."

Qas pointed at the knocked-out Tritans. "The 'soldiers' you have unconscious down there are like me. We're not soldiers at all, but scientists, engineers, one of them is a comedian for Elden's sake—"

Elden.

Lynn caught the slip, too.

Pablo smiled. "Are you a fan of the Verses?"

Black blood flushed the Tritan's face as he flustered over his mistake. "It's an executable offense here."

Miy called with a heavy note of sarcasm, "Well, we obviously don't mind." She even folded her arms and rolled her eyes. With the orange streaks in her black hair, she'd pass for a sullen teen girl on Earth.

Caedes gave his signature "humph."

Qas tried to explain something that really didn't need explaining to the Shadow. "Elden, and now Nox and Korac, are like your Robin Hood on Earth. They're stories to lift the spirits of the oppressed. But the difference with the Shadow is that you're all real and really declaring war on Enki. We don't want our Primaries to die—Any of our people to die. There are so few of us..."

Bethany appeared from nowhere and took his hand. He startled a bit and looked down at her as she reached out to Pablo, who took her other hand—

And fell down into a rabbit hole of memories. Ones Bethany already knew and easily led them to. Qas likewise witnessed the making of the Shadow.

When they returned to the here and now, Bethany let go and gazed up at both men expectantly. With an ability like hers, the Shadow could bring anyone to their side. At least, that was Pablo's hope, as Qas recovered across from him.

Both doctors stared at each other for a long time before the Tritan spoke first. "Imminent is real."

"It is." Lynn said from the level below. "And they want control over the entire Vast Collective."

Pablo ventured further. "You've been through enough, Qas. We're not asking you to join our crusade. Just help the wounded like an objective physician should."

Qas stared at Triss when Pablo said, "objective." The much older doctor blinked back water from his voids. A tear. "Yes. The others, if you can show them the way you showed me when they wake, will help anyway they can." To Twenty-One, Miy, and Caedes on the lowest floor, he called, "Prepare the bays. You'll need one of these patches in each device. We can activate the other facilities as needed.

"And you *will* need them."

{ENKI | NEW CINDER}

Ross hated cowering like this with full grown and terrified adults in the room. Some of them were thousands and even millions of years old. All of them hid from Celindria.

If Ross held Jack's hand any tighter, she might break his bones. He kept her beside him, not behind or in front, mirroring Bones and Para. Devis and Andrius exchanged nervous glances over T.A.O.'s pretend asleep body and Karter's actually sleeping one.

Then there was Tameka. Something about what happened to Chris gave Fury a signal not to needle Celindria as originally planned. Instead, she delved carefully into the First Progeny's motives. It was like watching someone tight rope between two buildings, but one building kept experiencing an earthquake.

No matter how much Ross tried, she couldn't grip onto Celindria's memories. Sometimes she'd catch static or a glimpse, but they all slipped through her fingers. Like downloading half a program and trying to run it. Ross exhausted herself trying. So she pressed herself closer to Jack and took comfort in the inhales of his scent. Clean, like a mahogany teakwood candle.

Elden, Ross could sniff him for days—

Suddenly realizing her bizarre behavior, she sat back and stopped smelling him.

Bones caught her gaze then. He gave a small smile that said he caught her being weird, but totally understood it with a gentle nod in Para's direction.

How embarrassing and comforting and just so not what Ross needed with the rest of this moment.

Celindria stood and stretched.

The people in the cell held their breaths, including Ross. She was so scared that she accidentally slipped into Atramentous.

Shit.

Jack looked down at her and gave her hand a reassuring squeeze, but Ross couldn't make it stop. In and out of Atramentous. That was one sure way to draw attention—

"After your brother invaded my memories in quite an excellent maneuver, caution forbids me from allowing your proximity." Celindria walked over to the cage with guns drawn and stared at Ross. "Struggling with your self-control?"

Everyone in the cell glared at her, but Jack's body increased the most in temperature to the point of forcing Ross to drop his hand. It burned. She didn't enjoy having Celindria's focus on her either, but there were more dignified ways of handling this. So with her chin high, Ross said, "I'm sure you can appreciate how fear affects the Icarean instincts in our DNA."

Celindria wasn't paying attention to her now. She was staring at Jack.

No.

"You're very much like your sister."

Jack opened his mouth to say something, but Tameka squeezed his shoulder until he clapped it shut. A tear spilled from his eye and evaporated into steam on his skin.

Celindria's eyes flashed. "What vexes you so? Was I threatening your mate?"

Jack poised to lunge at her—

No! Ross couldn't watch this, so she blurted out the first thing on her mind. "You're a real bitch for leaving me with Razor and killing Wiw."

The smile fell from Celindria's lips as she snapped to Ross, who wanted desperately to wince from her sudden focus, but bravery and all that. The First Progeny stared at Ross for so long, the younger woman saw something move behind her eyes.

Fuck bravery. Ross flinched from her.

Chris stood, fully recovered, and made his way over to the cage. Celindria never blinked and never took her eyes off Ross. Jack peered with a hopeful expression at his former guard. Their friendship was one of mutual support and guy jokes. Chris practically raised Jack into adulthood. Maybe that was enough to reach him.

As if reading Ross' thoughts, Jack called to Chris, "We'll get you out. I won't leave you here."

Meanwhile, Celindria finally blinked and backed over to her workstation. She pressed the mechanism which unlocked the cage and watched expectantly as Chris held out a hand to Ross.

He was under Celindria's volition, so it was really her holding out a hand. Still, Ross trusted him. She took it.

Para cried, "No! Don't!"

But not before Chris jerked Ross out of the cell and slammed her back against the bars in Jack's face. The mechanism locked with an audible gasp and many cries from the others.

Ross couldn't pay any attention to that right now. She had to breathe and remain calm. Those were her priorities as Chris picked her up by the backs of her thighs and spread her legs around him.

Jack shouted, "Stop, Celindria! He doesn't want to do this. Leave her alone!"

Tameka cursed. "I swear, if you'd just get to the point and fight me, woman, this would all be over by now! Let her go!"

Again, Ross ignored them, her heart beat like a frightened rabbit. Shallow breaths heaved out of Ross and threatened to hyperventilate her if not for her nacre. Chris gripped the nape of Ross' neck and gently tilted her mouth up to his.

Tears fell from her eyes. "I know this isn't you. It's okay, Chris. There's nothing to forgive, okay?"

Everything stopped there, and the Shadow's shouts died in the emptiness.

Chris wasn't as warm as Jack, but he was warm against places on Ross that were still unexplored. It wasn't his fault. She knew that, but she desperately wanted him to set her back down. He pinned her legs around him in a crushing grip. They were both dressed, so this was still salvageable. If only Celindria would let him put her down.

With a swift sweep of her skirts, the First Progeny left the lab through the tunnel without a glance in their direction. Left them locked up with someone strong enough to bust the bars, and left her and Chris pinned to them. Through his deep brown eyes, Ross knew she stared at Celindria in there, watching them. Who needed a gun for a threat when this display was enough?

"Ross, talk to me." Cautious concern filled Tameka's voice.

Jack echoed her, "Are you okay?"

Stuck in this awkward and emotionally stressful position, Ross swallowed and answered, "I'm okay." Her voice sounded thin and far away.

Para promised, "He would never do this to you."

"I know." Ross meant it.

Devis muttered close to Tameka, "T.A.O. can save us."

Andrius seconded the idea. "I'd like that very much."

Tameka reminded them, "Not yet."

They couldn't abort the plan. Not when they were this close.

Bones was near Ross when he said, "You're doing good. Hang in there."

That was the idea.

ELEVEN
YOUR FAITH, MY COURAGE, AND THEIR WEAPONS

{Enki | Cinder's Shrine}

Andrew was so grateful Kyle wasn't listening to his earpiece. He glimpsed Korac wincing from it and caught the Icarus' eye. With a raised brow, the Icarean General asked a wordless question.

Andrew answered the only way he could, with a nod. The Probability Matrix showed no one the full extent of happenings in a given instance. Spies of futures unknown only hoped to glean the most pertinent events and their outcomes. Although fucking traumatic to listen to, so far, the pertinent events in Tameka's current instance lined up with the successful Probabilities.

Korac understood and went back to his duties as a glamorous sentinel.

Kyle would *not* understand. Thus Andrew's relief.

Still, with both of them suffering like owners of lonely hearts, Andrew made his way across the gigantic and yet not gigantic enough station to find Kyle. Along the way, he scanned intentions. So many voices and all of them shouted battle cries. The entire Vast Collective was eager to rid themselves of Imminent—not the Tritan race. That was such an important distinction to make as they'd learned earlier today of several innocent Tritans swept up in the fray.

Among the throng of earnest fighters, some of the Generals' intentions intrigued Andrew the most. How long would Xelan get by with not talking to Tameka about this very important future the galaxy had planned for her? How would she react when Xelan finally confessed to knowing all along—

No. Never mind. They'd work through it. They were great together.

Their synchronism reminded Andrew of another couple, now toast—Or were they? How many times did Lucas and Andrew perfectly harmonize on so many major issues, but couldn't agree on what to eat for dinner—

Smiling.

Andrew was smiling without realizing it.

"Keep your faith in me a little while longer."

Kyle was right. How many times did someone say that to them? And how many times did 'keeping that faith' pay off? By their accounts, Xelan said it first when he shut the Valkyrie away for a million years or so. Andrew knew this from Korac's Verse. Iuo said it to Ross when he handed her over to Imminent to find Bethany. Tumu said it to Tameka when he found her snooping around the Pantheon. And then Lucas...

Such a strange assurance, but looking at its history... Well, it always paid off.

Renewed by this positive examination, Andrew slapped Kyle on the back. Hard.

"Ow. Dude."

Xelan was frowning too hard to chuckle, but Tumu laughed in Kyle's face, saying, "His eyes almost popped out of his head and everything. Humans make such funny faces with your eyelids and your lips."

Andrew and Tumu fistbumped.

When Xelan met Andrew's eyes, it was so similar to the gesture from Korac earlier that Andrew could see them being raised together. Andrew gave a nod of... reassurance? Guidance? He wasn't sure of this feeling he got from viewing the Matrix. It wasn't certainty, but something close. Tameka and the others were on their way into the sure-to-succeed category.

That's all that mattered.

Well, that and keeping Kyle from listening to Celindria torturing his sister with Chris' body.

What a mess.

"Are you free from screening duties and ready to check out the view?" Andrew was asking Kyle, but obviously everyone else in this circle was invited.

Kyle looked around and shivered as if brushed by something. "So many people. They're pressing in. Isn't it like that with you and their intentions?"

Andrew shrugged. "You've helped me gain better control of most of my abilities while you've exercised your lungs instead of practicing."

"And here I was thinking guarding Cinder's conduit for the last couple of years while you farmed under a balloon was exercise."

Xelan stepped between them, physically cutting off their bickering. "Anyone for a view?"

Tumu about-faced Kyle toward the other Generals. "Come along, Progeny."

Kyle lit a new joint, hit it, and took it from his lips to ask, "Hey, Tumu?"

"Yeah?"

"Why did the girls get cool and affectionate nicknames like Peaches, Star, Sparkles, and Little Tree, but me, Andrew, and Rayne were left out?"

That was a great question. Andrew stared expectantly up at Tumu.

Xelan spared him a pitying look before his eyes went vacant as he clearly listened for an update in the earpiece.

Tumu, abashed, straightened his robes and stuttered when he answered, "Well—"

Kyle pressed, "I'd say you were sexist, but you left Rayne out, too."

"Ahem. Peaches and Star were code names for the girls when referring to their influence in the Probability Matrix."

Andrew caught Kyle's eye across the other two men and raised a suspicious brow.

With another hit on his joint, Kyle nodded to Andrew and asked Tumu, "What about Ross and Karter's names? And that still doesn't explain why Andrew and I didn't get code names."

Tumu straightened his robes again. "How can you refer to Karter as anything but Sparkles? She's an Icarean Valkyrie with a rainbow mohawk."

Xelan gave an assenting nod. "That's fair."

"Your sister was easy because she was this little tree when I first met her. Humans grow so fast." Tumu's voice softened. "And we knew Rayne would destroy Enki. She is the storm and requires no other code name. She simply *is* 'Rayne.'"

Oh.

Well, that got dark.

But Kyle wasn't satisfied. "So, why nothing for me and Andrew?"

Tumu looked to Xelan as if for help, to which the Icarus simply shook his head. "You brought this on yourself by calling everyone pet names. Now tell them what you told me."

That rose both of Andrew's brows.

"Fine. Lamassau nicknamed you Thelma & Louise."

Although he'd clearly heard it before, Xelan let out a hearty laugh—

Oh.

He was laughing at Kyle's reaction. The young man's face shriveled into a confused pucker. "Thelma & Louise? Why in the fuck? Are we gonna runaway together at some point? And which one is Thelma—Fuck it. I'm Louise. You can be Thelma."

Andrew grinned and shrugged. "That's fine. I wouldn't mind hooking up with a young Brad Pitt. Might do me as much good as it did her right now."

{ENKI | CINDER'S SHRINE}

Xelan laughed without feeling relief. He was tense and wired, listening to Tameka and their people suffer. Some of them were only kids who happened to survive an apocalypse. They certainly didn't survive all of that to suffer through this.

Celindria's psyche had disintegrated much further than Xelan had predicted. Soon, nothing worth reasoning with would remain. Not that he'd ever managed to reason with her in the past. Xelan only ever pushed Celindria further away.

Tameka handled the situation fantastically. Calm and built from the kind of strength the Shadow could rely on. Even with Pax only a room away, she maintained her composure.

Soon, T.A.O. could set them all free and bring Karter with them. Xelan looked forward to seeing her for the first time since he awakened the Valkyrie from their stasis chambers in his stronghold. Years ago now to them. Months ago to him.

The Progeny had all grown and matured so much. Xelan was proud to call them his Shadow—

Korac glanced over at Xelan, and his words from earlier replayed in his head. *"The Progeny can see your mask, and I share their sentiment—We don't like it."*

But the General knew the Prince of Cinder as a lover and a friend. Korac couldn't know what it's like to mentor so many who relied on Xelan's composure during moments such as these. It allowed for bouts of levity, like earlier with Andrew, Kyle, and Tumu. Still... Perhaps Xelan came across as callous when he pretended to laugh, meanwhile the enemy had captured his son and soul mate on the brink of war.

Andrew shoved his elbow into Xelan's rib hard enough to make him look down at the younger man. Without taking his eyes off Torrentus, Andrew said, "You're overthinking it. We know you're worried. We all are, but we won't help Pax and the rest by pulling our hair out in front of our allies."

Allies. Diplomacy. Exactly what was on Xelan's mind. He could best help Tameka by organizing this army and using the advantage she'd afforded them. Wasting time on panic would mean wasting her efforts.

Xelan wouldn't have that. "Thanks, Conscience."

Andrew clicked his tongue. "That name sucks so bad."

Freely, the Prince of Cinder grinned. "I like it. It's not as cool as Story Taker, but..." He gave a half shrug at Andrew's grimace.

"Wingmaster. This is Fury. Over."

Relief washed over Xelan. "Go ahead."

Tameka breathed like she was shuffling around the others. "Celindria has us in the cage T.A.O. described. We have Karter. I wasn't sure if you heard that. Over."

The Shadow peered at him now through the gathering, those listening in, anyway. Kyle pressed closer to Sagan across the way, curious.

Xelan answered, "We heard everything. Is Karter all right? What about Chris and Ross? Over."

"Karter is unconscious, like Para was at first. Celindria stabbed Chris in the eye. I healed him pretty fast, and he seems okay. But he's in the room with us so Celindria will know I'm talking to you." There was a swallow before Tameka continued. "She uh... She's threatening us to keep still, or she'll use Chris to assault Ross. Over."

"What?!" Kyle heard that one.

Andrew muttered, "Better go calm him down," and took off in his brother's direction.

Xelan wet his lips and asked, "How is Celindria keeping you? Over."

"With nacre disabling guns, mostly." Tameka shifted, asking someone, "You still okay?"

Ross answered on the line in a slightly shrill voice, "I'm okay. No matter what happens, I want everyone to know that I'll be okay. It's not Chris' fault. Over."

"Fuck." That was Korac.

Sagan chafed his arm and helped Andrew placate Ross' fuming older brother.

Closing his eyes, Xelan assured, "You're the gold standard, Ms. Roberts." He swallowed and opened his eyes before the next. "Fury, you don't let it come to that. Over." Yes. That was an order to blow Chris' nacre if necessary. If roles were reversed, Xelan would rather someone killed him than forced him to rape an innocent girl.

Tameka hesitated, considering it, before saying, "Understood. How can I speed this along? Over."

"Ask her about Ishkur. Peaches, ask her to take your volition. Keep it centered on you. Over." Tumu's advice was sound.

Xelan nodded at him across the alcove. "That's right, Fury. Let us know when she returns. This was smart. Antagonizing her interest through Chris' watch—"

More of Korac's earlier words slammed into Xelan. *"But let Tameka see how much Pax's abduction affects you. She needs it."*

"Tameka, for you and for Pax—The second you think this mission feels out of hand, say the word and Sagan will bring me to you. I won't hesitate, Fury. Over." Xelan couldn't get more honest with his feelings than that.

Sagan waved from across the way. Korac bowed with his head.

Sparked by his words, Tameka sounded much more confident. "We got this. Over and Out."

Everyone agreed. Taking Pax was some kind of trap for Xelan. No one wanted him within miles of Celindria. Not even Xelan wanted it after he'd repeatedly tried and failed to reach his First Progeny. His very presence seemed to fuel her indignation.

In fact, Celindria dismissing any chance of Xelan being evil surprised him. He believed she understood him, but

Celindria still resented Xelan for the mistakes he made in her creation—

A hand clasped onto his shoulder. It was Tumu. "Peaches will be fine. Little Tree, too—"

"She'd better be." Kyle pushed his way through the other Generals. "Look, we haven't always gotten along, but I'm trusting you with this. Shit goes sideways, you and me are going in there to get them out. Got it?"

Xelan marked this as an improvement. He could remember a time when Kyle felt so little about Xelan's ability to protect the Progeny that he'd betrayed Rayne to Nox. Now, he asked to fight beside him.

In the only proper response, Xelan held out his hand, and Kyle clasped his wrist. They shook on it.

"Wingmaster. This is the Doc. Over."

Leadership never ended. "Go ahead."

Pablo sounded quite engaged and eager. "We met a friendly. He's helping us equip Triss and prepare some high-tech beds for the wounded. We're doing great here, all thanks to Bethany. Over."

Kyle flushed suddenly and shook his head. Both of his sisters were brave and making leaps without him. There was much pride to go around.

Xelan grinned and let it into his voice. "That's wonderful news. Thanks, Doc. Let us know if you need anything. Over and Out."

F8 rolled up next, and Xelan wondered how much more the galaxy would ask of him after this victory. She said, "I think you'll need to address the Generals. They're all ready to hear from you. They want a reminder of what they're fighting for."

Right.

Xelan peered over at Tumu, who winked at him. Lamassau gave two thumbs up. Iuo and Pehton stood with their respective armies side-by-side and gave him little encouraging waves. Sagan punched the air, and Korac smirked. Andrew and Kyle looked up expectantly at their mentor.

Time to see if all that education as the Prince of Cinder paid off.

May the rest of the galaxy be kinder to Xelan's excellent naming conventions.

{ENKI | NEW CINDER}

Bones hated everything about this. Ross' scent smelled of fear and inexperience. Both he and Para could sense it as Icari. Neither one of them liked the notion of watching that inexperience transform into experience through trauma. Ross and the King Regent recently cozying up to each other made the horror all the more awful. So, Bones asked, "Do you think I can pry them apart without getting us severely punished?"

As Bones asked the question, he realized the answer.

Tameka shook her head with her mouth in a tight, grim line.

Andrius confirmed it verbally. "It's ill-advised."

Devis gave him a pitying smile. "But we all share the sentiment."

Para whispered into Karter's ear. "Wake up and show these boys how it's done."

Jack stared unblinking at the sight. After a few years of getting to know these people, Bones understood Jack's relationship with Chris. Family. Like an older brother or a young dad, even. It must kill Jack to see his close friend pin his girlfriend in that position right in front of him.

Celindria fucking sucked.

And what about Tameka? All strong and powerful, but forced to cool her heels here with the rest of them while her son slept only a few feet away.

At least they got Karter back, but until Xelan and Pablo could cut into her motor cortex, she wasn't waking up. They couldn't even get T.A.O. to take her away because they still needed this plan to go through, and Celindria would punish them for escaping a few people.

That's how Bones took it all, anyway.

What he wouldn't give for a nice date with Para, splitting a slice of Colton's cheesecake while all their friends goofed around the house they could no longer live in because Imminent could kiss Bones' ass—

"Please don't kill him, Fury."

Jack said all that without moving a muscle from his view of Ross and Chris.

The young woman apparently agreed. "Please. Don't. I'll be okay." Ross' voice was a little reedy, but she still sounded quite certain.

Yeah, everyone was pretty sure Xelan had told Tameka to kill the soldier if it came down to it. As an Icarus—a male—who had dedicated his life to protecting his race, Bones understood Xelan. Because that's what Chris would likely prefer. No one wanted to live through involuntarily raping your almost-son's love interest. Too much post trauma for everyone.

Unfortunately, it was all up to Tameka, and she looked heavy with that knowledge.

Instead of acknowledging it, she said, "It won't come to that." Tameka increased the volume a bit, probably hoping Celindria would hear through Chris. "We'll get through this, Shadow. Ross, do you hear me? We'll make it through this."

It was true. They all felt a little more safe after Xelan's promise to rescue them if things steered too far off course. Bones only hoped they wouldn't need it.

Elden, he'd give anything to undo this. To somehow force himself to stay awake when the draining started back at the mansion. To protect Pax—

Para's warm hand slid into his, and she caught his gaze. "You're right, Fury. We'll make it through this." She said the words to Tameka, but the reassuring smile on her face was all for Bones.

His heart swelled—

The door to Celindria's room opened, and the First Progeny herself walked through it. What? Confounded, the

Shadow exchanged confused glances. She exited originally through the tunnel, not the bedroom. How did she...?

Para mouthed to Tameka, "Another. Door?"

With wide eyes, Tameka shook her head.

How the fuck did Celindria get in there?

Never mind that. *Why* was Celindria in there? Bones didn't like her near Pax. Especially with Pax in some kind of helpless coma—

Abruptly, Chris shifted until one hand gripped the front of Ross' jumpsuit and then he froze again.

Bones could hear Ross' heart pounding from over here. Para squeezed closer to the bars, between him and Jack, who lost all color to his complexion.

Tameka wasn't having it. "What are you doing, Celindria?"

The First Progeny rifled through some shelves and graced them with a response. "My father raised you to be so invasive. Or perhaps dense. Because surely you know why Chris has Ross. Now keep to yourself or risk her virginity."

Ross' whimper wrenched inside Bones' heart. All of their hearts by the looks on their faces.

Jack didn't just regain color. He turned bright red with rage. Abruptly, he sat up and gripped the bars near where Ross' arms rested. There, he brushed them with his fingers, reassuringly. It seemed to help because her heart rate lessened.

Smart kid.

Bones pat him on the back while Celindria wasn't looking.

Tameka went to work. "What is Ishkur, and why do you need me for it?"

Celindria laughed, and the sound rang as genuine. "You learn lessons the hard way, yes, girl? And my father is listening. You know, I know, of course."

Tameka took offense to the juvenile mention. "I'm a full-grown adult—"

Celindria dismissed her with a wave over her shoulder. "You're simply evidence of my father's midlife crisis. The mistress younger than his own children."

Ouch. That stung Bones from over here. He couldn't imagine how Xelan felt overhearing it.

Tameka's eyes twitched with it. "Who are you to criticize love—"

Again, Devis and Andrius did the thing where they gripped Tameka and shook their heads. A fierce warning. So many topics were off limits with Celindria as if she were some sensitive porcelain doll. The eggshells around her could fill the Blight Canyon in the Ignis Desert.

Chris ripped the front of Ross' jumpsuit open down to the waistline. She screamed at the abruptness of it.

Jack gritted his teeth and pressed his forehead to Ross' now bare back through the bars. "It's okay. I'm here." He repeated the litany as if they both could use the comfort.

Bones liked him.

Tameka cried, "Celindria, take my volition. I'm ready to give it."

The First Progeny whirled with a spin of her skirts. Celindria didn't miss a beat. "Repeat the words I say. 'Under my own will, I forfeit my volition. Perfectly and consensually until she returns me unto myself.'"

"After you separate Chris from Ross. We'll all give you our volition to keep her safe." Tameka walked a fine line here, giving away all their wills at once.

But Bones trusted her.

Chris lowered Ross' legs back to the floor, and Bones pitied her unsteady gait. She'd been stuck that way for over an hour. Nacres could only help so much. Next, the big human backed away and to the other side of the room, toward the mirror.

The cell door unlocked, and Ross hurried inside into Jack's arms. She buried her face in his chest while he rubbed circles on her back. The poor girl needed a new jumpsuit. This one exposed her bra and stomach all the way to other pieces of lingerie.

Bones wanted to hurt Celindria. Also aching with the desire to inflict some pain, Para clenched her jaw so hard he overheard it.

"You come out first, Tameka," Celindria called.

Tameka slipped out the gate and walked with a straight back to Celindria. Chris had already trained a nacre-disabling gun on her. Her ability to multi-task was terrifying.

Bones kept his eyes on the room and on their leader, walking her way to their destruction.

Without preamble, Tameka stopped in front of Celindria and said, "Under my own will, I forfeit my volition. Perfectly and consensually until she returns me unto myself."

Everyone in the room, including Celindria, held their breath.

{Enki | Medical Bay}

Lynn admired her husband for being such an amazing doctor and such an amazing person. The moment their side won, she wanted to have twelve of his babies. Until then, it was warming up bays, waiting for their hostages/potential partners to wake up, and listening to the intense situation unfolding in Celindria's lab. Although a little sore from missing out on all the action, Lynn was grateful she wasn't with Fury's team.

Poor Ross.

Poor Chris.

And poor Karter.

Poor Pax was a given. Lynn couldn't wait to hug that kid the instant she saw him next—Of course, only once Tameka let him go. Everyone foresaw potential for an overly protective period ahead.

No blame or shame there.

Sure, that also meant they'd need new digs. The idea of them all living under one roof again left Lynn conflicted. On the one hand, it was super comforting to share tears and laughs with her favorite people. But every now and again, she wanted to leave the room for a naked snack break during marathon sex. Not really an option in a house filled with forty-plus people. Those twelve babies might tack on a few extra difficulties to accommodate in one house. Then there was Pax and Echo. And all the other children surely on the way. They'd need room to grow.

So Lynn and Pablo would find a house of their own, but where would they end up after this ride? Close to family felt right, and their duties would only get more complicated as the galaxy became involved. Lynn supposed it was really a matter of climate preference. Someplace perpetually spring. She liked the idea of a flower garden for the twelve children to play in with warm days and frosty nights. Maybe even an occasional snowfall. Peaceful.

With a treehouse—

Oh, hey.

The new recruits regained consciousness and awoke in quite the panic. Clear across three bays, Lynn heard their shouts.

"Qas, you traitor!"

The doctor staved another Tritan with his hands out in surrender. "No, please listen. They left you unharmed because they're not here to wipe out the Tritans. They're here to take out Imminent."

Another one barked, "You sold us out for a fucking fairytale?!"

As Caedes and Twenty-One trained nacre-disabling weapons on them, Qas tried again. "No, listen. Primary Rem, Eminent Celindria, and Eminent Abresson are with Imminent. Along with the father of this woman's baby. It's all real."

The first one challenged Qas. "So what if it's real? Imminent is still more pro-Tritan than—"

"The Shadow want us to survive the destruction of Enki. They're here to help. Please. This girl can show you."

Lynn stayed still, watching, but separate. If she joined, another Shadow would only frighten the rabbits. One tentatively approached Qas and held his hand out to Bethany. Soon, they all would, and this mess would clean itself up.

Meanwhile, Lynn considered how many boys and how many girls she wanted. All of them should have

Pablo's eyes, brows, obviously his lips. Honestly, the only features they needed from their mother were her nose and complexion—

"Celindria, take my volition. I'm ready to give it."

Caught daydreaming, Lynn balked at Tameka's words and stumbled over the next device, nearly falling into it. Was this really happening?!

It was, and Celindria said so. *"Repeat the words I say. 'Under my own will, I forfeit my volition. Perfectly and consensually until she returns me unto myself.'"*

On the mic, Lynn heard Tameka's shoulders straighten. *"After you separate Chris from Ross. We'll all give you our volition to keep her safe."*

Shit.

Some shuffling followed, and then Ross' sobs were closer to Tameka, implying Celindria had released her.

Loud enough to pick up on the earpieces, the First Progeny called, *"You come out first, Tameka."*

After some movement, the brave Powerhouse that was Fury said, *"Under my own will, I forfeit my volition. Perfectly and consensually until she returns me unto myself."*

Lynn held her breath.

The moment of truth.

{Enki | Cinder's Shrine}

Pehton did *not* envy Xelan. His normal mid-tone gray complexion had paled to a shade which competed with Korac's skin—Ashen. The Traitor Prince of Cinder had to perform a rousing address under these conditions. Queen F8, sans earpiece, wasn't aware of the tumultuous exchange occurring on Tameka's frequency. Meanwhile, all the tuned-in Shadow bore the same tight expressions.

On the other end of the earpiece, Celindria had just returned to her lab while the Progeny were working together to spare Ross from a horrifying fate.

Pehton liked that girl, commiserated with her over their unrequited love for a man perfectly happy with his Seamswalker—

Overstimulated, Pehton closed her eyes to shut everything away.

What remained of the Lyriks formed a phalanx behind her, ready for marching orders. *General* Pehton. Sure, her forces were minute compared to the rest, but hers could fly and sing nacres to pieces. Not to mention that working in a prison under Triss and eventually forced to serve Razor left them all thoroughly ruthless. Deadly.

Pehton was so proud of how far they'd come in their rehabilitation, and they, in turn, trusted her to lead their army into battle. Again.

Progress.

A hand tapped her shoulder, and Pehton turned to find the Traitor Prince towering over her. All the Icari towered over her.

Kindly, he asked, "Will you join me up at the front, General Pehton?"

She liked Xelan, too. Her easy smile said so. "Of course."

Waving to the next in her chain of command, Pehton approached the window with Xelan and the other Shadow Generals. Korac stood on his Prince's left. Sagan to her man's left. Then Iuo and Pehton. Tumu, Kyle, Andrew, and Lamassau filled out the right side. They saved a space on Xelan's immediate right for Tameka. Those other planetary Generals, turned from their armies and faced the Prince in front of the glass.

With the spectacular view of Torrentus swirling in the background, Xelan addressed the armies of the Vast Collective.

"We don't ask for much, do we? We only ask for deliverance from a near omniscient parasite which begs our submission at every turn. I'm defying that parasite, and so are you or you wouldn't be here. Are you tired of it? The constant hindrance to the evolution of your people in every way—socially, intellectually, economically, and physically. Are you *sick* of it? Fearing the next opportunity because it always comes with a price which the parasite asks not only you to pay, but your race. Your planets. Your families..."

A pause.

Pax.

Xelan continued.

"I'll tell you what I am. I'm *done* with it. I'm here to end it. Every single one of you is here to free yourselves from this cancer, and finally meet some progress which doesn't cost you your souls—"

"Celindria, take my volition. I'm ready to give it."

Pehton clenched her fists until blood ran from her nails all to avoid crying out. With a glance at the others, she saw the same distress on their faces. Xelan's back was to her, but it didn't take a mind reader to know how badly it affected him. Everything on the man constricted.

"Repeat the words I say. 'Under my own will, I forfeit my volition. Perfectly and consensually until she returns me unto myself.'"

The other Generals and their armies stirred at Xelan's sudden freeze. The passion ignited by his words was already dousing from his unexpected silence.

Sensing this, Xelan continued, despite the transaction occurring on the other end of the mic.

Pehton pitied him.

"That's right. Imminent asks for your souls. I ask for your courage and your might. The Vast Collective asks for your will to win this fight."

A thunderous, deafening grunt erupted from the millions—possibly a billion—soldiers inside the station and trailing out of it into worlds beyond.

"After you separate Chris from Ross. We'll all give you our volition to keep her safe."

"Then you'll be free to guide your people into whatever ventures you seek, and *I* will be with you, fighting on your side to see you into all those opportunities you've turned away. All that progress you could have made—"

"You come out first, Tameka."

"I will lead you into battle today so I can take you into a tomorrow where your hope for a future can finally begin."

"Under my own will, I forfeit my volition. Perfectly and consensually until she returns me unto myself."

The Shadow held a collective breath as their allies cheered.

TWELVE

REVELATIONS FROM A WEEPING STATUE

{ENKI | NEW CINDER}

ROSS STARED UNBLINKING AT TAMEKA'S STRAIGHT BACK AND CELINDRIA'S STONY FACADE. T.A.O. laid on her side, facing the wall with her eyes wide open, listening. Jack gripped Ross' hand hard enough to hurt. Bones put a fist to his chest and closed his eyes, likely praying to Elden. Para looked ready to pounce. Devis and Andrius shrank into the corner. All of them held their breath. Except Karter, because she was still asleep.

A heartbeat passed.

Then another.

Until eventually, Tameka's shoulders relaxed, and Celindria's eyes narrowed a fraction.

Nothing happened, and the Shadow exhaled. Ross felt relief wash over her until the elation made her dizzy, and she leaned her forehead against Jack's sturdy frame. He brushed through her hair and murmured reassurances against it.

Icy, the First Progeny asked, "How?"

With her back to them, Tameka's grin was in her voice. "We're the Shadow. We're resourceful—"

The slap cracked across the room, and blood sprayed from Tameka's mouth.

But that didn't stop Fury. "You know, I used to look up to you. *The First Progeny*. The woman who threw the Icari back into Cinder—"

Another slap in the other direction. More blood.

Ross cried out.

Jack gripped the bars, ready to break them again.

Devis and Andrius turned to stone.

Para watched with calculation, waiting for her moment.

Bones went over and whispered in T.A.O.'s ear, preparing for an exit strategy.

Tameka, however, kept on, even with her head lolling on her shoulders. "You defied Nox and eventually parented my best friend—"

"How?!" Celindria wasn't angry or crazed. Simply professional as she slapped Tameka again.

The younger woman spat a nasty clog of blood at her assailant's bare feet.

Was that a tooth?!

Celindria raised her hand for another strike, and Ross couldn't watch this anymore. "A vaccine! I'm sorry, Tameka—"

"It's okay, Ross." She took labored breaths through the obvious pain. "You heard her, Celindria. We made a vaccine, and it worked." Tameka choked out a thick, exhausted chuckle which somewhat relieved the Shadow.

The First Progeny glared at her, but the dots connected on her frighteningly beautiful face. Quick calculations until she guessed aloud, "The shield virus deters *suggestion* like Rayne's blood so the Tenements of Volition can't apply to you." A strange and foreign smile spread across her mouth. Pride. Celindria was proud of them and impressed. "Not bad."

Tameka's strength was unwavering and an inspiration to Ross. "What will you do with me now that I can't be your puppet?" Again, she spat blood at Celindria's feet. Even now, Tameka held her head higher.

The ancient statue ignored Tameka, turned, and went back to her work. This time, Celindria reached for the shelf with the blood samples she'd collected from them earlier. Tameka was a dangerous person to leave at her back, and yet she spoke without turning around. "Is my father still listening?"

"Yes."

How Tameka mustered that much calm after losing a tooth escaped Ross.

Celindria performed some tests on someone's blood using a dropper and a centrifuge. "Ask him what he thinks I should do with you. Ask him how he disposed of his failed experiments while he bartered with his research in Enki."

"He's busy." Tameka was still unwavering.

It's true. Xelan was finishing up his rally for the allied troops, but no doubt he'd heard everything and—

"I'm here, Fury."

The sound of Xelan's voice alone sent a visible wave of relief through the caged Shadow, but what did Celindria mean by disposing of experiments? Ross and the others, no longer petrified, shared confused glances. Except Bones. He looked certain that nothing his Prince could say would shake his foundation.

That was true for all of them.

Tameka asked, "You heard her questions?"

Xelan said, "I heard. I'm getting somewhere less crowded to answer—All right. Tell her I want her to be better than me. That the mistakes I made were irreversible, and I don't want her to live with my regrets."

Ross' mouth fell open. This sounded dark.

Tameka repeated the words with a hint of concern in her voice.

A scary and pretty grin spread across Celindria's face. "Tell him I already live with his regrets, and I'll show them to you, Tameka. I'll show you how he disposed of the Children of Gait."

Tameka faltered. Ross gasped. Jack frowned harder and chafed her arm. Para's eyes fluttered closed. Bones shook his head as if he couldn't believe it. Andrius growled, "That was unfair, Celindria, and you know it. Father had no idea those were children—"

"He knew they were lives and counted them like data." Celindria looked her most serene in this moment, exposing the Progeny to the flaws in their leader.

Xelan astonished them further. "She's telling the truth."

Ross felt a little faint.

"But Andrius is right. I never knew. These are my sins, and they make me a monster, but you can't let her divide us now. We've almost defeated her. Please. I vow to confess everything. Soon."

Tameka shook her head. Not out of incredulity or confusion, but like her concussion was making her dizzy. "I can't think like this. Celindria, I trust him no matter what doubts you seed in your desperate attempt to divide and conquer. The Shadow aren't like you and Remorse. We actually enjoy each others' company and believe in one another."

Ross, along with the rest of the group, pressed against the bars, watching this unfold.

Celindria gave a single mocking laugh. "No wonder he went after someone so young. The naivety of you is astounding—"

Another crack, but this time it came from Tameka backhanding Celindria hard enough to turn her head. The group in the cell gaped, stunned, and for Devis and Andrius, terrified. A gap formed in Celindria's split lip, but there wasn't so much as a trickle of blood. It begged the question.

Could Celindria bleed at all?

Equally frightening was how little the woman had moved since the strike. No blinking. No breathing. Celindria simply stared at Tameka.

Ross admired Fury for declaring, "I'm tired of you. I'm *sick* of you. Fight me and get it over with. Or 'dispose' of me. Or whatever you think you can do to me. But there is nothing—nothing—you can do to hurt me—"

"Mommy, why did you hit sissy?"

{THE SEAM}

Sagan hid in the Seam so no one would see the General of the human army cry. The tears started with Celindria's first strike against her sister. It hurt too much to listen to it, but she refused to turn off the earpiece. If Tameka could endure it, the least Sagan could do was listen.

And it broke her heart.

The similarity between the anguish of Razor's ambush on Sagan at the Emporium and Celindria's cruel captivity sent Sagan into heaving fits, where she couldn't draw enough air.

Or maybe that was the several hundred enormous conduits Sagan was holding open.

Either way, she needed to catch her breath, and the Seam was as good a place as any. Sagan loved Korac with all her heart, but there were just some states he shouldn't see her in. It only got worse the more Celindria hit Tameka.

Sagan closed her eyes and tried not to worry about Xelan. What it must be like for him. No, that only increased her sorrow and made it impossible to breathe. But she was still ready at a moment's notice to open a conduit and get them the fuck out.

Unfortunately, the plan was working.

What a relief it was to find the vaccines had actually worked. High five to Pablo and Lynn for being geniuses. Sagan needed more of that positive thinking to remember what the Shadow were made of. They could do this. One more step, only a little nudge further, and Tameka could get on her way to complete her mission.

Sagan tried to rein in the panic.

Deep breath. Let go of her hair. Unclench her jaw. Relax her shoulders.

"I'll show you how he disposed of the children of Gait."

Oh no.

Pehton.

Sagan walked out of the Seam to find the Lyrik staring with wide eyes. Korac came to her side about the same time. They both spoke in unison, "Don't believe her."

Then Xelan confessed to it from wherever he dipped off to for this disturbing conversation.

Pehton paled, and Sagan stroked her orange feathers, whispering, "Please. This is a ploy."

Xelan and Tameka said as much over the earpieces.

Finally, those hard red eyes turned to Sagan's and focused. The pain in Pehton's voice brought another tear to Sagan's eyes. "Xelan owes me an explanation, but I trust him. I trust you."

Korac knelt down to meet her face-to-face. "General Pehton, we will make them pay."

Scooped out and hollowed through, Pehton said, "Yes. We will."

Sagan tried to wipe her eyes before anyone saw the fresh tears, and cleared her throat of emotion in time for Tameka to hit Celindria, own it, and encounter a nuclear bomb.

"Mommy, why did you hit sissy?"

Sagan cupped a hand over her mouth.

Frantic, and finally showing it, Xelan rushed through his words on the mic. "Tameka. Tameka, is he okay? Are you okay? Tell Pax we're taking him home today. Can you hear me—"

There was more such as that, but Xelan didn't seem to react to the one keyword in Pax's question.

Sissy.

Korac's warm hands were suddenly chafing on Sagan's chilled arms. She let him as everything went silent on Tameka's end.

Pehton muttered, "Do we go in now?"

Sagan answered honestly, "I don't know. Not until Xelan says so. Do you know where he went?"

Korac squeezed her arm before pointing to a far alcove. Sagan took off to find Xelan and the other two followed.

She welcomed them because they'd need the best to storm Celindria's lab and free Pax. They found Xelan gripping his hair, staring at the floor with his eyes wider than Sagan had ever seen them. He looked like he'd been put through the wringer.

Xelan startled when he spotted them and relaxed a touch at their presence. "She's not answering."

"Give her a minute," Sagan encouraged.

Andrew and Kyle rushed around the corner with matching frowns. Andrew asked first, "When do we go in?"

Kyle asked second, "Is Tameka—"

"Pax." Tameka's voice sounded breathy. "Pax, come here. Let me look at you. Are you okay, sweetie—Why are you looking at her? You can come to mommy."

Xelan took a deep breath and let it out like he was working through a countdown in his head. Sagan recognized it from the meditation techniques he'd taught them. So long ago now.

They picked up Pax's response over the earpiece. "Sissy, can I go to mommy?"

Sagan took in the frowns all around her. No one looked happy about this. Xelan mostly looked pale.

They heard Tameka swallow through the mic before she said, "Celindria. Please."

Celindria sounded not nearly as smug as Sagan expected. "Of course you can, sweetheart. For a little while, okay? Mommy has to go soon."

The blood in Sagan's veins dropped to zero degrees. Kyle and Andrew exchanged a sharp glance. Pehton hissed. Korac's eyes narrowed.

Xelan whispered, "Stay strong, Fury. I'm here. Sagan and I are standing by."

Iuo, Tumu, and Lamassau ran around the corner next, finding what they were searching for. Xelan looked up to meet Tumu's gaze with anguish written in every line of his royal Icarean face.

"Peaches is tough," Tumu assured.

Iuo hissed on his S's, his accent coming stronger with his anger. "Say the word, and I can have a unit ready."

Sagan loved these people.

Tameka said, "Mommy's so glad you're okay. Is Sissy being nice to you?"

"Sissy's always nice to me."

Again, that wave of unnerved alarm rippled through the group.

Another swallow from Tameka's end and a brushing sound. "Here, daddy wants to talk to you."

"Hi, daddy!"

For the first time since Sagan could remember, Xelan's voice broke. "Hey, kiddo. Are you having a fun adventure?" A tear spilled from his lashes.

Sagan couldn't take it anymore and sobbed into her hand. Fuck hiding her tears. Korac kissed the top of her head, and she leaned almost all her weight on him, needing it.

Pax giggled like he found Xelan silly. "Daddy, you're not s'posed to be here. Sissy said Uncle Nock was s'posed to be here."

"Well, I'm here, son, and you're coming home with me."

{ENKI | CINDER'S SHRINE}

Kyle had smoked his last joint out of Andrew's stash an hour ago. He rifled through his multiplying pockets, searching for more, and found Legir's gift from earlier. When Kyle was still screening the Icarean army into Cinder's shrine, the leader of Yu had approached him.

"Do you miss your forge?" The telepathic alien with no mouth gently invaded Kyle's mind.

Aloud, Kyle chuffed. "Every fucking day."

Straight to the point, Legir spoke into his gray matter. "You've lost a lot, haven't you?"

The Progeny sighed rather than answered. Kyle wasn't looking for a pity party, but yes, his 'have' column was shrinking as of late. Everything was slipping away from him. Rayne, his forge baby, his noble station at the desert fortress on Earth, the security of their house on Reipon, his sisters—One to trauma and the other to a snot-nosed, thug turned world leader—

Fuck it. Kyle missed Silence. She was his, and that felt right for the brief time they'd spent together. It felt right. It also didn't hurt sticking it to Xelan and Nox in the process. Kyle missed the exciting way she posed on furniture all wrong and turned whatever clothes someone loaned her into a sexy and amusing practice in apocalyptic fashion. Her scent...

Legir stood there silently for a good minute. Kyle turned to see why and found the alien holding out a flower. The most bizarre flower he'd ever seen. "It's glowing."

Yu's leader bowed his circular head on top of that upside-down triangle he called a torso. Inside Kyle's head, he elaborated, "It's made of a special organic phosphorous similar to some of your kelp on Earth."

The blue light from the flower reminded Kyle of Rayne's eyes. So bright it almost hurt to look at it. "Are you giving it to me?"

"Yes. A moment will come, as they always do, where you'll need your calm. This will provide it better than the weak Earth shit you've been smoking."

Bones, Twenty-One, Iuo, and Andrew could make Kyle chuckle. But Legir here made him snort on a bark of laughter. Kyle took the flower. "Do... do I smoke it? Or eat it?"

Legir's eyes smiled for his mouthless face. "One lick should suffice but be careful. The Progeny physiology is complex. Your reaction to it is unpredictable."

Kyle flagged the man a salute. "Thanks for the warning, Chief. I'll save it for a special occasion."

Waiting for Pax to respond while Ross' life hung in the balance counted as a special occasion in need of more calm. With shaking hands, Kyle reached into his pocket and retrieved the flower. Everyone was staring at Xelan, leaving no prying eyes on Story Taker while he brought the glowing bloom to his mouth and licked it.

When Andrew was six, he asked for nail polish for Christmas, and his parents got him a bebe gun. Sagan secretly took cooking lessons from Tempest to impress Korac with one hell of a spread from all over the Vast Collective. Iuo, the Porn Baron, was a virgin. Lamassau's original occupation on the Tritan homeworld was as an author of children's books. Pehton burned every prisoner with a history of pedophilia in her first week as Executive Warden. Korac was afraid of Chihuahuas. Xelan never learned how to ride a bike. And Tumu was closed to Kyle entirely.

Story Taker didn't go looking for stories. He couldn't turn it off. All their lives he experienced in real time all at once. It reminded him of Andrew's view of the Probability Matrix, but more concrete and less fluid. The area of effect spread and spread—

Control. Kyle needed control, and fast before it affected someone in the allied armies with no tolerance for this level of an obtrusive invasion.

Out and out and out—

Focus. Breathe. Seek shelter somewhere safe from this storm—

Quet.

Remorse.

The loneliest existence.

Escape and Cascading Light.

Elden.

Happiness.

Confusion and hurt.

Pain.

Loss.

A baby girl.

Sleep.

"Kyle."

Cinder's shrine melted into the carousel of Silence's—no, Surra's—memory scape. Vast and full, it spun. Each scene was sprinkled with black fire. Standing upside-down on the ride in the most beautiful ceremonial dress was the Mother of all their existence. The layered necklaces covering her breasts and her skirt stayed fixed as if gravity obeyed her will. Even her unusual hair stayed in place. But of course it did. Everything about Silence was extraordinary.

"How did you reach me?"

How should Kyle explain this? He started with shoving his hands into two of a zillion pockets in his jumpsuit and wandered closer to the magical merry-go-round, displaying various windows into her life with each turn.

Silence kept her eyes on him with unveiled, sensual hunger strong enough to make Kyle's ears burn. The maker of their galaxy paid him a greater compliment than he'd ever assumed. And she apparently liked the jumpsuit. Win. The girls could dress him anytime.

Self-conscious, Kyle rubbed his neck. "So… I'm kinda in the middle of a trip, and I needed somewhere safe to hide until it goes away."

Damn. Silence's movie star smile always blew Kyle away. Her eyes even sparkled, and he felt rather proud of himself. Her husky voice did a number on him, too. "You seek me for sanctuary?"

"I seek you for comfort." The words spilled out of Kyle with no thought. He didn't want to waste time on pretensions. "I miss you."

Silence's lashes fluttered, and she looked at the carousel. Standing almost directly beneath her put him about a meter under her eyes. The images reflected on the steel in them. Softly, she confessed, "I wanted us."

Kyle held out his hand to her. "We can have us. There's no need to hide anymore. I know everything now, Silence." Sorta. The images stopped when she met him on Earth. He didn't know where she was in Enki or what she'd done since coming here, but he believed in her. "You're Shadow."

When the carousel turned between images, the breaks cast Silence in darkness. In one such pass, a glowing blue light pulsed under her skin. Frowning, Kyle asked, "What *is* that?"

Silence smiled, but not the thousand-watt grin Kyle loved. It was sad. It ladened her voice when she said, "So... not *everything*, then." To his surprise, she took his hand and, with a little hop, flipped onto the floor before him without a single hair out of place.

Gentle. Don't scare her away. Kyle lifted Silence's knuckles to his lips and kissed each one, assuring, "You can tell me anything."

She slipped her hand from his to unzip his jumpsuit. He wasn't about to argue, but... her features put a stop to any erotic thoughts. Instead, Silence pressed her hand over Kyle's chest between his heart and his throat. Over his nacre. She stared at her hand and said, "Tritans have a cruel sense of ownership. They aren't kind masters."

This was heading in an unexpected direction, and Kyle frowned as Silence went on.

"Rayne has it, too. They hate her as much as they hated me. They hate what they fear, as all things do." When Silence met Kyle's eyes, the full weight of a lifetime serving the Twelve Worlds in her gaze staggered him. "The frequency increases. Not long now. For me or for her. Soon, our stories will end."

No, no, no. No.

Kyle cupped both sides of Silence's face. "What?! Tell me. You don't mean—"

"It's why I went to sleep. It afforded me a few more months to find the means of freeing my children. I stayed long enough to bring Savis into a world which treated her as unkindly as it had treated me. And Elden..."

Panic and concern clogged Kyle's throat until he had to swallow it all to speak. "What can we do? For you and Rayne? Is there anyway?!"

A tear fell from Silence's ancient eyes and splashed into his hand where he still held her face. Only then did Kyle feel the moisture on his cheeks. She wiped it away and brushed his lip with her thumb until he tasted the salt.

With her voice in six pitches, she said, "Ishkur will save us. Tameka is the key."

Silence's memories on the merry-go-round dimmed.

This rung a little wrong in Kyle's ears. It was too close to what Celindria had said, and it bothered him enough to force a step back. Reevaluate. With a little suspicion in his voice, Kyle said, "Tell me I can trust you. Tell me you won't break my heart again."

The carousel spun slower, and the darkness lingered on her.

Silence's hand fell to her side slowly as Kyle moved out of her reach. Her little hiccup of a sob pulverized his heart, but he couldn't blindly trust anyone, especially her, again. Almost as if she understood, Silence answered with a force of honesty in her multi-octave voice which touched him. "I will break your heart one last time. To save my children, I would do anything. This cannot exclude causing you more pain. Forgive me, Kyle."

End of the ride.

Kyle blinked and saw Xelan standing in the alcove, waiting for a response from his son. Not even a second had passed since Kyle had licked the flower. But... the conversation with Silence was real—

A glance down at his exposed chest confirmed it. Kyle *really* talked to Silence, and she really told him the Tritans who created her—Quet and Remorse—stamped her and Rayne with an expiration date like they were a gallon of milk—

Andrew clutched Kyle's shoulder in a comforting gesture. At Kyle's distraught glance, the other man leaned in to say, "This almost has me in tears, too. Poor Pax."

Right. The here and now.

Work through this shit first.

Tell Xelan and Tameka about Rayne, Silence, and Ishkur.

Never lick that fucking flower again.

Attainable goals mattered in a time of recovery, and Kyle would find a way to salvage this.

{Enki | New Cinder}

"Well, I'm here, son, and you're coming home with me."

Tameka glowed. Truly radiated warmth as her chest swelled with pride and love for the father of her child. Even though Xelan was changing the plan, she *believed* he'd make improvising work. It was a comfort to contrast the icy concern for why Pax was wearing robes, which fit him perfectly. Helped her ignore the dread at the extra foot he'd grown since Celindria had snatched him despite his toddler speech. And maybe protect her from the fear welling in her at the sight of his small midnight blue wings.

Like a cherub.

And this little angel crushed Tameka's soul when he said, "I don't want to, daddy," into the spare earpiece she gave him.

The ache in her jaw from losing a molar couldn't compare to the ache in her heart. Tameka cradled her son's freckled face in her hands. "Why not, baby?"

"I *am* home."

Tameka knew Celindria gloated behind her, but she still couldn't fathom what was happening.

Xelan said over the earpiece, "Did uh... Sissy tell you that?"

Pax placed his not as little hands on Tameka's and shook his head in her gentle hold. "I'm always with Sissy. Every time."

Without turning from her son, Tameka asked, "Celindria?"

"Yes, child?"

Tameka popped her jaw to keep from cussing the other woman out in her son's presence. "Do you have anything to say for yourself?"

"I think I know." Andrew's voice trembled over the earpiece. "Oh, Elden, Tameka... I..." He took a steadying breath before continuing. "I don't know how to say this, but I think... Well, remember when I said someone new had touched Cascading Light?"

The rest of what Andrew or anyone else said turned to static in Tameka's ears as she gazed into her son's midnight eyes. Perfect replicas of his father's. Pax's sweet freckles which matched Tameka's own on that beautiful brown skin of his. The red coils which foamed from his head, so much longer now than when she last saw him.

Pax smiled, and Tameka's ears popped.

Permanent teeth had grown into his mouth over a matter of hours.

"—Tameka? Tameka, are you there?!" Xelan sounded near to action, but that wouldn't be necessary.

Tameka knew what she had to do. "I'm okay. Everything's okay, Xelan." To Pax, she said, "You were a good boy for Sissy, weren't you? You helped her bring Karter, Chris, and Para here. You told her where our house was so she could find you. And then you helped her bring mommy here, didn't you?"

All those teeth showed so cute and white in a grin taken straight from his daddy's playbook. Pax looked beyond Tameka to Celindria. "Hee. She figured it out. She always figures it out."

Tameka choked, let her hands fall, and hung her head. She didn't dare spare a look at the others in the cell. This grief was private. Between her and Xelan. His silence was heavy, but she understood. What could he say?

"I love you, mommy."

A strangled gasp broke into a sob straight from Tameka's heart. The lights brightened into harsh beacons and blew one by one. Scalding tears squeezed from her eyes. But don't let him see. Don't frighten him.

Tameka raised her face to the light of her life, went to her knees, and pulled Pax in for a hug with a kiss on his curls. "I love you, too, baby. Mommy has to go away for a bit, but I promise I'll come back."

Pax's heart beat against her chest as he said, "You always say that, and you never come back."

No fears. No doubts. "This time, nothing in the galaxy will keep me from you." Celindria stepped behind Pax, and Tameka let her see the promise in her eyes. "And no one will stop me."

The other woman reached out and gently tugged on Pax until he let go of Tameka. "Come along, short stuff. You woke too early from your rest."

Pax rubbed his eyes with his not so chubby fists. "I *am* sleepy. Can we play with Chris before I go to bed?"

Someone in the cell hissed, and Tameka fought the urge to look away. To erase the thought of Pax mistreating people under Celindria's guidance, but Tameka clenched her aching jaw and stared. She stared at the back of Celindria's head and imagined it missing. Stared between her shoulder blades and imagined a hole clear through her.

The ancient creature turned as if she'd sensed Tameka's thoughts and said, "None of that, girl."

Deep breath in. Exhale out. Not in front of Pax.

They walked into the room with Celindria saying, "Not right now. I'm entertaining our guests." She picked Pax up and laid him on the bed. "But later. I promise." She poked his nose and kissed his forehead. "Rest well, darling."

"G'night, Sissy."

Wait.

Wait...

Celindria closed the door behind her, and the second it latched, Tameka launched with an uppercut. With no time to waste, she punched the other woman in the gut. Once. Twice.

In the dim light of the darkened room, Celindria disappeared.

Ross cried out, and Jack yelled, "Behind you!"

Arms locked around Tameka and crushed her with obscene strength. She couldn't breathe—

With one terrifying crack, Tameka couldn't feel anything. Not her toes or fingertips. A strange wheezing followed—

It was Tameka, trying to breathe. Breathe dammit!

Against her ear, Celindria rubbed salt in the wound. "He never forgets that you leave him. In every Probability, he knows you fail him absolutely from his first breath. Multi-lives. That's what it means to be Imminent."

Tameka was *not* dying. Her hard tissue repair system already worked its magic on her broken back enough for Tameka to draw air. She rasped between breaths, "You... need me." She knew this for certain.

Celindria laughed against her. It was horrifying and beautiful all at once. "You are the only way to find Ishkur, not that you ever have. But we've all inherited our maker's infinite capacity for trying. We never stop."

"Say the word, Tameka." Xelan's voice stole a gasp from her at its pure reassurance from all the trauma.

Healed and revitalized with gritted teeth and clenched fists, Tameka vowed, "I'll never help you."

"Disposal then. I'll relay your farewells to Pax. *My* son."

{ENKI | GAIT}

Matt laid his last explosive charge and narrowed his gaze at the horizon. His zone could use at least two hundred more. Where was the refill he'd asked for? And the rations? It wasn't like the shrine team to take this long, but maybe they partied too hard and needed a food coma. He could use one himself.

With a stretch, Matt stared out at the ocean in the sky. It grew larger as they flew closer. They were definitely moving faster. Why hadn't their team informed them yet?

On cue, Puk came over the line. "I've been done for an hour. I want to request a transfer to help with your zone, but they're not responding to me."

Yup. Sounded about right. "You called it."

"I did. You owe me three rounds at the driving range."

Matt grinned and shook his head, incredulous. "I'm still reeling over your deep love of golf."

Puk's voice hinted at indignation. "It's a game of finesse. That's not exactly a skill I get to flaunt a lot, seeing as people only hire drones for muscle or porn." He was understandably sensitive about it.

Or Matt assumed it was understandable. He wasn't sure of his own grasp on sensitivity. In his assumption of the best friend role, Matt said, "Preach, man."

After a pause, Puk corrected, "But you know I don't mind me some porn."

Of course not. He'd starred in four of Iuo's films in the short month they'd spent at the Reipon Villa before coming here.

To die.

"Do you think she'll save us in time?" There was no fear or actual concern in the drone's voice. Only mild finality.

Lucy. Incredible, insatiable Lucy. Not only would she save them in time, she'd amass some army at her back, change into the sexiest battle gear, and turn up drenched in the blood of their enemies in the nick of time. Perfection.

"Yeah. I *know* she will."

In a soft voice, Puk asked, "How many people did Imminent kill up there? Fourteen? Twenty?"

Matt counted on his fingers before saying, "If you count the secret Tantamount team more like forty or sixty."

Again, that righteous fire burned in the other man's words. "And that doesn't even include the ten thousand on the surface of this hemisphere." Puk gave a disdainful snort. "They really think they'll get by with this."

In some ways, the redhead understood justice or right from wrong. Razor was very much an example of Matt on the wrong course. Both men enjoyed wrenching death from a life. The only trouble with the Pain Curator was his inability to discriminate a worthy life from a worthless one. All the Justices in the Cult of Night had deserved their ends. Razor deserved his. But those people who'd worked to save the Tritans' home only wanted to help. A worthy cause, and Remorse murdered them with their prize for helping.

Matt's blood quickened at the thought of crushing that bastard's skull. "On a scale of 'Rayne killing Nox' to 'Sagan bisecting Enki,' how excited are you to make sure they won't get by with this?"

Without hesitation, Puk said, "Easy. I'm as excited as Tameka when Xelan resurrected."

That's pretty excited. "That's what I wanna hear—"

Among the rubble surrounding Matt, several granules of gravel rose about hip-height and lingered in the air. He glanced around to find it was happening everywhere. As far as he could see, the tiny rocks hovered—

Faster than they lifted, they fell back to the ground.

Weird.

Puk's frown was in his voice. "Hey, man. I'm seeing some weird shit."

That couldn't be good. "Over here, too—"

The gravel rose again, slowly. Almost straining. This time, Matt's stomach kinda followed. The sensation was foreign and concerning—

When they fell, his stomach flopped like taking a hill too fast in a car.

"The inertia dampeners are wearing off," Puk warned over the mic.

It didn't explain why the rocks were somersaulting—

Gravity.

The artificial gravity they'd installed required constant monitoring, and with the team all dead, well...

A little shaky, Puk said, "Remind me again why we wanted to do this job."

Easy. Matt recited the answer on his way to the nearest building with an intact ceiling. "Because as long as Gait hurdles toward Enki's hull, Rayne stands a chance. If the Dyson's Sphere is destroyed first, she may not have to die like all those zealots said she would."

The rocks hovered longer with each interval, and Matt's stomach felt it.

Puk's labored breathing over the line indicated he was also seeking shelter. "So how did my ass end up on the planet laying explosive charges?"

A derelict space scraper would suffice as shelter from floating away. For now. Crouched in a corner, Matt said, "Because you and your cousin's entire demo team are experts in diffusing construction charges, and if we'd let any other team win the bid, then the Shadow would lose one more avenue of hope for Rayne."

"So I'm one noble motherfucker. That's what you're saying? Xelan and Tameka will erect monuments in our honor?" Puk's way of asking obvious questions never failed to amuse Matt.

Clinging to the surface of a spinning rock, Matt said, "Something like that."

"Cool. I'd look fabulous in bronze."

THIRTEEN

MIRACLES AMONG PREDATORS ARE READILY DEVOURED

{CINDER | 2,000,000 YEARS AGO}

AT ANOTHER CONQUEST CELEBRATION ON CINDER, UMBRA DRESSED HIS HAIR IN SUCH A WAY TO DISPLAY HIS UGLY, SCARRED FACE. The reason escaped Remorse. After all, Nox as a mere child had scarred his father with that hideous mug. Then again, most of what Elden's Coalition lieutenants such as Umbra found pride in befuddled Primary Rem.

Now. The woman on Umbra's right, Remorse understood.

Savis carried herself with a poise befitting a daughter of Elden. Despite her obvious weakness, her chin was high and her eyes shone with clarity. Savis wore the same severe expression meant only to invoke Umbra's dismay. Never happy in his presence. The King of Cinder often wept at their incompatibility. Privately, of course.

But when one lurked in the shadows of this Spire, they could witness everything meant for an audience of one. Remorse had learned so much from spying here. Like Amolot spent hours on her knees praying to Elden for Umbra's demise. Savis met with rebels in secret. And Nox was more father to Xelan than Umbra could ever claim.

This was not a home.

Disguised as a tall Thailean Mystic, Remorse gleaned more secrets from this festival. Karter, the Valkyrie with the rainbow hair, walked by, and he admired her carriage. Para followed Karter, with the most endearing smile—

Xelan.

The half-Icarean toddler rushed by with an emphatic giggle and squealed, "No, Nock!" He kept looking back for his older brother, presumably in chase.

Primary Rem plucked him from the crowd so fast it left the boy—*Remorse's son*—blinking in his face.

After a hiccup, Xelan said, "Hi!" Then he grinned so big it showed off his missing tooth.

Remorse's heart melted. "Hello, *son*."

"Give him to me."

The ice in Savis' voice instantly chilled Remorse. A threat lay beneath it. Although quite ill for some time now, Remorse knew her to be a pragmatic woman. She was quite capable of murder, especially if she felt her son was threatened.

Primary Rem turned with deliberate slowness. Xelan bubbled at him, unaware of the strife between his parents. Nox appeared behind his mother and stared harder to see under the Thailean robe's hood.

Savis' eyes were mystical. Iridescent and shining. They complimented her delicate bone structure and the waves in her hair, but it was the shrewdness in her eyes which had attracted Remorse to her. It's why he chose her to bear this important merger of their races, and something in those intelligent eyes glinted with knowledge of the truth.

Savis *knew*.

"*My* son, sir." Savis held out her arms.

Xelan reached for her.

Remorse held on. He liked the warmth and play emanating from his son. The sweetness in him, so foreign now to the rest of Primary Rem's existence. He and Vi parented many sons, but none like him. "I think I may keep him."

Without taking those shimmering eyes off Remorse, Savis instructed, "Nox, find your father and sound the alarm. Tell them a Tritan invaded—"

"No. That will *not* be necessary." A Primary could level a battlefield with a single blow. He wasn't concerned for his life, but more for Imminent's future use for the Icari until they were no longer required.

Xelan giggled for his mother as Remorse handed him to her.

Nox was a child, but his eyes narrowed with suspicion as he gazed between the two adults. Perhaps he'd inherited more of his mother's intelligence than Remorse had acknowledged in prior interactions.

With her two boys in tow, Savis swept away without another word.

Or so she thought. "You will keep my secret then?" Why Remorse called to her like he had any right escaped him. As a scientist, his impregnating her was clinical and necessary, and Remorse could deceive the others all day why he chose her, the woman so similar to his long gone Vi. Right down to her secret revolution against her unioned partner.

No. Remorse knew exactly why he called after Savis. One last look. A final moment to memorize every feature of her face which fate had denied him of Vi.

Savis stopped with Xelan in her arms and Nox ready at her side. A heavy pause filled the space between them. One she broke with a flat tone. "You understand little of why a woman tolerates the presence of a man. You give us children, and we rear them in love while you plan their futures in war and breeding. Consider your cankerous influence on the Icari? What love will they know with my father gone, and all of them left cowing to the likes of Umbra?"

Remorse needed Silence's army, and Umbra was a necessary evil. One he despised.

The proud daughter of Elden continued. "No. I keep your secret within my arms." Xelan giggled like Savis had tickled him. "Never force me to tolerate your presence again or risk learning a hard truth: all women would rather die than endure more of your cancer."

How did Savis...

Those were Vi's last words to him.

Remorse winced beneath his hood and a tear squeezed from his voids.

Without a backward glance, denying him a final glimpse of her beauty, Silence's daughter continued down the hall. "Come, my sons. Let us retire and speak of the future Elden had intended. A future of love and a Cinder free of Li."

{ENKI | NEW CINDER | NOW}

Remorse punched the cave wall with a guttural roar, sending a concussive shockwave through the mountainside and creating an entirely new splinter of tunnels.

Why?! Why was he plagued with this endless stream of frustration?! Every single ordeal in his life centered around a *fucking* woman. And he tried. Oh, did he try. Primary Rem respected their intelligence and impressive capabilities, but for some reason reason which escaped him, engaging with these women always went horribly wrong.

This was the last time.

Celindria could subdue Remorse inside Karter's—another *fucking* woman—formidable, yet inadequate body compared to his own, but even the First Progeny was no match for a Primary. It was beyond time for Remorse to demonstrate how far off she'd underestimated him.

To think. There was a time when he considered loving Celindria.

Hah!

Nothing about her knew of love or its virtues. No, that lonely hollowed-out facsimile of a person couldn't grasp it, even with her expansive imagination. Remorse pitied Nox for gaining the focus of her attentions, and Rayne for ever pitting herself as a rival.

Now they all spun around this pool of lava, funneling to the end.

Enki.

This was someone's doing, and Remorse no longer attributed it solely to Project Surra. This stank of...

Aegis.

Remorse stopped charging for Celindria's lab and peered down the tunnel on his left. Black rock lined the cave and glowing water lit the way. At this junction, the tunnel on the right led to her lab. After he used Aegis blood from his precious store to travel here, should he risk a detour? It would catch her unawares.

One benefited from the element of surprise when killing someone like Celindria, and who didn't like a grand entrance?

Vi would approve. *"Cripple your enemy with their own arrogance."*

Remorse took the tunnel on the left.

{ENKI | NEW CINDER}

Chris couldn't take much more. Lead-lined his skull, too heavy to lift it. Sand swallowed his limbs to the knees and elbows, too deep to raise them. Tears poured endlessly from his eyes, too salty to blink them.

Let Chris' heart finish breaking.

Let him die.

Never—*never*—would he forget the forgiveness in Ross' eyes as he—

When he almost—

Chris' hands...the warmth from Ross' thighs would burn him into Eternity and branded him with an irreversible sin.

Jack...how could Chris begin...

Then surviving all that to witness the rupturing of Tameka's heart, with the love for her son bleeding from the fissure like magnesium tears, unable to help her at all. To sweep Pax up and escape with them. All of them together.

Chris was ready to die.

Now, Celindria forced him to watch over the very people she forced him to betray, holding guns on them while she shackled their leader in nacre cuffs.

Jack called out, "Don't worry, Fury. We'll get you back."

Infected, infested, and invaded, Chris groaned as Celindria raised his arm and aimed the gun right in Jack's face.

"Eventually, I suppose you'll fade." Her words to him inside his mind brought no comfort. "As your will disintegrates, I will become you. I thought you'd endure longer than this, but..." She shrugged. "Better you accept your fate sooner rather than later."

Was this a gift? An end to this existence? Or would the perpetual awareness remain?

With little strength left in him, Chris muttered, "I'll live long enough... to see you finished."

The slight smile on Celindria's face was approving, and Chris could give a shit for her approval.

In reality, her actual body placed a warm kiss on his cheek. "Good guard dog. Keep them in line while I'm gone. I'll give you a treat when I return."

Someone else—Bones, maybe—gagged.

Oh, did Chris feel that.

In his real peripheral vision, Celindria brought Tameka before the cage. "Any rousing last words for your troops, *child*?"

A shudder overtook him. Chris *hated* the way she infantilized the brave woman leading this rescue mission, who proved herself more than a match when Tameka said, "Don't forget Chris. Leave Pax to me."

Did Celindria clench her jaw at that?

Chris was surprised his throat could even form a chuckle, but there it was.

"Silence, toy. Or pay the price you abhor the most."

Why was Celindria such a bitch?

Her actual body left with Tameka. Unfortunately, as much faith as Chris placed in the young galactic leader, Celindria could reduce her to a puddle even without nacre cuffs. Chris cheered Tameka on so hard when she uppercut the bitch, but Elden dammit, he knew how it would end before it started.

The First Progeny was absurdly powerful and swift. No, Chris supposed it'd take an Aegis or a god to bring her down. The combined might of the Progeny. Something—

"Don't worry, Chris. We'll get you out."

Jack's reassurances tugged on Chris' heart strings. His head lightened a touch, and he lifted it from the ground.

Inside his mind, Celindria glared at him, and Chris spent the last of his strength to pull his lips into a knowing smirk.

They would win.

"Thanks, kid."

The words came from Chris' actual mouth.

{CINDER | 7,000,000 YEARS AGO}

"Elden, would you like to hold your daughter?"

Familiar with the mess of birth, Silence cherished her time holding Savis before the nurses cleaned her. Elden had stayed with Silence the entire delivery and never balked once, as she expected of this great man. He held his arms in a cradle to hold their first child, and when he smiled, she knew Savis was the first of many children.

Gently, Elden swayed with her, gazing down with the adoration of a man who yet knew how much raising a daughter could change a father. The sweetest expression.

The nurses helped Silence clean and dress herself while he held her. It was so important to hold them.

"Will she always be this soft?"

Eternity, his questions were so endearing. It made Silence stare at her own hands. Were they as soft as in the beginning—

Azure light pulse under her skin, and she swallowed. The frequency... It had increased recently—

"Silence, my silence. Looking at you while holding her, I find you more radiant than the day you first claimed Cinder."

Why were these tears so hot?

"Shh." Elden came to stand beside her and bent to kiss her temple. "We live this glorious day, together—"

"Elden?" Umbra deigned to stand in the doorway of Silence's chambers. She must have glared because he quickly straightened. "Forgive me, Silence, but the Coalition demanded an emergency forum at the audience house." His eyes clung to Elden, still holding Savis.

Her lover and unioned mate handed over their daughter to the nearest nurse. On his way over to Silence, Elden said, "Forgive me. This regards the most recent quest pods, and the results they delivered this morning. We may yet find the foreigners. Tonight, we feast."

Elden leaned down to kiss Silence. Before he could break it, she gripped a handful of his hair at his nape and pressed him into a deeper embrace. Even as they parted, Silence's fingers lingered in the blending of the colors in his hair. Dual strands. So unusual for an Icarus.

With a broad grin, Elden left. His Silence retrieved their daughter from the nurses and sung to her of their beautiful world. Until...

Fire burned in Silence's sight. Black and cold. Misery stretched far in her vision. No one particular instance clarified their future for her, only the whisper of their names. Savis, Umbra, Elden, Nox, Xelan, and—

It starts with *him* and ends with *her*.

When Silence returned to herself, Savis was wailing in her arms, twisted in the blanket. Her nurses begged Silence to handover the infant before she accidentally strangled herself. Instead, the mother straightened Savis' swaddled blanket and held her closer. "No. Not my child. They can't have another one of my children—"

Azure pulsed under Silence's skin.

The Exalted and Ishkur were her last hope. She shielded herself from the truth, closing her eyes. All the peoples in the galaxy were ablaze in black flames. With every blink, the Probability Matrix showed Silence only the worst futures.

Where no one would know happiness.

{ENKI | OPAL MEZZANINE | NOW}

"Mother, why do you cry?"

Silence blinked away the tears, aware of the here and now. Lucas stared at her with expectation on his face, waiting for his answer. Smith smiled kindly at her without words or curious prodding.

These boys were her family.

With a dry swallow, Silence said, "Do you remember the day I knew it was over?" Chills pricked her skin, but she ignored this body seeking comfort. This heart seeking joy. Both sought Kyle and Elden and the life she'd never attained. That happiness Cascading Light had promised her…

Lucas opened his arms to Silence.

Why did this hurt so much?

Silence fell into them, and Lucas squeezed with a fraction of his strength but enough to wring tears from her. Smith's arms pulled them both into his embrace, and she held on with her life in the balance.

"Not long now," Silence muffled against them.

Lucas shook his head in her shoulder. "It won't come to that."

"We won't let it." Smith still sounded as if he were smiling, but sadly.

The golden-eyed Icarus confessed, "I woke you."

Silence pulled back enough to search Lucas' eyes for the truth.

His subsequent nods confirmed it. "I repaired the stasis mechanism and awakened you. This Probability's Shadow showed potential in their capabilities, which might bring you to Ishkur. Forgive me for concealing it from you during your forgetting. I knew you'd remember and hate anyone who forced you to do so."

Azure light pulsed under Silence's skin, echoing throughout the colored lights of the room. Echoing in Rayne.

Silence said, "Thank you, old friend. After my encounter with Story Taker, we can trust they'll find it now."

They separated, and Silence lifted the pendant to stare into Rayne's blood. The mezzanine swirled in pink and purple.

Smith returned to monitoring the girl's journey in the projection with respect in his smile for her.

Lucas peered at the tiny Pretiosum Cruor on the chain. "Will it afford you more time?"

"We cannot know everything for certain." Silence's voice no longer trembled with the emotions she'd confined for the sake of her sanity. Such a long existence. Such a hard one. "I only wish to taste her extravagant optimism once more." The last time Silence drank Rayne's blood, it broadened the frequency of the pulses by one additional week, and it tasted like stardust.

Smith chuckled. "Optimism. There's more than enough to go around."

Lucas grinned. "Rayne didn't come by it on her own, Mother. All the wonderful people in her life keep her bolstered. Something I still struggle to convince you of to this day."

His words entered Silence as a truth she had long since denied. Hard to trust. "When you give birth to an entire galaxy with your neck under a boot, you return to me and we can discuss 'trust issues.'"

Lucas sighed, losing a long-fought argument. "Trust the Shadow. Trust Rayne."

This insistence rang of more than concern for Silence's mental well-being. She cocked her head to the side and accused, "Are you certain this isn't your bid to reunite with a certain intention-reader? He was sized quite nicely."

Lucas gaped like a fish, gasping for air, and choked on her assumptions.

Smith shook his head incredulously and pat the other man on the back.

Bristled by Lucas' incessant bid for an alliance with Rayne, Silence asked an obvious question with an obvious answer. "Why did you bring Andrew to Cascading Light?"

Her companion looked away from her and stared down into the projection of Rayne's flight across Enki. Softly, Lucas said, "So much promise and such vision. He sees into lives in ways we cannot. I thought it was a perfect marriage of his talents and his potential."

Silence unfurled her wings and stretched one pinion until it touched a particle of floating water. Disturbed, the bubble burst. As one did. "I apologize for pricking you, Lucas. It was unkind." She held her hand out to him.

He took it and cupped his face with it, drawing something from the contact. All beings reacted to her thus. "All is forgiven."

"Rayne's arriving." Smith grinned down at the projection with eager anticipation. "I haven't been this excited since—" He shot a sheepish glance at Silence. "Well, since her fight with Nox, but before that it was millennia."

In a tone laced with mock-pity, Silence asked, "Was your life so empty?"

"Oh, yes. These are the best days of my existence, and I can't wish for better company."

An exchange took place between Lucas and Smith which spoke of their mutual esteem for the Shadow and their time shared with them.

Silence felt it deep in her marrow. An appreciation and allegiance worth dying for. But until it came to that, Silence would watch the girl with two nacres and an azure pulse uncover the secret which would ignite the greatest pyre this galaxy would ever witness.

And it would be the last.

FOURTEEN

ON AND ON, THE NIGHTMARE STRETCHED INTO THE HORIZON

{Enki | Ocean Landing}

Elden, Rayne had so much explaining ahead of her, but she couldn't wait to tell Xelan all about it. With her sitting upside-down in a chair, him rolling his eyes and gently chiding for her to sit properly, and them both knowing that would never happen. His approving grin. Her legs dangling over the back of the seat. Hair draped everywhere. Then Tameka would come in with Pax, and Rayne could show him the right way to drive his dad crazy. Meanwhile Nox—

Nox.

Inside her head, Rayne looked up at her predecessor. There was this carriage about Nox lately. Once upon a few years ago, he only ever stood in a fighting stance, on guard and ready to strike first. A posture of 'the frightened,' but one capable of so much destruction. Now, he folded those arms of his—as wide as the diameter of her waist—like he wasn't sure what to do with them, but still ready to defend himself if trouble should find him.

Rayne pitied whatever the next trouble was because Nox fought like the savage she remembered from the battlefield. Quick for such a behemoth, he enjoyed using his hands to rip flesh apart. A death machine and damned fierce about it—

"You're staring. And smiling."

Caught in her examination of him, Rayne looked forward and tried to force her metaphysical body not to flush with embarrassment. "I . . . uh . . . Look, we're close to the last conduit before the big empty space. Do you think there's more ocean? I hope not." Nervous chatter.

Mercifully, Nox let her off the hook. "If it is, I hope there are more sea creatures. I could use the exercise. Or maybe an army to demolish on my own?"

Rayne wasn't sure how to feel about all this. Her ex-enemy voiced her exact longing. One army wasn't enough. Despite being a good warm-up fight, she still withheld a few surprises, and Rayne couldn't wait to see the look on Nox's face when he realized why she didn't need saving. It was enough to make her smile with mischief.

"You wear the same expression on your face that Xelan wore when he'd completed some new invention he wanted us to test."

Nox couldn't know how much his words meant to Rayne. "Really?!"

"I live in fear of that face." He shot her a wry smirk. It said he knew exactly the worth of his sentiments, but also that he awaited whatever mischief she intended to cause.

Trusting Nox came easily after the last two years together, but how could Rayne explain this to Xelan and the rest in a way they'd accept him? Because that's what Rayne wanted, despite fearing their judgment or disappointment.

"Your brain and your heart are not always in concert." These words from Korac's Verse often replayed in her head lately. About her violence. About her confinement. About her shadow.

"'An Icarus thinks deep on the eve of war, but only the brave think on their future with no heed for mortal concerns. Those are prisons for the obvious.'" Nox brought Rayne once more to the present.

She *was* thinking of the future to avoid thinking of her fate. "That's beautiful. Is it from a Verse?"

Nox unfolded his arms to rake fingers through his hair in a recurring gesture Rayne recently noticed. "Uncle Vinco's. I want to speak with... with my grandmother of the wars the Icari fought. The ones he often referred to but which we were never taught in our histories. The wars my mother never knew."

Rayne wet her lips before asking, "How—how would you like me to tell everyone about us—I mean, you?" A voice inside her head told her to keep her eyes forward. Cowardice. Ignoring the impulse, she turned and looked up at Nox.

He turned and looked down at her. His eyes widened a touch. She'd surprised him with her question. Emotion thickened Nox's deep voice as he asked, "You wish to?"

Resolute, Rayne gave a definitive nod. "Yes." In saying so, she agreed to fight her family for his place in this world, in her mind, and in her shadow. She bit her lip.

Nox's stare fell to her mouth and quickly raised to Rayne's eyes. He cleared his throat before saying, "Tell them however makes you the most comfortable, but we both know they will argue to remove me."

Rayne frowned at him. "I'm not so sure anymore. Do you remember how Sagan said she forgave you? And the way Korac talks... Xelan read your Verse and was receptive of it. I trust them."

"I defer to you on this matter, your majesty." Nox dipped his chin in a bow, folded his arms, and returned to his vigilance outside this space.

Staring at him, Rayne wasn't entirely convinced of this quiet reservation—

His black eyes... they shimmered.

"Nox, are you—"

Calibrated.

Optimized.

Stabilizing...

Unable to stabilize.

Warning: Fifty-six hours and forty minutes until maximum destabilization.

"The final conduit." The giant in her mind pointed ahead.

Rayne focused on the coup at hand and stopped. It was the same energy barrier as all the other conduits, but this one gave none of its secrets away. All dark. "What do you think is on the other side?"

"Abresson."

Rayne, uh...tried not to think too hard about how much she savored the growl in Nox's voice. "Right. Let's kill us a Tritan." Inside her head, she punched her palm. Outside of her conscience, Rayne stepped across the threshold.

It was *not* another ocean.

A blanket of darkness threatened to suffocate Rayne, the surface beneath her feet clanged of metal, and heat suffused the air. The uncomfortable aroma of living bodies accompanied the stifling warmth.

But none of this was why Rayne stopped breathing.

Heartbeats.

Paralyzed by the sound, she forgot how to breathe. Rayne fell forward until she found something to support her—a metal rail.

Inside her mind, Nox gripped her biceps and forced her to look at him. "Rayne—"

Light, blinding and intrusive, exposed a simulated sky above and black rock below. Rayne couldn't focus on it while also relearning how to breathe. For this, she stared into Nox's grave eyes. He held her steady, and she still couldn't speak to explain. To tell him of the danger. Of—

She finally looked out.

Rayne and her shadow stood on a scaffolded platform, one of several overlooking the expanse below. On and on, the volcanic rock stretched to an endless horizon covered with people.

Not just any people.

A girl stood with pale skin, long black hair tied in a braid, and blue eyes. She wore armor of black banding over her entire body except her exposed back. Face forward, and hands relaxed at her sides.

A man stood beside her with medium gray skin, long black hair with half of it pulled up in a high knot and the other flowing down his back, and black eyes. Black leather pants, no shirt, and war paint covered his tremendous body. He stood at attention.

"Us," Rayne breathed. "A continent of us."

"Surviving our steward is impressive, but I'm afraid this is where you meet your end. Imminent can't have you warning the Vast Collective of their new Overseers."

{ENKI | DEPOSITORY}

The smug intonation of Abresson's voice broke through Nox's initial shock and apparently through Rayne's because she asked, "Are they all like us?! Are they all Weapons?" With her voice breaking, she shouted at him, where he stood below with the most deadly army.

Abresson groaned and rolled his voids. "Contain your martyrdom, girl. They're not real people. We programmed them only to obey orders without sentience. They *are* Weapons. You and Nox were merely stepping stones to our finest achievement."

"Our." "We." Nox growled at the hubris. As if this toddler of a Tritan ever touched the technology or architecture that went into an endeavor of this magnitude. A true military genius devised this.

Celindria.

"She'll flay you for taking credit for her work." Nox's words came out of Rayne's mouth.

She shot him a wide-eyed glance, but returned her focus to Abresson. They'd deliberate on that later.

"Oh, she would, but I can claim some credit. After all, it was my idea to use your likeness." Abresson reached out and brushed the cheek of one Rayne replica, gazing into her empty, unblinking eyes. There was something wrong with them. "My favorite contribution." He dropped his hand and looked back at the authentic Rayne. "Your guardian can claim some credit as well. The Traitor Prince designed the prototype." He pointed at her. "The one in you."

Nox muttered so it wouldn't release from Rayne's mouth, "Even if he speaks truth, you know it isn't in my brother to harm you."

Without taking her eyes off Abresson, Rayne said, "I know." Her voice was soft, consumed with some contemplation.

"Tell me." It usually took some coaxing to draw out her concerns.

Rayne turned the full weight of her gaze on him, and Nox knew what was wrong with the copies. Her genuine eyes were the color of lightning in a velvet night sky, bright and electric. The artificial ones were dull and lifeless. He'd wager they couldn't transform into Atramentous at all. Abresson lacked the imagination to think of that.

While staring into Nox's eyes, Rayne asked outside of her mind, "Abresson, how many more continents in Enki are like this? Depositories?"

Nox and Rayne didn't need to look at him to hear the smug smirk on his face. "All but one."

A tear rolled down Rayne's cheek.

This was it. This would be the reason.

"Rayne." With his knuckle, Nox brushed the tear from her chin and the next one and the next.

She swallowed her decision, her responsibility—what she chose to take on herself. This martyr he loved. He loved her more presently.

Understanding, Nox nodded, and Rayne nodded with him. They would see this through. With hard swipes, she cleaned her face of tears and straightened her shoulders. That fire was back in her eyes, and she shifted into Atramentous without warning.

Rayne opened her wings, gripped the rail, and jumped off the scaffold before Abresson could see her move. She slammed into him with a strangled cry as Nox split from her in time to catch the Tritan's wrist, stopping his fist from freezing her in retaliation.

Abresson screamed in terror and frustration.

Rayne chewed into his neck with her fangs, while Nox broke the arm he held down—

The air shifted right before a blow sent Nox flying into the scaffolding hard enough to bring it down on top of him. Another Nox had delivered that blow. Abresson had activated the army. While Nox shifted his shadow form through the debris, Rayne cried out in pain.

No. No!

Beams and slabs kept Nox from her—

"Bitch, forget destroying Enki." Abresson's voice came from the opposite platform. He'd shifted from below, where Rayne last screamed. "You'll die in this pit. Fuck Remorse's orders. Good luck seeing daylight again."

Nox threw an entire concrete pad off him to get to her.

The army swarmed Rayne. He ran, almost as fast as she, to her side in time for her blinding light to dissipate his form. The other Rayne's and Nox's responded by cowering, but made no pained sounds while their eyeballs melted in their sockets. It made sense the artificial Weapons couldn't produce the magnesium field. It was Rayne's Progeny gift. Not her nacre's, and certainly none of the fakes had inherited a Gargantuan Primary nacre.

So Rayne still reigned.

Calibrated.

Optimized.

Stabilizing...

Unable to stabilize.

Warning: Fifty-four hours and fourteen minutes until maximum destabilization.

Once his shadow form reconstituted, Nox took up at her side. Rayne bled from many places, but the wounds had already healed as he checked her over. Several dozen kilometers away, a distance safe from her field, more ran toward them, slower than even Nox moved. Still quick enough to hurt—

Rayne nudged him, and he looked down at her. She was grinning with black blood staining her lips. Nox had to contain his reverence. Presumably without seeing his admiration on his face, Rayne said, "Remember when I told you I didn't need saving?"

"Yes."

A hint of mischief graced that grin as Rayne reached a hand over her nacre and pushed in through her sternum. She bit her lip to keep from screaming and scrunched her face in agony, but persisted all the while. Eventually, she touched the amber core and... and...

Pulled.

Rayne pulled at something from her nacre—

No...

Nox felt his eyes widen completely. Both brows went up with them.

This crazy, gorgeous, lethal woman retrieved the grip from Night Killer, her staff from their Volcano Day battle. With it withdrawn from her body, the wounds healed, and Rayne beamed at the weapon. The longer she stared at it, the more of it she constructed, like her clothes, until that Xelan-named staff finished forming. As long as her body, sharp at both ends, and made of nacre glass, it was a magnificent weapon. The swirled, ornate grip was equally sharp, and when unlinked, acted as gold-bladed batons.

"Never leave home without it." Rayne kissed the weapon and grinned once more up at Nox while an army of them descended.

He refrained from professing his respect and admiration for her, and instead pressed his fist to his chest and bowed to his ruler. "Most impressive, your majesty."

She twirled Night Killer and faced the army, now minutes away. "We can't let Abresson get far, and we can't leave these people to exist like this."

No. Always half alive and poised to kill was an unpleasant fate all too familiar to Nox. "Agreed."

Rayne swallowed and met his eyes full-on. She searched for something in them. Wetting her lips, she asked, "You understand? None of them can make it through this."

"To the end, I will follow my King."

Closer.

Closer.

One authentic Nox and one authentic Rayne versus twelve million deficient copies.

There was nowhere else he'd rather be.

FIFTEEN

WALK THE FINE LINE BETWEEN JUSTICE AND VENGEANCE

{ENKI | MEDICAL BAY}

BETHANY WAS HAPPY SHE DIDN'T NEED TO EAT QAS AND HIS TRITAN FRIENDS. Her ability brought the two groups together and let her keep the precious little of herself she'd gained during walks with Korac.

How was he doing with his internalized trauma and high expectations of self, leading an army once more under Xelan's leadership?

Was Ross okay with Rayne's brother, the boy she finally noticed, on a mission together?

Would Kyle's broken heart mend enough for him to find peace amongst his friends and put the self medication to rest?

Sat alone in a neighboring operating theater, Bethany let her thoughts wander onto the people in her life who begged her to find another Bethany, long gone. Not everyone knew that girl, and she found herself drawn to their company.

Like Caedes. The gravelly Icarus didn't force words from Bethany. He hadn't said two syllables to her the entire time they'd lived in the Villa on Reipon, and she liked the way he looked at Pehton.

Miy. On two occasions, the Lyrik with black feathers and orange streaks sat beside Bethany, opened a case, and applied makeup on her eyes, touching her only with brushes. It made the Progeny girl feel grownup. She'd been too young to wear makeup when... when...

Cut. Burn. Scratch. Hurt. Break.

Bethany pulled her knees into the chair and hugged them, staring off to the side and trying not to think. She didn't see or hear anyone walk in, so Chief Lynn startled her when she said, "You did good. Your brother and sister will be proud. Korac and Xelan, too."

After jumping back into her skin, Bethany raised her head and met the well-intentioned woman's eyes. Bethany gave a nod.

In the doorway, Chief Lynn folded her arms, leaned, and sighed. "This was a rough one. I believe the Shadow can pull anything off, and I wish you'd been there to see most of it. But this one... I can't imagine what could possibly complicate matters worse—"

As if summoned, Twenty-One appeared in the door frame beyond Chief Lynn with wide eyes and a finger pointing back toward the medical bay. "Chief, it's Triss. Pablo says he needs you. The baby's coming."

Bethany bolted out of her seat, anxiety driving her limbs.

Chief Lynn gestured for the girl to follow. "C'mon, we'll need your help."

Help? How could Bethany help bring another being into this world? She followed anyway, curious about meeting someone who never knew pain in their life. The baby would be Korac's niece and adopted daughter—

Was there a chart keeping up with all these relationships somewhere?

Bethany followed Chief Lynn back into the medical bay where Qas and Pablo surrounded the tank housing Triss' unconscious body. Bethany liked the way the woman's outside matched her insides now, despite how much Triss' appearance seemed to trouble the doctors. This was how she'd always looked to Bethany.

Monstrous.

"Okay, Bethany, can you please wait by the intravenous cylinder—Yes, there, please."

Dr. Suarez always spoke so gently to her. Bethany could never eat him. With that decision made, she stood, poised with a bag of Aegis blood, ready to administer it at his notice.

Qas nodded at a drawer built into the big bank of terminals. "Lynn, the top drawer has only one thing in it. Please grab it for Triss."

"Gotcha." Chief Lynn hopped the steps up to the next tier and opened the draw. What she saw there paled her deep complexion. Bethany watched curiously as Chief Lynn lifted something very familiar to the girl. Good for the teeth.

A little shaky, Lynn asked, "Will this be necessary?"

Dr. Suarez sounded concerned but grounded. "Yes. We're waking her, and she'll need the bit in her mouth when we do."

Triss devoured entire lives, yet Bethany tried to restrain her delight at the other woman's pain, no matter how well deserved. Korac's daughter was on her way, and the joy of that miracle took precedence.

Chief Lynn fit the bit in the sleeping woman's teeth in time to see the impression of a hand press against the box in Triss' womb. "So, Triss will give birth? We can't perform a c-section?"

Qas shook his head. "Surgery isn't an option. Her uterus is hardened with nacre glass."

Two tiers down, Miy, Twenty-One, Caedes, and the other Tritans watched. All of them turned a little green.

Bethany glanced over at the instruments in time to see the pain meter fully spiked before Dr. Suarez announced, "Ten centimeters. Bethany, the blood. Qas, I'm waking her. Lynn, I know how you feel, but if you could—"

His wife promised to comfort the dying woman with a nod.

"Right. Go!"

Yellow blood spilled into the cylinder from the bag Bethany squeezed. Twelve more bags were stacked beside her for subsequent dosing, all to be administered on Dr. Suarez's say. Qas operated the tech side of things to manage Triss' pain levels—

Shrieks filled the bay as the pregnant woman awakened.

Instantly, Chief Lynn clasped Triss' straining hand and said, "The baby's coming. Razor told us to give you blood. We're here—"

Ugly and primitive, the Lyrik screamed spit in the Chief's face between sharp, gnashing teeth. She even snatched her hand back.

Five fingers and a palm pressed from inside her, and Triss stopped screaming. Her eyes locked onto that nightmarish hand with exhaustion and love.

Chief Lynn tried again. "That's your baby. The one you're giving everything up for. It's all I admire about you, you fucking crazy bitch. But we're here to bring her into this world with you. Can you tolerate us for that long? Listen to us?"

Dr. Suarez gave Triss a reassuring smile for good measure, while the Tritan doctor at her side—a stranger—tried his best to look small.

"Where is Razor? I want him here."

Chief Lynn looked at Dr. Suarez, who cleared his throat before saying, "Uh... Korac is kinda in the middle of taking down Enki. That's where we're at. Triss, I'll be honest with you." He swallowed hard, and sorrow filled his eyes. "You won't survive this birth, but if we can sustain you long enough to see him again, will you work with us? Otherwise, baby Echo will die."

Triss let her head fall back on the pillow and rolled her eyes dramatically.

Lynn snapped. "What? You don't like the name?"

On a groan, the Lyriki warrior said, "No, it's perfect. Who named her? Xelan?!"

Caedes, of all people, barked out in laughter.

Dr. Suarez let his smile show until Triss cried out in pain. "Triss, please."

Through gritted teeth and a wail of pain, she said, "On your honor. I work with you, hold my child, and see Razor's eyes one last time." A pitiful smile cracked her dry lips. "Not bad for a finale." Triss held out a hand gnarled from a spasm, and Lynn took it. The Lyrik jabbed, "I never liked you."

The Chief ground, "The feeling is fucking mutual."

Bethany made lots of screams in the years she'd spent under the Emporium's roof. She never made one like the sound dragging out of Triss' mouth. It was beautiful, with the lilt of a whistle beneath the harmonic tones.

Did it call the troops outside the bay?

Or did one of the new Tritans betray them?

Either way, Bethany focused on her part in Echo's birth, while Caedes, Miy, Twenty-One, and the other Tritans defended the miracle happening inside.

{ENKI | ABRESSON'S RESIDENCE}

"Hang in there, Morning Star."

Lucy liked Yito. She was talking to him over their earpieces. He, Dolton, Praw, and the others waited outside the room to make her case to Abresson. Meanwhile, Gait's unhindered half headed for Enki's hull, sure to kill everything inside the Dyson's Sphere.

Matt and Puk would need rescuing, no doubt.

Here, Lucy tended to some finishing touches. Polishing a few edges and tying some loose ends. "Thanks, Yito. Be careful."

Dolton sounded more than a little concerned about her well-being, which just added a cherry to Lucy's sundae. "I worry about how Abresson will interrogate you. You don't know what he's like." He had an earpiece too. Dolton was a teacher in his past life, so he enjoyed fancying himself as a spy.

Sat on her knees in the middle of the Eminent's residence, Lucy could see how this looked from his point of view. He didn't know her. "Thank you for caring, really. I promise I'll be all right. Over and Out."

One quick fluff of her hair, a little rip to her smock neckline, and some biting of her lips should do the trick—

Abresson stormed into the hallway up to his door. He growled at his guard. "Do you know Primary Rem's whereabouts?!"

Yito, standing at attention outside Abresson's residence, said, "No, sir. And there's a matter to attend to in your quarters."

In the hour since Lance had exposed Lucy as a Shadow traitor, she'd convinced her Tritan guard of their own cover story and turned them over to her side. The preferred veneer was that Matt, not of the Shadow, brought her along for work on the demolition project using a fake marriage as pretense and, when she turned down his advances, he betrayed her by lying about her agency with the Shadow.

Personally, Lucy thought it was complicated; however, the boys convinced her Abresson was one of those people who believed complex stories because it confused his basic intelligence.

Yito and the others reported the situation and followed the Eminent into his foyer, where Lucy waited.

"You mean, you left a young woman in my residence?" Abresson didn't sound at all put out.

Dolton asked a good question. "Will you see to her before you find Primary Rem, sir?"

Abresson ignored him and walked into Lucy's line of sight. He took one look at her and said, "Leave us."

Yito tensed like he wanted to defend her, Dolton wouldn't meet Lucy's eyes, and Praw glared at the back of Abresson's head.

"I am Eminent, and you will leave my residence. Now." He bit the last word in a snarl.

They left.

Abresson stepped around Lucy to somewhere in the space, out of her line of sight. He worked with something, and it chinked. When he came back around, he held two glasses in his hand. "Thirsty?"

Lucy reached for the drink, nodding gratefully on her knees. She licked her lips when he chilled the glasses in his hands and gave her one. Wide-eyed, she gaped. "How did you do that?"

Abresson chuckled and sat down on the seat across from her, favoring an injury to his arm. "I'm gifted... Lucy, is it? That's a pretty name. I'm Eminent Abresson."

"I've looked forward to meeting you."

In the middle of bringing the rim to his lips, Abresson stopped at her words, and sat the drink back down. "Have you?" When he reached to put the glass on the nearest table, his jumpsuit pulled back enough to reveal the white scars on his indigo wrist.

Lucy licked her lips again and sighed the words out, "Yes. For some time now."

{ENKI | CINDER'S SHRINE}

Three years ago, Sagan had recited the Tenements of Volition for Korac. Before Razor—Before Imminent reared its ugly head. It was a beautiful and selfless act. The gesture came from a place of love meant to share her experiences at his hands.

What an ugly thing which became of something so beautiful. This was why the Shadow fought against Imminent. Xelan was right. The order leeched the goodness out of everything and left the worlds with nothing but despair.

Xelan hung his head with it, pressed to a wall while Korac leaned his side against it within reach, in case the Prince of Cinder required restraining. Andrew pulled Sagan closer against him as she cried into his chest, warm tears for Pax. Corrupted so young and for the rest of his life. Tameka's ability to soldier on garnered more respect than Korac thought possible for the young mate of his ex.

Celindria escorted Tameka to the rest of her mission while the Shadow waited for her signal. Once given, they'd migrate the armies to the Pantheon and stage the battlefield. They couldn't afford for Xelan to lose his composure in some half-cocked rescue—

For fuck's sake. The strangest look had been on Kyle's face for a few minutes now, and it had ruffled Korac's feathers. "What's on your mind, Story Taker?" He knew the codename would rankle the other man.

With a grimace, Kyle joined them in the present, irritated. "The same as what's on all our minds, *Silver General*."

Xelan muttered into the wall, "Please, not now."

Korac shot him a pitying look before mouthing to Kyle, "Truce."

The younger man flipped him off on his way to Xelan's side. "Wingmaster, I... I met with Silence in her memory."

Stiffly, Xelan turned to look at Kyle. "Go on."

Overhearing, Andrew and Sagan drew closer, with her joining Korac against the wall. Korac shifted slightly to conceal the pocket containing his secret. To say right now wasn't the right time to ask was an understatement.

Tumu acted as sentinel to their small reprieve, and Lamassau looked ready to breathe some fire. Iuo and Pehton had returned to their armies to maintain morale, which was honestly where they all should be. Both Xelan and Tameka were hurting, but they both had roles to fill. Korac was familiar with supporting the leadership through unbearable obstacles, but Elden, they seemed to get more unbearable with each hurdle.

Kyle looked like he finally decided how much he wanted to tell. "I saw Silence's life, who she is and some of why she's like this." He licked his lips in a nervous gesture before continuing. "She was the Tritans' main attempt at reviving their species—"

"Project Surra," Lamassau gasped on a whirl. "She was a *real* experiment?! And that's Silence?!"

Tumu sounded grim as he spoke with his back to them. "No one deserved her existence."

Xelan pushed. "You know of her?"

Sober as hell, the Primary said, "Ugly gossip rumored that Remorse and Quet hid a secret experiment gifted to them by the Exalted himself for destroying our females. I investigated, but found no trace of such an endeavor."

Lam's face soured. "But if that's Silence, she's ancient and threadbare—"

"That's exactly how it was for her," Kyle argued. "They used her up, and she populated all the planets with their initial species. That's why they call her 'the Mother.'"

Korac looked down to see if Sagan looked how he felt. Overwhelmed and exhausted. This news of Silence certainly illuminated some of her motives. Except… "Why is she working with Remorse?"

Xelan nodded his agreement with the question. "Why so many things?"

Kyle rubbed his forehead and groaned. "It'd be easier to show you, but I…"

Andrew softly confirmed, "You don't want to break her trust."

Everyone went quiet and looked away. Korac didn't want to touch that with a Primary-sized pole. Each of them was guilty of trusting the wrong people at one time or another. It left scars. He squeezed Sagan closer against him, grateful for the honesty between them. Korac was ready to ask her the moment things were right.

Xelan mustered his best reasoning voice, warm and reassuring. "Kyle, I know your relationship with her was complicated. My relationship with her isn't exactly straightforward, either, but if there's one iota of something useful in the memory you downloaded—Something that could save Pax, help Tameka, take down Enki, or even help us retrieve Silence for our side—then please. Trust me to be open-minded. I'm willing to hear her Verse."

The Prince's arguments were always so damned convincing. It was endearing and annoying all at the same time.

Kyle thought so, too, because he grabbed Xelan's shoulder, and they both fell still.

Tumu confessed, "I hate my brothers the more I learn about them."

Lamassau rubbed his back consolingly. "It's okay, Tumi. I always knew they sucked."

Korac suppressed a smirk. That was one thing about the Shadow. They could make him smile even in the most dire of straits. A little furrow formed in Sagan's brow, and her nose scrunched as she concentrated, listening to the quiet on the other end of the earpieces.

Nothing much was happening, aside from Celindria and Tameka's footsteps. New Cinder must connect to the Pantheon for them to simply walk there. Unless Celindria could Seamswalk, which might explain why she suddenly came over the earpieces, despite the Shadow saying she'd left the room. Of course, Korac knew about the Seamswalking capsules. He and Nox had bought them from Celindria's arms-dealer back when they'd invaded Earth the second time, but those capsules' capabilities were limited. Maybe Celindria reserved the heartier stuff for herself—

Kyle and Xelan returned on a gasp, both of them separating. The Prince's eyes shone with tears.

Korac raised a brow and asked, "That bad?"

When Xelan met his eyes and nodded, it was with a broken expression. He breathed. "Yes."

Kyle pushed his hair back from his face. "So, you understand? Silence isn't evil; she's dying."

Tumu and Lamassau exchanged a look.

Xelan pressed his bent arm to the wall and rested his head on it, staring at the corrugated floor. "Not just her."

Sagan separated from Korac and took a step toward her guardian. "Who else?"

Xelan swallowed hard and turned his haunted eyes to Sagan. The destroyed look on his face said it all.

Sagan cupped her hand to her mouth and gasped, "Rayne."

When Tameka's voice came over the earpieces, Xelan melted away his anguish into a separate compartment and transformed into the supportive spouse. "Fury, I'm here. Just say the word." Liquid in his responsibilities.

Korac could see Xelan's meltdown approaching on the horizon and vowed to do anything in his power to diffuse the bomb that was the Prince of Cinder.

{ENKI | PANTHEON}

Xelan's words over the mic meant the worlds to Tameka, especially as she and the First Progeny approached the target. Celindria didn't say a word, probably concentrating on the strange things happening with Chris inside his mind. Over the earpiece, Tameka thought he'd spoken on his own. If so, she'd count that as a win.

Soon, Tameka would get what they came for, save her son, and kill Celindria. Tameka *knew* Rayne was awake and out there somewhere. She felt it in her Progeny blood. They were winning. But first...

Celindria kept a nacre-disabling gun trained on Tameka's back. "I like your weapon. Few people are skilled with a chain dart. I'll add it to my collection."

The redheaded Progeny marched along with her hands cuffed behind her, certain she could overload and break them. Feeling sore, Tameka quipped back, "You keep a lot of trophies from your victims? You know that makes you a serial killer, right?" Losing her favorite weapon—one she should really get Xelan to name—only added to a growing list of things she'd reclaim from the First Progeny.

It disgusted Tameka that Celindria sounded impressed. "You're still full of so much fire after I stripped everything away from you."

With all the love of her family within, this next statement came from Tameka's heart. "Not everything, and not as much as you think."

"That's the truth," Xelan said, most perfectly.

The Pantheon's white-on-white shelves and books climbing to the atmosphere fell away to an empty field of white dirt. It was level with no cover of any kind for kilometers. This was where the Shadow would soon stage their armies. Tameka left the task in excellent hands that wouldn't fail her. It's how she knew they'd retrieve Pax and rebuild the Twelve Worlds together.

After about thirty minutes, a split shimmered ahead. The conduit. The target.

Celindria said, "You think you know something of the Wrong Side of Eternity—Of Hell? You will now."

Tameka didn't want to come across as eager, so she bit back her initial response of, "Bring it, bitch." Instead, she said, "You can never take everything from someone."

Xelan's voice in her ear lent her so much strength. "I love you, Fury."

In a move so sudden it choked Tameka, Celindria pulled the other woman's back to her front. Celindria bit down on her own lip and dripped actual blood on Tameka's shoulder. It was red, viscous, and smelled of jasmines. This would send her through the conduit despite the DNA lock programmed to Celindria.

The First Progeny whispered in Tameka's ear, "Father, you should have told her what you taught me of Hell."

Then Celindria pushed Tameka into the conduit.

It didn't transport her to the ground, no. Tameka fell through the sky in a storm, roaring with wind and thunder and strobing with lightning. She was soaked in rain almost instantly. Thinking quickly, she opened her wings, but they struggled against the turbulence. There was a spin to the gusts which threatened to cyclone her down. It took a bout of patience, buffeting, and intentional falling to travel to the ground miles away.

If Celindria disposed of all her experiments this way, they likely died from the fall alone—

Lightning split the sky beside Tameka in a beautiful branching arc that sent her heart racing. When she alighted, she closed her wings and tried to find shelter anywhere, speaking into the earpiece, "Can you hear me? Come in? Over."

No response.

Okay. Focus.

Seek the source of Torrentus and drain it, all while avoiding deadly lightning strikes. Another one blasted nearby and sparks chased along the muddy ground to Tameka's inert boots.

Deep breath. Eyes closed—

Wait.

Tameka opened her eyes. Did she glimpse something in the distance? What could it be in this wasteland? No, it was a trick of the lightning flash.

A second attempt. Meditate and locate the heart of Torrentus like all the suns Tameka had explored—

There.

The energy felt different from a star. More suffused with life and the allocation of it. It breathed fresh air and tasted like rich soil. Tameka reached for its source and opened the well inside her to drain—

A roar—the loudest noise—guttural and desperate, busted her eardrums.

The storm screamed at Tameka and turned rain into fire.

{ENKI | CINDER'S SHRINE}

Xelan felt the eyes of the people he loved on him. Each of them wondered what Celindria's last words meant.

"Father, you should have told her what you taught me of Hell."

Why couldn't Celindria understand he tried—Elden, did he try! Xelan loved her like a daughter, and she continued to punish him for a mistake he could never take back—

No.

This doubt and heartache was exactly what Celindria wanted. For Tameka and for Pax—for the entire Vast

Collective—Xelan needed to maintain his composure more than ever before.

The Prince of Cinder turned and faced the people he loved and refused to give them explanations or excuses. Xelan met them in the eye. Korac straightened from where he leaned against the wall, unfolded his arms, and almost stood at attention. Nox was right. The best soldier. Beside him, Sagan's tear-stained face hardened to the pitiless expression she wore when the Seamswalker split Gait apart. Ready to do what was necessary. Andrew's eyes said he knew already, invaded Xelan's mind and read his intentions. He didn't look sorry about it. He simply looked primed to address it. Kyle's eyes were clearer and a little brighter after his memory walk with Silence. The good it did him would rally him through the rest of the fight to figure things out with her. A worthy cause. Lamassau donned his Pil platinum gauntlets, prepared for this battle. Even though Tritan faces were near-featureless, resolution wasn't hard to decipher from Lam's expression.

Tumu.

The thirteen-foot tall Primary stared at Xelan not with pity, but with mercy. In that deep voice of his, he said, "The past asks us to pay for mistakes of its making. What will you do, Prince Xelan? The Icarus, once so young when he first came to me for help, looks at me now with old eyes from a life of harsh lessons. What will you do?"

Mid-stride, Xelan said, "I'm finishing it," and walked back into the fray.

Imminent had stolen so much from Xelan, and the more connections he made to the underground organization, the less like a person he felt. An experiment, like everything else—

No.

This experiment went rogue long ago, and Xelan would *not* let his family pay any further for the sins of someone else's past and futures. Imminent could swallow his life, but he'd make certain they'd choked on it.

The Collective Generals waited at the glass view of Torrentus. They stepped back to make way for Xelan and his people. Standing in the shrine closest to the Torrentus continent, he peered through the glass and waited.

The signal.

"If we do our jobs right, my signal will be a lot of non-responsive static and clear skies, but I know I'll deliver."

Xelan whispered into his mic to try once more. "Fury—Tameka, come in."

Nothing but static.

Out of his periphery, Sagan gave him a thumbs up. She was right. This was part of the plan. Xelan needed to trust the plan and trust his partner. Tameka was capable, amazing—a force of nature, really. With beautiful skin, cute freckles, the most fun hair, and a radiant smile. He was so happy to love someone who let it shine so freely, so often. Perfect in combat with the strongest kick ever delivered to Xelan's sternum. He couldn't wait to beg Tameka for more children with her eyes and maybe his hair. He'd teach them and Pax all how to grin—

Sagan pointed at the storm and drew Xelan from his reverie. As planned, the storm pulsed.

Pehton shouted, "Fury's got it!"

Someone else cried, "The Shadow have done it!"

Again Torrentus pulsed, and Xelan loved his fierce warrior on the ground battling a storm which had raged for thousands of years—

Orange.

Orange and red.

The once gray storm clouds whirled in a blaze—a hurricane of fire no one could survive.

"Ta—Tameka..."

EPILOGUE

{CINDER | 6,000,000 YEARS AGO}

SILENCE LOVED THIS MOUNTAINTOP. IT OVERLOOKED THE SPRAWLING CITY BELOW, FILLED WITH THRIVING ICARI. The highest point, referred to as Li Mountain, meant the wind kited her hair and tugged playfully at her wings. Her sharp eyes made out Elden's audience house from this distance. A humble, squat structure meant to feel welcoming and not at all intimidating. Like her mate. An attribute of Elden she loved very much and would deeply miss.

Silence hugged herself at the thought and turned her back on the view.

The Exalted had been generous and kind, meeting with her in Quet's Sanctum. "I lament your condition, Surra, but I will not surrender Ishkur to you or Primary Rem. Your intentions are not as pristine as you think. Very few are worthy of owning that kind of power."

While he spoke, azure light pulsed under Silence's skin, marking a week left for her. His strange eyes filled with pity, but he held fast to his convictions. Softly, she said, "You know Primary Rem will take Enki from you. He has asked for my army, and I am tempted to let him have it."

"To force my hand? I would sooner cut it off."

Silence liked Zero. With a sigh, she decided. "I will retract my support of an Icarean invasion in Enki." At his relieved smile, she held up a hand. "Your people will die without my race's involvement. Your species faces destruction. He tells me there is a stratagem the Aegis will employ in desperate times. One which may benefit my search for your Ishkur."

The Exalted shook his head. "Forgive me, but even if I make such a reckless ploy, you will be long gone."

Another pulse. Silence smiled, sadly. "I will discover a means to outlast you."

So, she found herself on the mountain. Along one of its cliffs, Silence discovered the perfect cave to hide her stasis casket, and Remorse assembled it for her. It was powered by her nacre and the sun, and it promised to prolong her life. Without it, she would die soon. Silence tried to tell Elden, but she couldn't. She would try again when she awakened. Although she'd miss raising her daughter, it was better Savis thought she lost her mother in childbirth.

All the Probabilities said so. Silence would wake in time to stop whatever happens to Li, to find Ishkur, and to prevent the shadow which clouded Savis in the Matrix. Every Probability showed all but the slightest chance of something interfering with her waking—

But that was only slim enough to install a failsafe into the device.

Silence would wake on time and save her family. She'd suffered enough for fate's toll. Destiny wouldn't dare ask more from her.

It wouldn't *dare*.

{Enki | Opal Mezzanine | Now}

Silence sought the comfort of her wings to ward off the chill of her cruel past. Rather, she embraced the blazing fire coming from the projection feed. Rayne's magnesium field was truly impressive. It swallowed the Mezzanine in blinding white light until it receded back from the blue and green hues covering the walls.

"Des."

Lucas and Smith spared her a questioning look.

Touching a hand to her nacres, Silence said, "Des was her donor. The Tritans typically hid their abilities, but each of them possessed a special gift exclusive to them, like the Progeny. Des could manipulate his nanite field and widen it. The light is all her own, but how it expands is very much from him."

Smith's smile took on a bewildered edge. "Why would he give up his life for Rayne's nacre?"

"Oh, he didn't give up anything." Silence nodded with certainty at their curious glances. "The other primaries imprisoned him before they arrived in Enki. They only kept him alive because of their eroded numbers."

Lucas sounded impressed. "I'd like to hear more about this rogue Primary."

With her eyes fixed on the action within the projection, Silence said, "In a way you have. He was Tumu's twin."

They both peered at her for more, but Rayne and Nox were interacting, and Silence wanted to hear them. Wait… Why was Rayne rooting into her nacre—

Oh.

They all stared wide-eyed as the young woman formed a glorious weapon from nacre ore.

Lucas wore a wry smile as he said, "Rayne named it 'Night Killer.'"

Bemused, Silence rolled her eyes. "Of course she did."

Smith argued, "Nox found it flattering. Your grandson has a few issues and many of them center around Rayne."

The look Nox gave Rayne in the projection confirmed Smith's observations. So much adoration and respect. So much like his grandfather.

"You've cried more in the last few hours than in the entire lifetime I've known you." Lucas' observations were less welcome only because they exposed a vulnerability Silence would rather keep private.

A vulnerability hollowed out by the same Tritans which Nox and Rayne now defied.

Silence changed the subject. "What of Fury?"

Smith answered automatically, "Celindria deposited her into the Torrentus conduit, and the terraformer reacted as expected."

Lucas asked with more than a little concern. "Do you think she survived?"

Smith grinned. "Fury versus an eternal storm. Who *would* I place my money on?"

Lucas spared the other man an incredulous shake of the head.

So, they believed Fury would survive, but that storm was raging when Silence was known by another name. It would make for quite a formidable foe, assuming Tameka survived the firestorm. Something Silence wanted for Xelan's sake. She wished no ill will on the Shadow. She loved them, but they threatened her mission, and that couldn't be allowed—

"Look at all those Weapons, and Rayne is simply fearless." Smith sounded so proud.

Lucas sounded utterly confident. "What has she to fear?"

They both turned and looked at Silence. She spread her wings wide. "Let's ensure they find Ishkur. Do either of you object to your parts?"

With a sparkle in his golden eyes, Lucas opened his wings with a nod. Smith stepped around to the other man's back and climbed on when Lucas knelt. The human assured, "We're prepared, Mother. We'll come when you call."

Good.

Silence understood and appreciated their allegiance, even when she wasn't sure of her own. Her views on 'family' had complicated and simplified, shrank and grew for her over the eons she'd lived. It was a funny thing that Silence only realized the meaning of 'family' in the last few months. Her last days.

Ishkur would save Silence and the galaxy.

Xelan, her family, would lead her to it.

THE VAST COLLECTIVE CHRONOLOGY

7M BCE	Enki Terminates Li, Elden's Sacrifice, Umbra Seizes Control of Cinder, Nox is born
3M BCE	Xelan is born, Nox becomes a weapon
2M BCE	Gait's children disappear, Korac joins Cinder's royal family
1.7M BCE	Umbra invades Lacceirus Capra
1M BCE	Umbra invades Monarch 3
500K BCE	Valkyries & Lyriks Revolt
250K BCE	Savis & Umbra pass into eternity, Nox becomes King of Cinder
6K BCE	First Icarean invasion of Earth, Nox invades Thailea, Xelan creates the Progeny
5.5K BCE	Celindria's uprising, Disbursement of Progeny lines, Formation of The Brethren, The Vacating
100 CE	Celindria 'dies' in Thailea incident
400 CE	Razor introduces Nox to Cascading Light, Xelan is banished to Earth, Nox & Korac plan their next invasion of Earth
1987 JAN	Tameka Phillips is born, Xelan builds Iona-oo
1993 May	Xelan saves Rayne Callahan from a fateful car accident
2002 SEP:	Xelan trains the Progeny, Icari commence 'soft' invasion of Earth
2006 APR	Full-Scale Invasion Day
2006 AUG	Volcano Day Battle
2008 JUL	Gait's destruction

AUTHOR'S NOTE

"It starts with him *and ends with* her.*"*
We're getting closer to the end.
Keep reading for a sneak peek at *Flood*, Book XI of the Vast Collective Series.
And head over to my website to sign up for news of future books.

FLOOD

{ENKI | NEW CINDER}

"THANKS, KID."

On all fours in his own conscience, Chris focused sharply on the manifestation of Celindria, who glared at him with no small amount of alarm.

The words. Came from *his* mouth. His actual mouth, currently under her volition control, but somehow—some fucking how—Chris had managed to speak.

This was it.

The volition exchanged hands by forfeiture from his own lips.

"I give up."

That didn't work.

"I give my will back."

Still nothing, but now he was so desperate to see this through that he refused to look at the Shadow watching him from their cell. Their hopeful gazes would put too much pressure on this delicate operation. Already, Chris sensed Bones and Para crowding the cell's bars. Jack's eager hopefulness and Ross' undeserved kindness both emanated an energy, like optimistic radiation. Devis and

Andrius gasped, crowding the unconscious Seamswalker, T.A.O., and the love of Chris' life, Karter. Both women would receive medical help once Chris got his shit together, returned his volition, and they all escaped.

Likewise, he couldn't look at Celindria. She was working on a way to subdue him any minute. Chris only knew this because, out of his periphery, her eyes were doing something truly terrifying.

Spark.

Dull.

Live wire.

Lights out.

Think! What did Karter say when Remorse relinquished control of Karter only two hours ago? Celindria was hurting the Valkyrie leader, hurting the Tritan inside her by default, and Primary Rem screamed—

"I relent!"

The words came out of Chris' mouth on a bellow, and everything changed.

Ears popped. Eyes strained. Every muscle contracted. Tendons tightened—

Pulled.

Chris was being pulled inside-out. Would he fall unconscious like Karter? Why was he awake and aware but blind and deaf at the same time—

Sound hit him all at once.

"Chris! Chris, it's Jack. Can you hear me?!"

Para's sweet voice cracked. "Chris! Please tell me you're all right?!"

Everyone came loud and clear, but he still couldn't see—

Oh.

Chris' eyes were closed. He opened them and found himself on all fours, staring at a rug on the cave floor. Blood dripped onto it—His blood from his mouth. With a lick of his lips, Chris knew he bit his tongue in the process.

All the while, the others shouted.

Alone.

Chris was alone in his body, in his conscience. The space he shared with Celindria was gone. "I'm me."

www.ingramcontent.com/pod-product-compliance
Lightning Source LLC
Chambersburg PA
CBHW020459310726
48979CB00016B/2720/J

* 9 7 8 1 7 3 7 8 3 7 9 8 5 *